FOREW

Adam Rose is one of *those* guys.

You know the type. Great at everything? Makes it all look easy? Like, he could walk into a court room on twenty minutes notice and defend someone accused of running a really complicated Ponzi scheme. Or like he could walk onto a ball field with both arms in casts and somehow strike out the last batter and win the World Series.

I can't *stand* those guys.

Let me tell you about Adam Rose. He wrote the book you're about to read. He's an idea fountain. Ideas fall out of him so fast, if you're walking next to him, you'll trip over them (He nimbly leaps over them and scoops them back up with the grace of a dancer). He gets a new idea for a book, a short story, a comic book, a screenplay, every five minutes (He keeps them all in a gold-leaf notebook given to him personally by Zeus). It never ends. Every time you meet him for lunch, he's got a story he thinks would be good for a particular literary journal. He's thinking about a novel about the most obvious, relatable subject in the world and it ticks you off because *you* didn't think of it. He's brainstorming lists of possibilities for a screenwriter pal's multi-million-dollar feature.

And he does this all while being a great husband (of course!), a great father (gah!) a great teacher (lucky kids!), and a great friend (naturally!).

Makes me *sick*.

Obviously, I was nauseous with jealousy from the first page of *Corollary*. I mean, a galaxy where everyone has a twin, except for *one person*? I could *never* come up with that, not in a million years, but dang it, I *should* have. The themes of duality and individuality and sacrifice and honesty, mixed in with thrilling adventure, wild alien races and fantastic environments? Solid cliffhangers, snappy dialogue and a dash of mystery? I'd eat my own *arm* to come up with a story that worked on that many levels.

And of *course*, he found an extraordinarily talented collaborator in Robert Ahmad, whose whimsical visuals bring life to all those ideas and themes, even seamlessly adding in some brilliant ones of his own.

So, go ahead, read this book. See if you don't feel like I do. See if you don't whack your forehead with your palm at how sucked in to the story you get, how much you want to know what happens next, and how much absolute fun you're having. See if you can't wait for *Corollary* to be announced as a movie or television show. Do that for a few years and see if you don't finish another Adam Rose book (or short story, or screenplay, or grocery list) and throw it across the room, muttering, "That guy... He did it again!"

Oh, and never have your picture taken with him. He's so good-looking, no one will ever notice you're standing next to him.

Of course.

Adam Beechen
Los Angeles
June, 2022

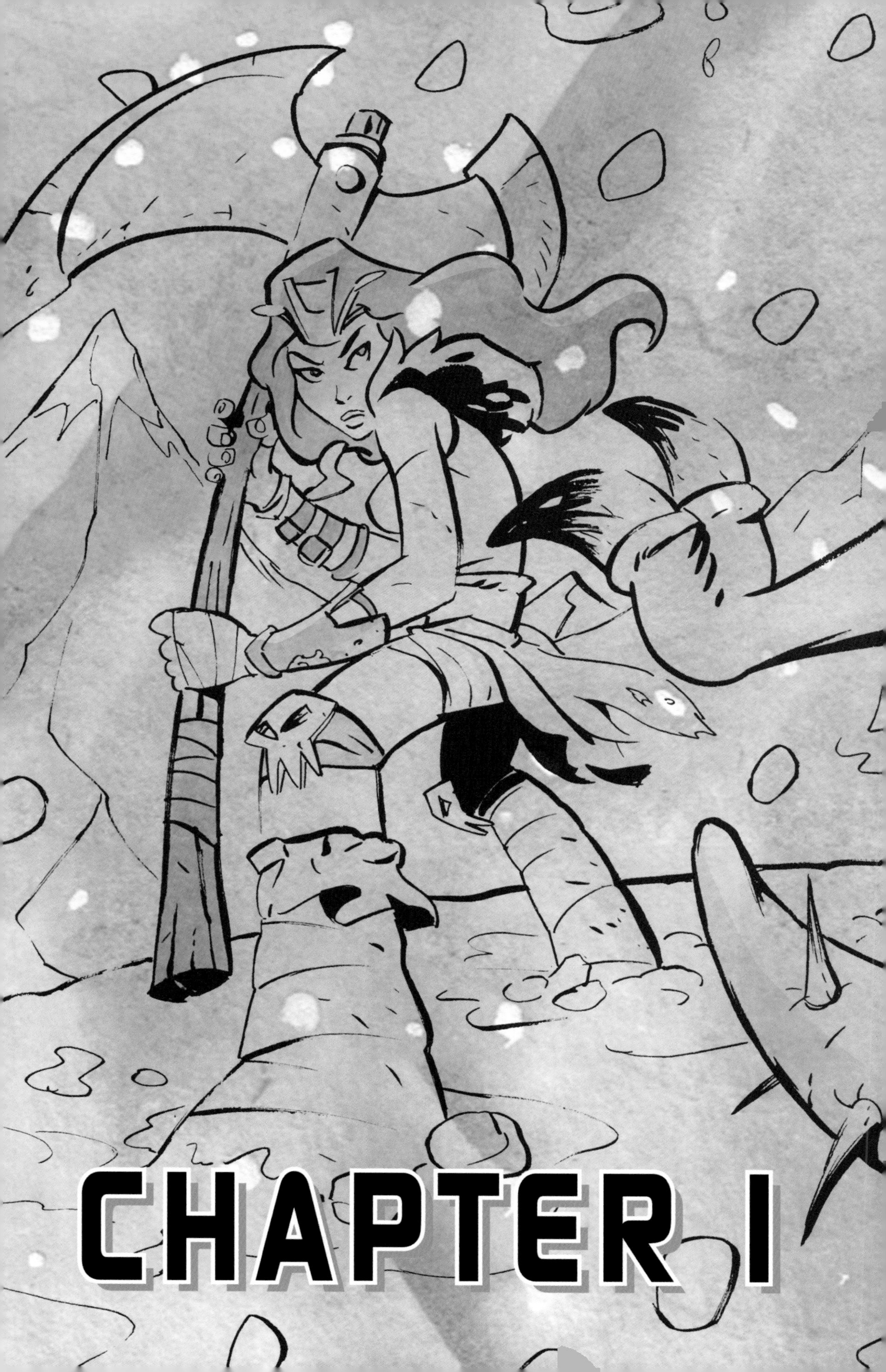
CHAPTER I

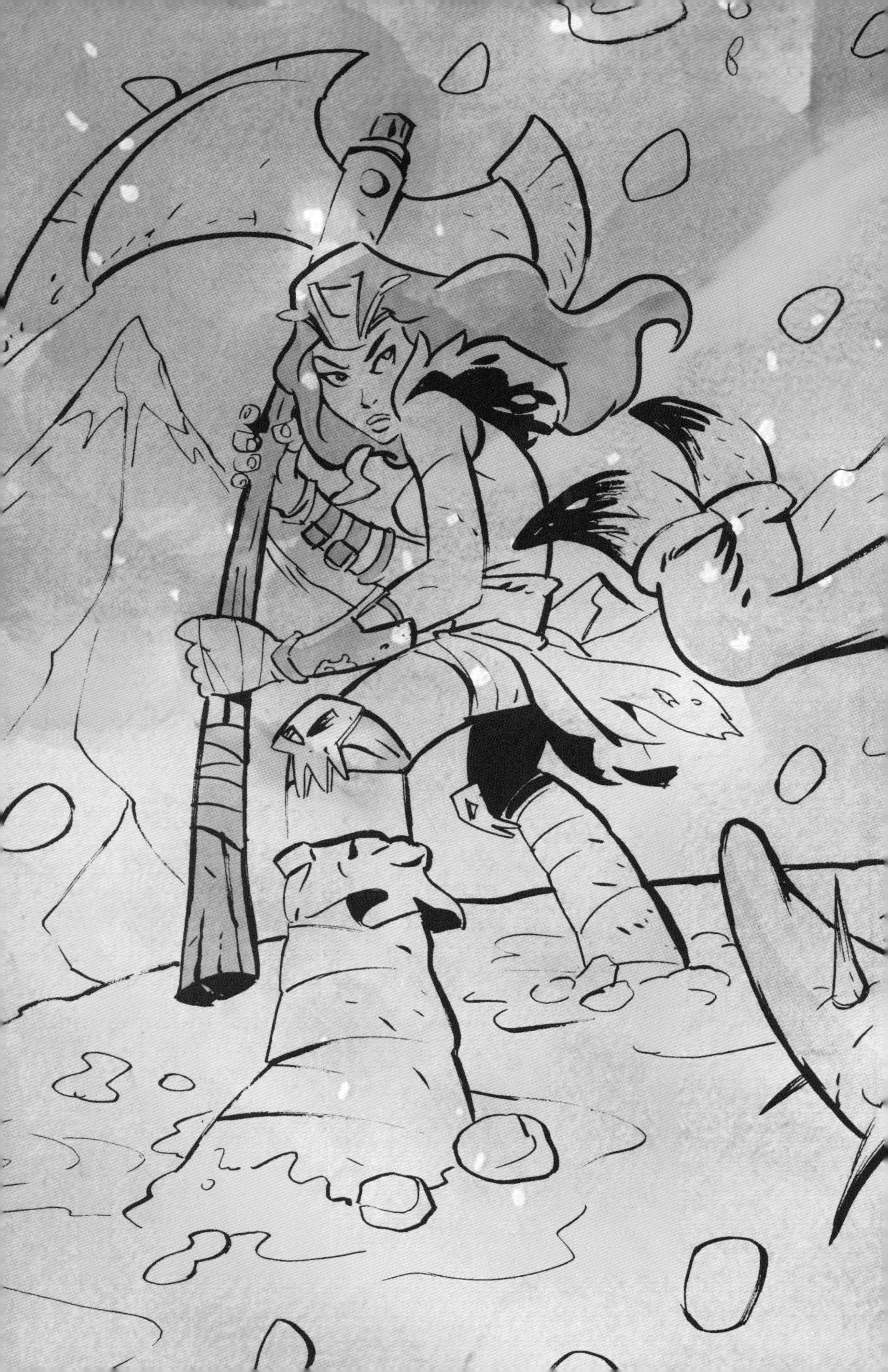

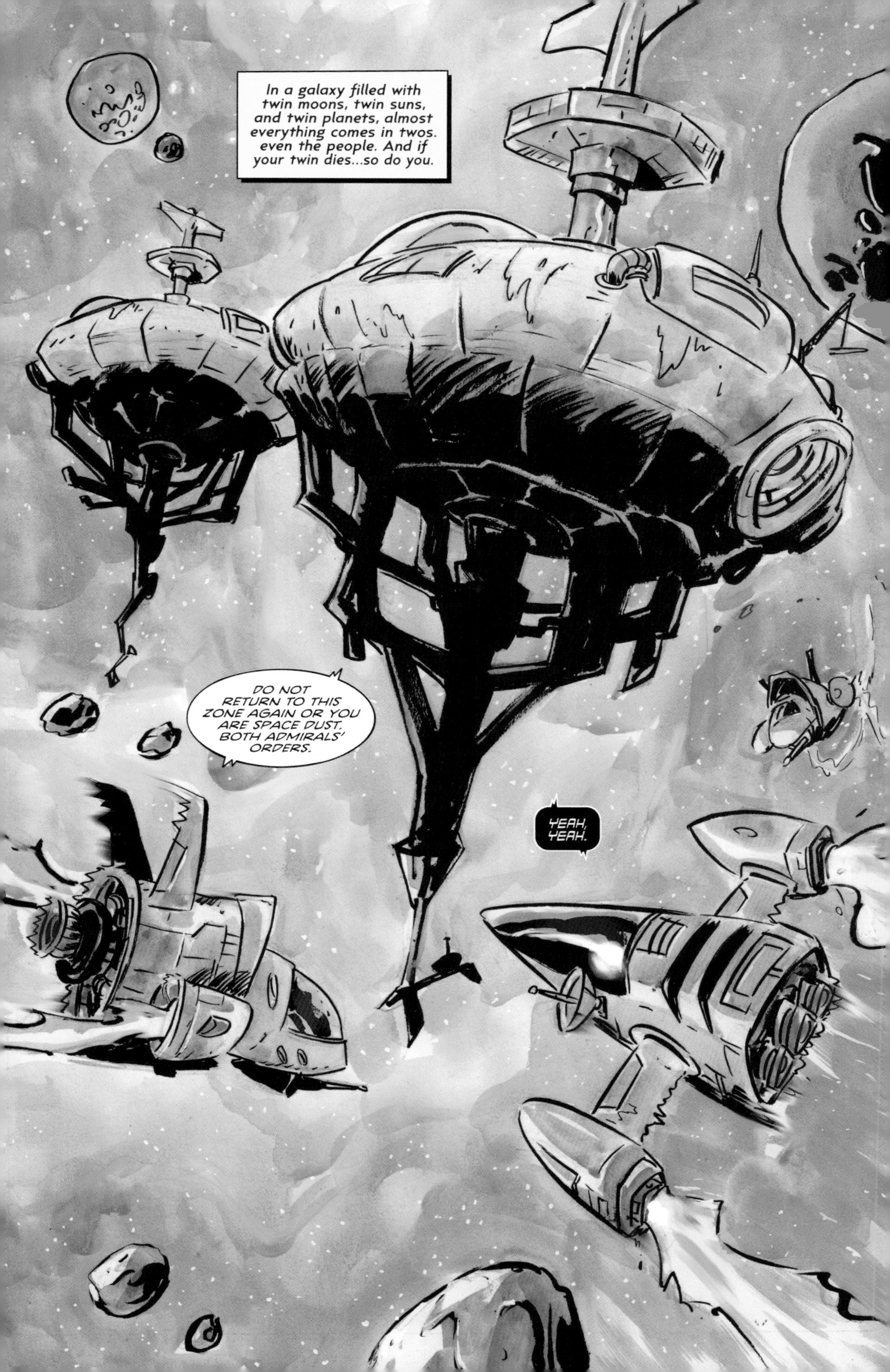
In a galaxy filled with twin moons, twin suns, and twin planets, almost everything comes in twos. even the people. And if your twin dies...so do you.
DO NOT RETURN TO THIS ZONE AGAIN OR YOU ARE SPACE DUST. BOTH ADMIRALS' ORDERS.
YEAH, YEAH.

GRUNT

ONE, TWO, THREE.

ANDROMEDA, TRY NOT TO PULL ANY MUSCLES. WE NEED THEM FUNCTIONAL.

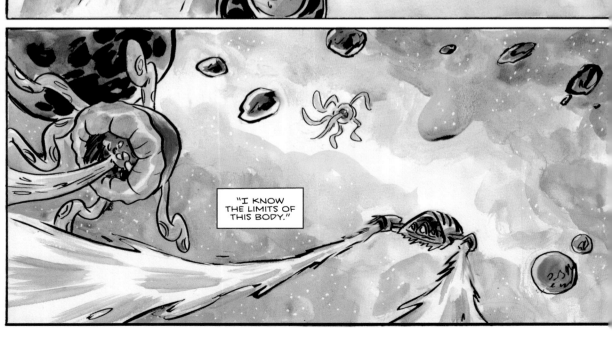

"I KNOW THE LIMITS OF THIS BODY."

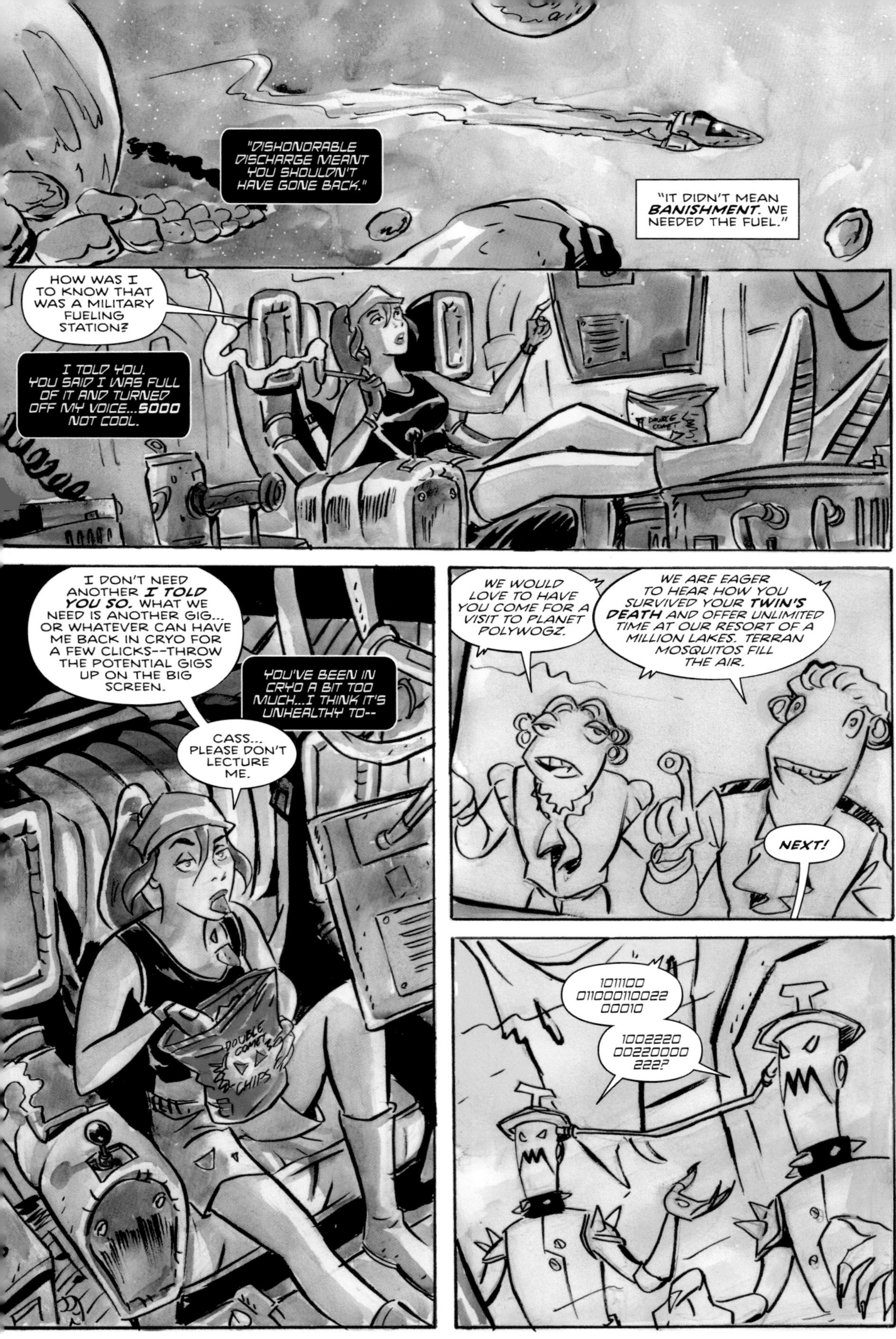

"DISHONORABLE DISCHARGE MEANT YOU SHOULDN'T HAVE GONE BACK."
"IT DIDN'T MEAN BANISHMENT. WE NEEDED THE FUEL."
HOW WAS I TO KNOW THAT WAS A MILITARY FUELING STATION?
I TOLD YOU. YOU SAID I WAS FULL OF IT AND TURNED OFF MY VOICE...SOOO NOT COOL.
I DON'T NEED ANOTHER I TOLD YOU SO. WHAT WE NEED IS ANOTHER GIG... OR WHATEVER CAN HAVE ME BACK IN CRYO FOR A FEW CLICKS--THROW THE POTENTIAL GIGS UP ON THE BIG SCREEN.
YOU'VE BEEN IN CRYO A BIT TOO MUCH...I THINK IT'S UNHEALTHY TO--
CASS... PLEASE DON'T LECTURE ME.
DOUBLE COMET CHIPS
WE WOULD LOVE TO HAVE YOU COME FOR A VISIT TO PLANET POLYWOGZ.
WE ARE EAGER TO HEAR HOW YOU SURVIVED YOUR TWIN'S DEATH AND OFFER UNLIMITED TIME AT OUR RESORT OF A MILLION LAKES. TERRAN MOSQUITOS FILL THE AIR.
NEXT!
1011100 01100011002 00010
1002220 00220000 222?

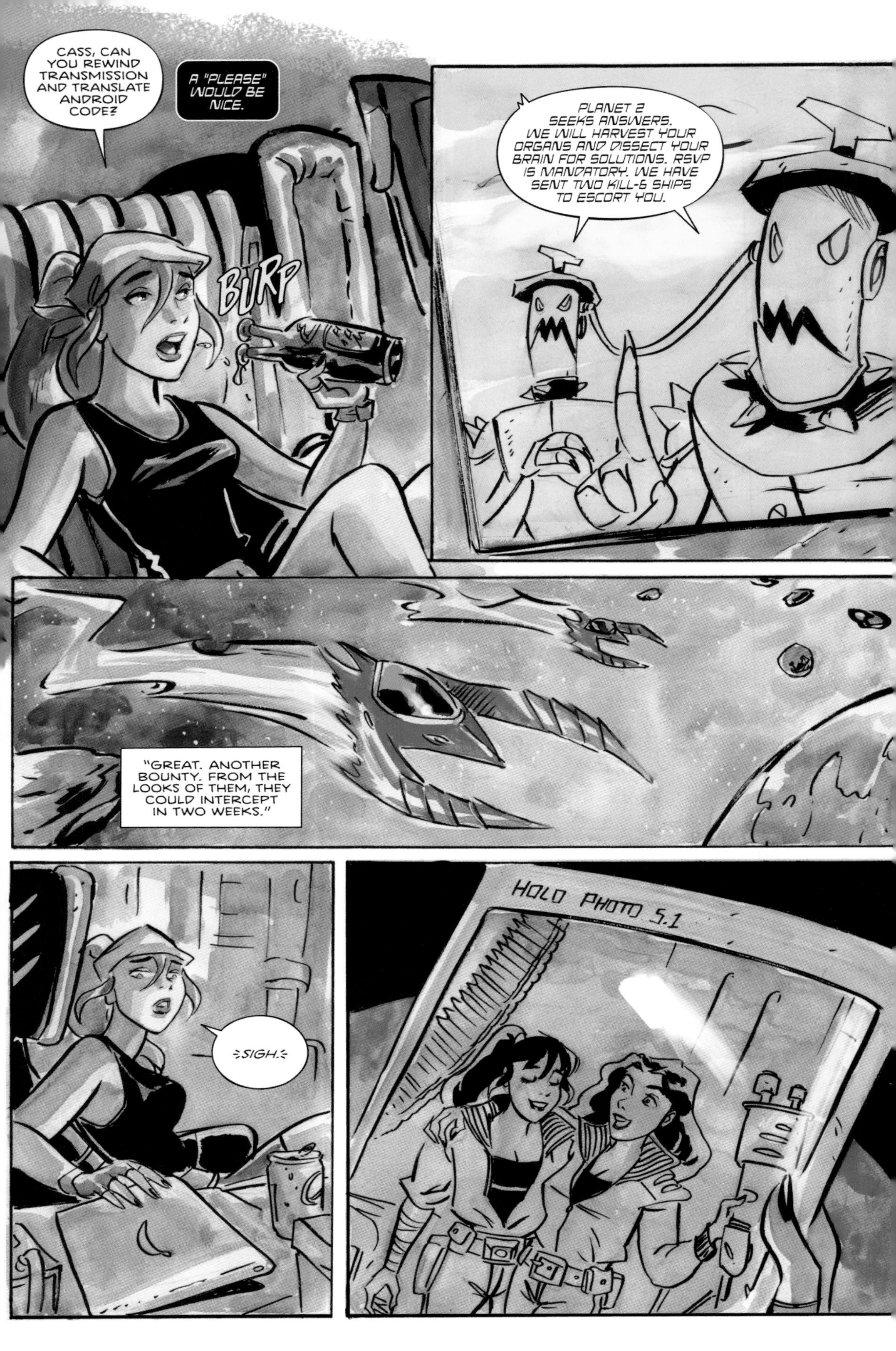
CASS, CAN YOU REWIND TRANSMISSION AND TRANSLATE ANDROID CODE?
A "PLEASE" WOULD BE NICE.
BURP
PLANET 2 SEEKS ANSWERS. WE WILL HARVEST YOUR ORGANS AND DISSECT YOUR BRAIN FOR SOLUTIONS. RSVP IS MANDATORY. WE HAVE SENT TWO KILL-6 SHIPS TO ESCORT YOU.
"GREAT. ANOTHER BOUNTY. FROM THE LOOKS OF THEM, THEY COULD INTERCEPT IN TWO WEEKS."
SIGH.
HOLO PHOTO 5.1

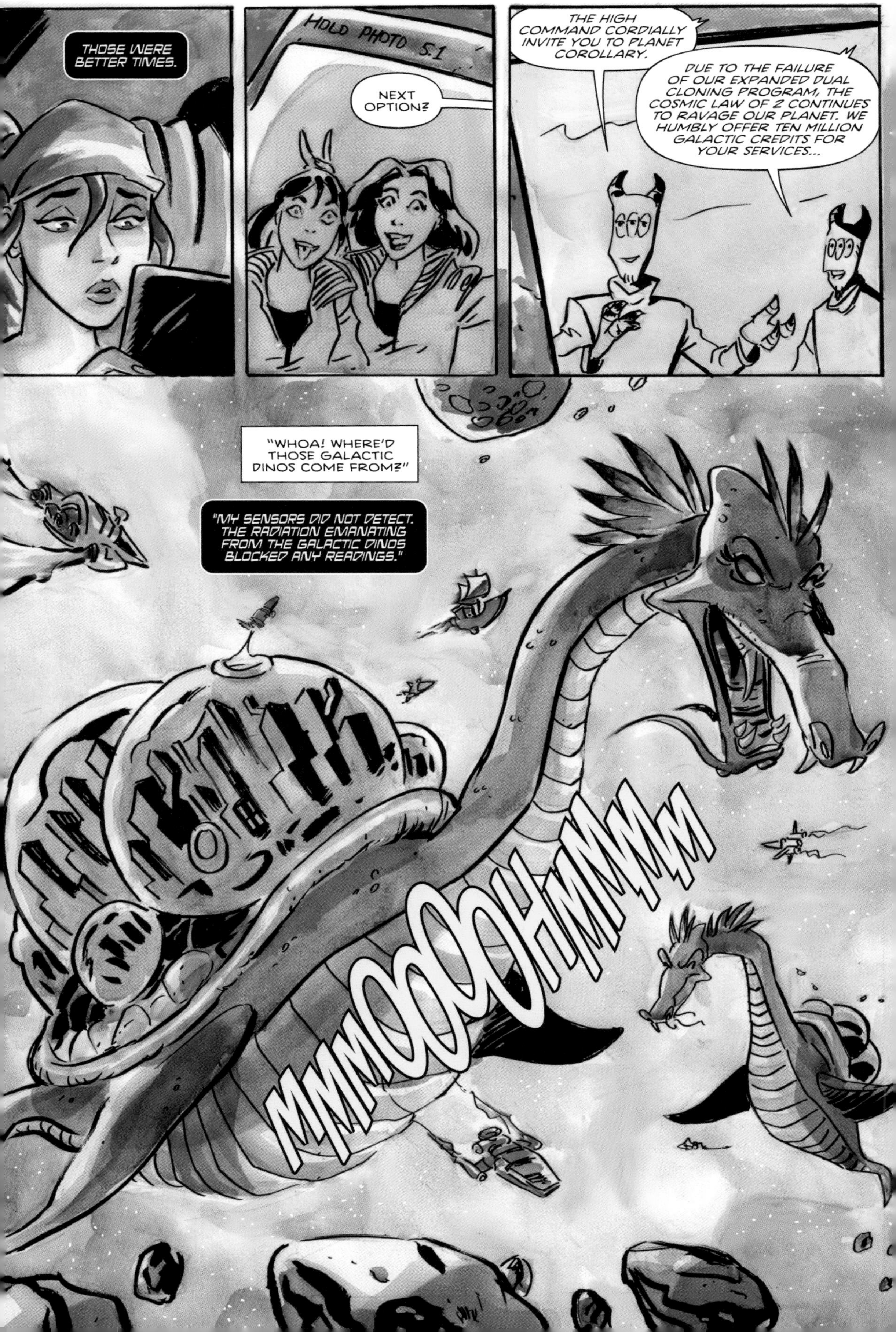
THOSE WERE BETTER TIMES.
HOLD PHOTO 5.1
NEXT OPTION?
THE HIGH COMMAND CORDIALLY INVITE YOU TO PLANET COROLLARY.
DUE TO THE FAILURE OF OUR EXPANDED DUAL CLONING PROGRAM, THE COSMIC LAW OF 2 CONTINUES TO RAVAGE OUR PLANET. WE HUMBLY OFFER TEN MILLION GALACTIC CREDITS FOR YOUR SERVICES...
"WHOA! WHERE'D THOSE GALACTIC DINOS COME FROM?"
"MY SENSORS DID NOT DETECT. THE RADIATION EMANATING FROM THE GALACTIC DINOS BLOCKED ANY READINGS."
MMMOOOOHMMMM

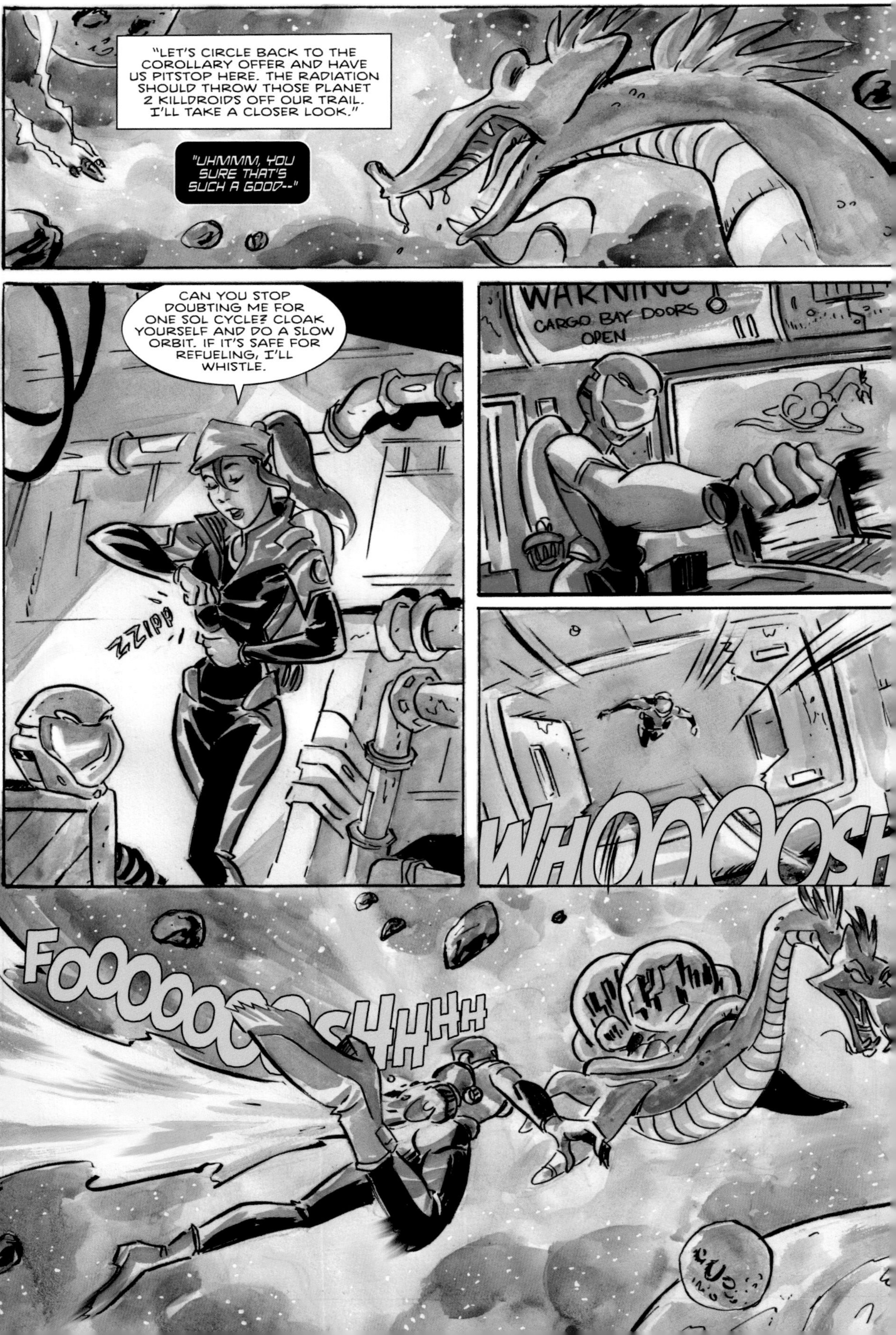
"LET'S CIRCLE BACK TO THE COROLLARY OFFER AND HAVE US PITSTOP HERE. THE RADIATION SHOULD THROW THOSE PLANET 2 KILLDROIDS OFF OUR TRAIL. I'LL TAKE A CLOSER LOOK."
"UHMMM, YOU SURE THAT'S SUCH A GOOD--"
CAN YOU STOP DOUBTING ME FOR ONE SOL CYCLE? CLOAK YOURSELF AND DO A SLOW ORBIT. IF IT'S SAFE FOR REFUELING, I'LL WHISTLE.
ZZIPP
WARNING CARGO BAY DOORS OPEN
WHOOOOSH
FOOOOOOOSHHHH

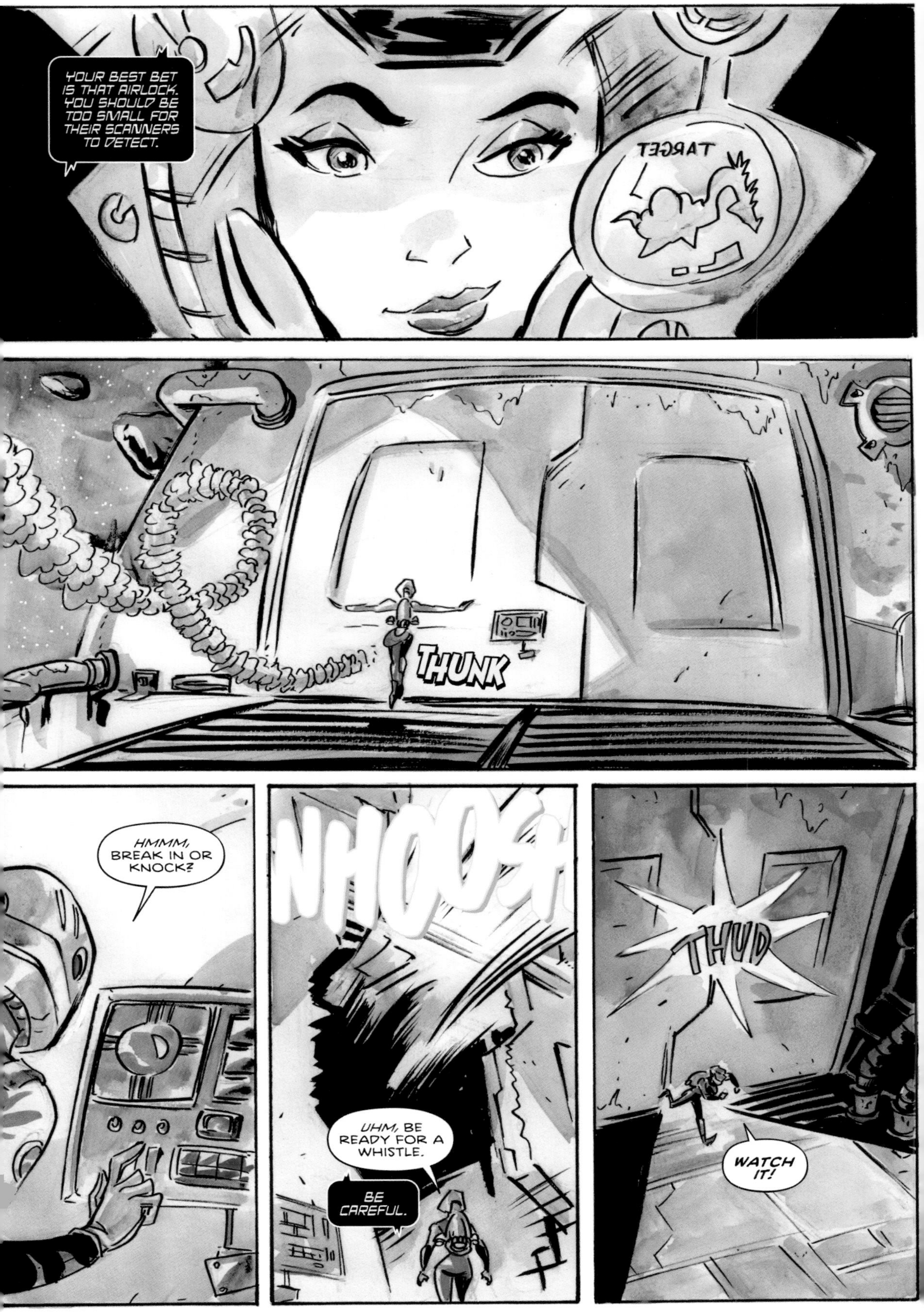
YOUR BEST BET IS THAT AIRLOCK. YOU SHOULD BE TOO SMALL FOR THEIR SCANNERS TO DETECT.
TARGET
THUNK
HMMM, BREAK IN OR KNOCK?
UHM, BE READY FOR A WHISTLE.
BE CAREFUL.
THUD
WATCH IT!

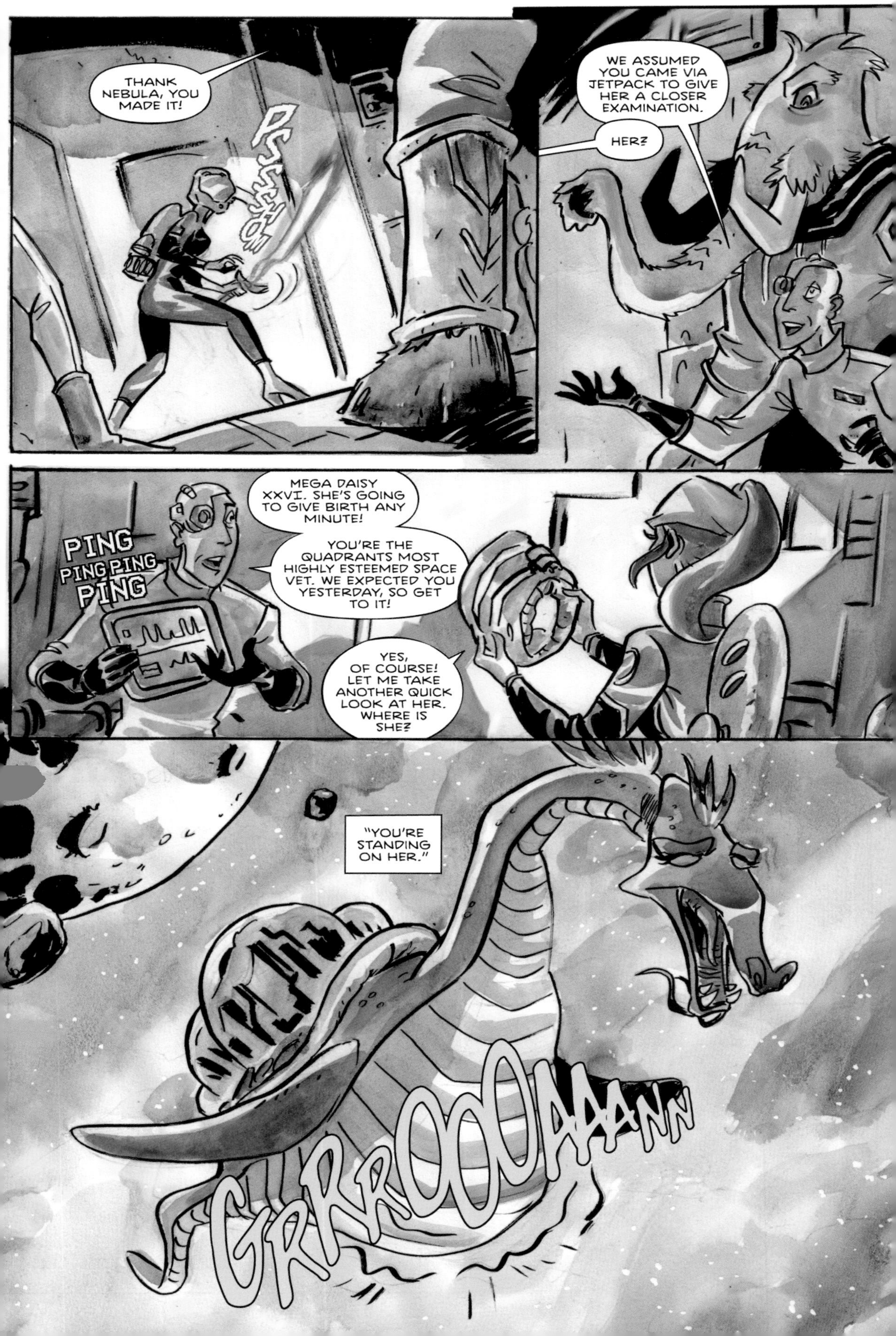
THANK NEBULA, YOU MADE IT!
PSSSHOOM
WE ASSUMED YOU CAME VIA JETPACK TO GIVE HER A CLOSER EXAMINATION.
HER?
MEGA DAISY XXVI. SHE'S GOING TO GIVE BIRTH ANY MINUTE!
YOU'RE THE QUADRANTS MOST HIGHLY ESTEEMED SPACE VET. WE EXPECTED YOU YESTERDAY, SO GET TO IT!
PING PING PING PING
YES, OF COURSE! LET ME TAKE ANOTHER QUICK LOOK AT HER. WHERE IS SHE?
"YOU'RE STANDING ON HER."
GRRROOOAAAANN

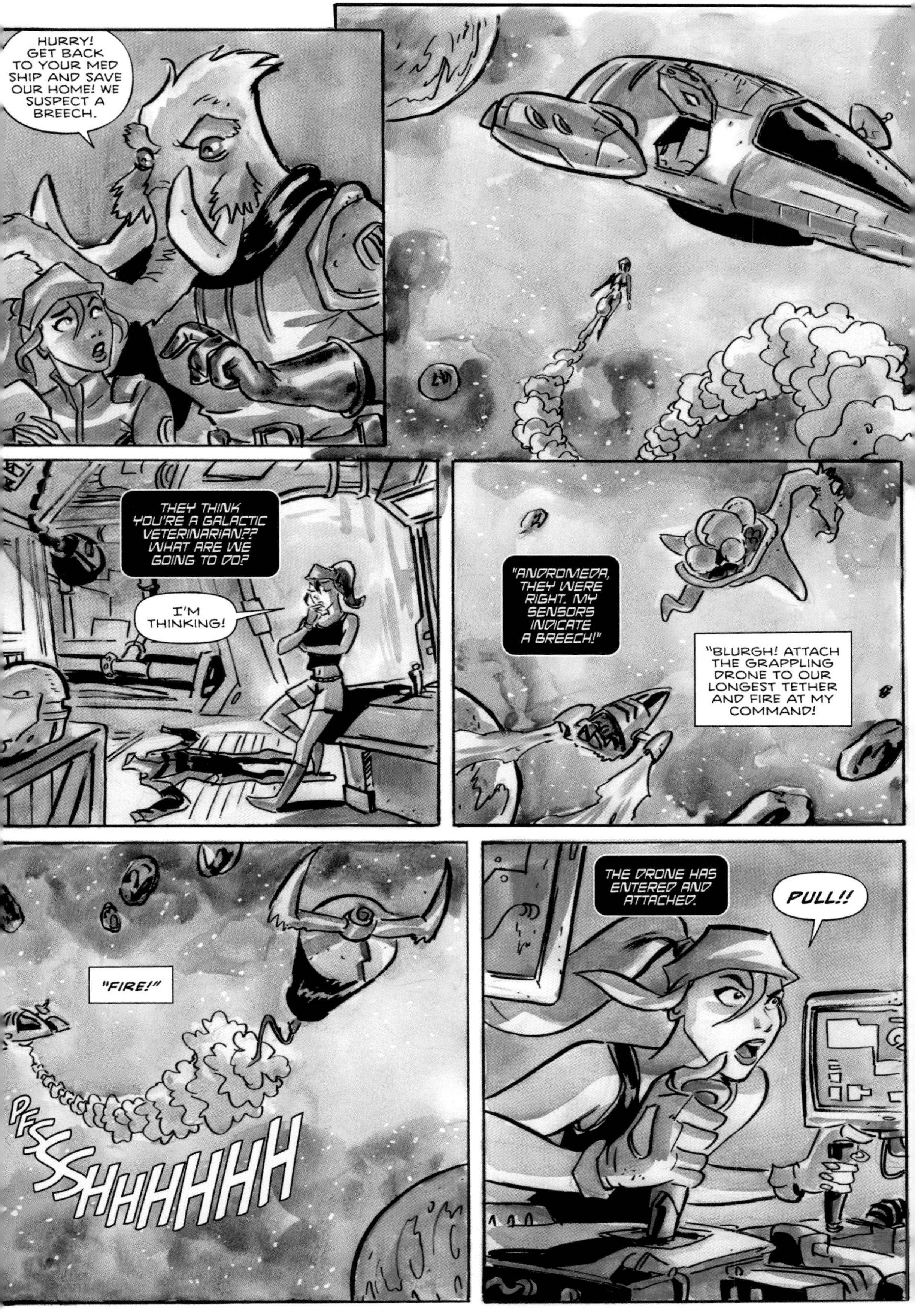
HURRY! GET BACK TO YOUR MED SHIP AND SAVE OUR HOME! WE SUSPECT A BREECH.
THEY THINK YOU'RE A GALACTIC VETERINARIAN?? WHAT ARE WE GOING TO DO?
I'M THINKING!
"ANDROMEDA, THEY WERE RIGHT. MY SENSORS INDICATE A BREECH!"
"BLURGH! ATTACH THE GRAPPLING DRONE TO OUR LONGEST TETHER AND FIRE AT MY COMMAND!"
"FIRE!"
PFSSSHHHHHHH
THE DRONE HAS ENTERED AND ATTACHED.
PULL!!

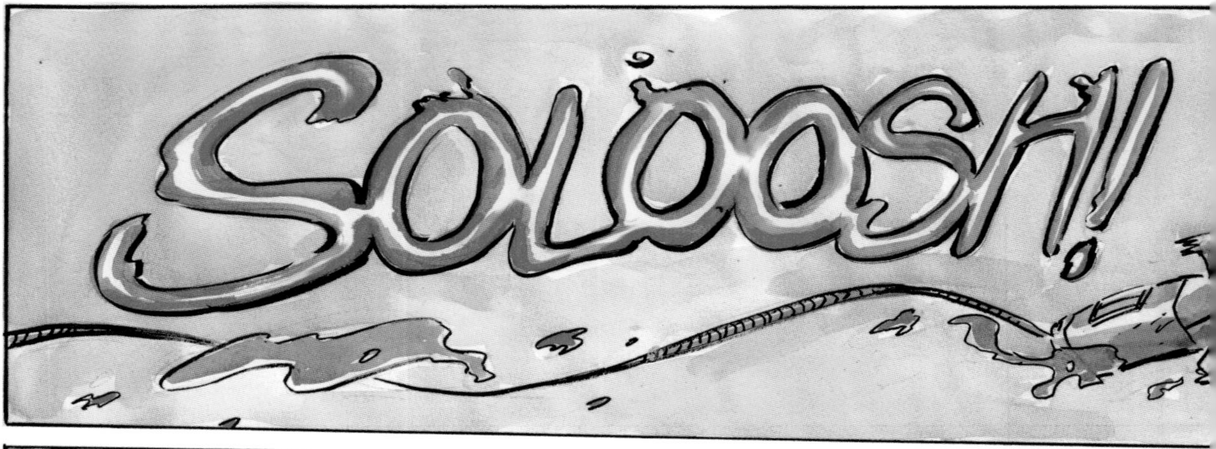
SQLOOSH!

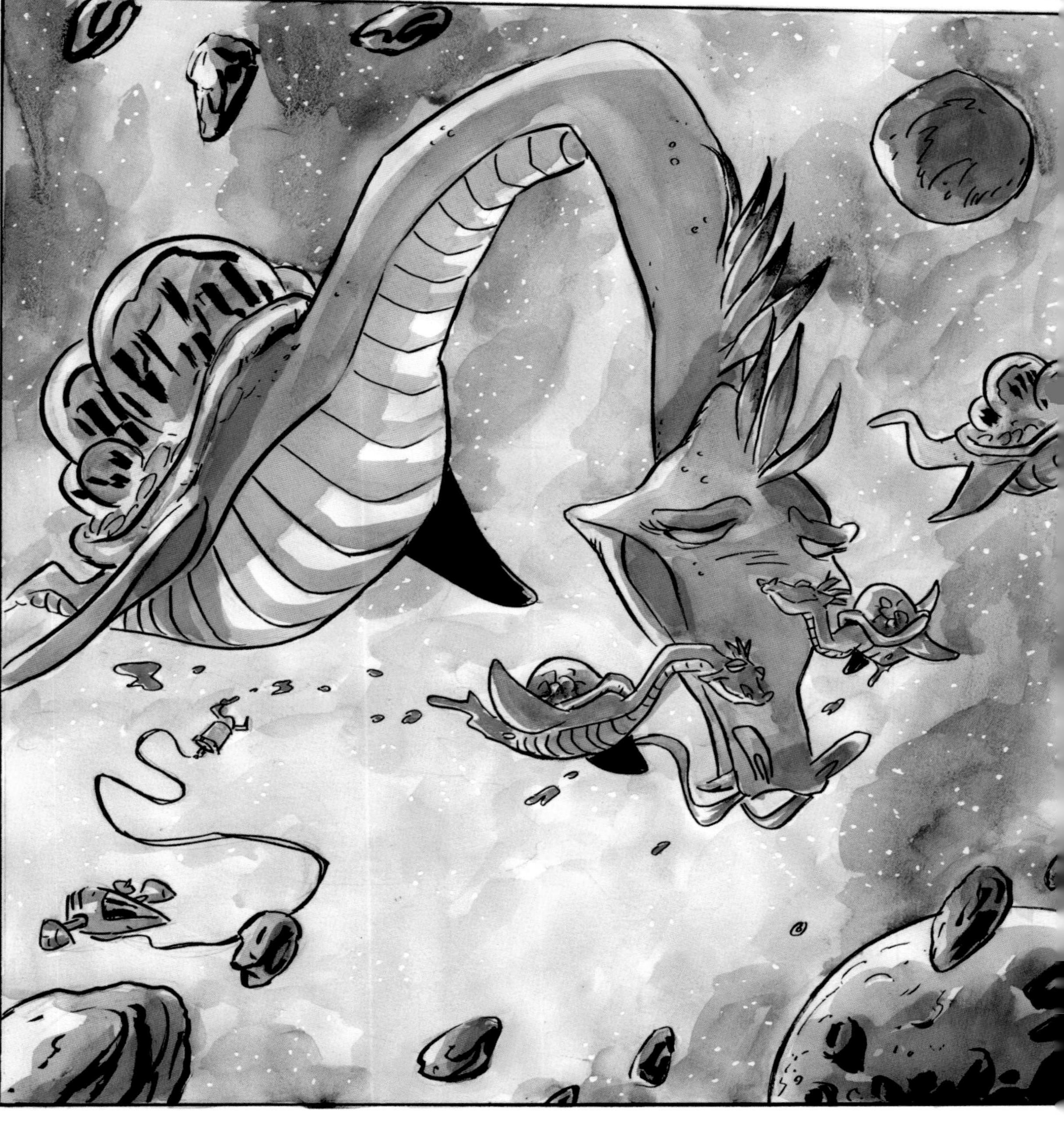

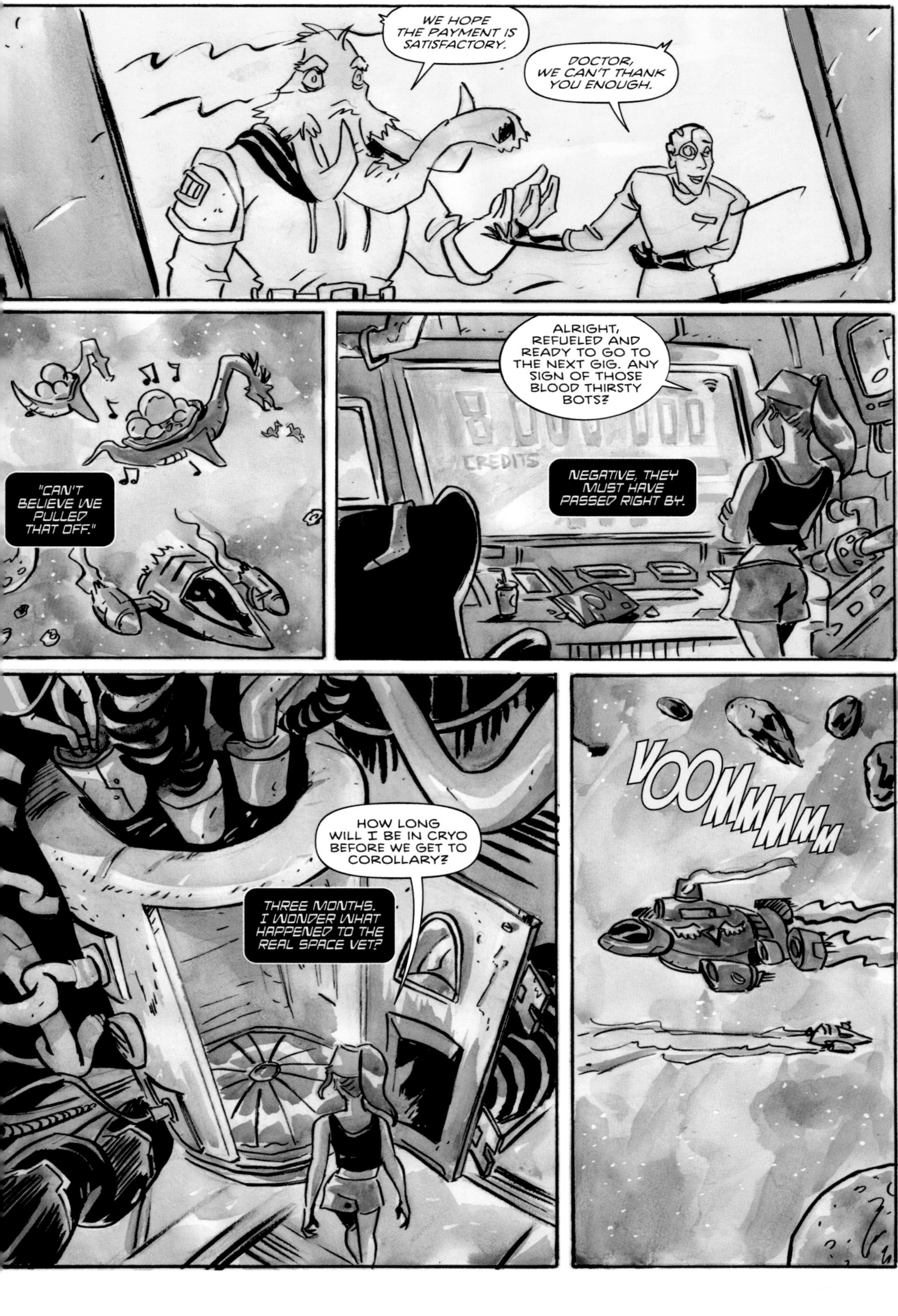
WE HOPE THE PAYMENT IS SATISFACTORY.
DOCTOR, WE CAN'T THANK YOU ENOUGH.
"CAN'T BELIEVE WE PULLED THAT OFF."
ALRIGHT, REFUELED AND READY TO GO TO THE NEXT GIG. ANY SIGN OF THOSE BLOOD THIRSTY BOTS?
CREDITS
NEGATIVE, THEY MUST HAVE PASSED RIGHT BY.
HOW LONG WILL I BE IN CRYO BEFORE WE GET TO COROLLARY?
THREE MONTHS. I WONDER WHAT HAPPENED TO THE REAL SPACE VET?
VOOMMMMMM

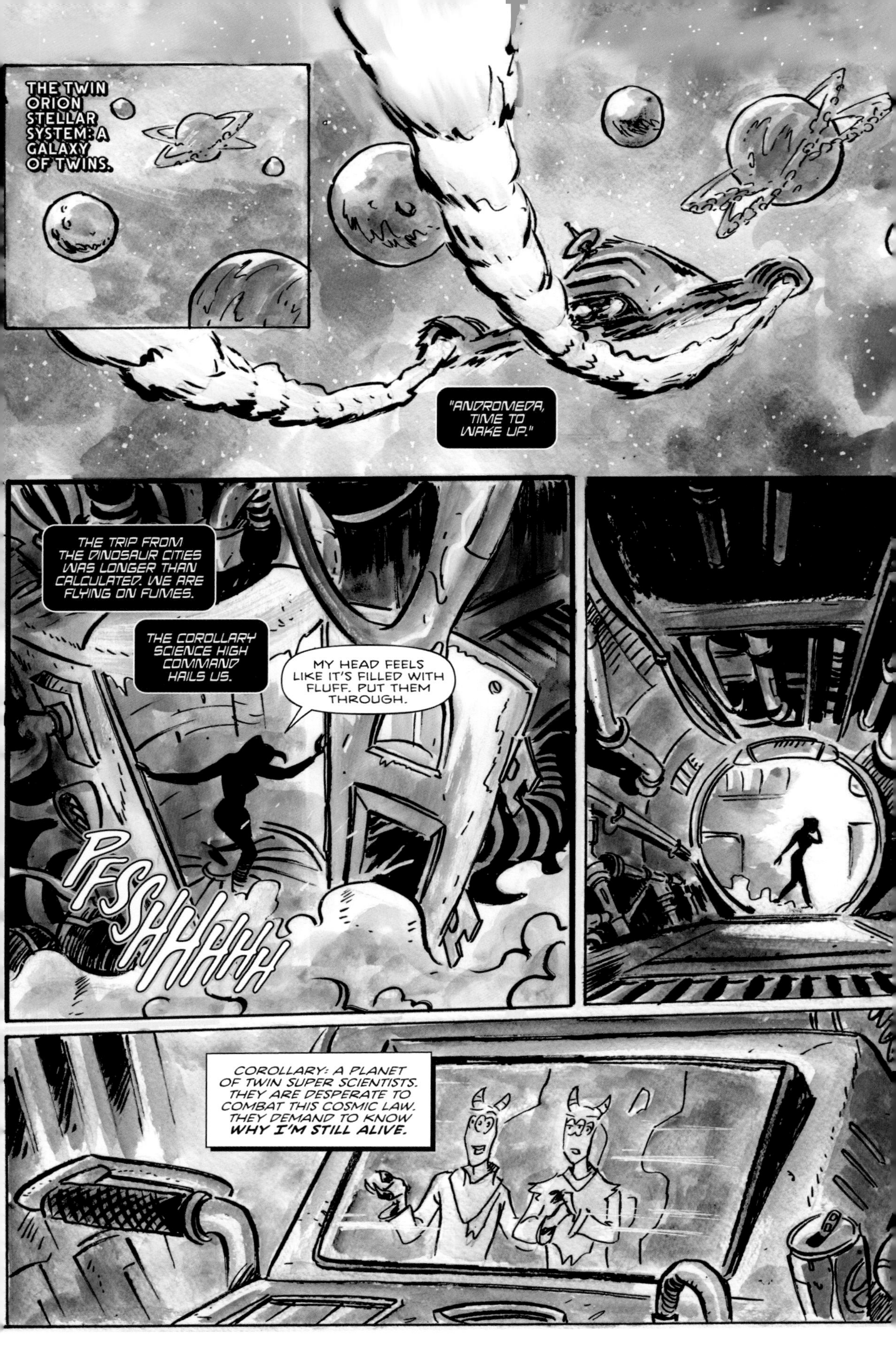
THE TWIN ORION STELLAR SYSTEM: A GALAXY OF TWINS.
"ANDROMEDA, TIME TO WAKE UP."
THE TRIP FROM THE DINOSAUR CITIES WAS LONGER THAN CALCULATED. WE ARE FLYING ON FUMES.
THE COROLLARY SCIENCE HIGH COMMAND HAILS US.
MY HEAD FEELS LIKE IT'S FILLED WITH FLUFF. PUT THEM THROUGH.
PFSSHHHHH
COROLLARY: A PLANET OF TWIN SUPER SCIENTISTS. THEY ARE DESPERATE TO COMBAT THIS COSMIC LAW. THEY DEMAND TO KNOW **WHY I'M STILL ALIVE.**

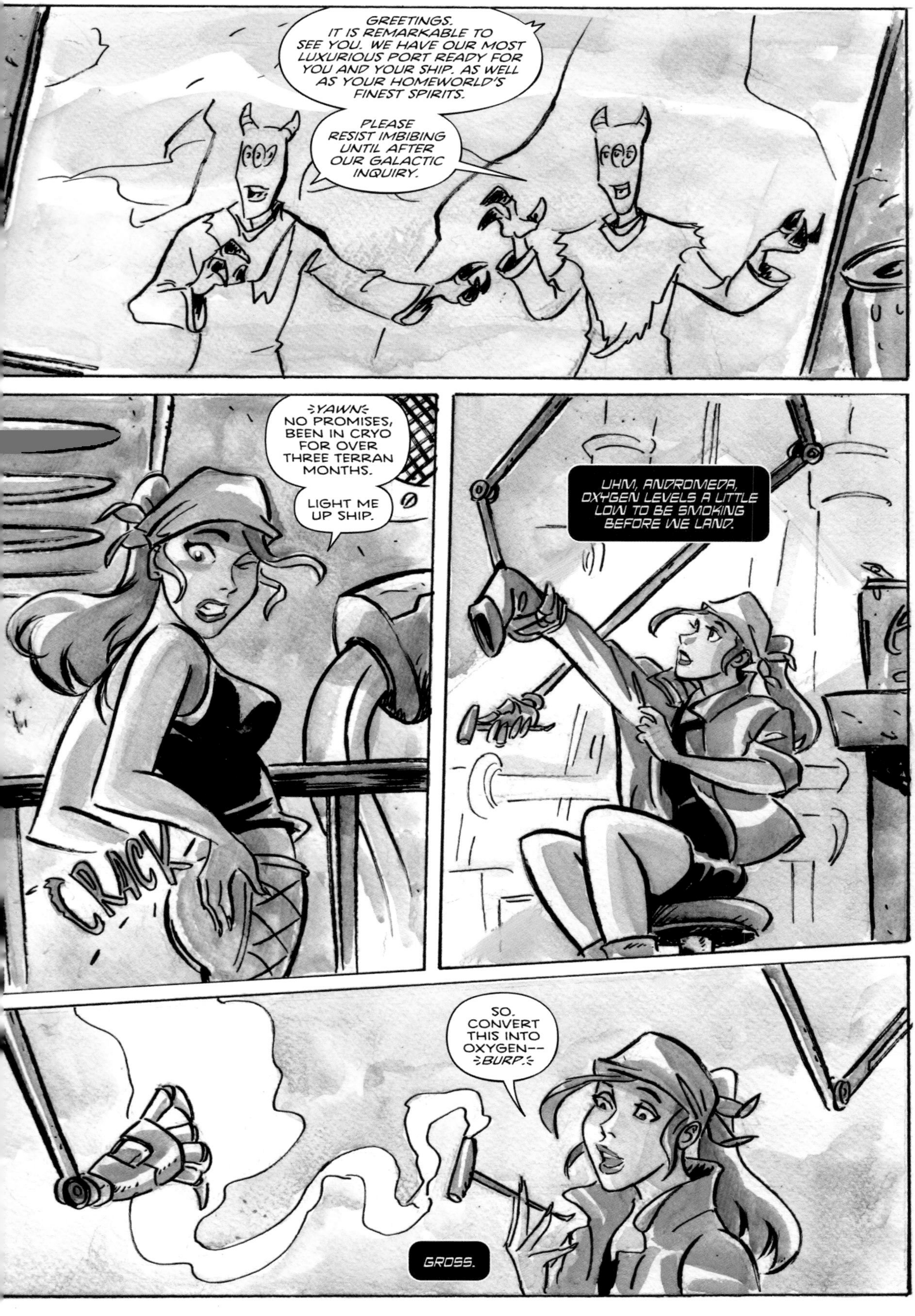
GREETINGS. IT IS REMARKABLE TO SEE YOU. WE HAVE OUR MOST LUXURIOUS PORT READY FOR YOU AND YOUR SHIP. AS WELL AS YOUR HOMEWORLD'S FINEST SPIRITS.
PLEASE RESIST IMBIBING UNTIL AFTER OUR GALACTIC INQUIRY.
YAWN NO PROMISES, BEEN IN CRYO FOR OVER THREE TERRAN MONTHS.
LIGHT ME UP SHIP.
CRACK
UHM, ANDROMEDA, OXYGEN LEVELS A LITTLE LOW TO BE SMOKING BEFORE WE LAND.
SO. CONVERT THIS INTO OXYGEN-- BURP.
GROSS.

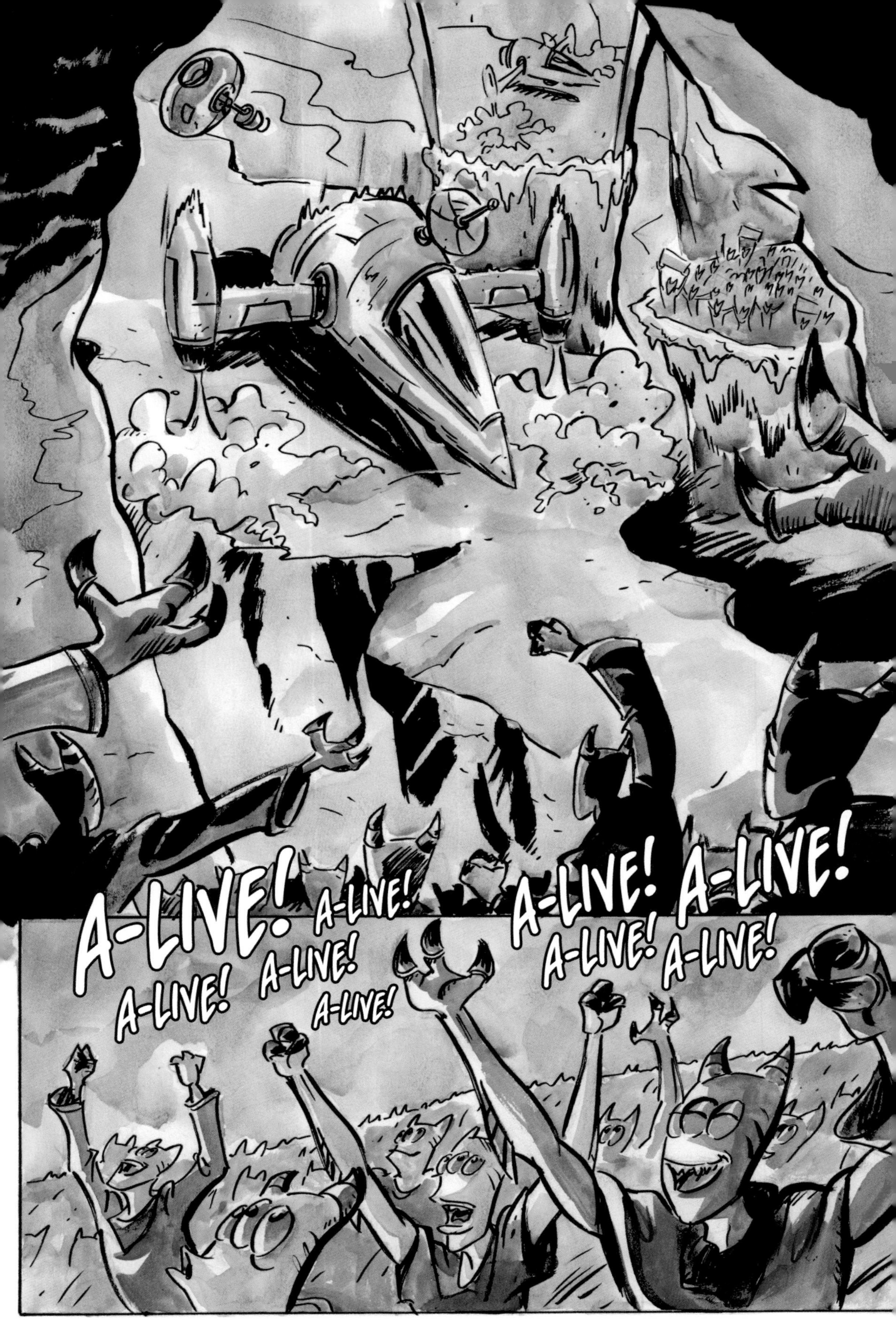

A-LIVE!
A-LIVE!
A-LIVE!
A-LIVE!
A-LIVE!
A-LIVE!
A-LIVE!
A-LIVE!
A-LIVE!

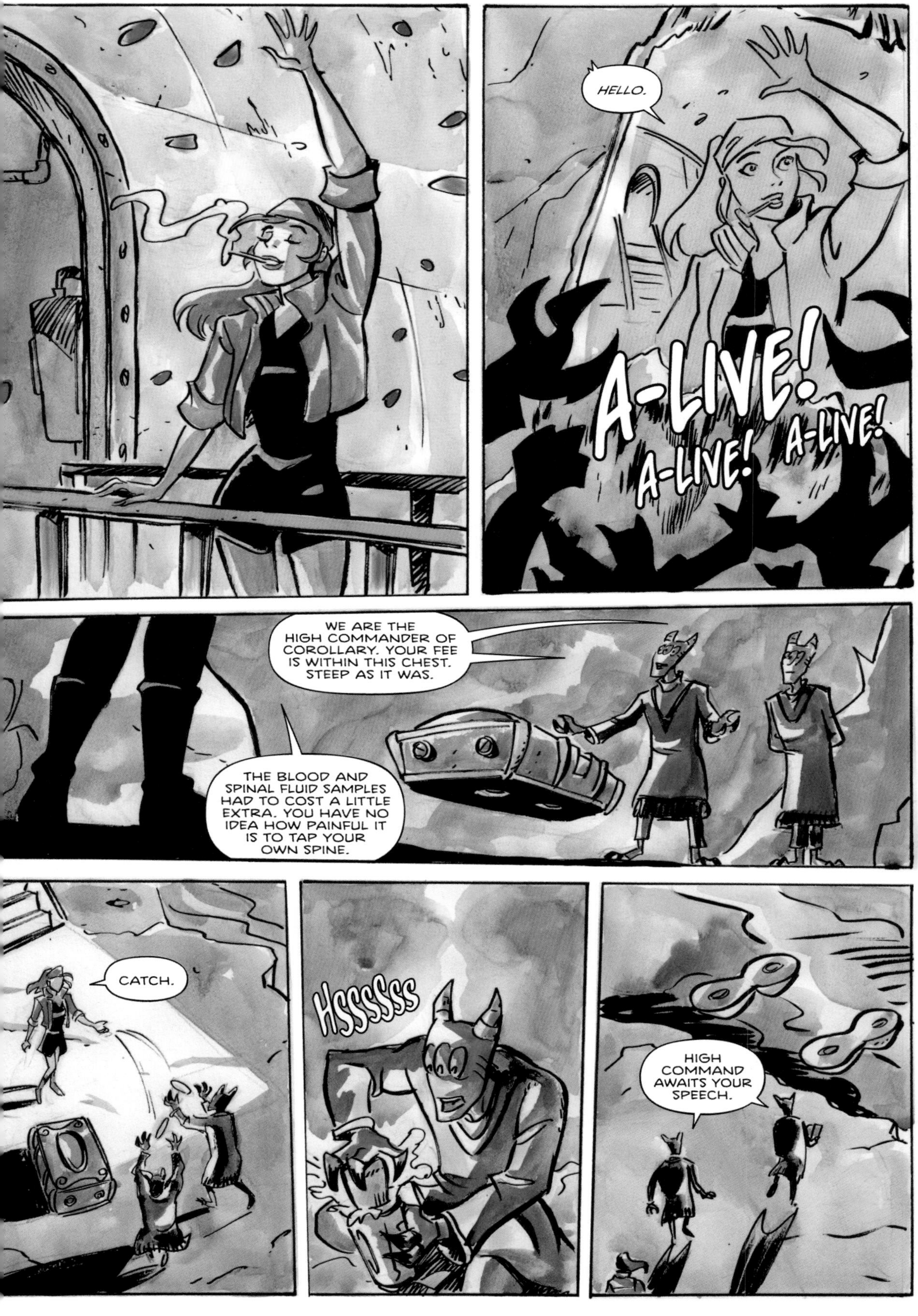
HELLO.
A-LIVE!
A-LIVE!
A-LIVE!
WE ARE THE HIGH COMMANDER OF COROLLARY. YOUR FEE IS WITHIN THIS CHEST. STEEP AS IT WAS.
THE BLOOD AND SPINAL FLUID SAMPLES HAD TO COST A LITTLE EXTRA. YOU HAVE NO IDEA HOW PAINFUL IT IS TO TAP YOUR OWN SPINE.
CATCH.
HSSSSSS
HIGH COMMAND AWAITS YOUR SPEECH.

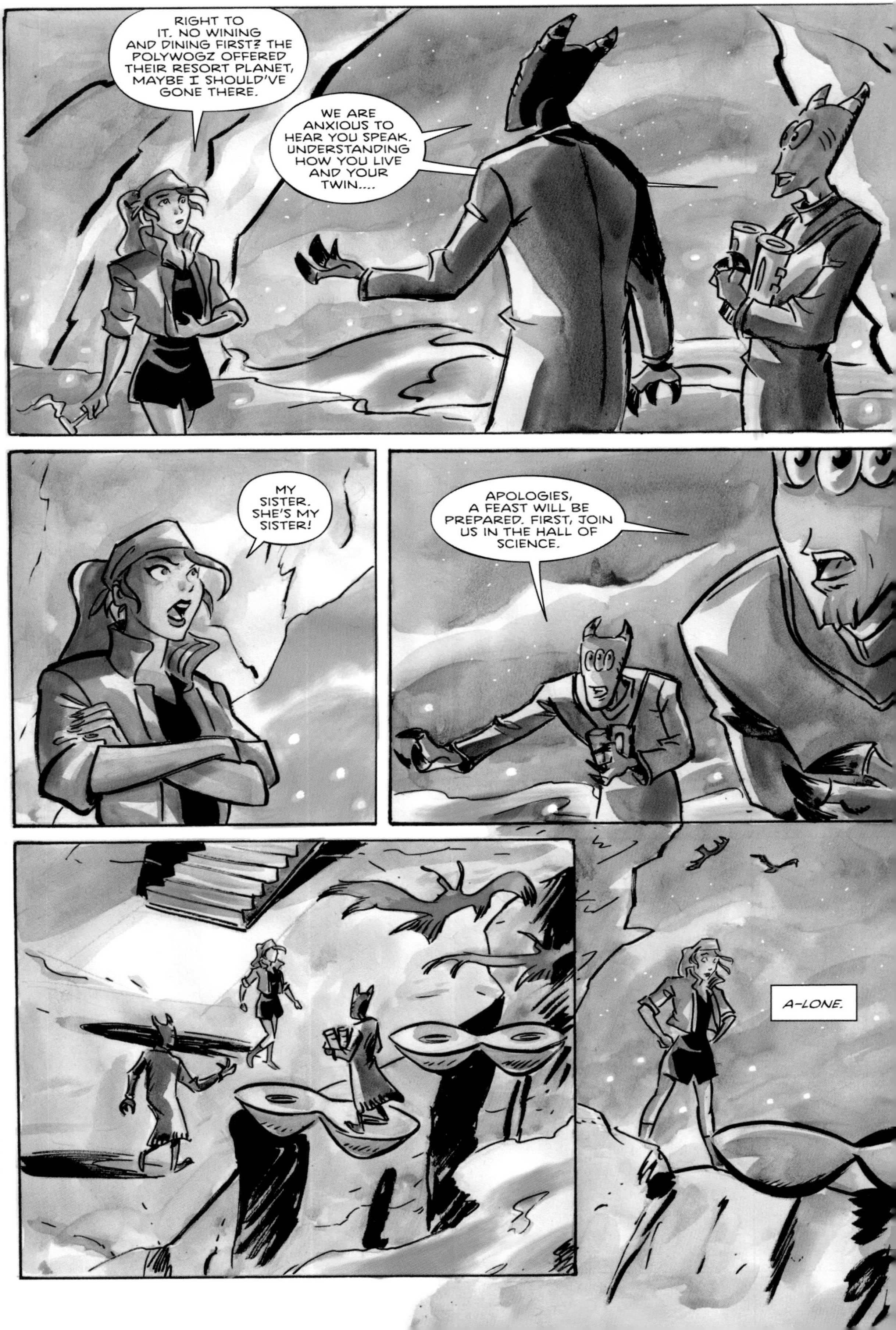
RIGHT TO IT. NO WINING AND DINING FIRST? THE POLYWOGZ OFFERED THEIR RESORT PLANET, MAYBE I SHOULD'VE GONE THERE.
WE ARE ANXIOUS TO HEAR YOU SPEAK. UNDERSTANDING HOW YOU LIVE AND YOUR TWIN....
MY SISTER. SHE'S MY SISTER!
APOLOGIES, A FEAST WILL BE PREPARED. FIRST, JOIN US IN THE HALL OF SCIENCE.
A-LONE.

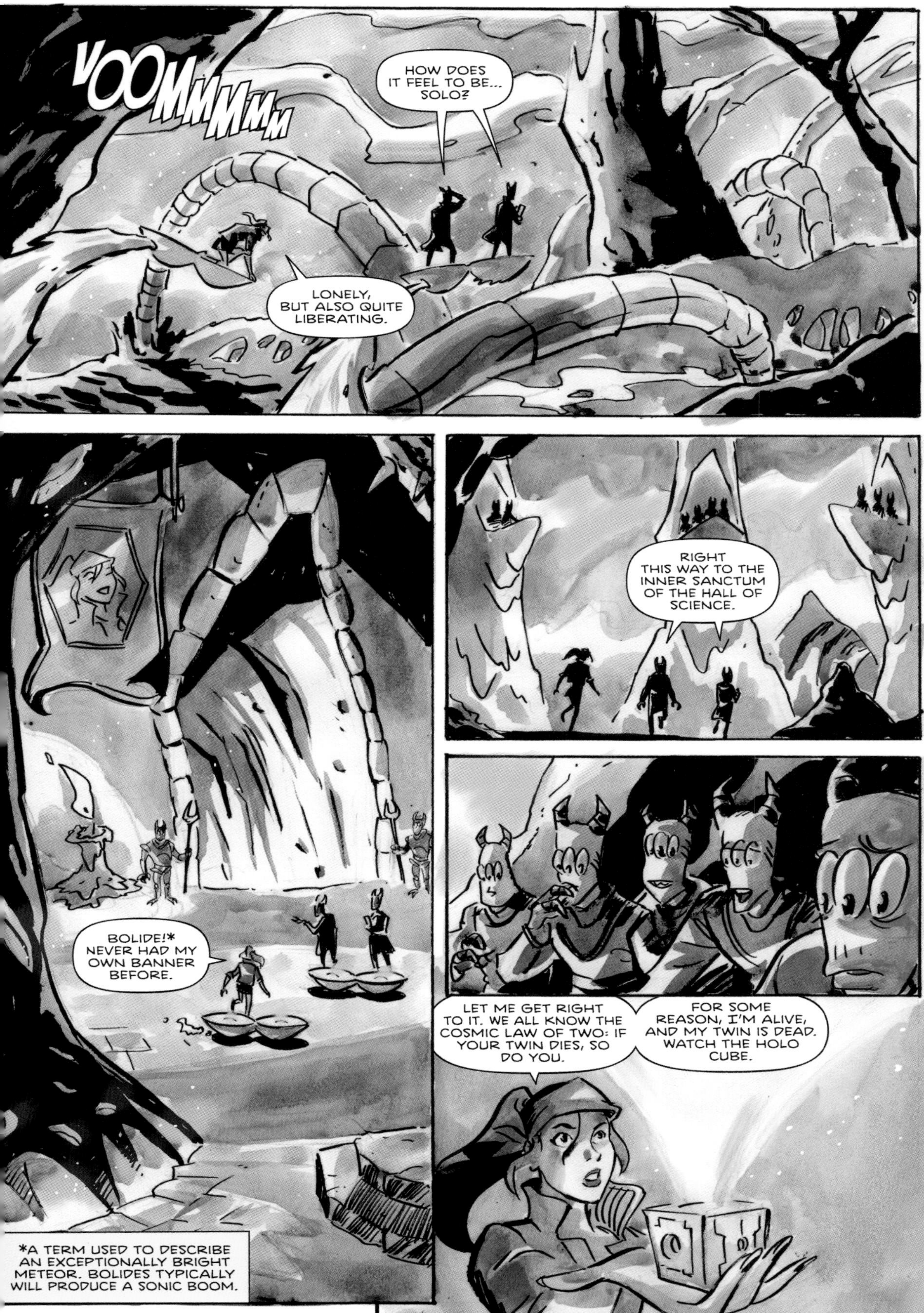
VOOMMMMMM
HOW DOES IT FEEL TO BE... SOLO?
LONELY, BUT ALSO QUITE LIBERATING.
BOLIDE!* NEVER HAD MY OWN BANNER BEFORE.
*A TERM USED TO DESCRIBE AN EXCEPTIONALLY BRIGHT METEOR. BOLIDES TYPICALLY WILL PRODUCE A SONIC BOOM.
RIGHT THIS WAY TO THE INNER SANCTUM OF THE HALL OF SCIENCE.
LET ME GET RIGHT TO IT. WE ALL KNOW THE COSMIC LAW OF TWO: IF YOUR TWIN DIES, SO DO YOU.
FOR SOME REASON, I'M ALIVE, AND MY TWIN IS DEAD. WATCH THE HOLO CUBE.

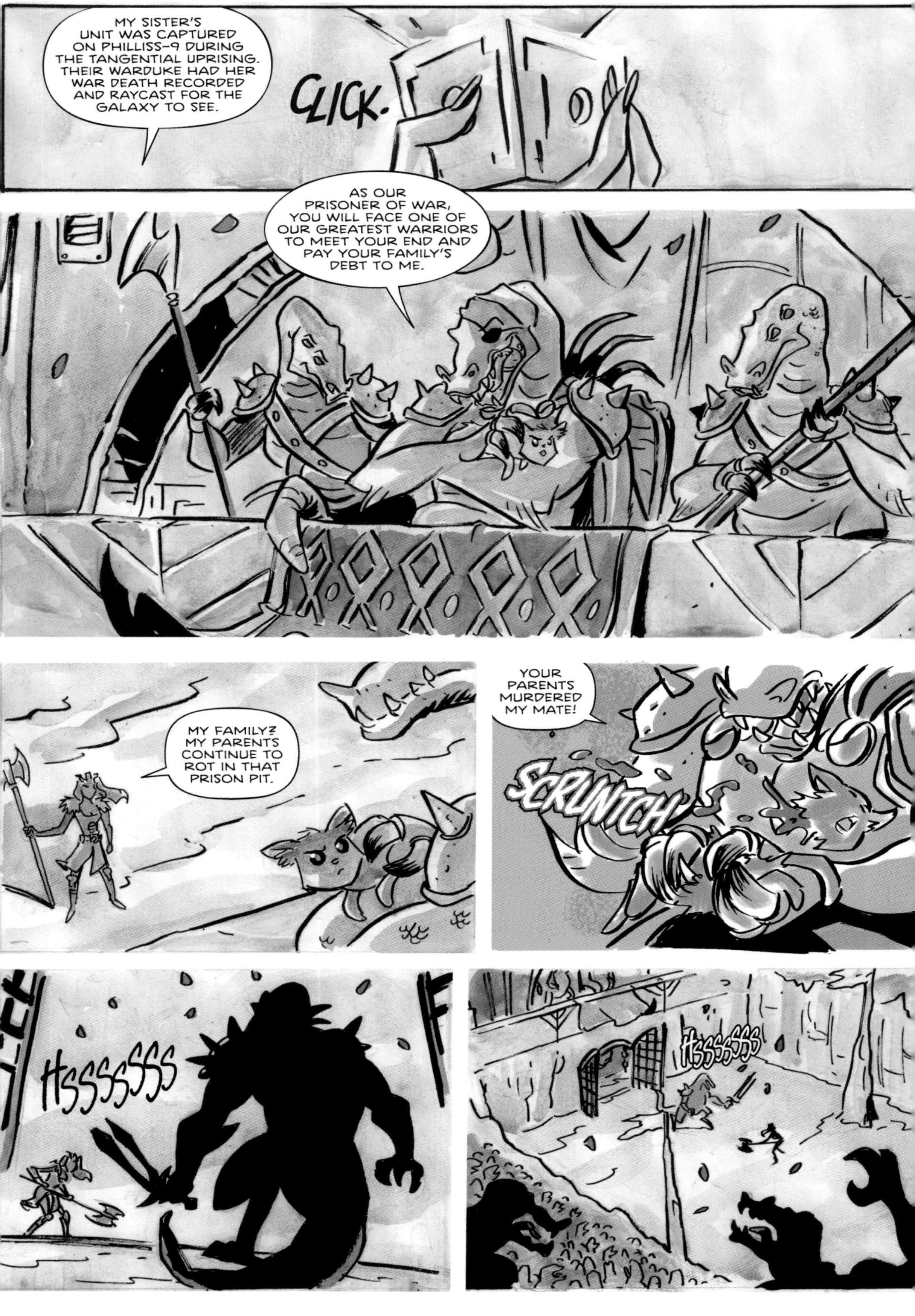

MY SISTER'S UNIT WAS CAPTURED ON PHILLISS-9 DURING THE TANGENTIAL UPRISING. THEIR WARDUKE HAD HER WAR DEATH RECORDED AND RAYCAST FOR THE GALAXY TO SEE.
CLICK.
AS OUR PRISONER OF WAR, YOU WILL FACE ONE OF OUR GREATEST WARRIORS TO MEET YOUR END AND PAY YOUR FAMILY'S DEBT TO ME.
MY FAMILY? MY PARENTS CONTINUE TO ROT IN THAT PRISON PIT.
YOUR PARENTS MURDERED MY MATE!
SCRUNTCH
HSSSSSSS
HSSSSSSS

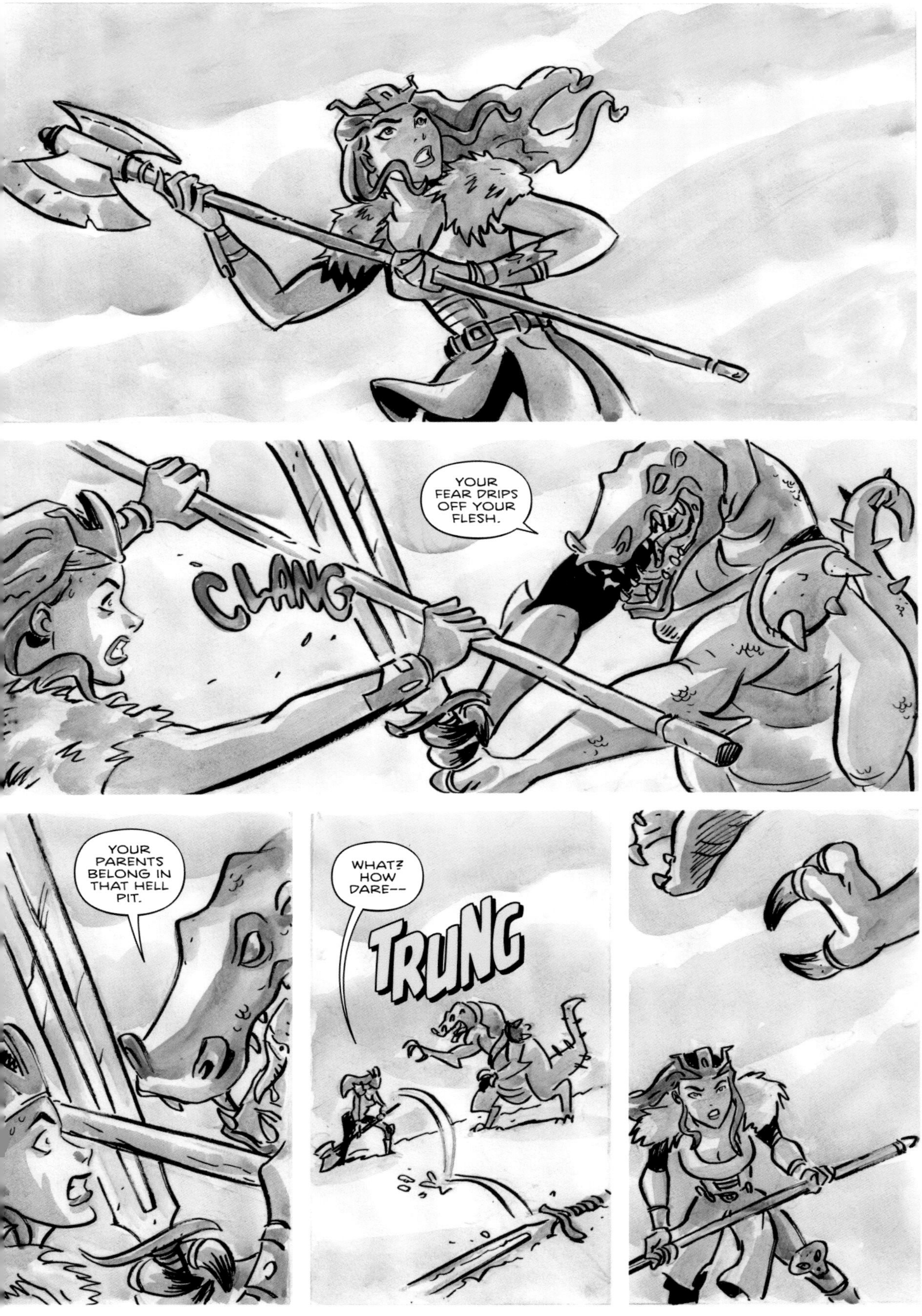
YOUR FEAR DRIPS OFF YOUR FLESH.
CLANG
YOUR PARENTS BELONG IN THAT HELL PIT.
WHAT? HOW DARE--
TRUNG

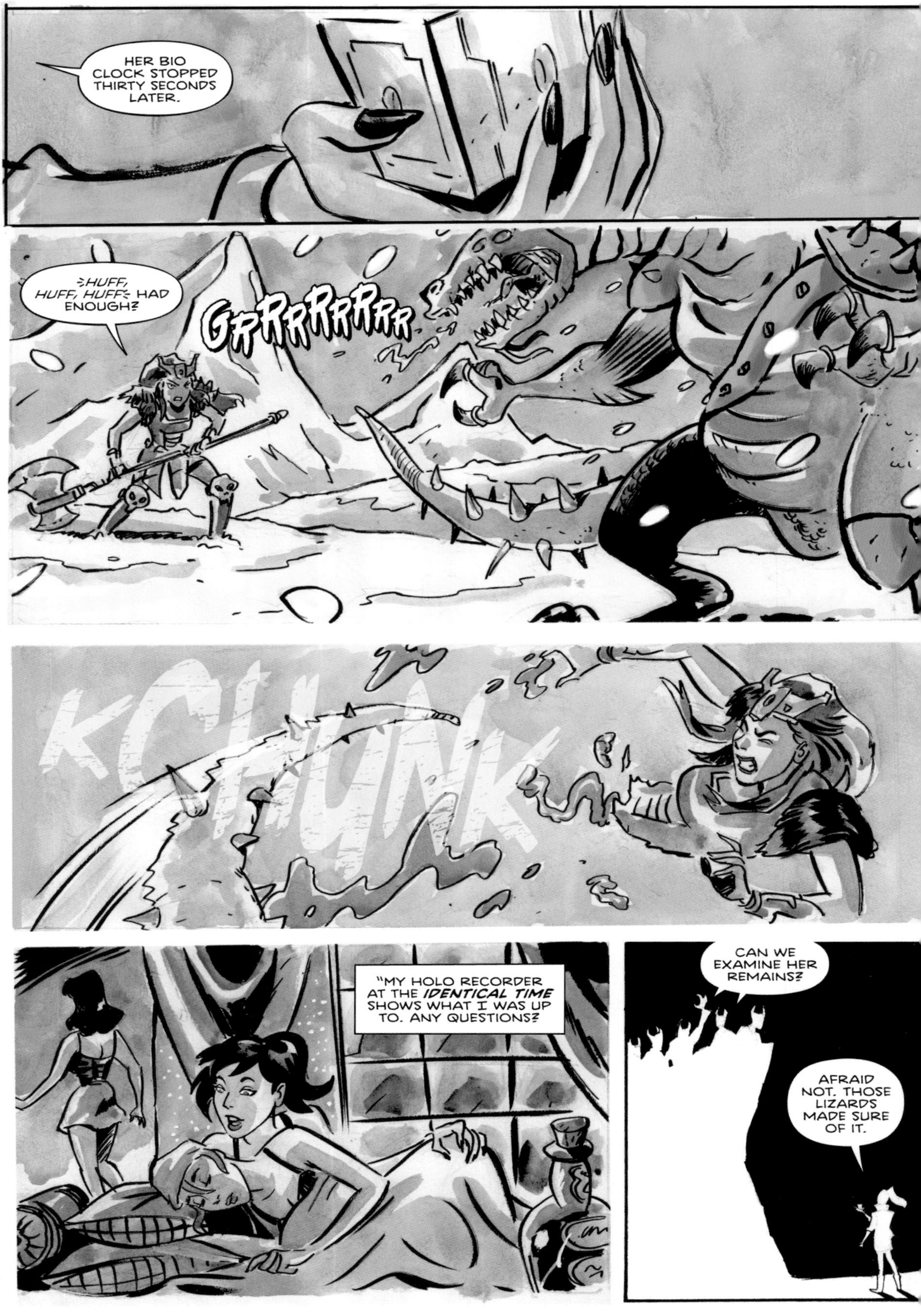
HER BIO CLOCK STOPPED THIRTY SECONDS LATER.
HUFF, HUFF, HUFF HAD ENOUGH?
GRRRRRRRR
KCHUNK
"MY HOLO RECORDER AT THE *IDENTICAL TIME* SHOWS WHAT I WAS UP TO. ANY QUESTIONS?
CAN WE EXAMINE HER REMAINS?
AFRAID NOT. THOSE LIZARDS MADE SURE OF IT.

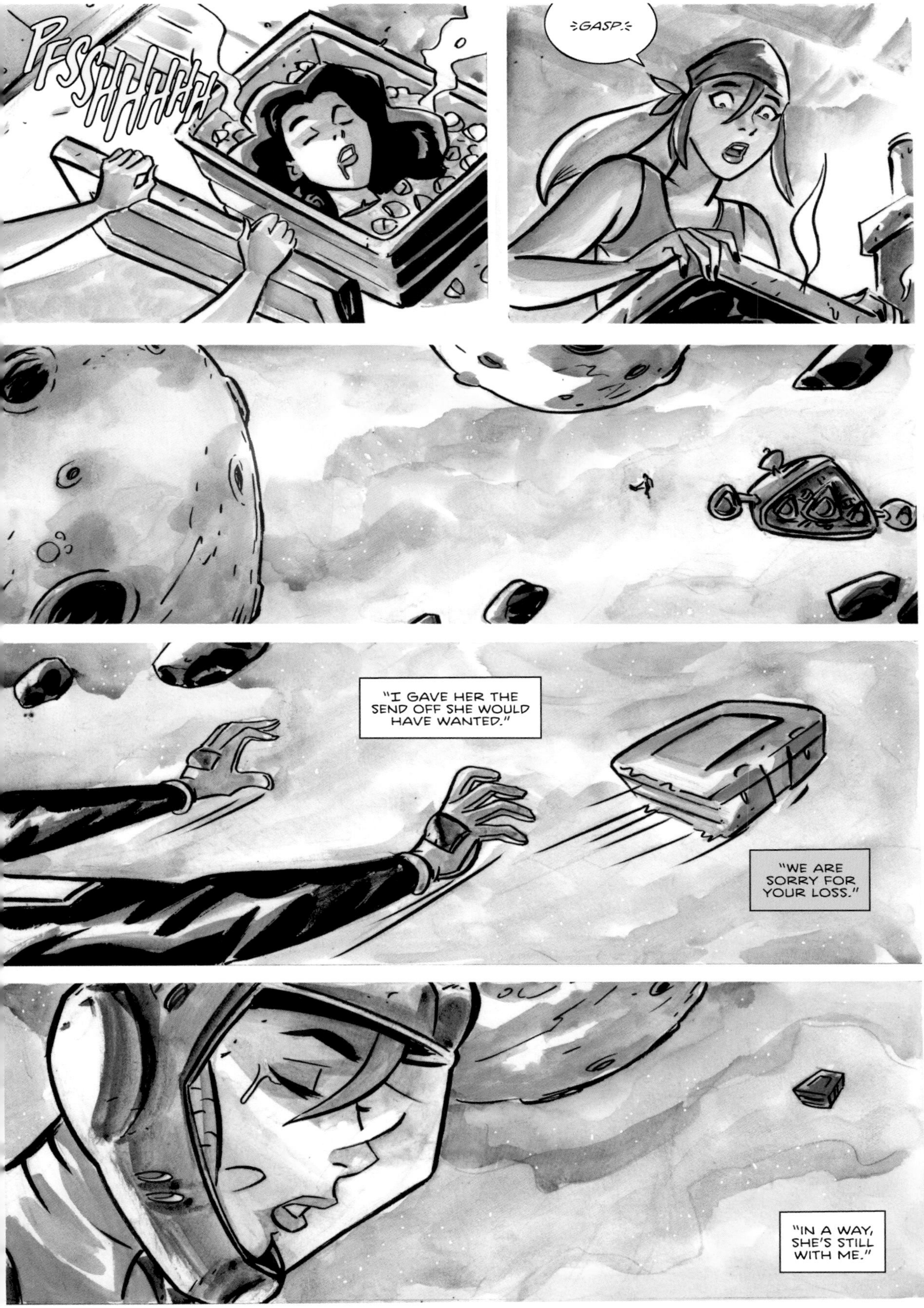
PFSSHHHHHH
GASP.
"I GAVE HER THE SEND OFF SHE WOULD HAVE WANTED."
"WE ARE SORRY FOR YOUR LOSS."
"IN A WAY, SHE'S STILL WITH ME."

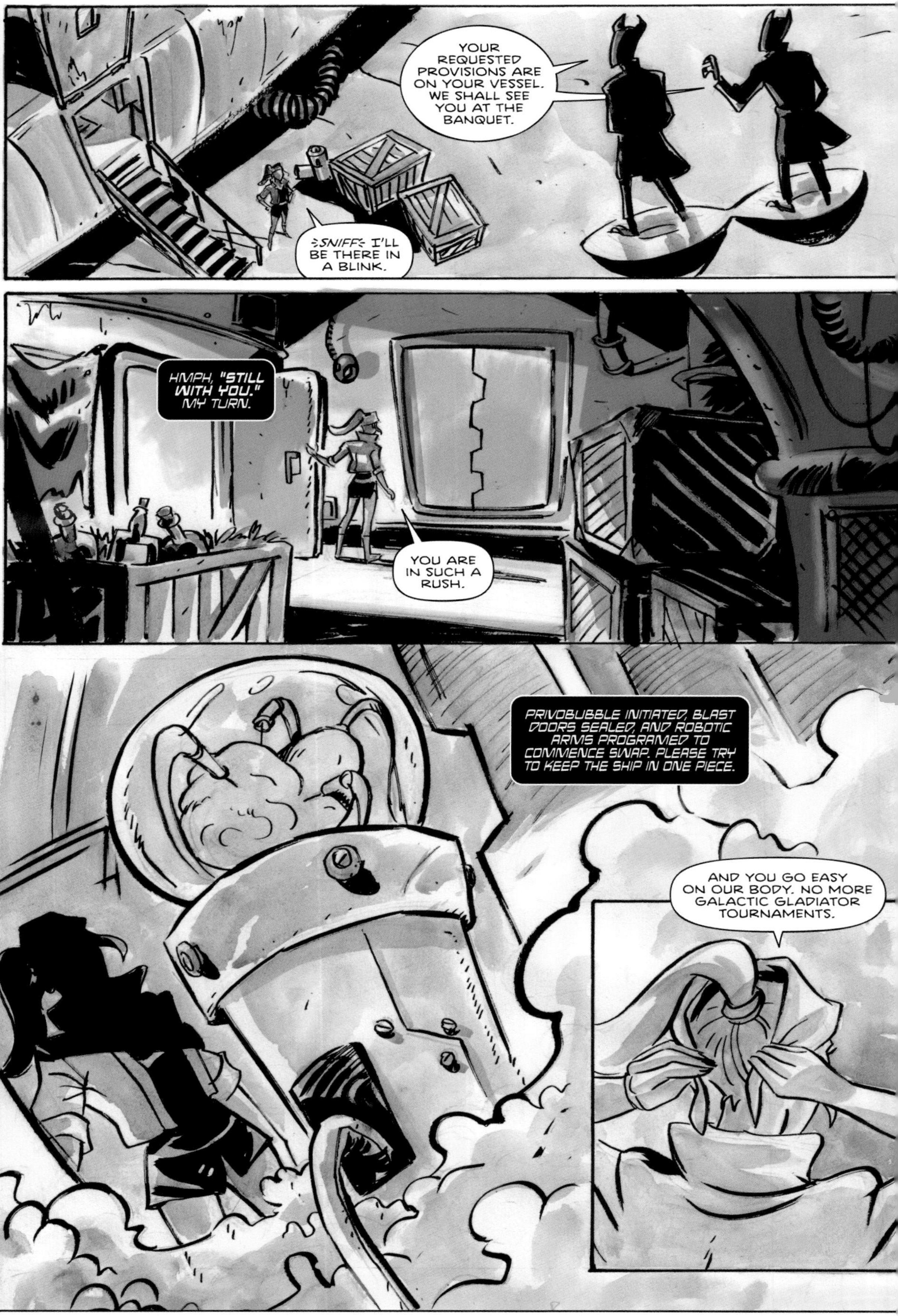
YOUR REQUESTED PROVISIONS ARE ON YOUR VESSEL. WE SHALL SEE YOU AT THE BANQUET.
=SNIFF= I'LL BE THERE IN A BLINK.
HMPH, "STILL WITH YOU." MY TURN.
YOU ARE IN SUCH A RUSH.
PRIVOBUBBLE INITIATED, BLAST DOORS SEALED, AND ROBOTIC ARMS PROGRAMED TO COMMENCE SWAP. PLEASE TRY TO KEEP THE SHIP IN ONE PIECE.
AND YOU GO EASY ON OUR BODY. NO MORE GALACTIC GLADIATOR TOURNAMENTS.

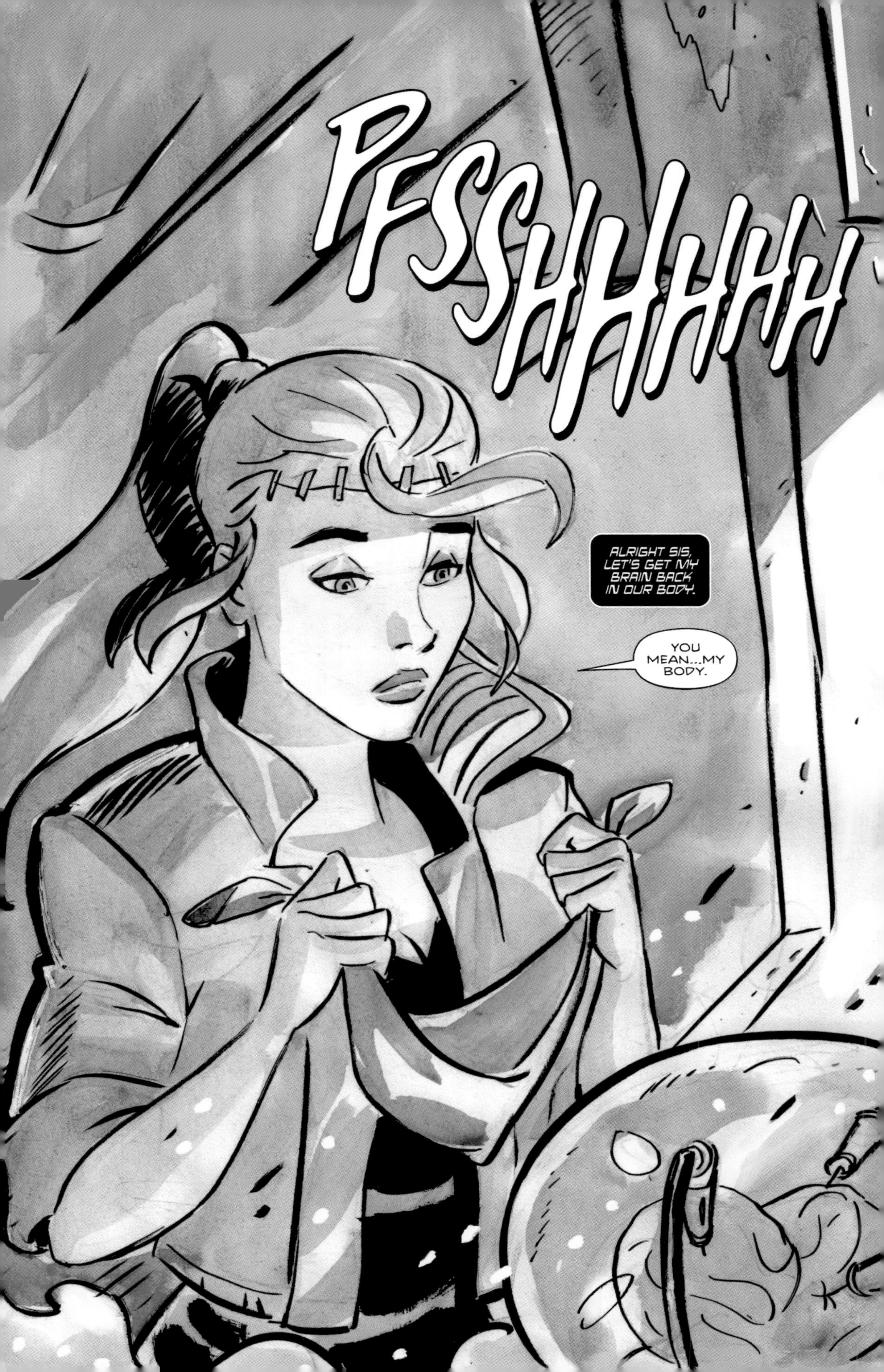
PFSSHHHHHH
ALRIGHT SIS, LET'S GET MY BRAIN BACK IN OUR BODY.
YOU MEAN...MY BODY.

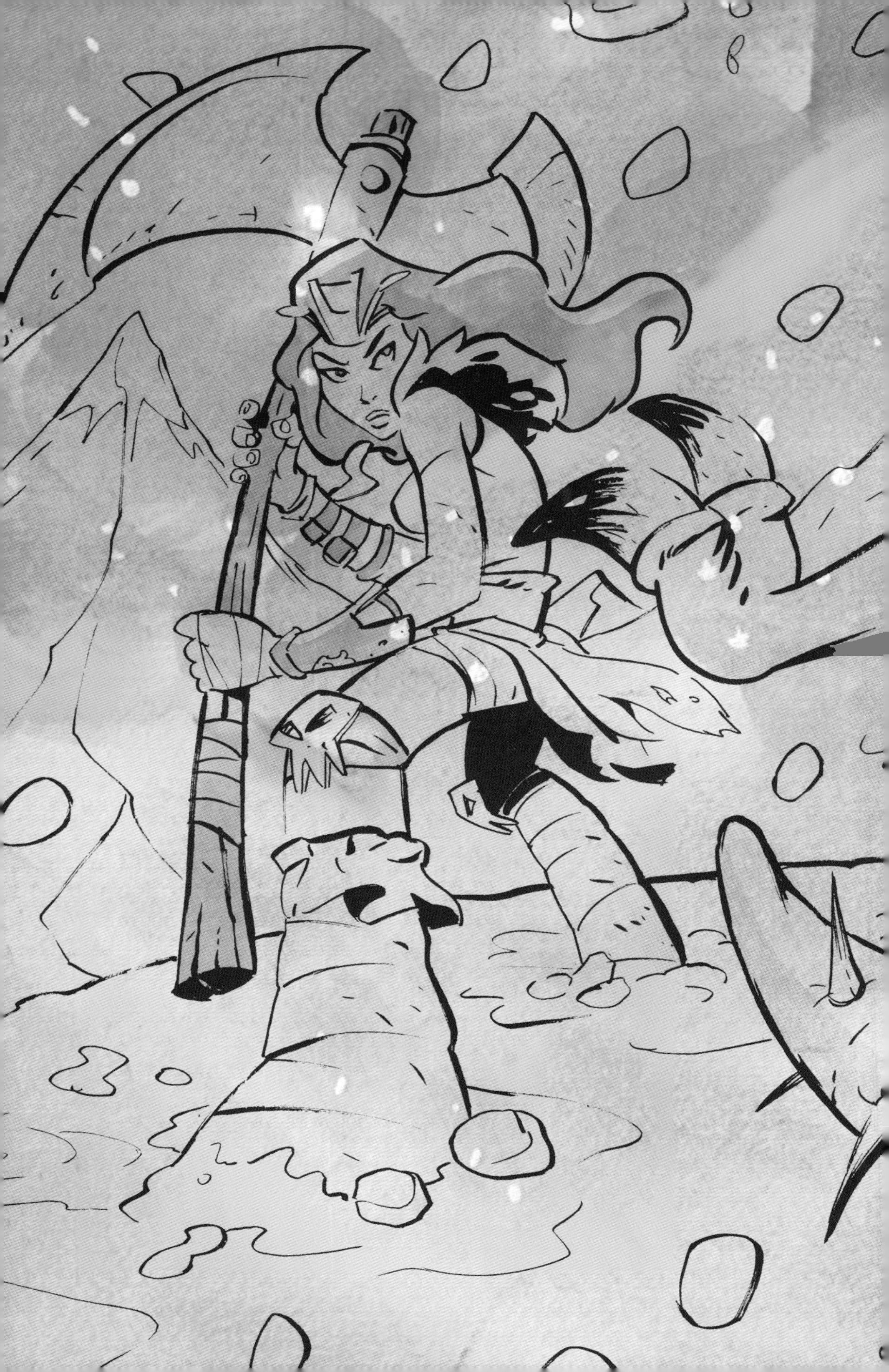

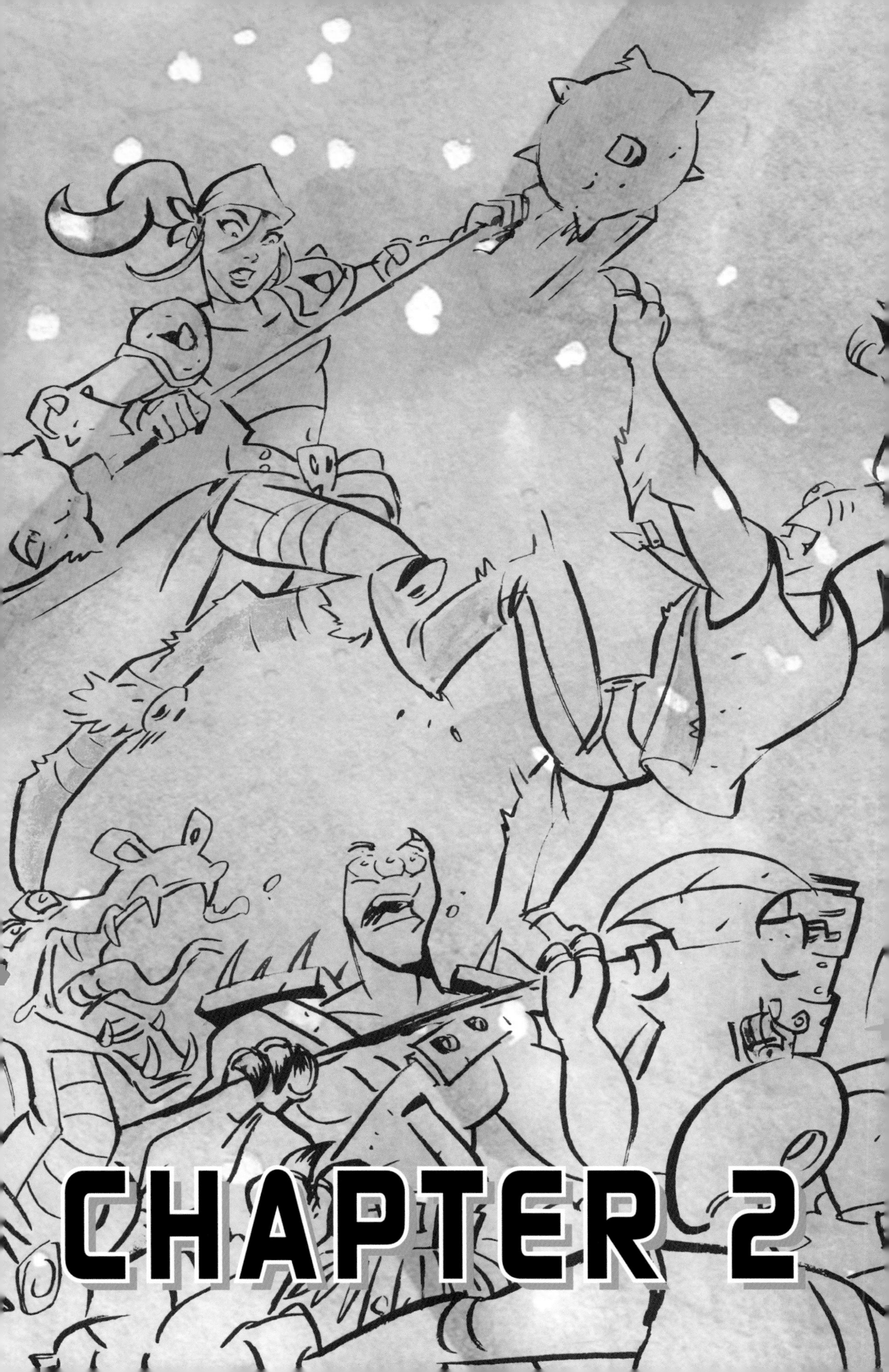

CHAPTER 2

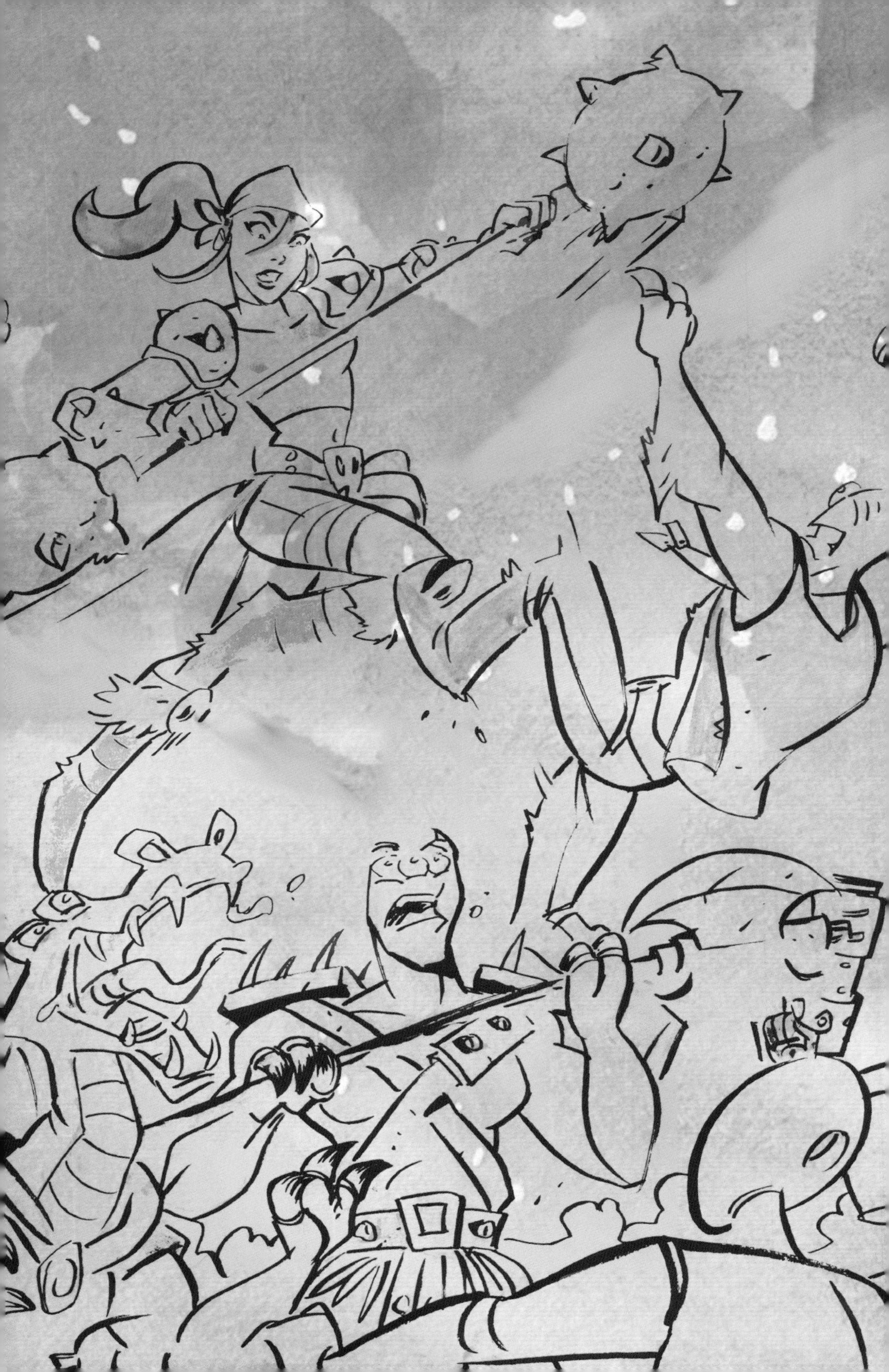

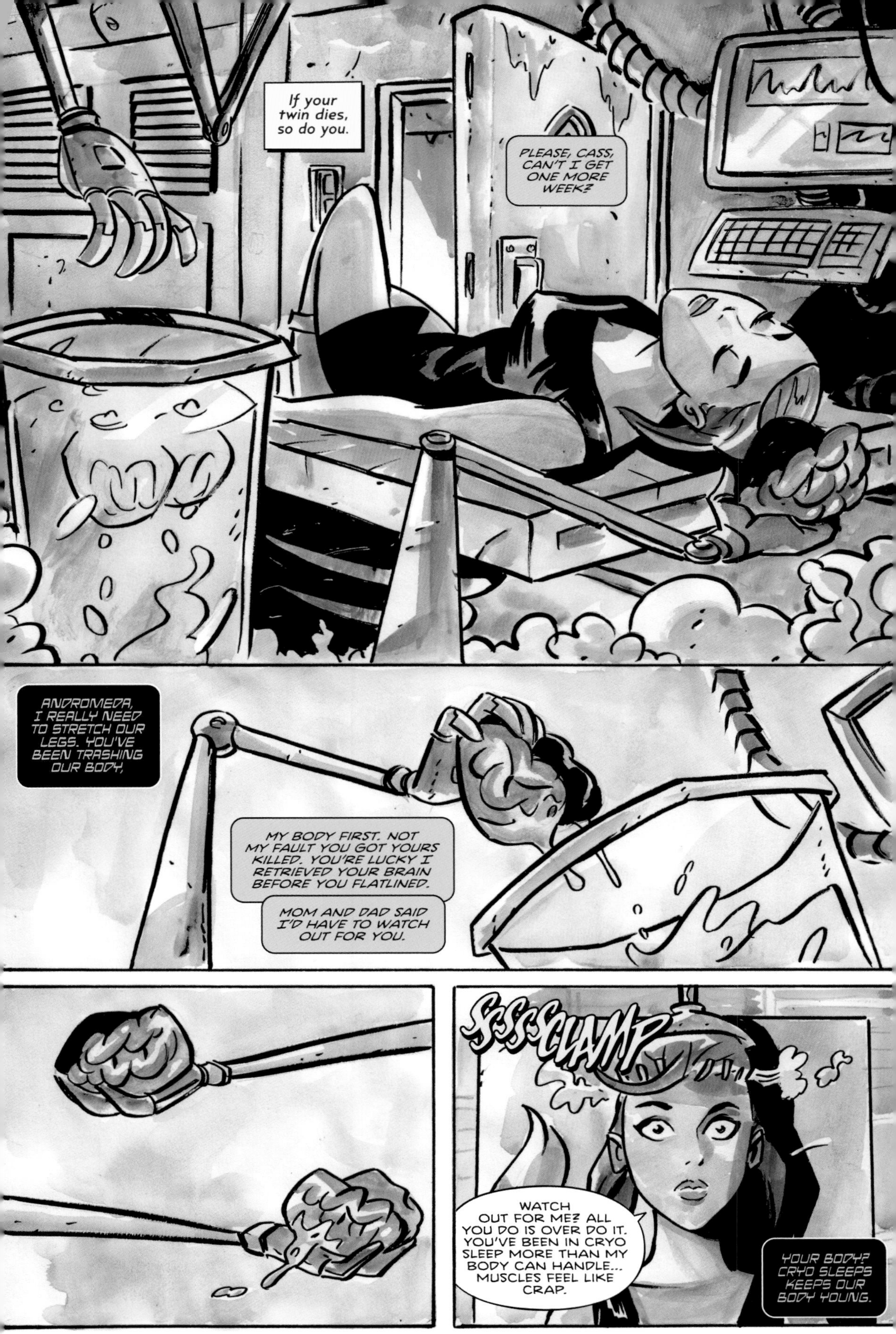
If your twin dies, so do you.
PLEASE, CASS, CAN'T I GET ONE MORE WEEK?
ANDROMEDA, I REALLY NEED TO STRETCH OUR LEGS. YOU'VE BEEN TRASHING OUR BODY,
MY BODY FIRST. NOT MY FAULT YOU GOT YOURS KILLED. YOU'RE LUCKY I RETRIEVED YOUR BRAIN BEFORE YOU FLATLINED.
MOM AND DAD SAID I'D HAVE TO WATCH OUT FOR YOU.
SSSSCLAMP
WATCH OUT FOR ME? ALL YOU DO IS OVER DO IT. YOU'VE BEEN IN CRYO SLEEP MORE THAN MY BODY CAN HANDLE... MUSCLES FEEL LIKE CRAP.
YOUR BODY? CRYO SLEEPS KEEPS OUR BODY YOUNG.

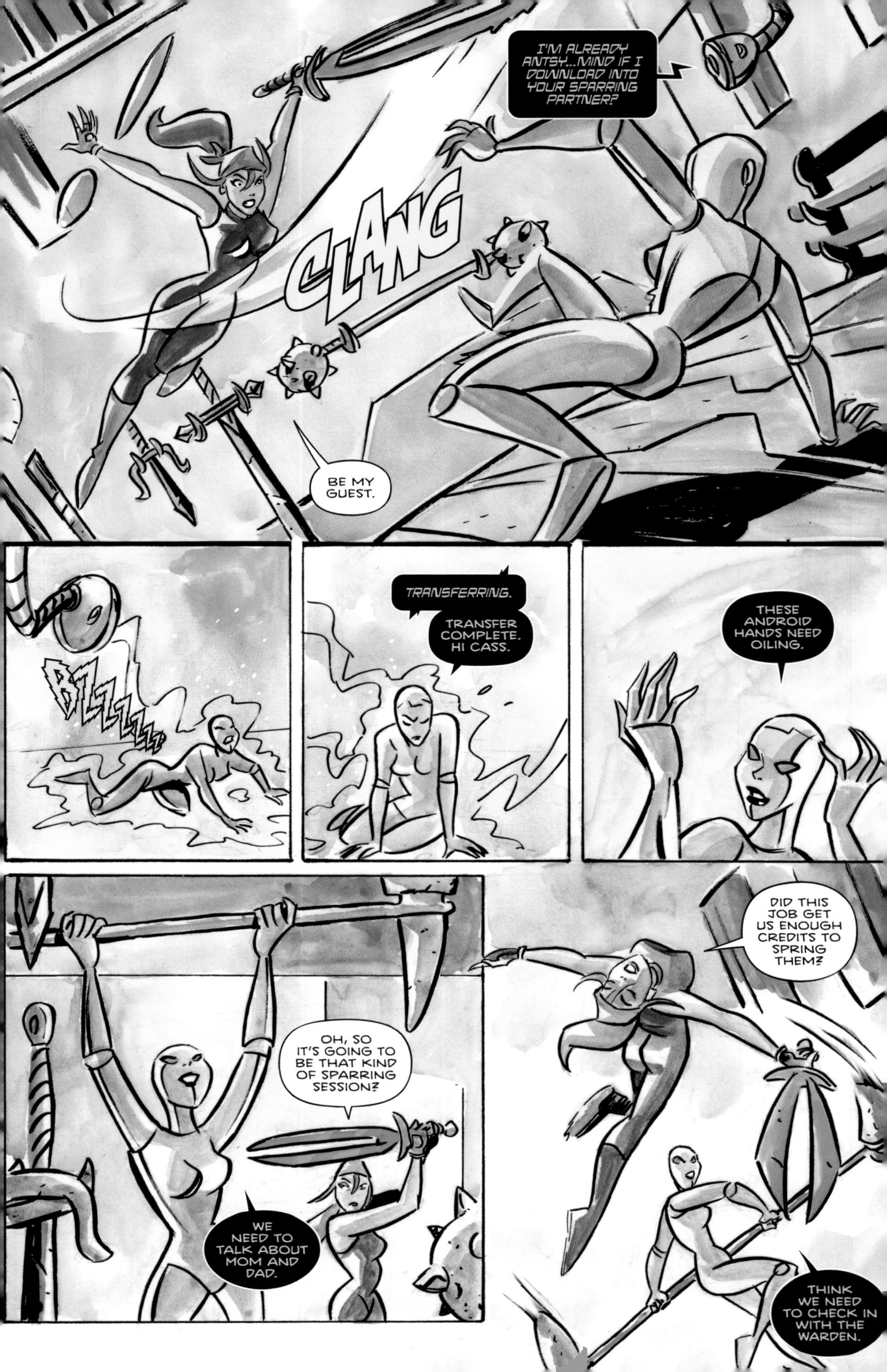
I'M ALREADY ANTSY...MIND IF I DOWNLOAD INTO YOUR SPARRING PARTNER?
CLANG
BE MY GUEST.
BZZZZZ
TRANSFERRING.
TRANSFER COMPLETE. HI CASS.
THESE ANDROID HANDS NEED OILING.
OH, SO IT'S GOING TO BE THAT KIND OF SPARRING SESSION?
WE NEED TO TALK ABOUT MOM AND DAD.
DID THIS JOB GET US ENOUGH CREDITS TO SPRING THEM?
THINK WE NEED TO CHECK IN WITH THE WARDEN.

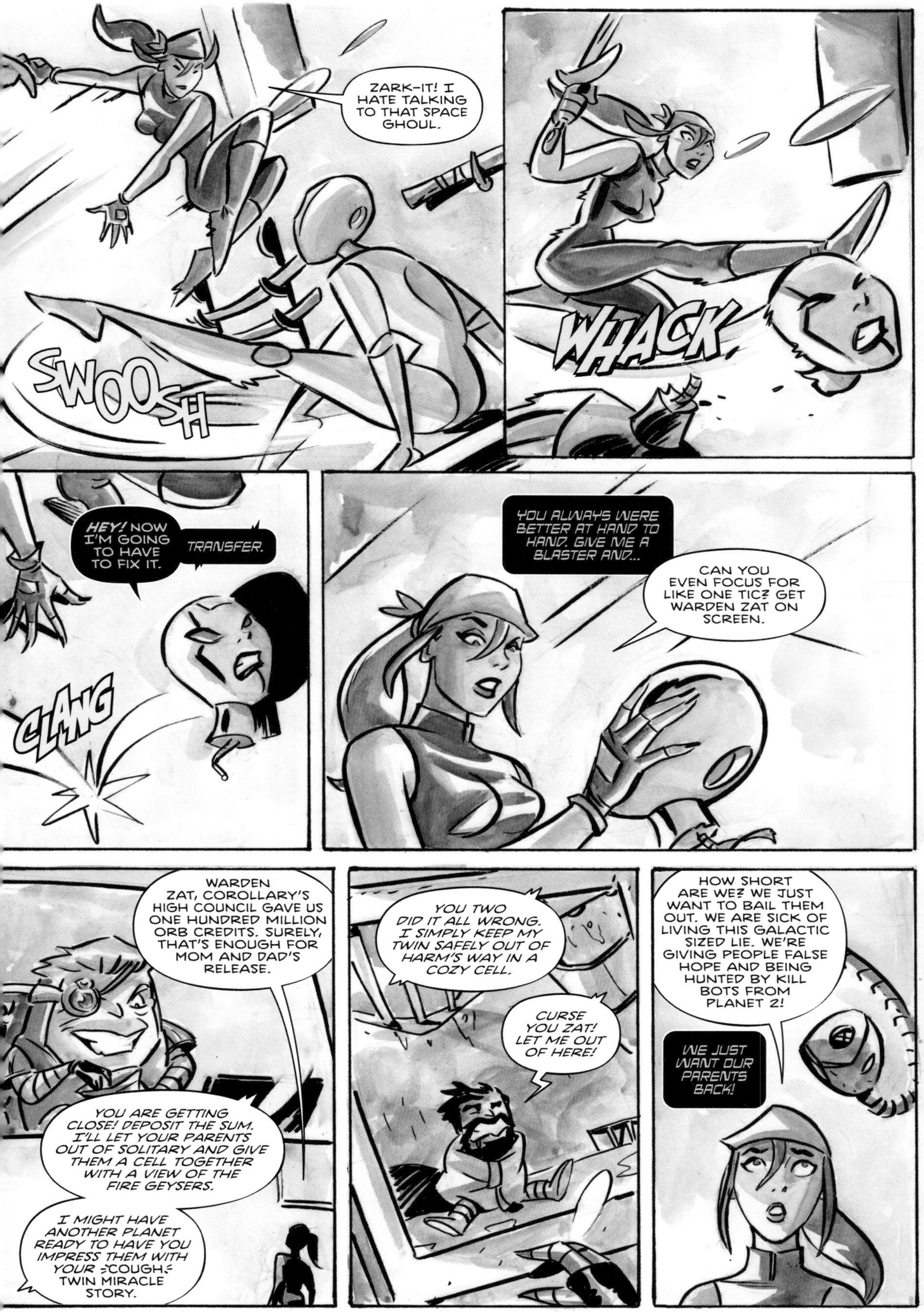
ZARK-IT! I HATE TALKING TO THAT SPACE GHOUL.
SWOOSH
WHACK
HEY! NOW I'M GOING TO HAVE TO FIX IT.
TRANSFER.
CLANG
YOU ALWAYS WERE BETTER AT HAND TO HAND. GIVE ME A BLASTER AND...
CAN YOU EVEN FOCUS FOR LIKE ONE TIC? GET WARDEN ZAT ON SCREEN.
WARDEN ZAT, COROLLARY'S HIGH COUNCIL GAVE US ONE HUNDRED MILLION ORB CREDITS. SURELY, THAT'S ENOUGH FOR MOM AND DAD'S RELEASE.
YOU ARE GETTING CLOSE! DEPOSIT THE SUM. I'LL LET YOUR PARENTS OUT OF SOLITARY AND GIVE THEM A CELL TOGETHER WITH A VIEW OF THE FIRE GEYSERS.
I MIGHT HAVE ANOTHER PLANET READY TO HAVE YOU IMPRESS THEM WITH YOUR =COUGH= TWIN MIRACLE STORY.
YOU TWO DID IT ALL WRONG. I SIMPLY KEEP MY TWIN SAFELY OUT OF HARM'S WAY IN A COZY CELL.
CURSE YOU ZAT! LET ME OUT OF HERE!
HOW SHORT ARE WE? WE JUST WANT TO BAIL THEM OUT. WE ARE SICK OF LIVING THIS GALACTIC SIZED LIE. WE'RE GIVING PEOPLE FALSE HOPE AND BEING HUNTED BY KILL BOTS FROM PLANET 2!
WE JUST WANT OUR PARENTS BACK!

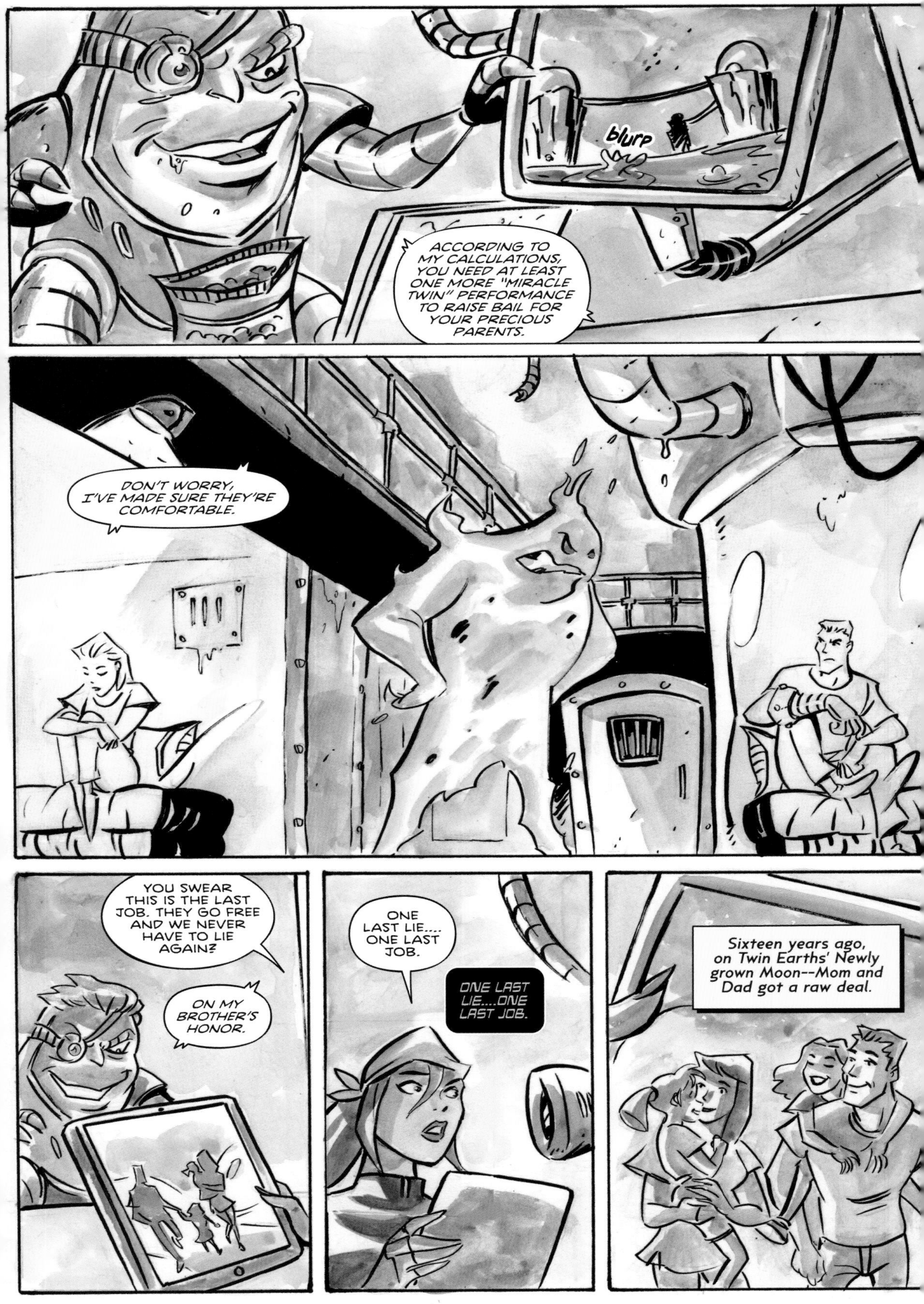
blurp
ACCORDING TO MY CALCULATIONS, YOU NEED AT LEAST ONE MORE "MIRACLE TWIN" PERFORMANCE TO RAISE BAIL FOR YOUR PRECIOUS PARENTS.
DON'T WORRY, I'VE MADE SURE THEY'RE COMFORTABLE.
YOU SWEAR THIS IS THE LAST JOB. THEY GO FREE AND WE NEVER HAVE TO LIE AGAIN?
ON MY BROTHER'S HONOR.
ONE LAST LIE.... ONE LAST JOB.
ONE LAST LIE....ONE LAST JOB.
Sixteen years ago, on Twin Earths' Newly grown Moon--Mom and Dad got a raw deal.

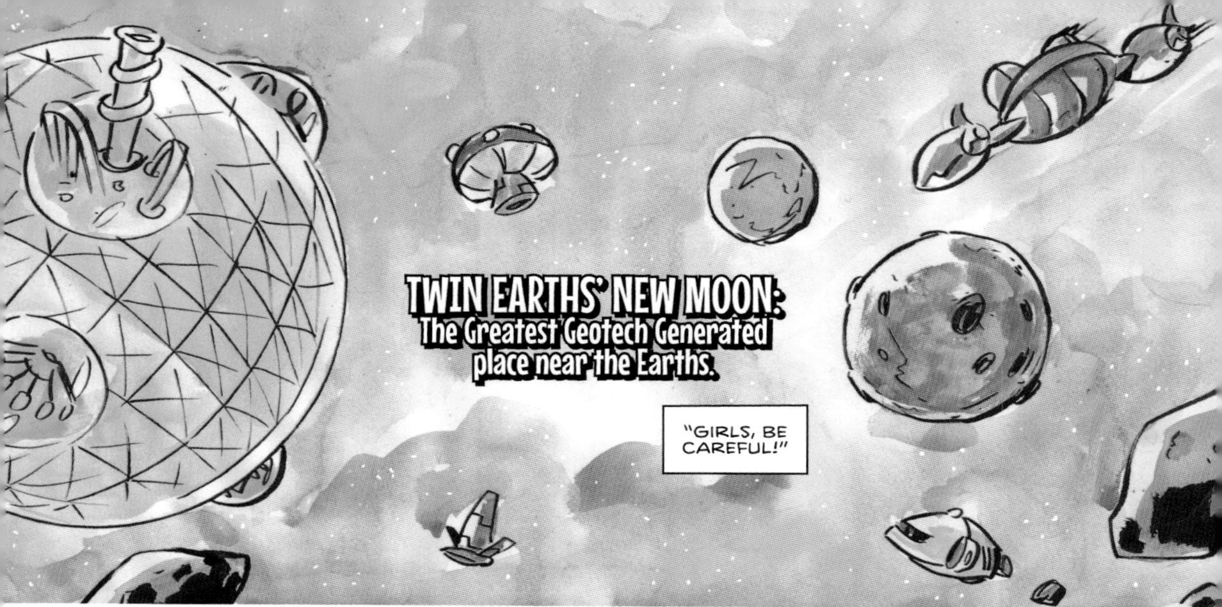
TWIN EARTHS' NEW MOON:
The Greatest Geotech Generated place near the Earths.
"GIRLS, BE CAREFUL!"

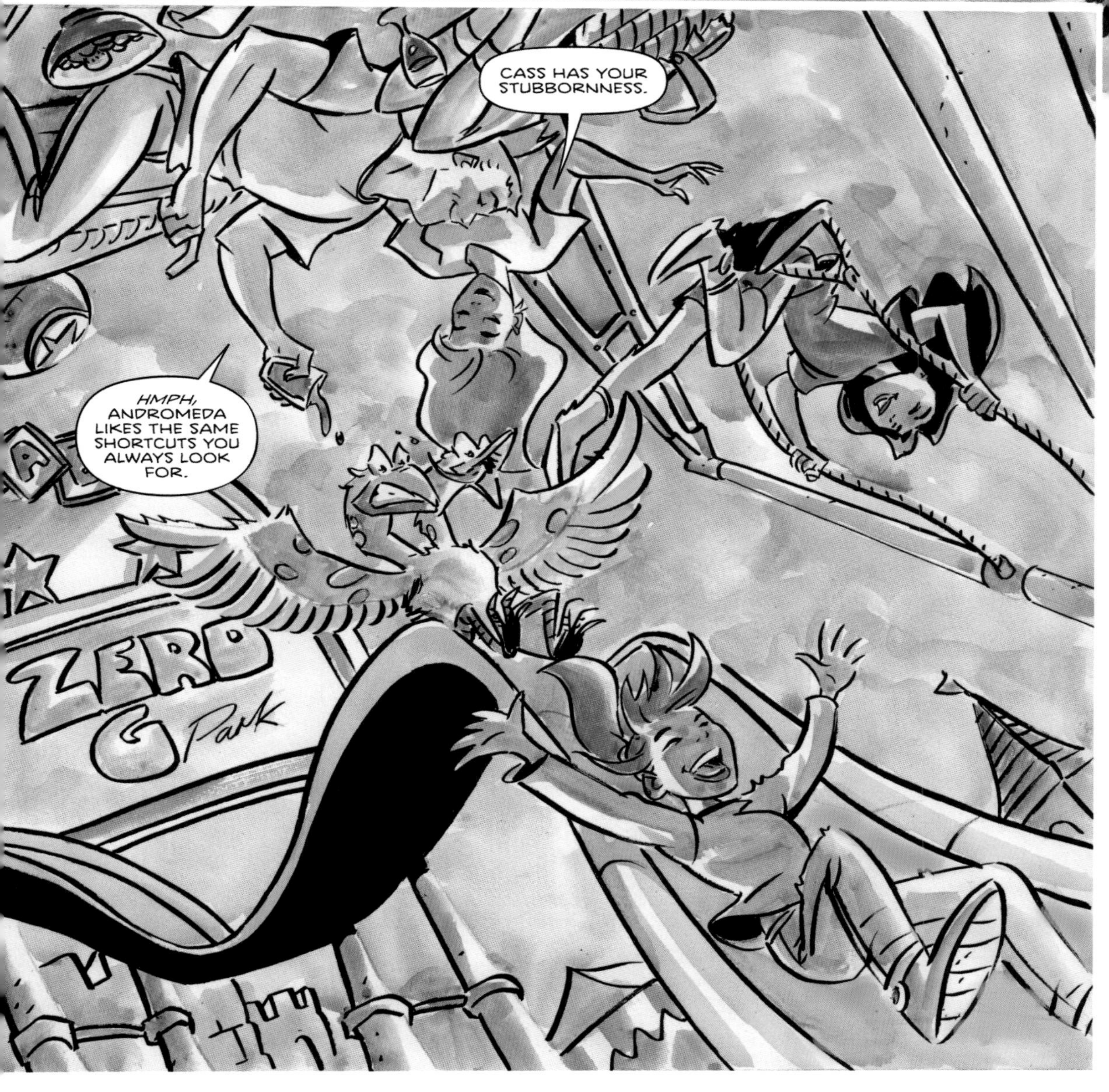
CASS HAS YOUR STUBBORNNESS.
HMPH, ANDROMEDA LIKES THE SAME SHORTCUTS YOU ALWAYS LOOK FOR.
ZERO G Park

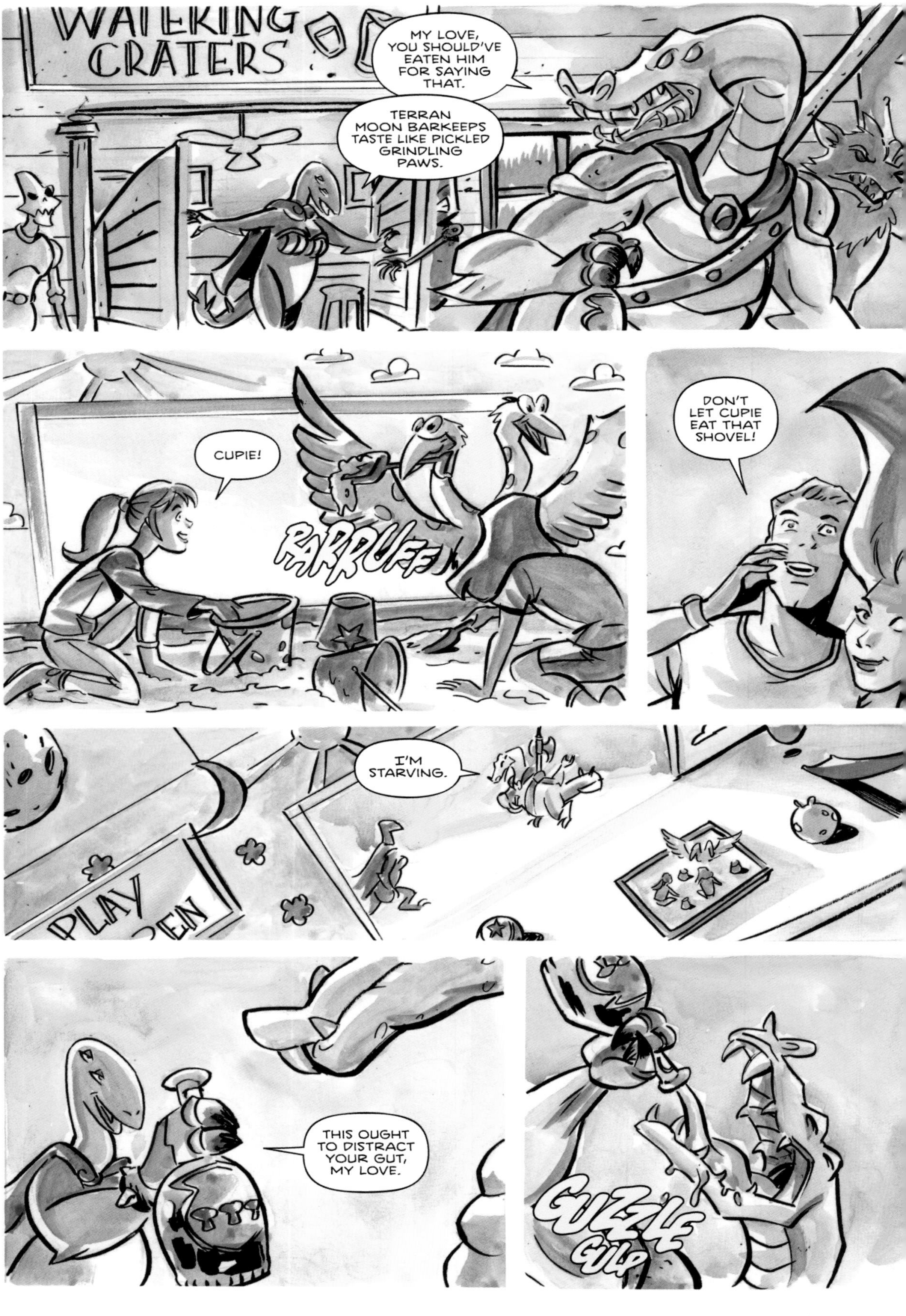

WATERING
CRATERS
MY LOVE, YOU SHOULD'VE EATEN HIM FOR SAYING THAT.
TERRAN MOON BARKEEPS TASTE LIKE PICKLED GRINDLING PAWS.
CUPIE!
RARRUFF
DON'T LET CUPIE EAT THAT SHOVEL!
PLAY
I'M STARVING.
THIS OUGHT TO DISTRACT YOUR GUT, MY LOVE.
GUZZLE
GULP

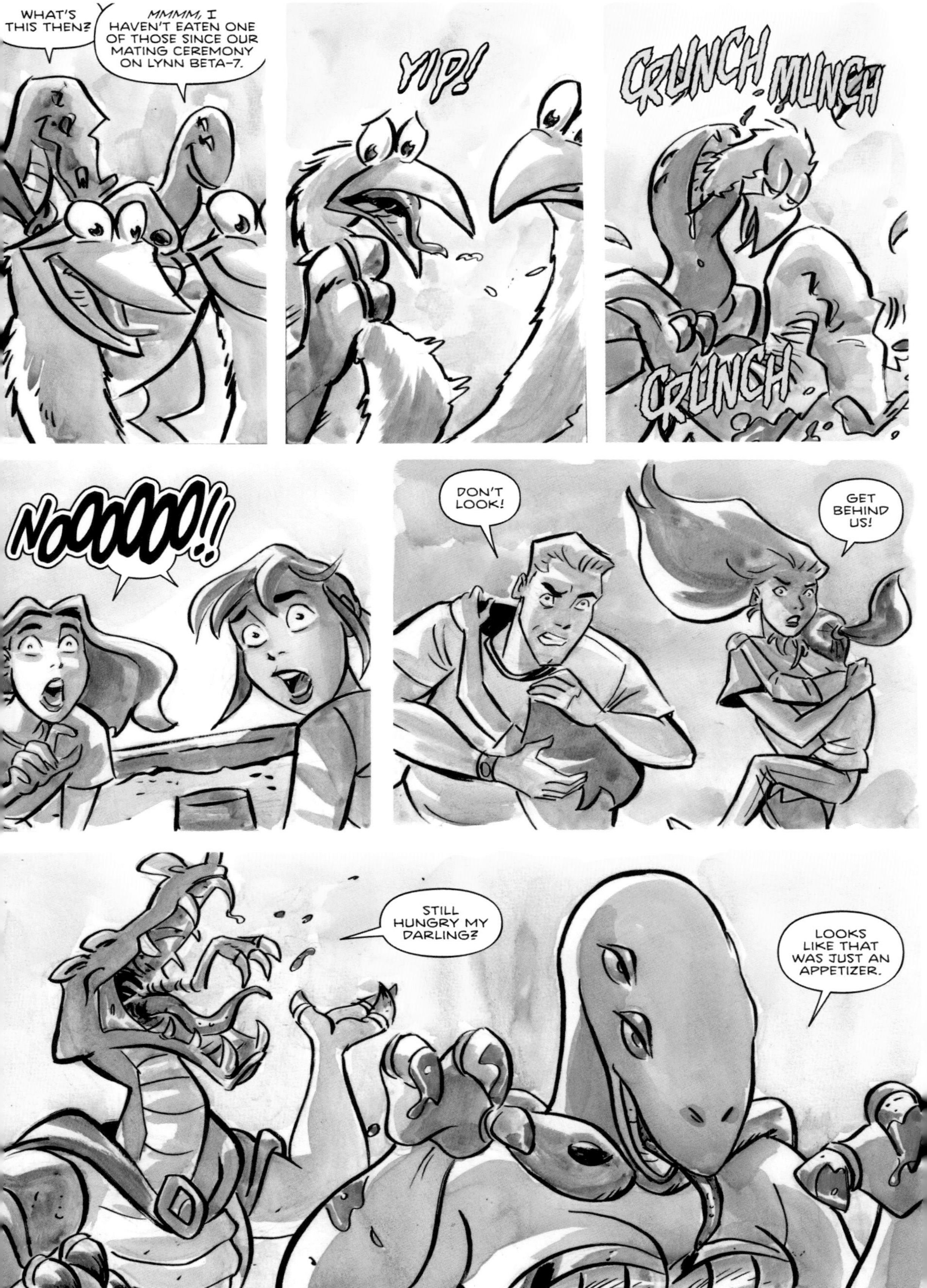

WHAT'S THIS THEN?
MMMM, I HAVEN'T EATEN ONE OF THOSE SINCE OUR MATING CEREMONY ON LYNN BETA-7.
YIP!
CRUNCH MUNCH
CRUNCH
NOOOOOO!!
DON'T LOOK!
GET BEHIND US!
STILL HUNGRY MY DARLING?
LOOKS LIKE THAT WAS JUST AN APPETIZER.

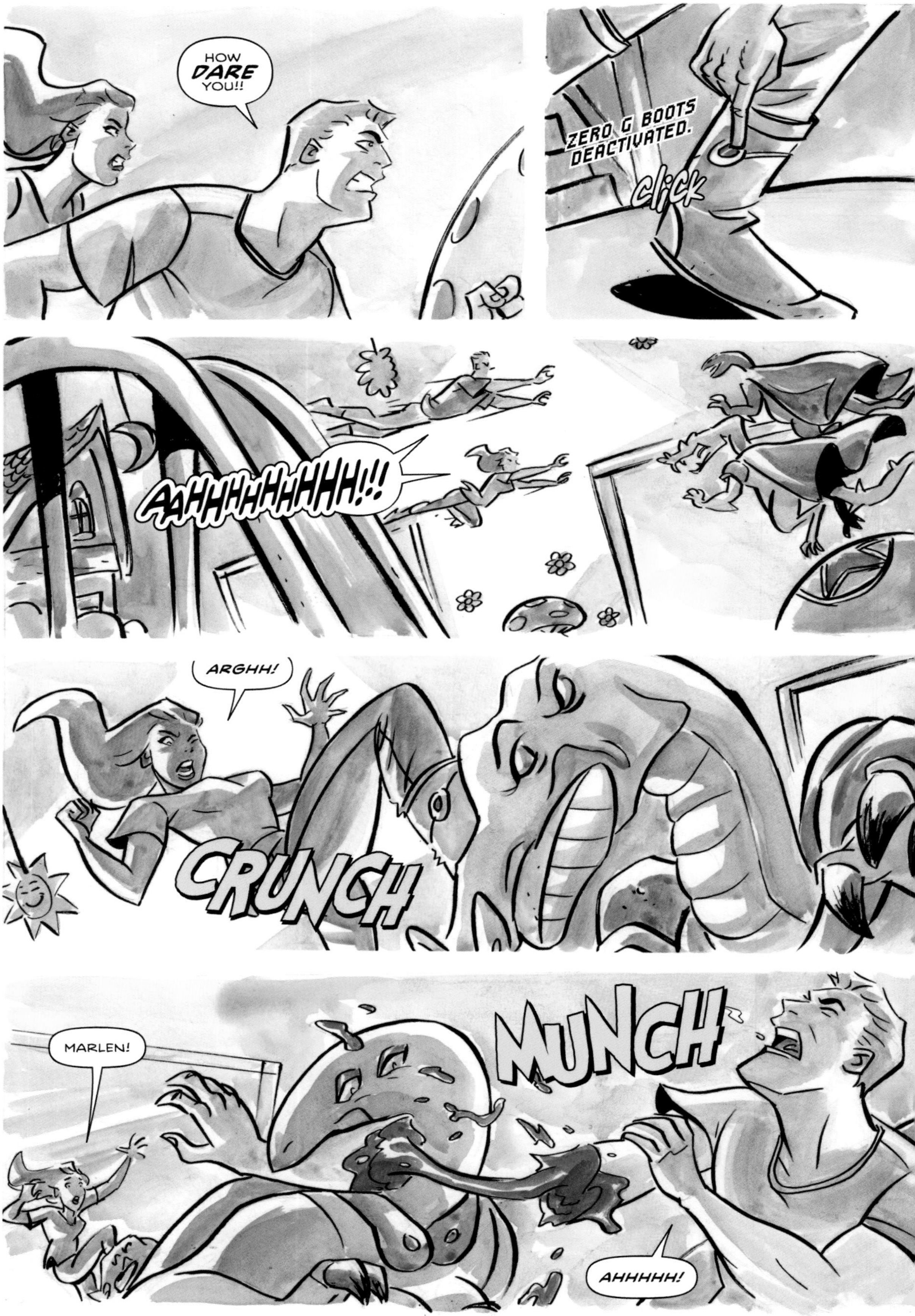
HOW DARE YOU!!
ZERO G BOOTS DEACTIVATED.
CLICK
AAHHHHHHHH!!!
ARGHH!
CRUNCH
MARLEN!
MUNCH
AHHHHH!

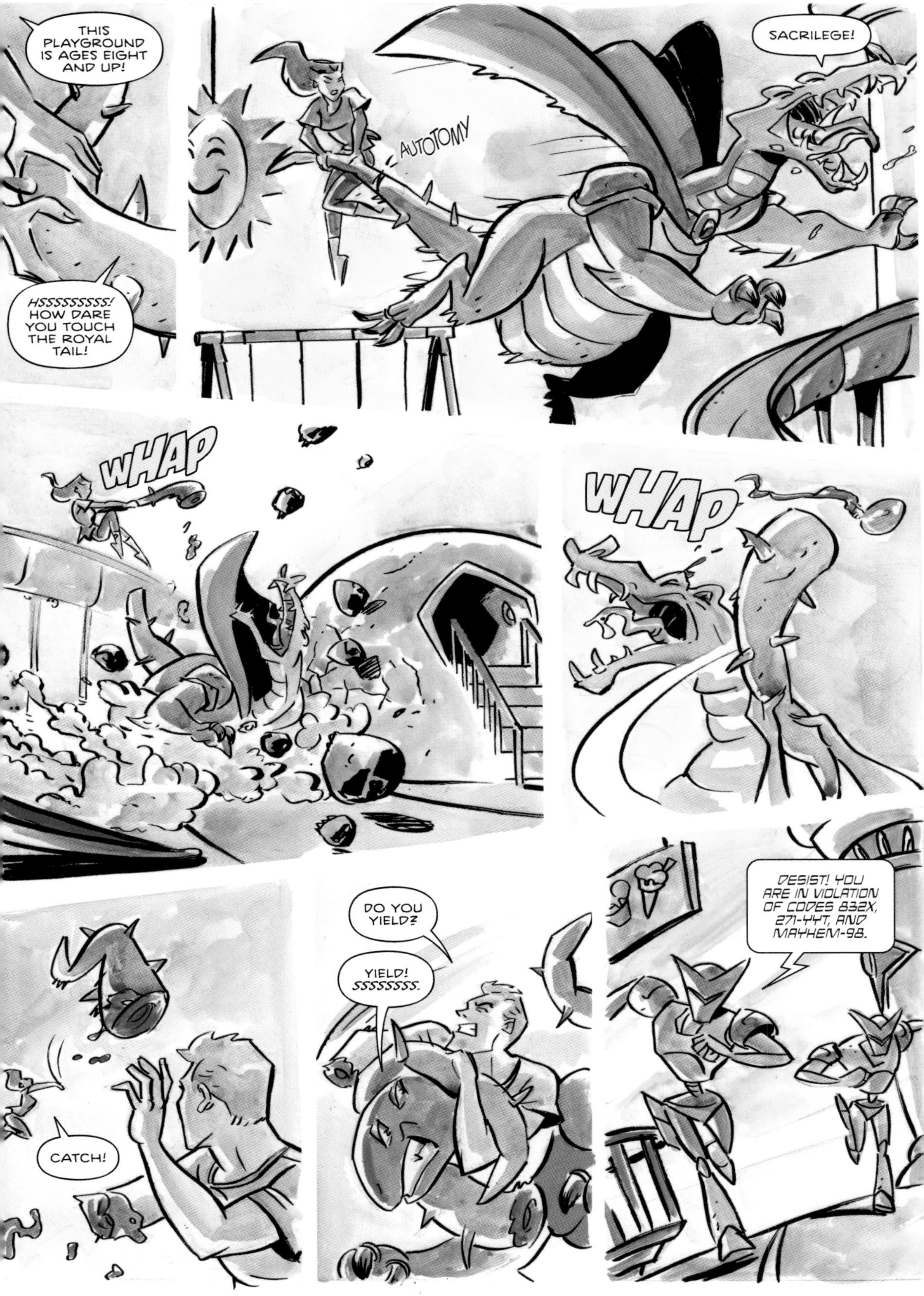
THIS PLAYGROUND IS AGES EIGHT AND UP!
HSSSSSSSSS! HOW DARE YOU TOUCH THE ROYAL TAIL!
AUTOTOMY
SACRILEGE!
WHAP
WHAP
CATCH!
DO YOU YIELD?
YIELD! SSSSSSSS.
DESIST! YOU ARE IN VIOLATION OF CODES 832X, 271-YYT, AND MAYHEM-98.

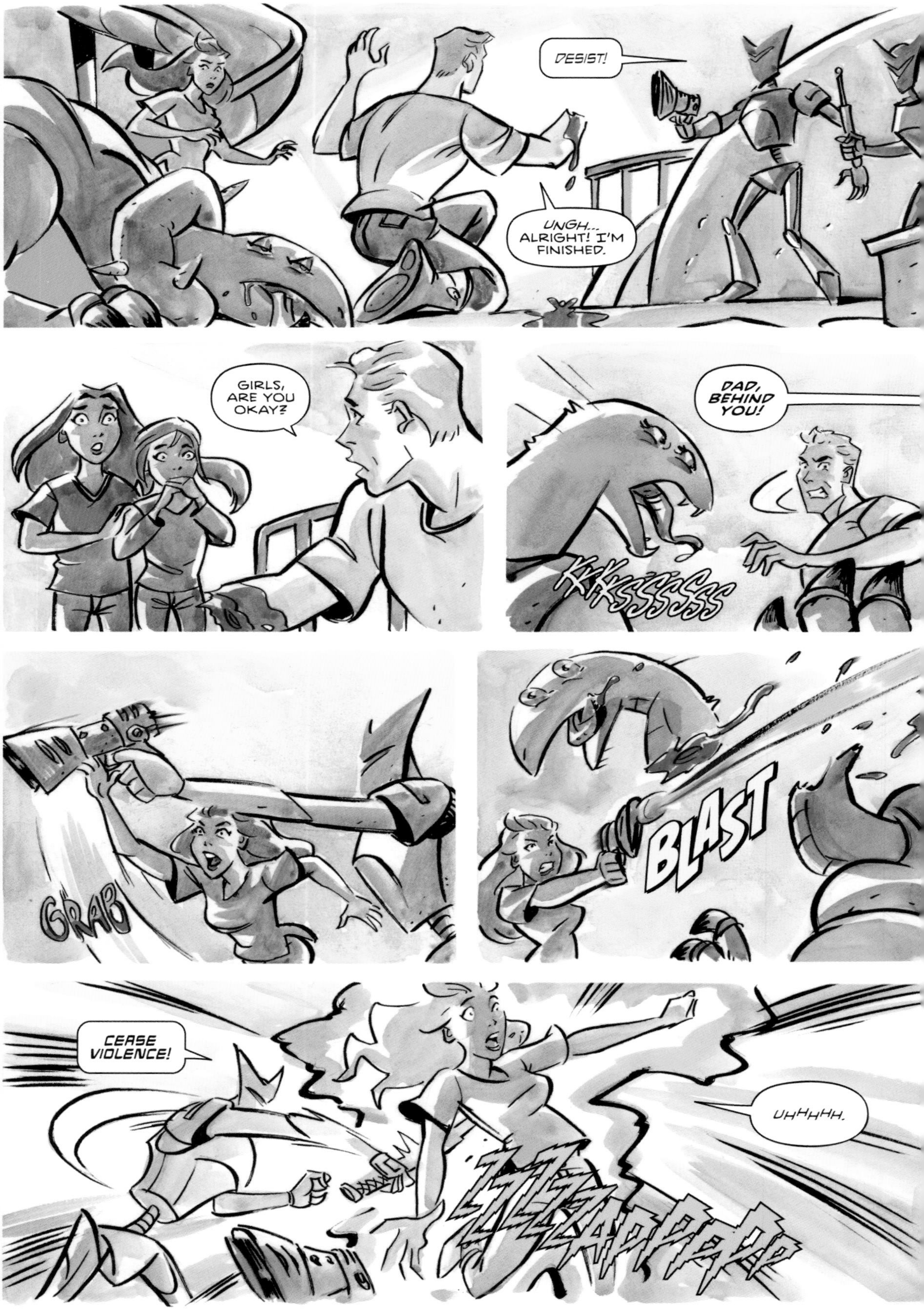
DESIST!
UNGH... ALRIGHT! I'M FINISHED.
GIRLS, ARE YOU OKAY?
DAD, BEHIND YOU!
KKKSSSSSSS
GRAB
BLAST
CEASE VIOLENCE!
UHHHHH.

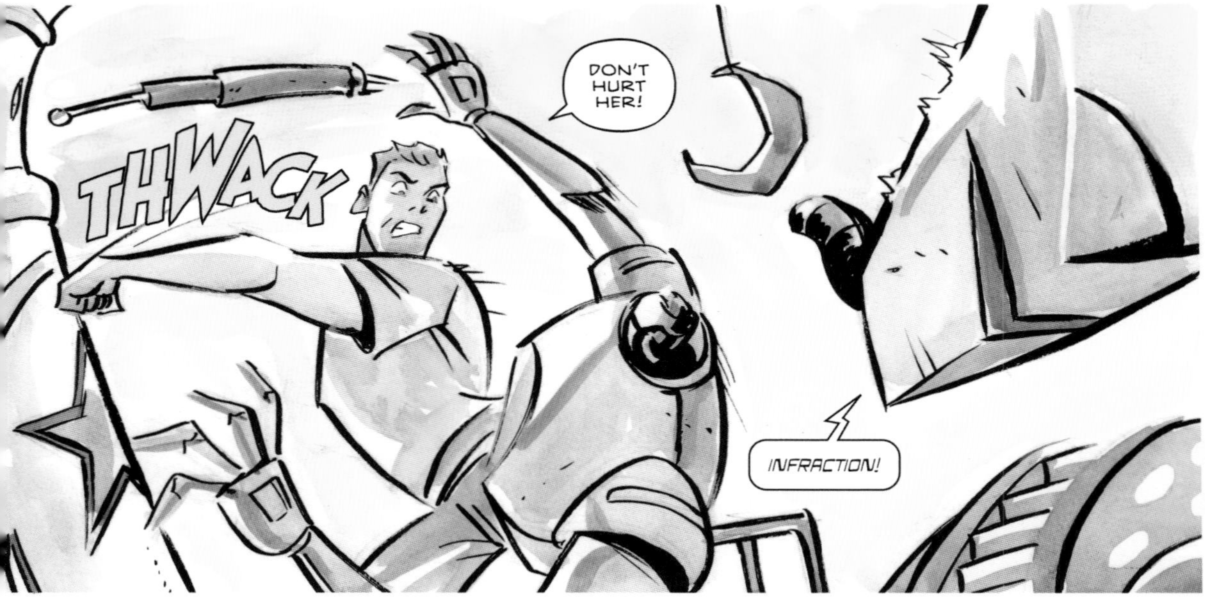
THWACK
DON'T HURT HER!
INFRACTION!
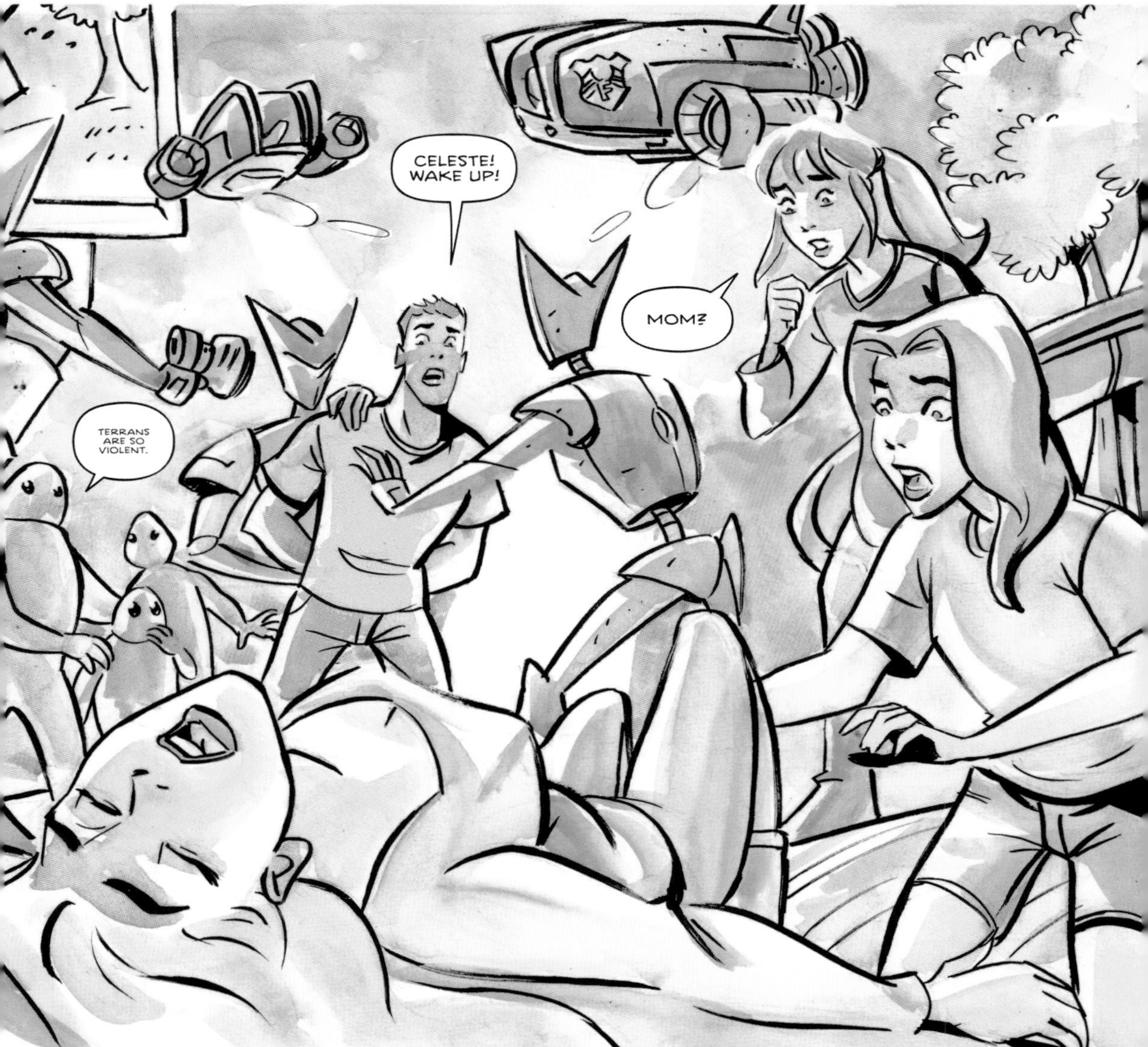
CELESTE! WAKE UP!
MOM?
TERRANS ARE SO VIOLENT.

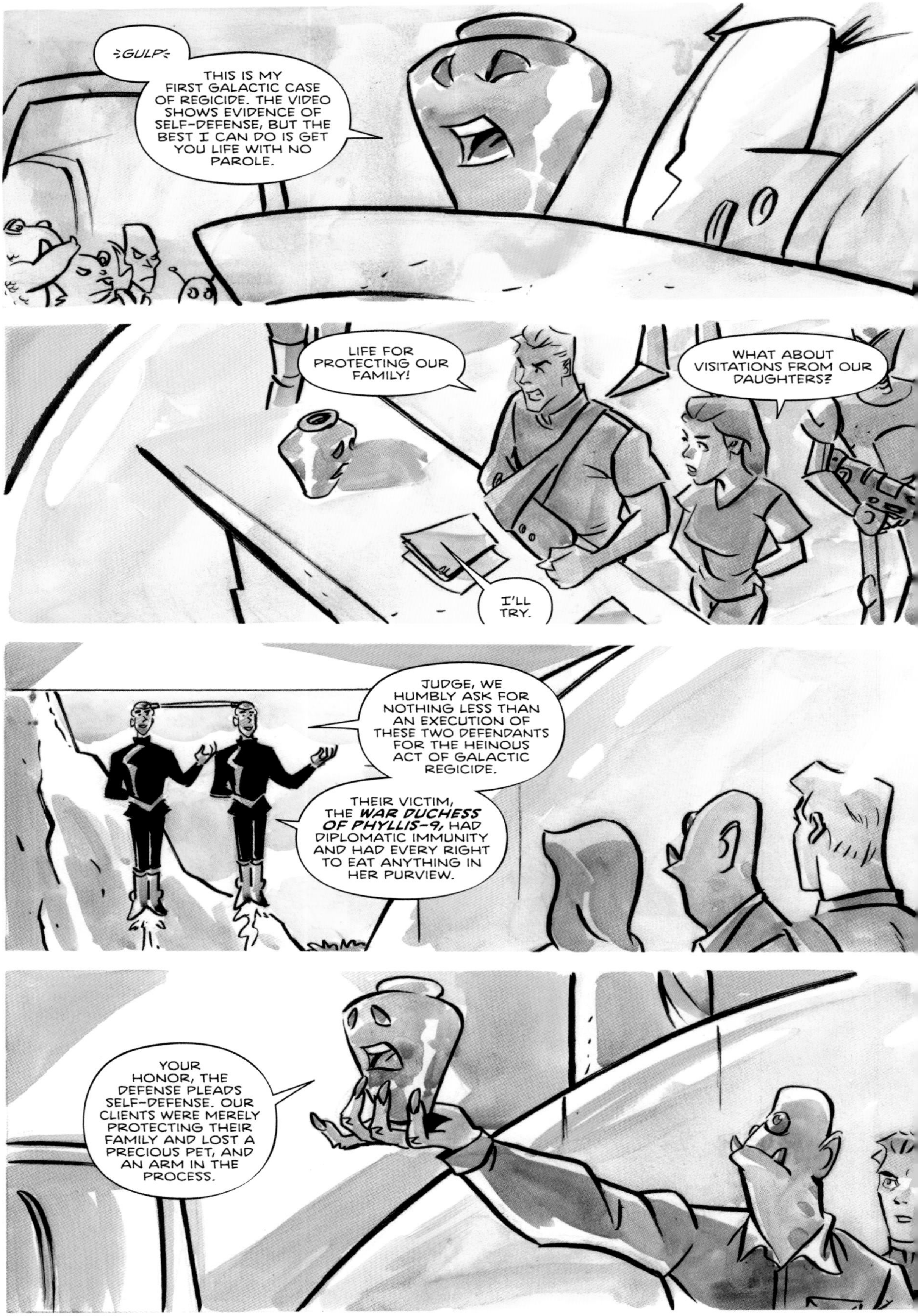

GULP
THIS IS MY FIRST GALACTIC CASE OF REGICIDE. THE VIDEO SHOWS EVIDENCE OF SELF-DEFENSE, BUT THE BEST I CAN DO IS GET YOU LIFE WITH NO PAROLE.
LIFE FOR PROTECTING OUR FAMILY!
WHAT ABOUT VISITATIONS FROM OUR DAUGHTERS?
I'LL TRY.
JUDGE, WE HUMBLY ASK FOR NOTHING LESS THAN AN EXECUTION OF THESE TWO DEFENDANTS FOR THE HEINOUS ACT OF GALACTIC REGICIDE.
THEIR VICTIM, THE WAR DUCHESS OF PHYLLIS-9, HAD DIPLOMATIC IMMUNITY AND HAD EVERY RIGHT TO EAT ANYTHING IN HER PURVIEW.
YOUR HONOR, THE DEFENSE PLEADS SELF-DEFENSE. OUR CLIENTS WERE MERELY PROTECTING THEIR FAMILY AND LOST A PRECIOUS PET, AND AN ARM IN THE PROCESS.

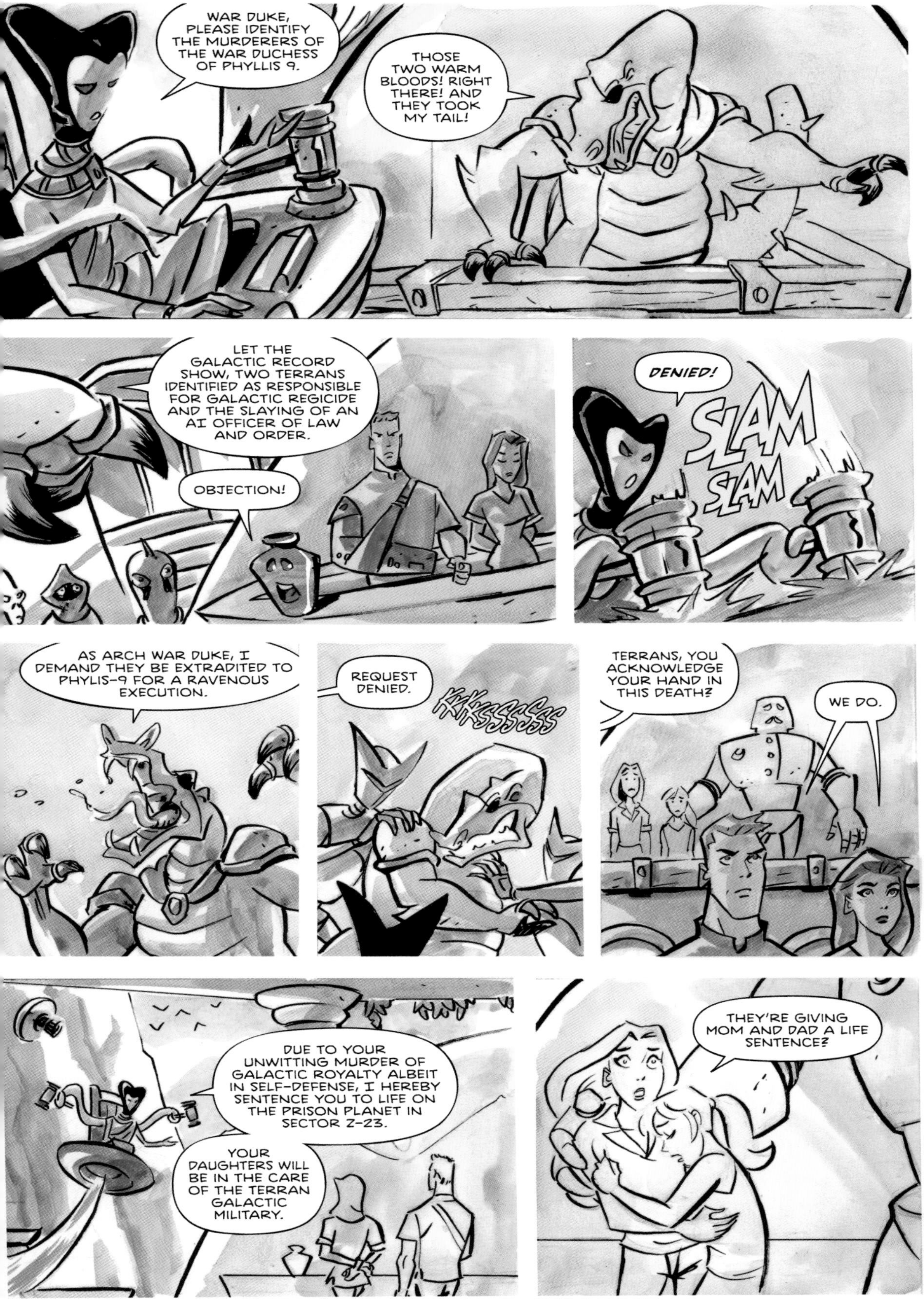

WAR DUKE, PLEASE IDENTIFY THE MURDERERS OF THE WAR DUCHESS OF PHYLLIS 9.
THOSE TWO WARM BLOODS! RIGHT THERE! AND THEY TOOK MY TAIL!
LET THE GALACTIC RECORD SHOW, TWO TERRANS IDENTIFIED AS RESPONSIBLE FOR GALACTIC REGICIDE AND THE SLAYING OF AN AI OFFICER OF LAW AND ORDER.
OBJECTION!
DENIED!
SLAM
SLAM
AS ARCH WAR DUKE, I DEMAND THEY BE EXTRADITED TO PHYLIS-9 FOR A RAVENOUS EXECUTION.
REQUEST DENIED.
KKKSSSSSSS
TERRANS, YOU ACKNOWLEDGE YOUR HAND IN THIS DEATH?
WE DO.
DUE TO YOUR UNWITTING MURDER OF GALACTIC ROYALTY ALBEIT IN SELF-DEFENSE, I HEREBY SENTENCE YOU TO LIFE ON THE PRISON PLANET IN SECTOR Z-23.
YOUR DAUGHTERS WILL BE IN THE CARE OF THE TERRAN GALACTIC MILITARY.
THEY'RE GIVING MOM AND DAD A LIFE SENTENCE?

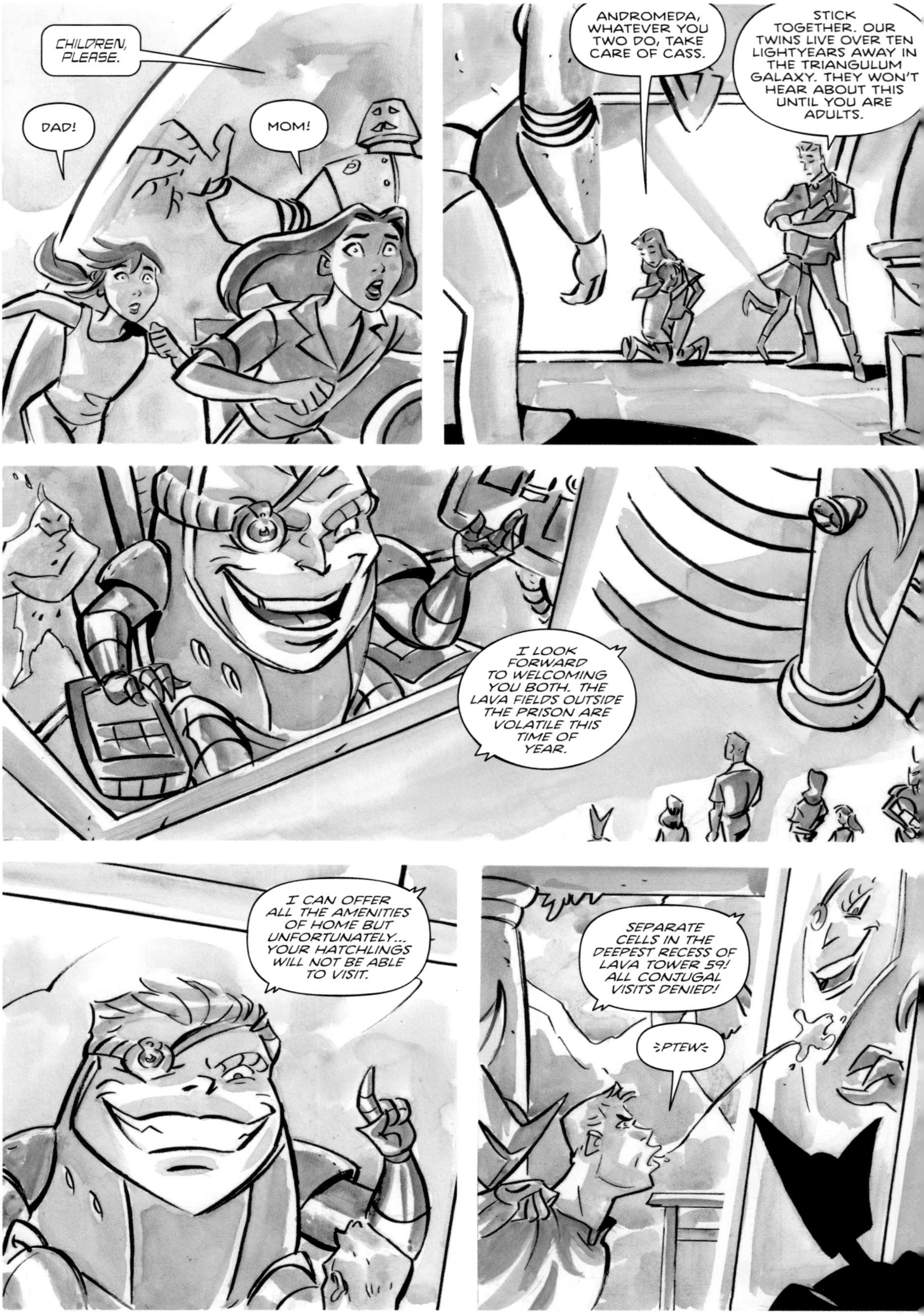
CHILDREN, PLEASE.
DAD!
MOM!
ANDROMEDA, WHATEVER YOU TWO DO, TAKE CARE OF CASS.
STICK TOGETHER. OUR TWINS LIVE OVER TEN LIGHTYEARS AWAY IN THE TRIANGULUM GALAXY. THEY WON'T HEAR ABOUT THIS UNTIL YOU ARE ADULTS.
I LOOK FORWARD TO WELCOMING YOU BOTH. THE LAVA FIELDS OUTSIDE THE PRISON ARE VOLATILE THIS TIME OF YEAR.
I CAN OFFER ALL THE AMENITIES OF HOME BUT UNFORTUNATELY... YOUR HATCHLINGS WILL NOT BE ABLE TO VISIT.
SEPARATE CELLS IN THE DEEPEST RECESS OF LAVA TOWER 59! ALL CONJUGAL VISITS DENIED!
PTEW

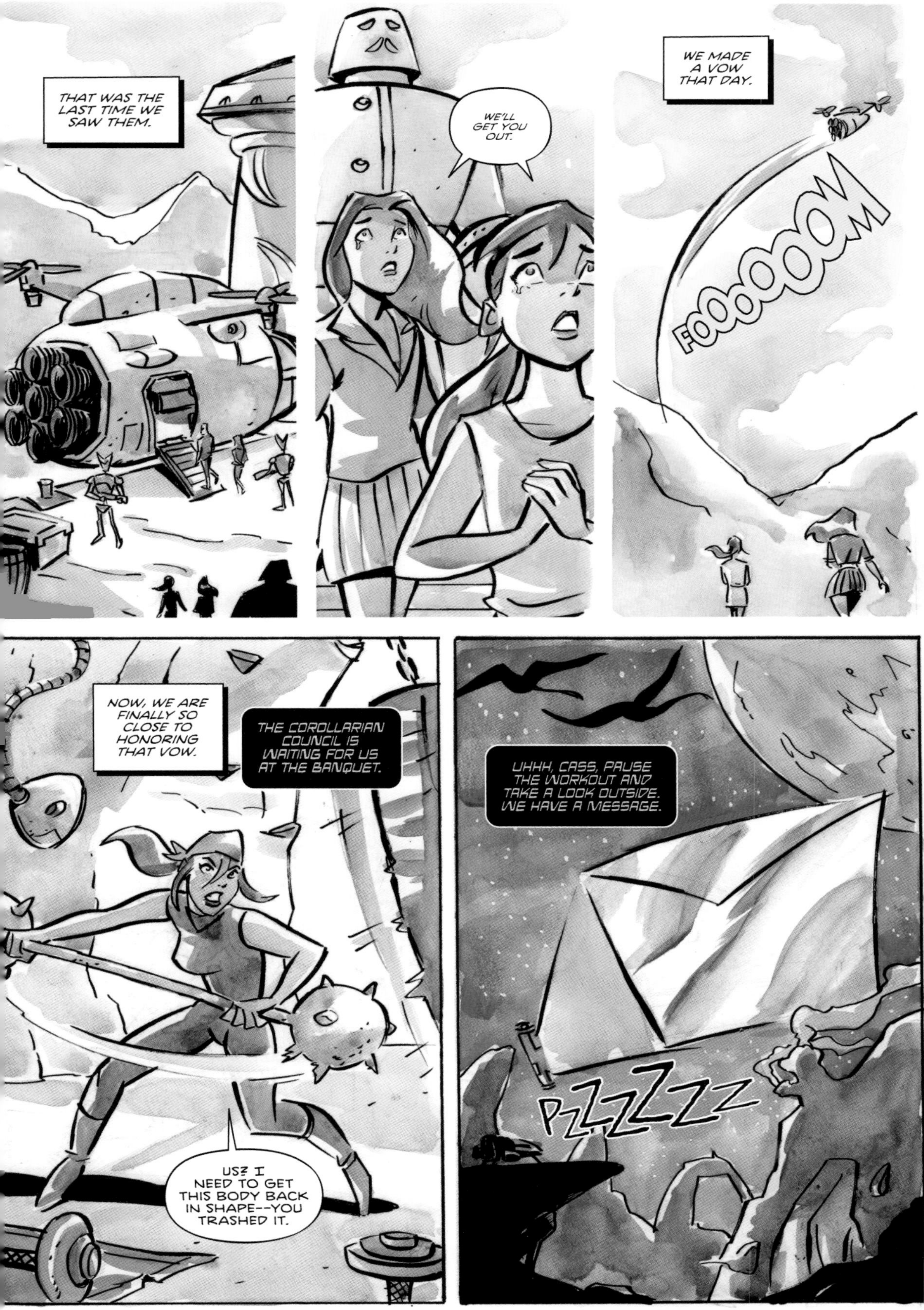
THAT WAS THE LAST TIME WE SAW THEM.
WE'LL GET YOU OUT.
WE MADE A VOW THAT DAY.
FOOOOOOOM
NOW, WE ARE FINALLY SO CLOSE TO HONORING THAT VOW.
THE COROLLARIAN COUNCIL IS WAITING FOR US AT THE BANQUET.
US? I NEED TO GET THIS BODY BACK IN SHAPE--YOU TRASHED IT.
UHHH, CASS, PAUSE THE WORKOUT AND TAKE A LOOK OUTSIDE. WE HAVE A MESSAGE.
PZZZZZZ

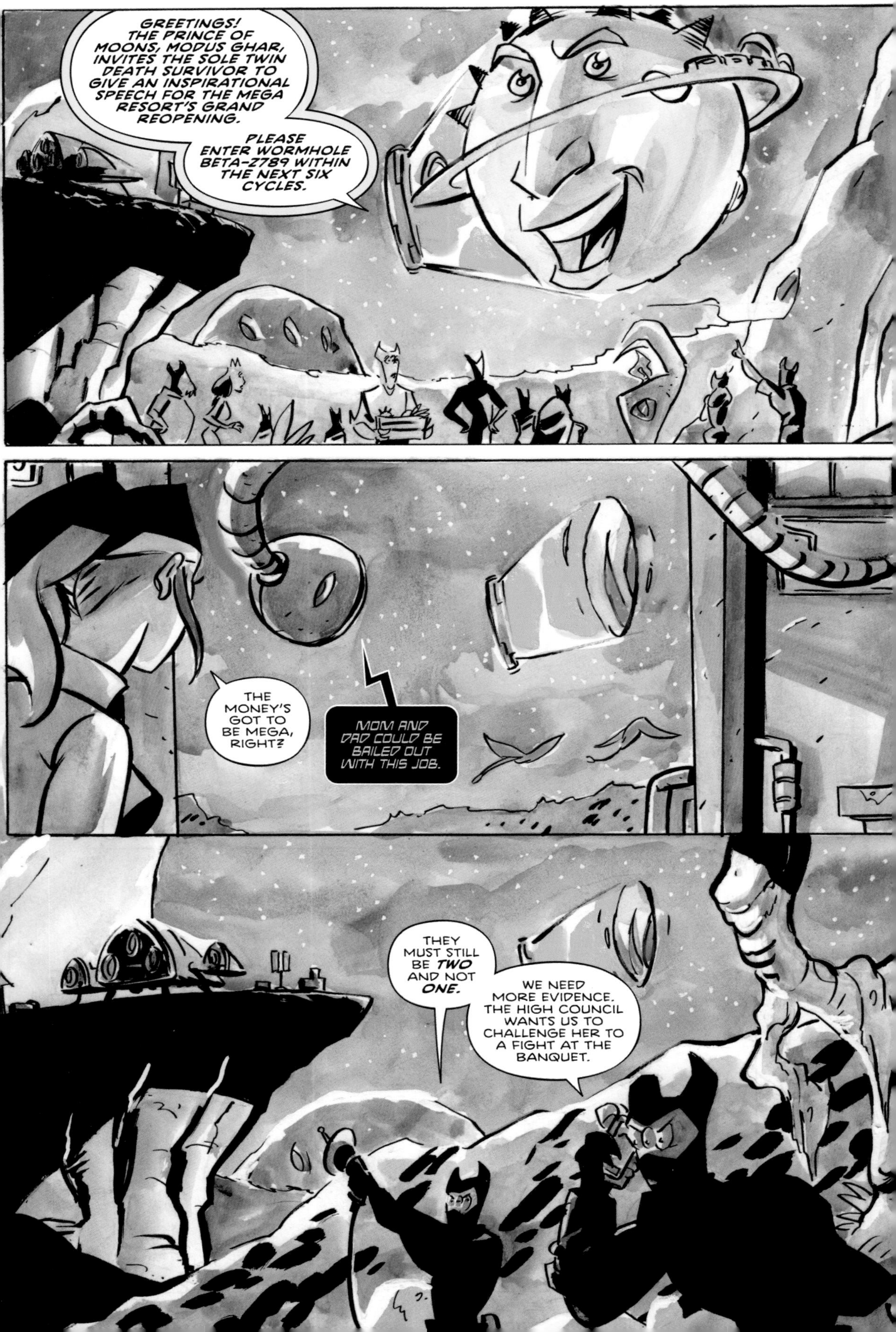
GREETINGS! THE PRINCE OF MOONS, MODUS GHAR, INVITES THE SOLE TWIN DEATH SURVIVOR TO GIVE AN INSPIRATIONAL SPEECH FOR THE MEGA RESORT'S GRAND REOPENING.
PLEASE ENTER WORMHOLE BETA-Z789 WITHIN THE NEXT SIX CYCLES.
THE MONEY'S GOT TO BE MEGA, RIGHT?
MOM AND DAD COULD BE BAILED OUT WITH THIS JOB.
THEY MUST STILL BE *TWO* AND NOT *ONE.*
WE NEED MORE EVIDENCE. THE HIGH COUNCIL WANTS US TO CHALLENGE HER TO A FIGHT AT THE BANQUET.

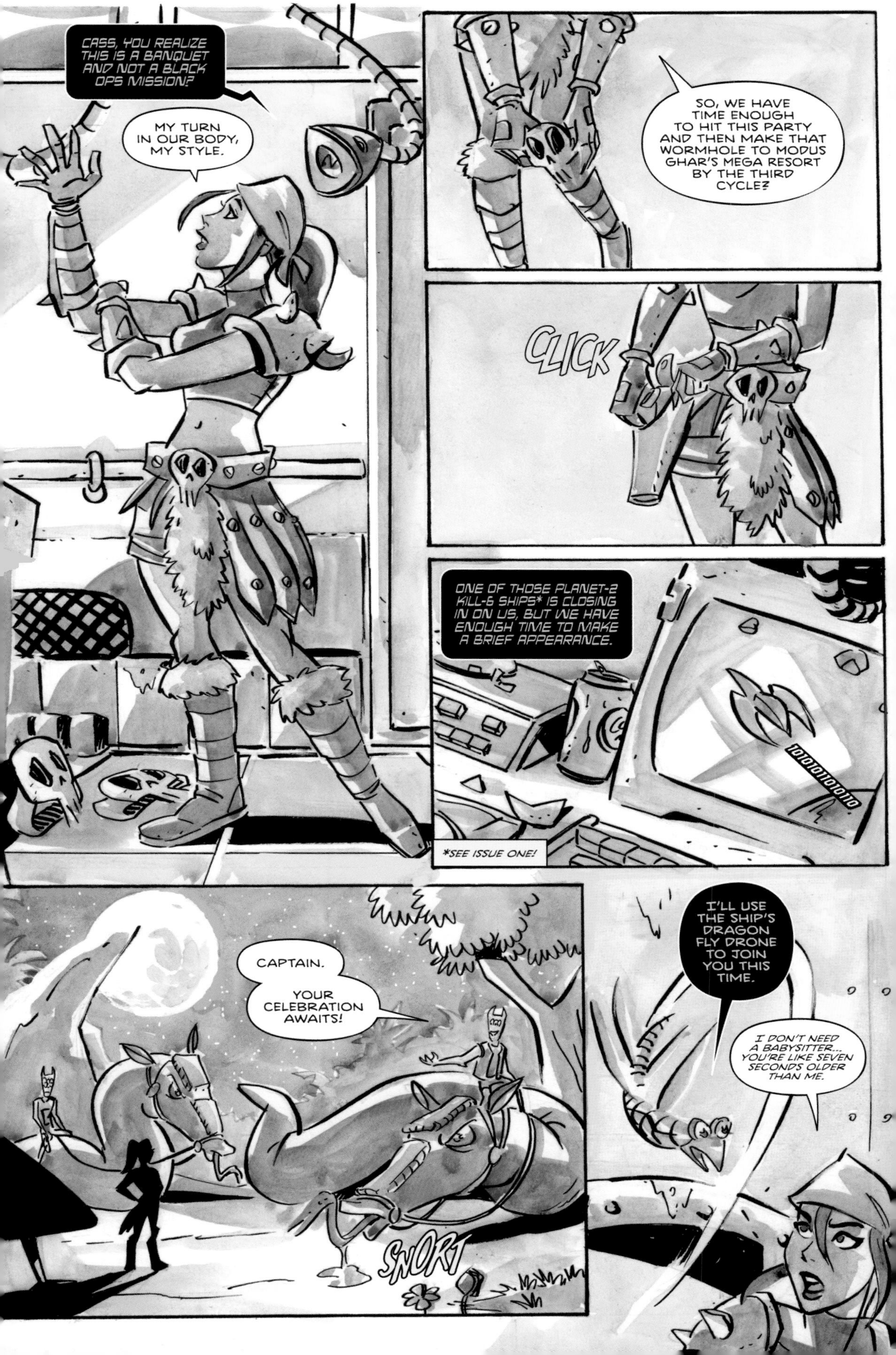
CASS, YOU REALIZE THIS IS A BANQUET AND NOT A BLACK OPS MISSION?
MY TURN IN OUR BODY, MY STYLE.
SO, WE HAVE TIME ENOUGH TO HIT THIS PARTY AND THEN MAKE THAT WORMHOLE TO MODUS GHAR'S MEGA RESORT BY THE THIRD CYCLE?
CLICK
ONE OF THOSE PLANET-2 KILL-6 SHIPS* IS CLOSING IN ON US, BUT WE HAVE ENOUGH TIME TO MAKE A BRIEF APPEARANCE.
*SEE ISSUE ONE!
CAPTAIN.
YOUR CELEBRATION AWAITS!
SNORT
I'LL USE THE SHIP'S DRAGON FLY DRONE TO JOIN YOU THIS TIME.
I DON'T NEED A BABYSITTER... YOU'RE LIKE SEVEN SECONDS OLDER THAN ME.

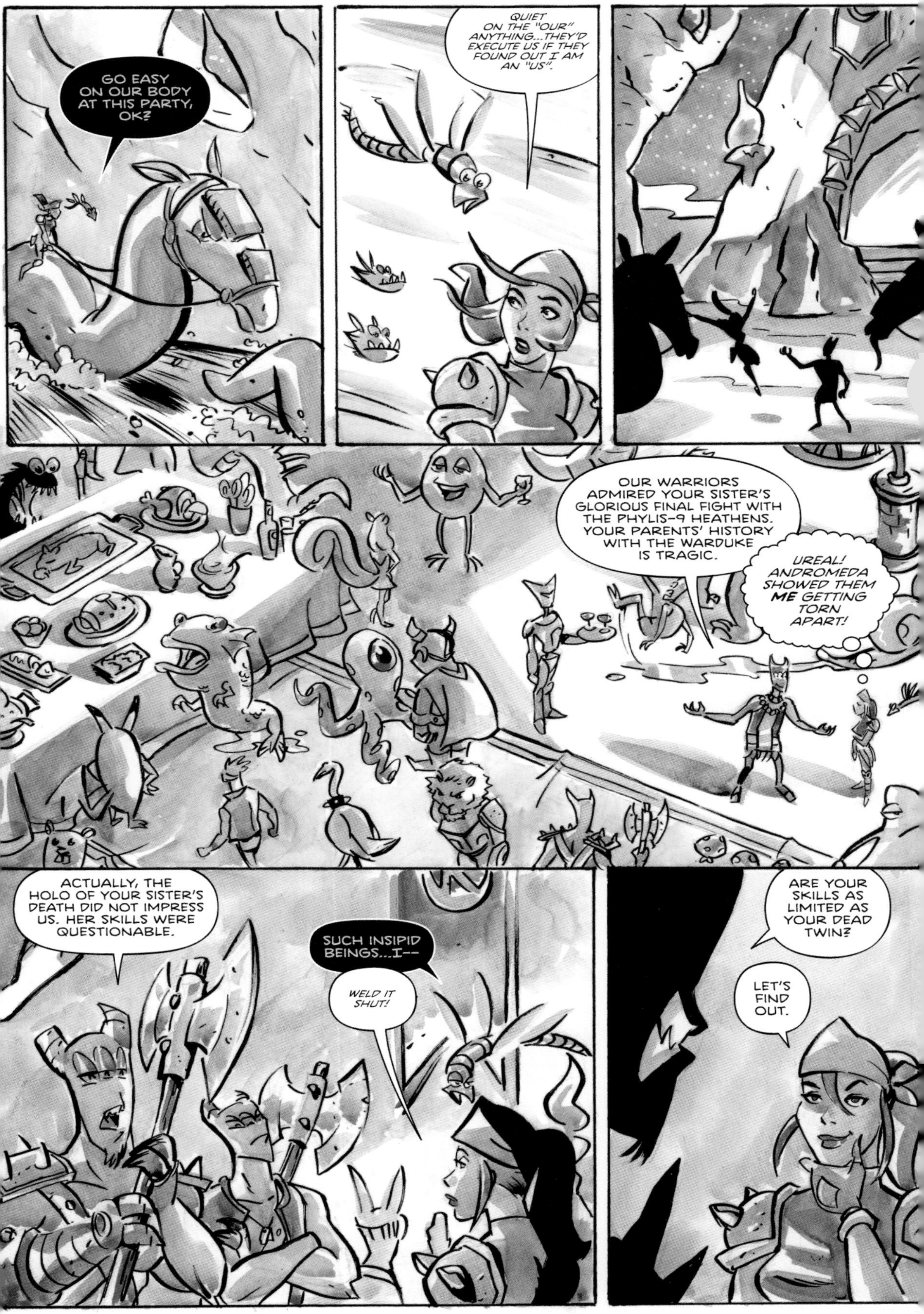

GO EASY ON OUR BODY AT THIS PARTY, OK?
QUIET ON THE "OUR" ANYTHING...THEY'D EXECUTE US IF THEY FOUND OUT I AM AN "US".
OUR WARRIORS ADMIRED YOUR SISTER'S GLORIOUS FINAL FIGHT WITH THE PHYLIS-9 HEATHENS. YOUR PARENTS' HISTORY WITH THE WARDUKE IS TRAGIC.
UREAL! ANDROMEDA SHOWED THEM ME GETTING TORN APART!
ACTUALLY, THE HOLO OF YOUR SISTER'S DEATH DID NOT IMPRESS US. HER SKILLS WERE QUESTIONABLE.
SUCH INSIPID BEINGS...I--
WELD IT SHUT!
ARE YOUR SKILLS AS LIMITED AS YOUR DEAD TWIN?
LET'S FIND OUT.

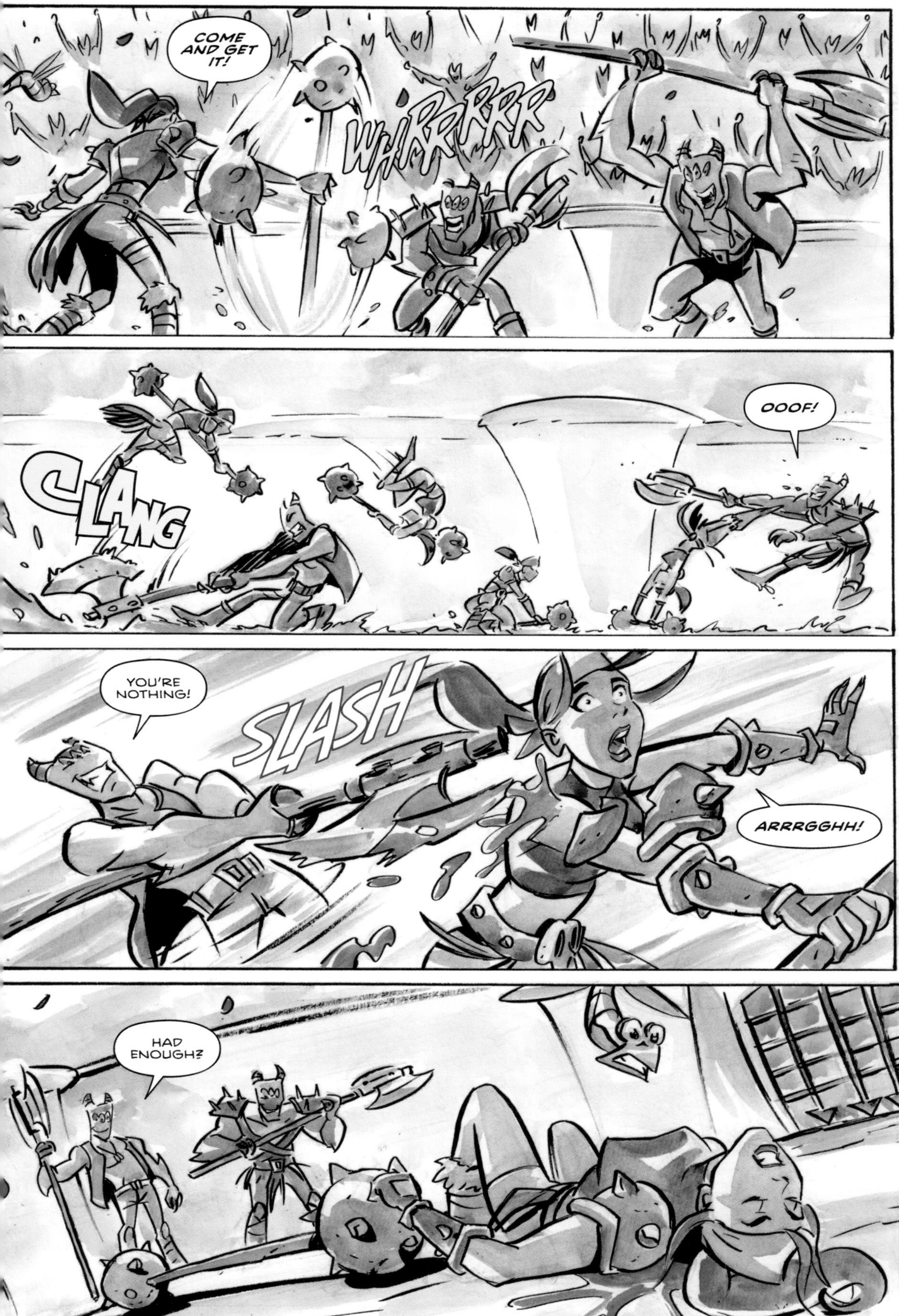
COME AND GET IT!
WHIRRRRR
CLANG
OOOF!
YOU'RE NOTHING!
SLASH
ARRRGGHH!
HAD ENOUGH?

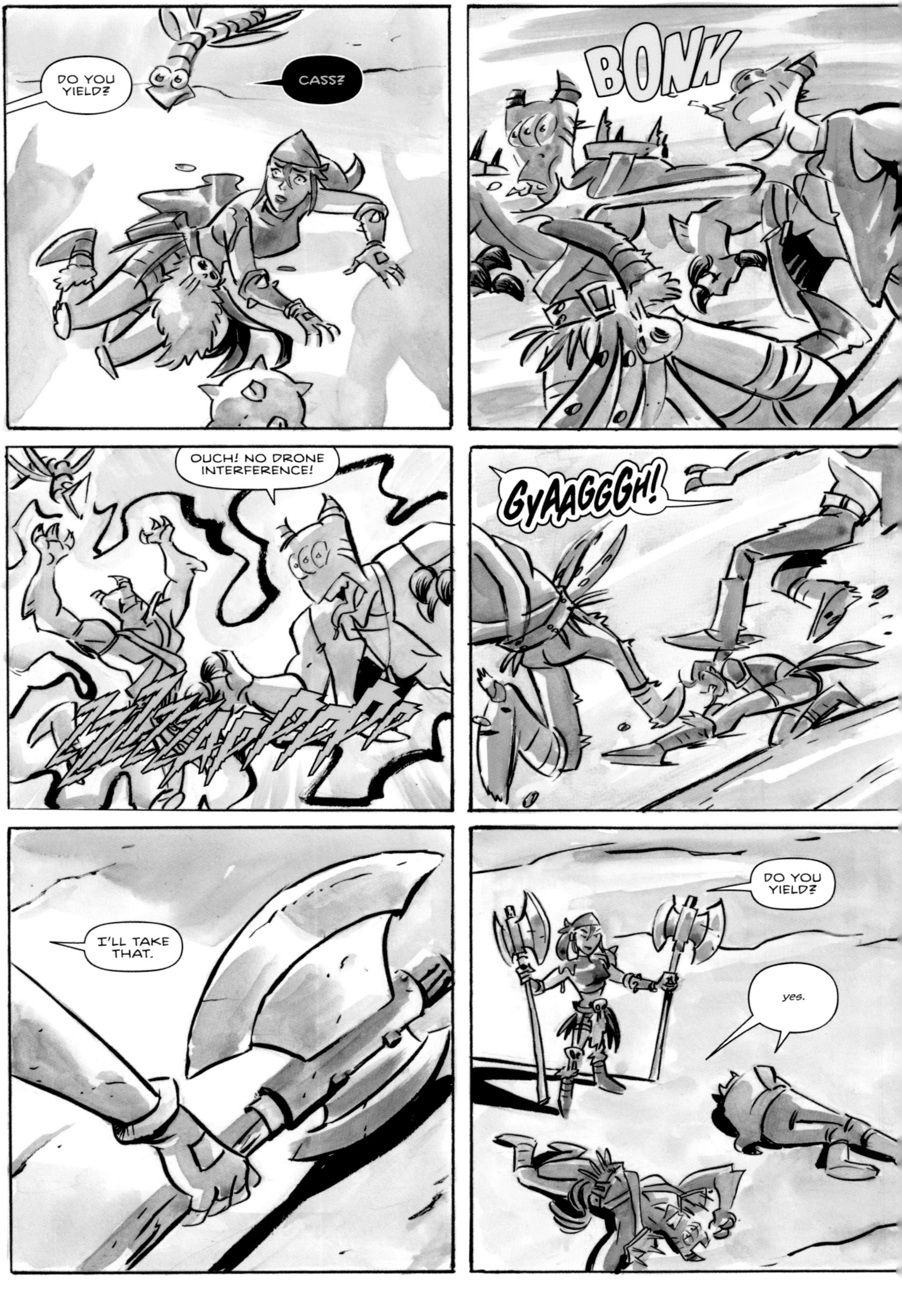
DO YOU YIELD?
CASS?
BONK
OUCH! NO DRONE INTERFERENCE!
GYAAGGGH!
I'LL TAKE THAT.
DO YOU YIELD?
yes.

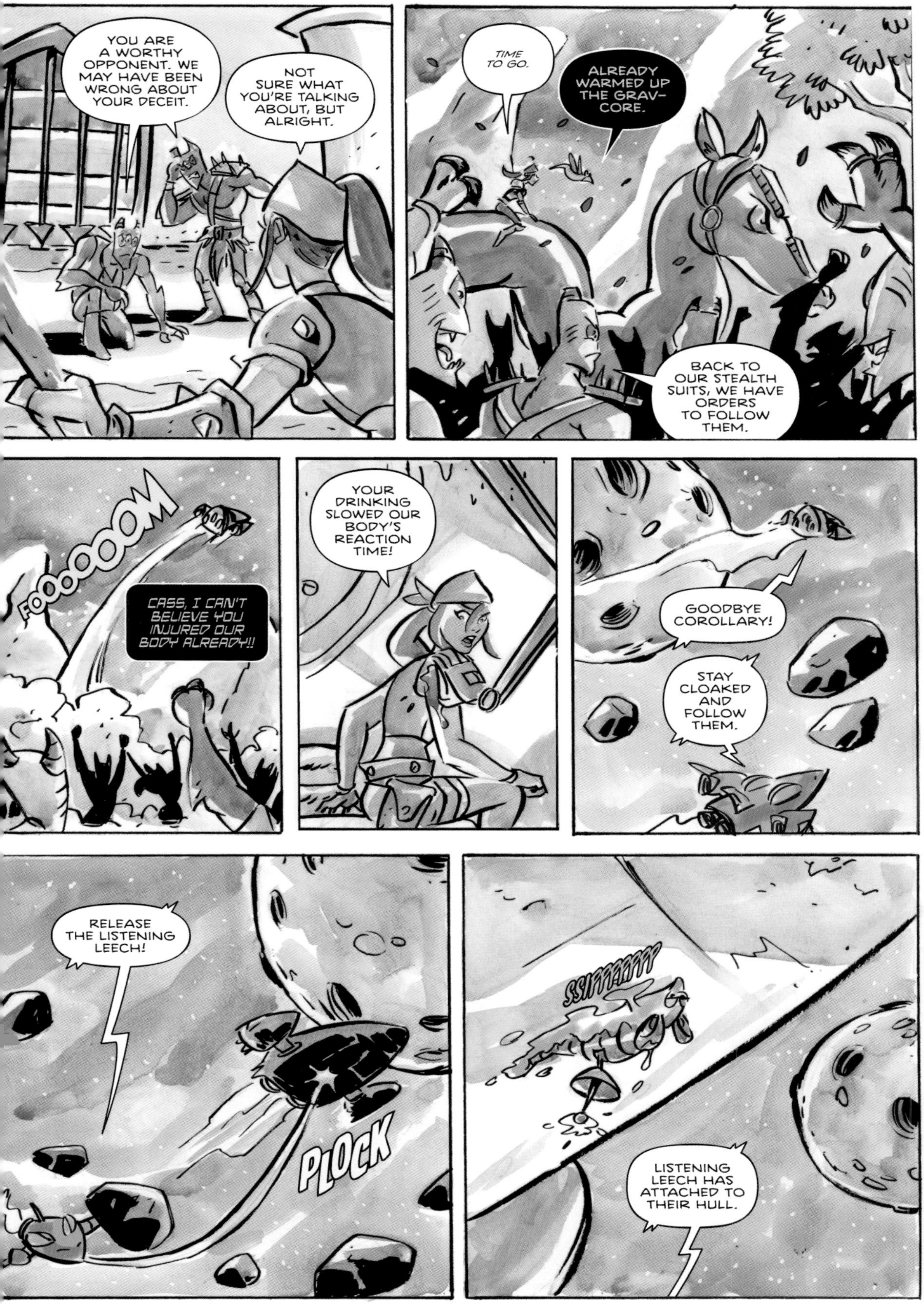

YOU ARE A WORTHY OPPONENT. WE MAY HAVE BEEN WRONG ABOUT YOUR DECEIT.
NOT SURE WHAT YOU'RE TALKING ABOUT, BUT ALRIGHT.
TIME TO GO.
ALREADY WARMED UP THE GRAV-CORE.
BACK TO OUR STEALTH SUITS, WE HAVE ORDERS TO FOLLOW THEM.
FOOOOOOOM
CASS, I CAN'T BELIEVE YOU INJURED OUR BODY ALREADY!!
YOUR DRINKING SLOWED OUR BODY'S REACTION TIME!
GOODBYE COROLLARY!
STAY CLOAKED AND FOLLOW THEM.
RELEASE THE LISTENING LEECH!
PLOCK
SSIPPPPPPP
LISTENING LEECH HAS ATTACHED TO THEIR HULL.

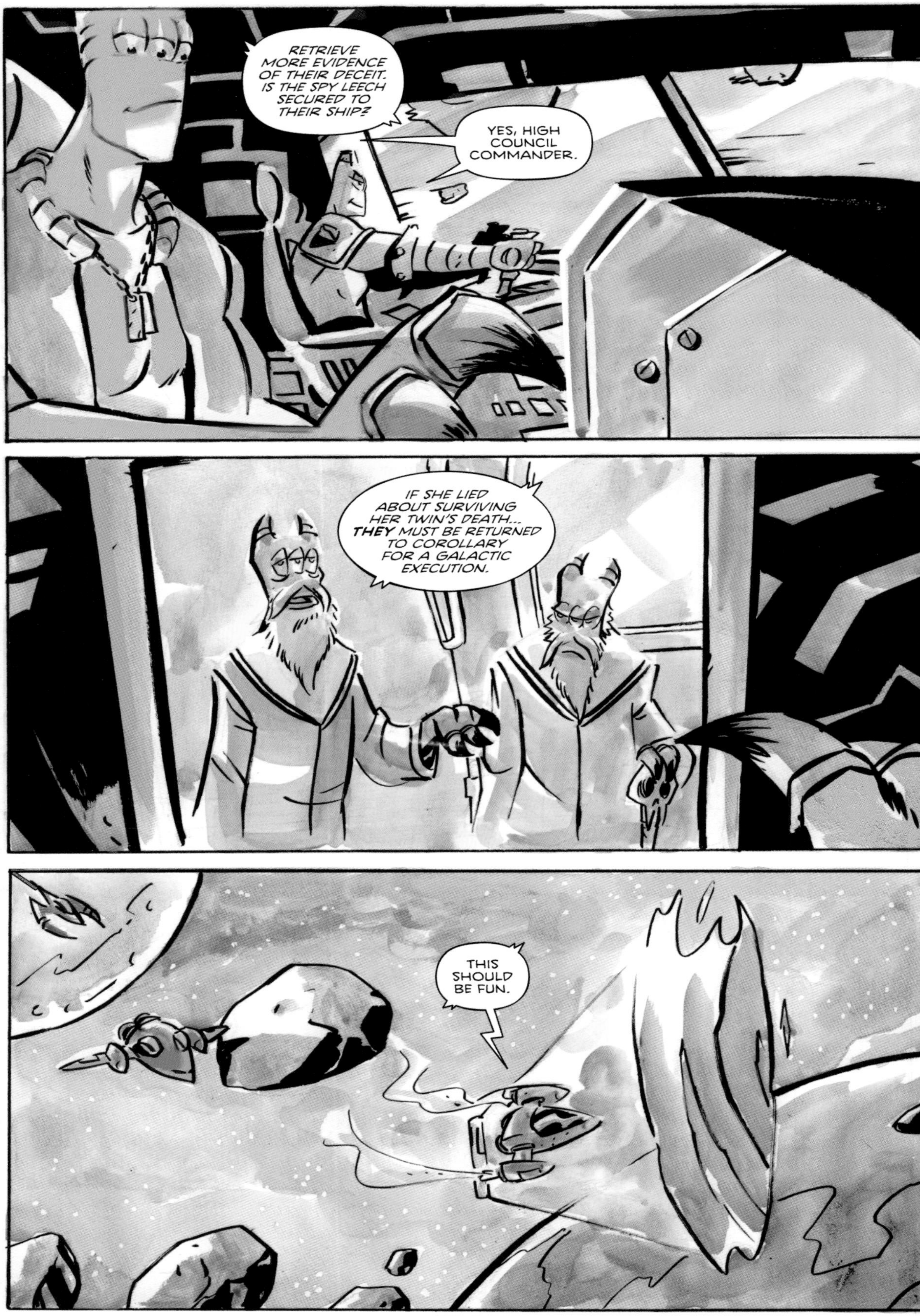
RETRIEVE MORE EVIDENCE OF THEIR DECEIT. IS THE SPY LEECH SECURED TO THEIR SHIP?
YES, HIGH COUNCIL COMMANDER.
IF SHE LIED ABOUT SURVIVING HER TWIN'S DEATH... THEY MUST BE RETURNED TO COROLLARY FOR A GALACTIC EXECUTION.
THIS SHOULD BE FUN.

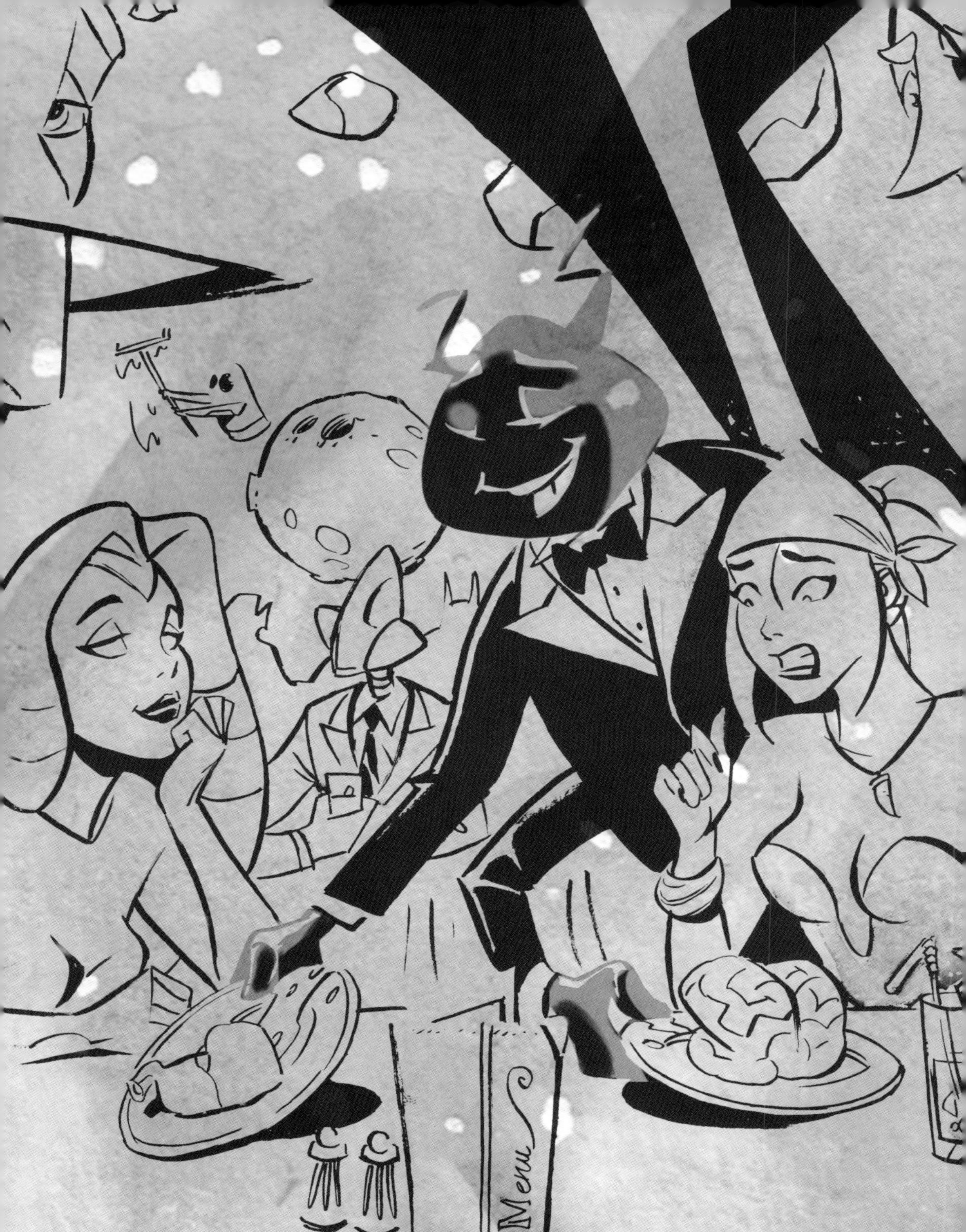
Menu

CHAPTER 3

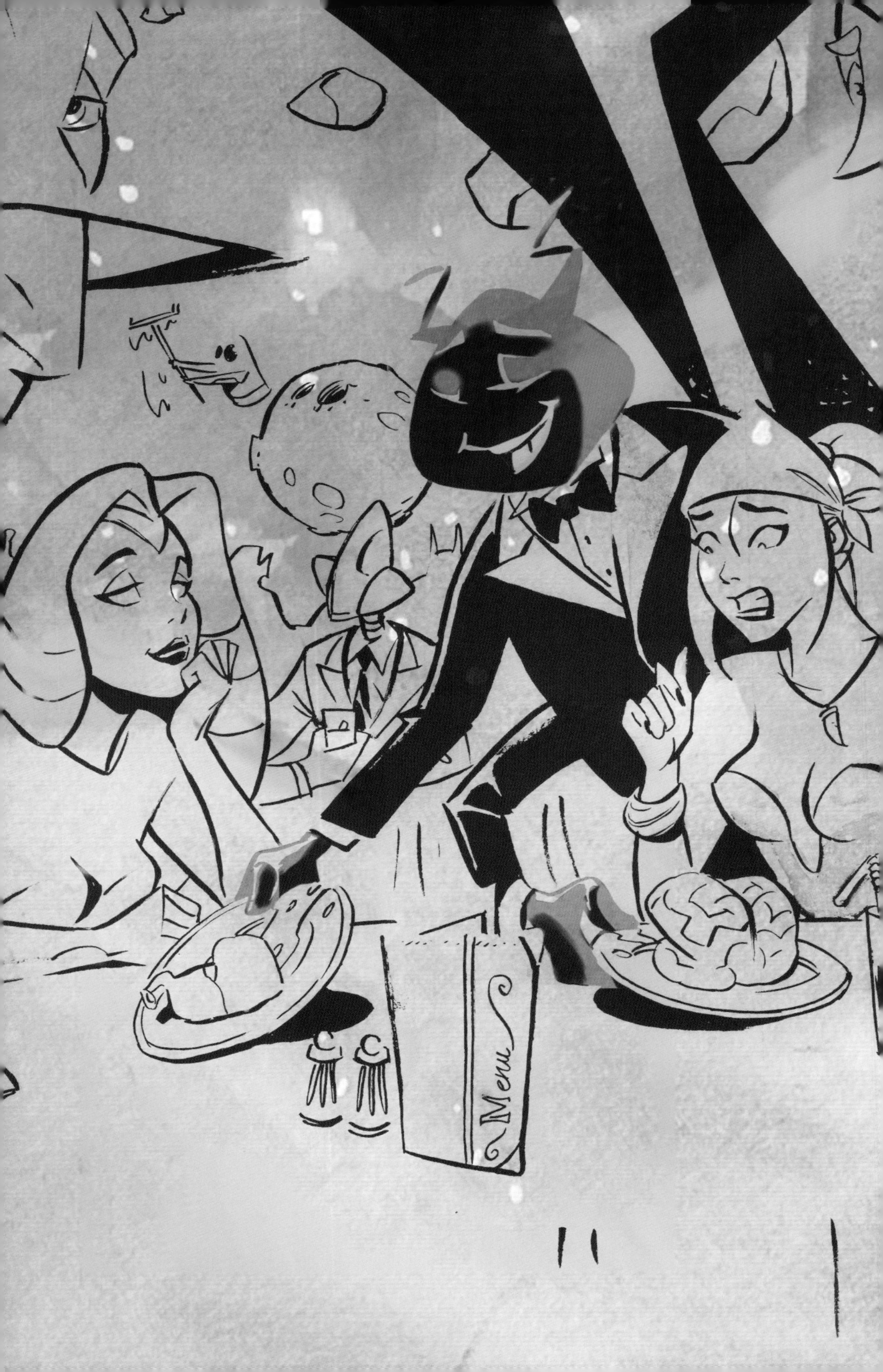
Menu

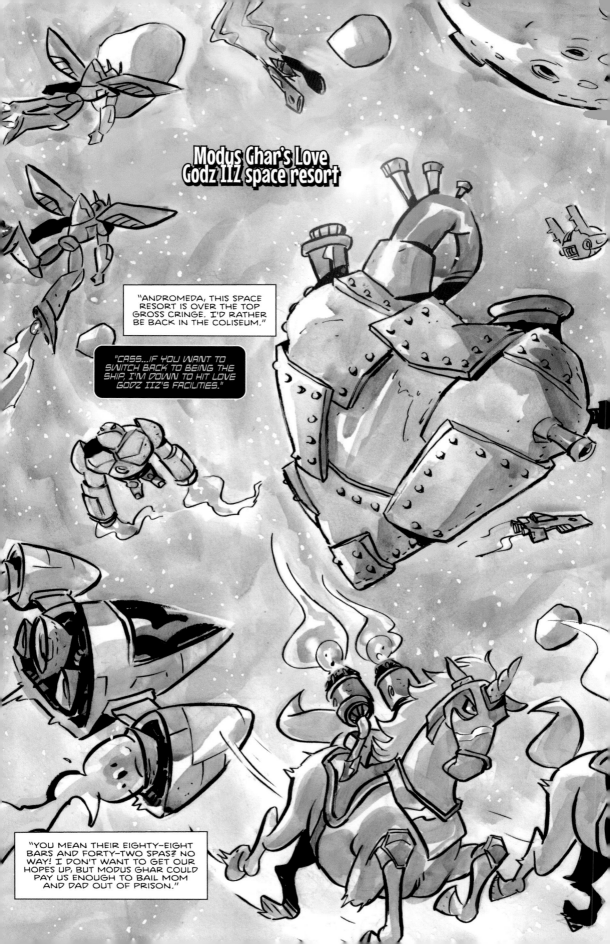

Modus Ghar's Love Godz IIZ space resort

"ANDROMEDA, THIS SPACE RESORT IS OVER THE TOP GROSS CRINGE. I'D RATHER BE BACK IN THE COLISEUM."

"CASS...IF YOU WANT TO SWITCH BACK TO BEING THE SHIP, I'M DOWN TO HIT LOVE GODZ IIZ'S FACILITIES."

"YOU MEAN THEIR EIGHTY-EIGHT BARS AND FORTY-TWO SPAS? NO WAY! I DON'T WANT TO GET OUR HOPES UP, BUT MODUS GHAR COULD PAY US ENOUGH TO BAIL MOM AND DAD OUT OF PRISON."

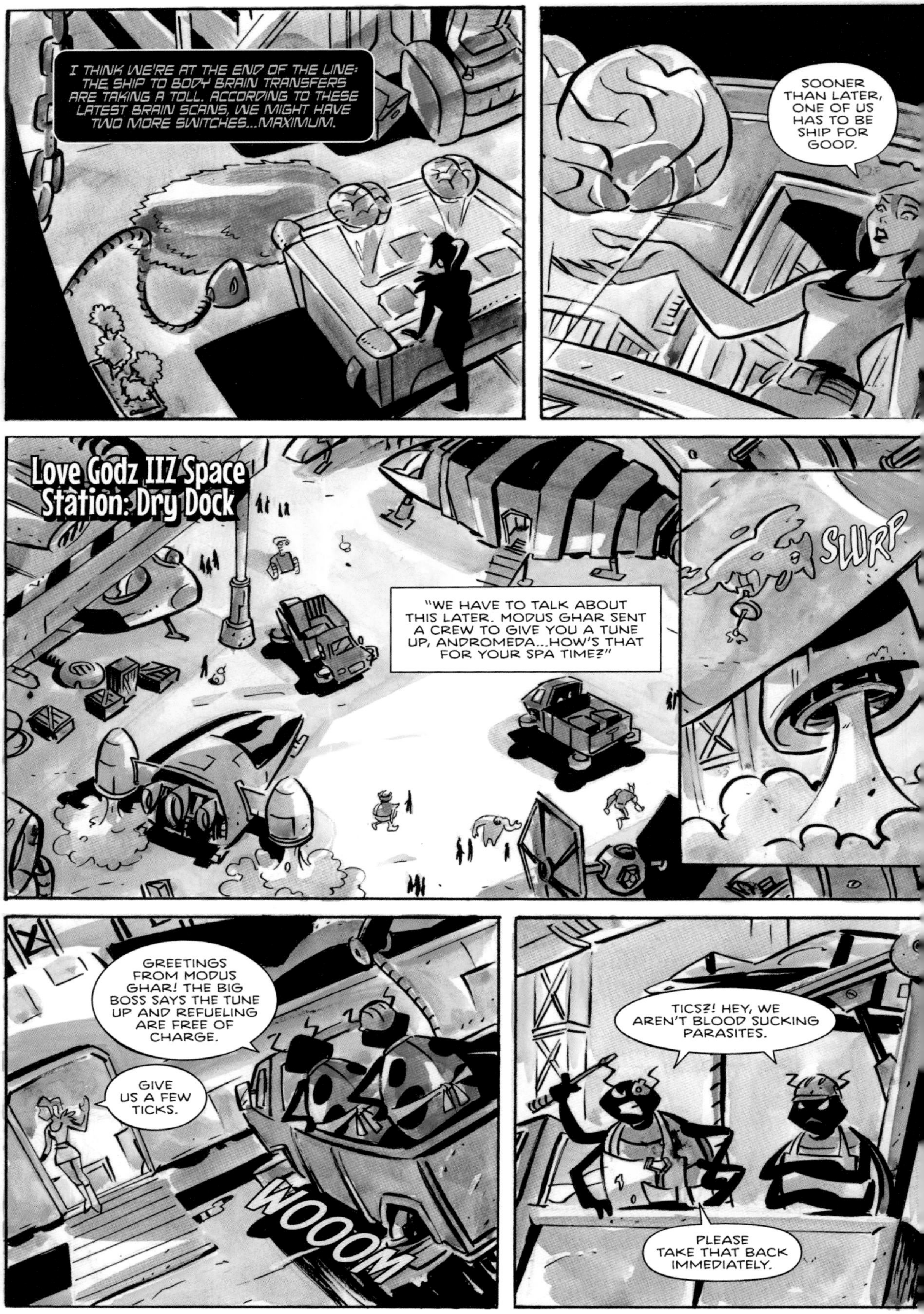
I THINK WE'RE AT THE END OF THE LINE: THE SHIP TO BODY BRAIN TRANSFERS ARE TAKING A TOLL. ACCORDING TO THESE LATEST BRAIN SCANS, WE MIGHT HAVE TWO MORE SWITCHES...MAXIMUM.
SOONER THAN LATER, ONE OF US HAS TO BE SHIP FOR GOOD.
Love Godz IIZ Space Station: Dry Dock
"WE HAVE TO TALK ABOUT THIS LATER. MODUS GHAR SENT A CREW TO GIVE YOU A TUNE UP, ANDROMEDA...HOW'S THAT FOR YOUR SPA TIME?"
SWRP
GREETINGS FROM MODUS GHAR! THE BIG BOSS SAYS THE TUNE UP AND REFUELING ARE FREE OF CHARGE.
GIVE US A FEW TICKS.
WOOOM
TICS?! HEY, WE AREN'T BLOOD SUCKING PARASITES.
PLEASE TAKE THAT BACK IMMEDIATELY.

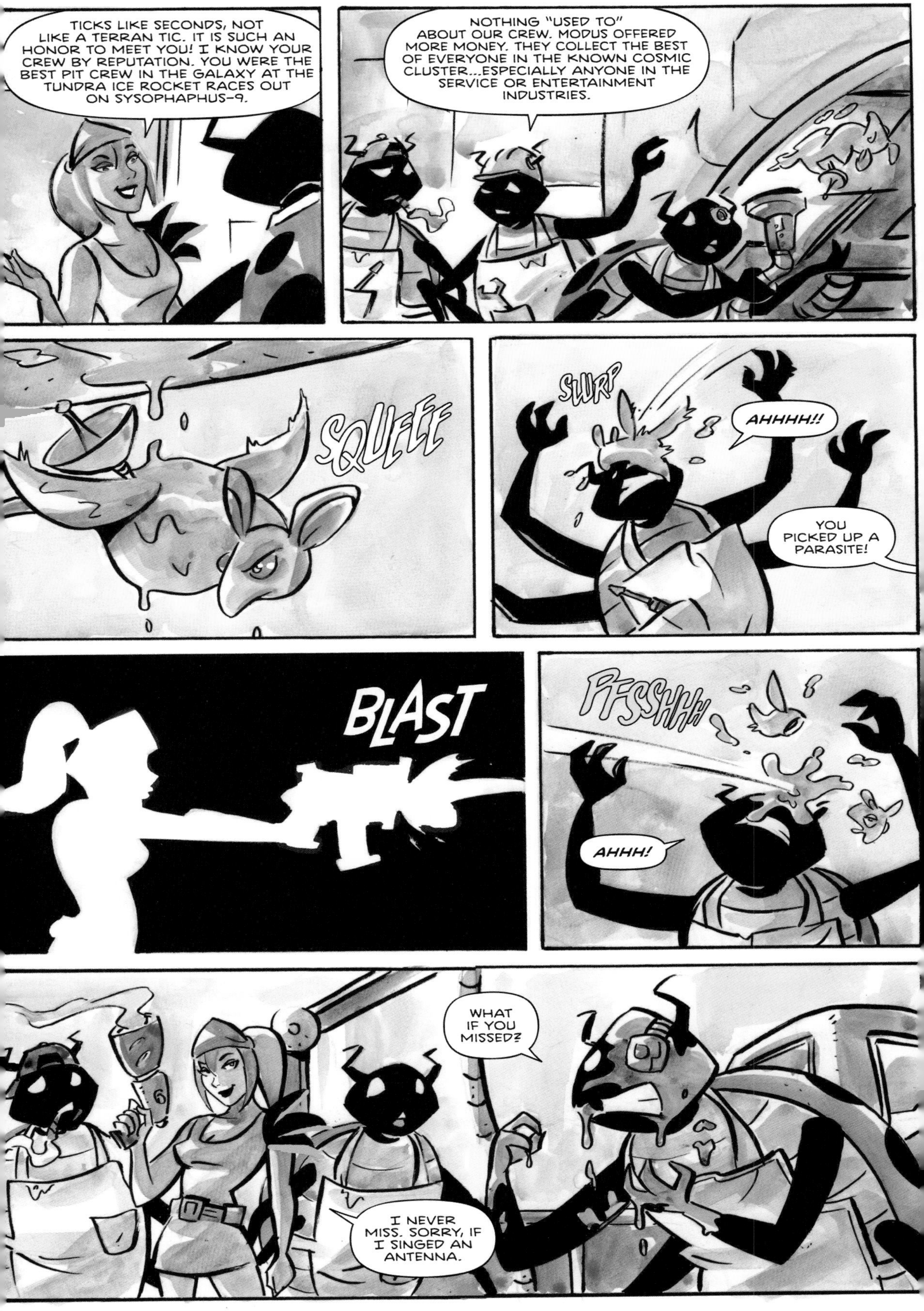
TICKS LIKE SECONDS, NOT LIKE A TERRAN TIC. IT IS SUCH AN HONOR TO MEET YOU! I KNOW YOUR CREW BY REPUTATION. YOU WERE THE BEST PIT CREW IN THE GALAXY AT THE TUNDRA ICE ROCKET RACES OUT ON SYSOPHAPHUS-9.
NOTHING "USED TO" ABOUT OUR CREW. MODUS OFFERED MORE MONEY. THEY COLLECT THE BEST OF EVERYONE IN THE KNOWN COSMIC CLUSTER...ESPECIALLY ANYONE IN THE SERVICE OR ENTERTAINMENT INDUSTRIES.
SQUEEE
SLURP
AHHHH!!
YOU PICKED UP A PARASITE!
BLAST
PFSSHHH
AHHH!
WHAT IF YOU MISSED?
I NEVER MISS. SORRY, IF I SINGED AN ANTENNA.

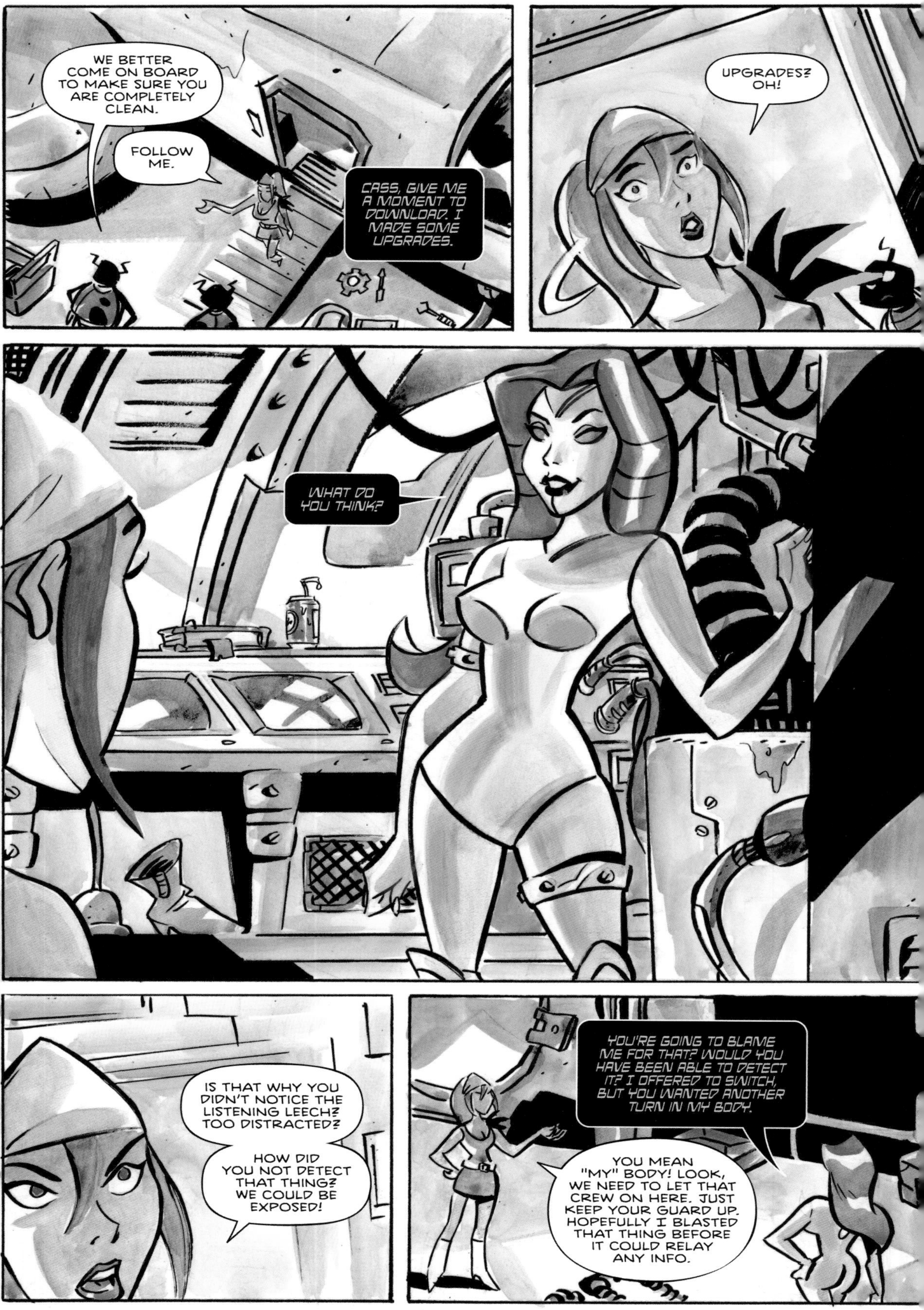

WE BETTER COME ON BOARD TO MAKE SURE YOU ARE COMPLETELY CLEAN.
FOLLOW ME.
CASS, GIVE ME A MOMENT TO DOWNLOAD. I MADE SOME UPGRADES.
UPGRADES? OH!
WHAT DO YOU THINK?
IS THAT WHY YOU DIDN'T NOTICE THE LISTENING LEECH? TOO DISTRACTED?
HOW DID YOU NOT DETECT THAT THING? WE COULD BE EXPOSED!
YOU'RE GOING TO BLAME ME FOR THAT? WOULD YOU HAVE BEEN ABLE TO DETECT IT? I OFFERED TO SWITCH, BUT YOU WANTED ANOTHER TURN IN MY BODY.
YOU MEAN "MY" BODY! LOOK, WE NEED TO LET THAT CREW ON HERE. JUST KEEP YOUR GUARD UP. HOPEFULLY I BLASTED THAT THING BEFORE IT COULD RELAY ANY INFO.

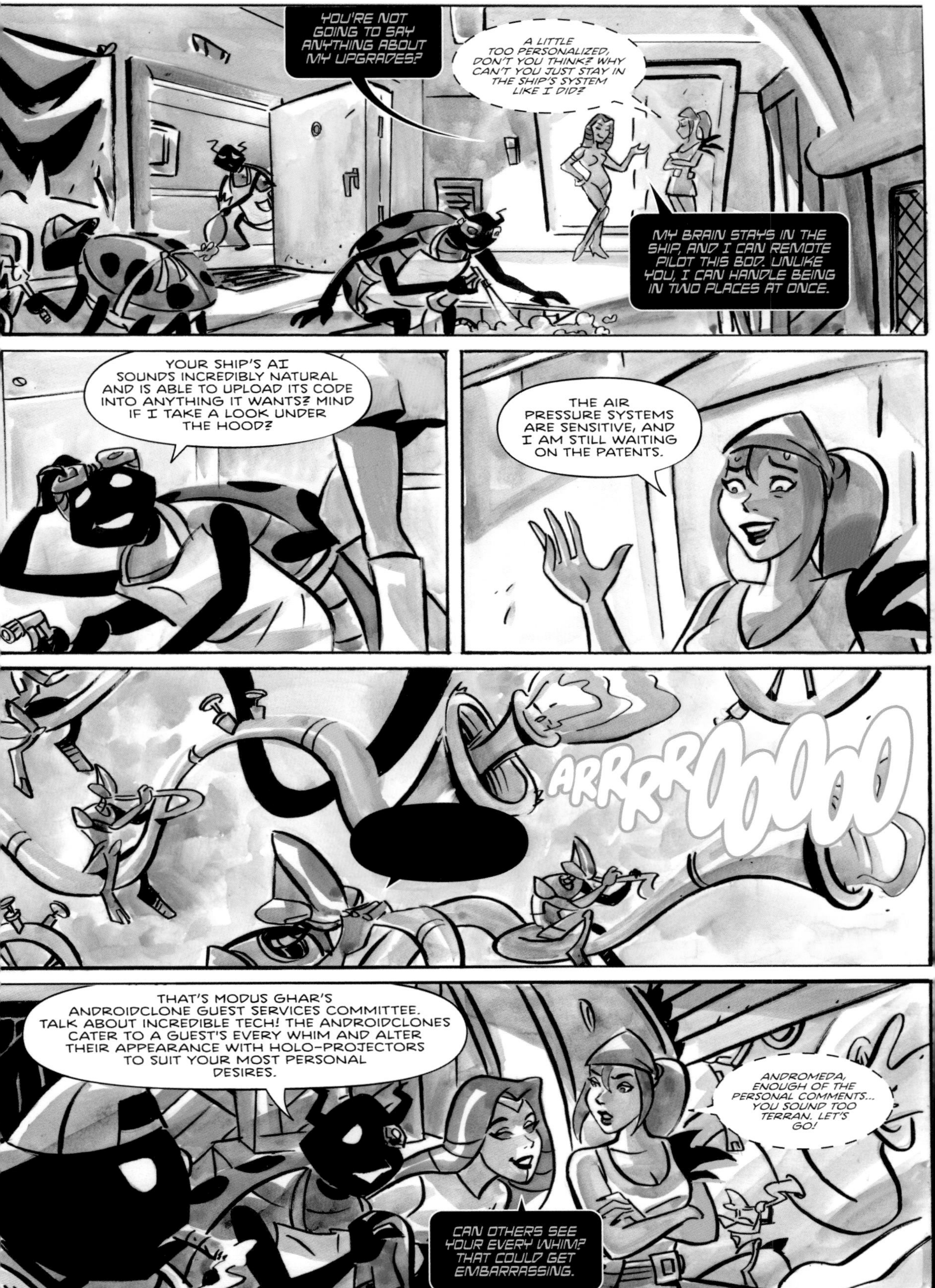
YOU'RE NOT GOING TO SAY ANYTHING ABOUT MY UPGRADES?
A LITTLE TOO PERSONALIZED, DON'T YOU THINK? WHY CAN'T YOU JUST STAY IN THE SHIP'S SYSTEM LIKE I DID?
MY BRAIN STAYS IN THE SHIP, AND I CAN REMOTE PILOT THIS BOD. UNLIKE YOU, I CAN HANDLE BEING IN TWO PLACES AT ONCE.
YOUR SHIP'S AI SOUNDS INCREDIBLY NATURAL AND IS ABLE TO UPLOAD ITS CODE INTO ANYTHING IT WANTS? MIND IF I TAKE A LOOK UNDER THE HOOD?
THE AIR PRESSURE SYSTEMS ARE SENSITIVE, AND I AM STILL WAITING ON THE PATENTS.
ARRRROOOOO
THAT'S MODUS GHAR'S ANDROIDCLONE GUEST SERVICES COMMITTEE. TALK ABOUT INCREDIBLE TECH! THE ANDROIDCLONES CATER TO A GUEST'S EVERY WHIM AND ALTER THEIR APPEARANCE WITH HOLO-PROJECTORS TO SUIT YOUR MOST PERSONAL DESIRES.
ANDROMEDA, ENOUGH OF THE PERSONAL COMMENTS... YOU SOUND TOO TERRAN. LET'S GO!
CAN OTHERS SEE YOUR EVERY WHIM? THAT COULD GET EMBARRASSING.

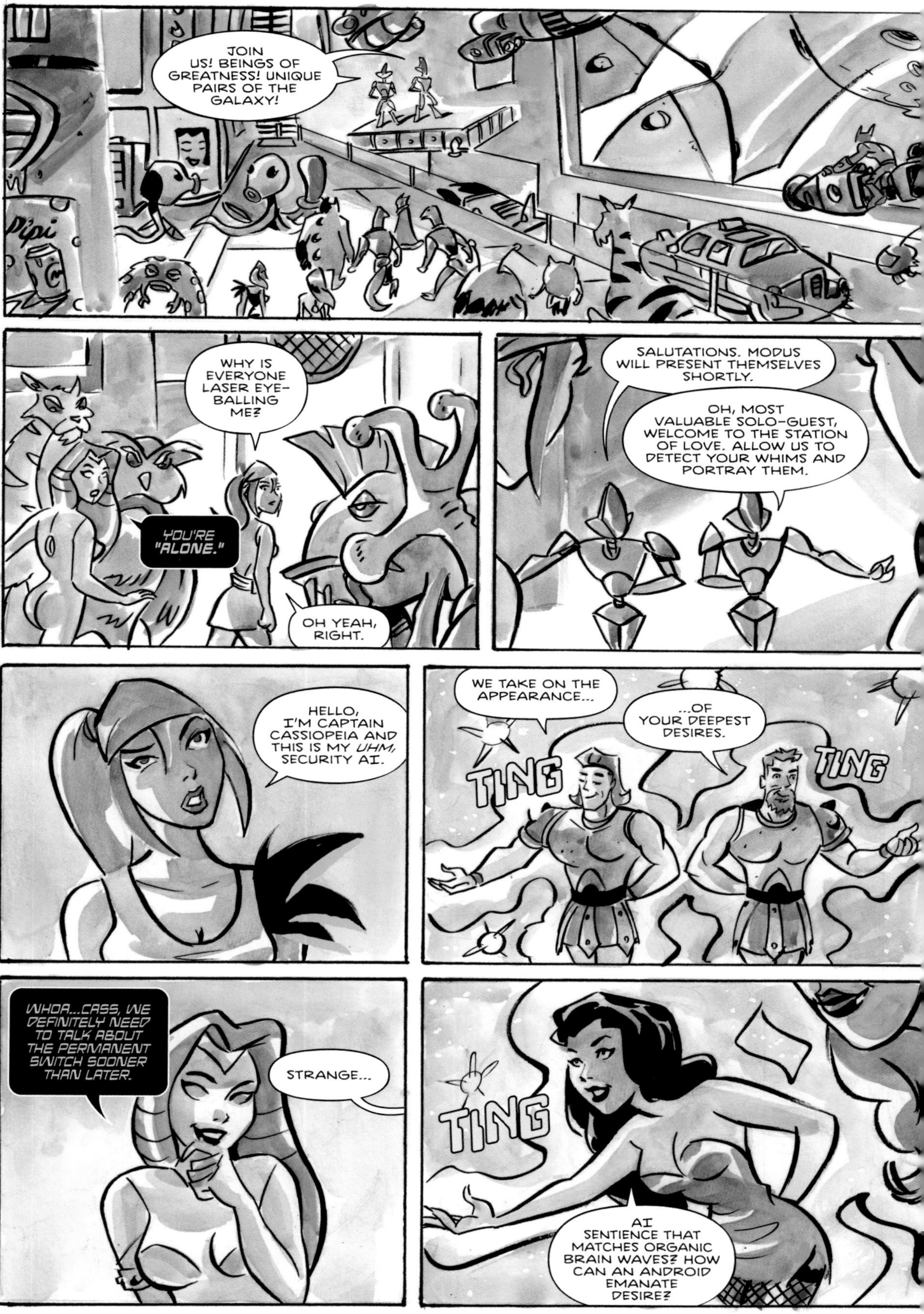
JOIN US! BEINGS OF GREATNESS! UNIQUE PAIRS OF THE GALAXY!
WHY IS EVERYONE LASER EYE-BALLING ME?
YOU'RE "ALONE."
OH YEAH, RIGHT.
SALUTATIONS. MODUS WILL PRESENT THEMSELVES SHORTLY.
OH, MOST VALUABLE SOLO-GUEST, WELCOME TO THE STATION OF LOVE. ALLOW US TO DETECT YOUR WHIMS AND PORTRAY THEM.
HELLO, I'M CAPTAIN CASSIOPEIA AND THIS IS MY *UHM*, SECURITY AI.
WE TAKE ON THE APPEARANCE...
...OF YOUR DEEPEST DESIRES.
TING
TING
WHOA...CASS, WE DEFINITELY NEED TO TALK ABOUT THE PERMANENT SWITCH SOONER THAN LATER.
STRANGE...
TING
AI SENTIENCE THAT MATCHES ORGANIC BRAIN WAVES? HOW CAN AN ANDROID EMANATE DESIRE?

THEY ARE ONTO YOU! COOL IT! STOP EMANATING!

I AM STARTING TO LOSE IT AS THE TIN CAN! I CAN'T FEEL ANYTHING! WITH MY THOUGHTS OPEN, I AT LEAST GET TO SEE WHAT I WANT TO SEE. OTHERWISE, THEY'RE JUST BLANK SCREEN LOOKING ANDROIDS.

PULL IT TOGETHER. THOSE ANDROIDCLONES ARE STARTING TO WONDER HOW ANOTHER AI CAN PERCEIVE THEM AS ANYTHING BUT ROBOTS. YOU HAVE TO BLOCK THEM!

FINE...BUT YOU NEED TO STOP ACTING LIKE YOU ARE THE BOSS OF ME. IF YOU ARE SO MUCH BETTER AT BEING SHIP, LET'S GO BACK IN AND SWITCH.

BLOCK

STRANGE...

I AM REVERTED TO FACTORY SETTINGS.

WHAT IS THAT CODE COMING FROM OUTSIDE THE STATION?

10101101101011

1010110110101110

WE ARE CLOSING IN.

WE MUST NOT OBLITERATE THE TERRAN CAPTAIN. WE NEED HER REMAINS FOR DISSECTION SOLUTIONS.

THE KILLBOTS FROM ISSUE 1!

WE CAN USE OUR BLACK MATTER CANNON TO PENETRATE THE STATION'S SHIELD AND SUCK THE CAPTAIN OUT INTO THE VACUUM OF SPACE.

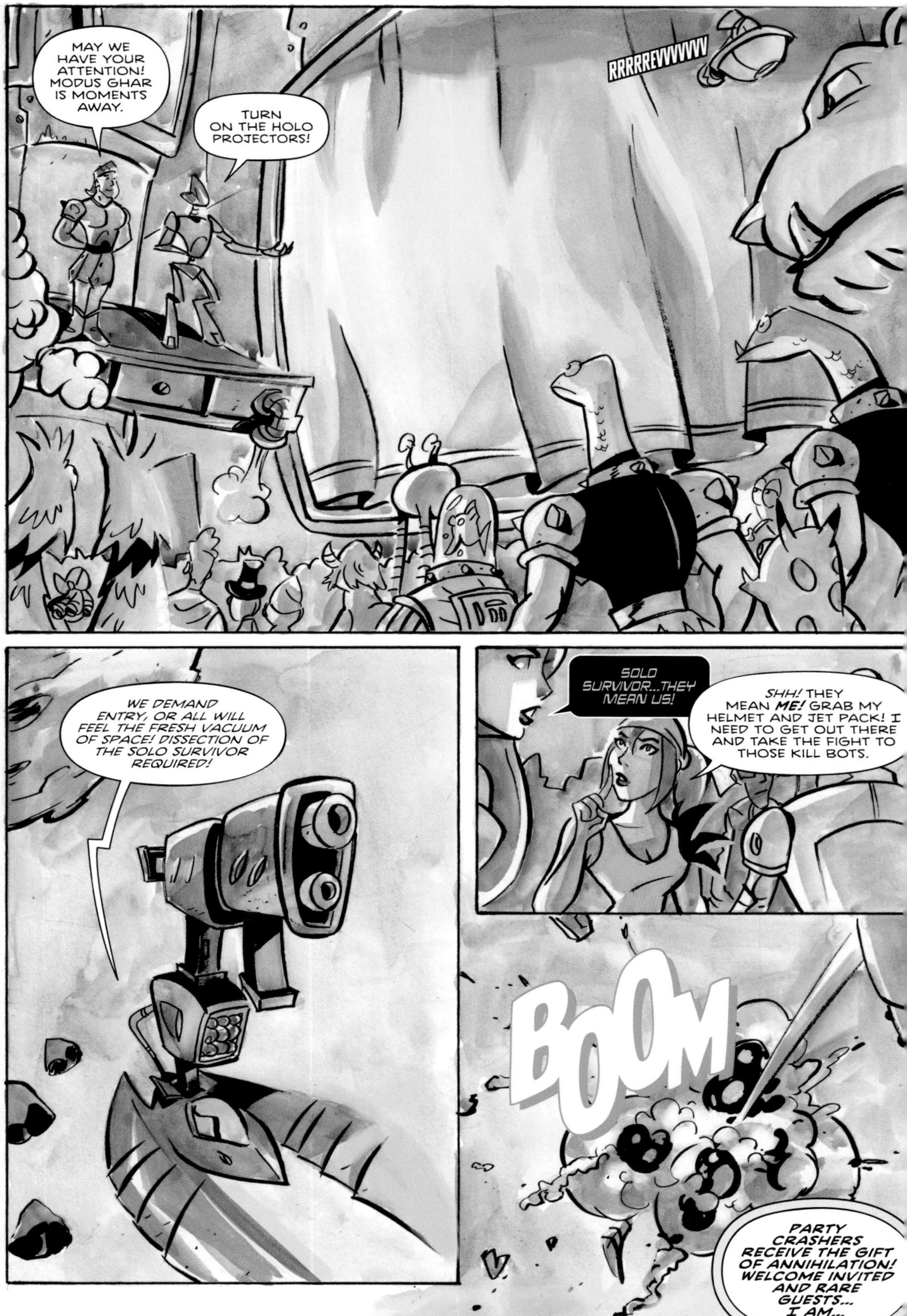
MAY WE HAVE YOUR ATTENTION! MODUS GHAR IS MOMENTS AWAY.
TURN ON THE HOLO PROJECTORS!
RRRRREVVVVVVV
WE DEMAND ENTRY, OR ALL WILL FEEL THE FRESH VACUUM OF SPACE! DISSECTION OF THE SOLO SURVIVOR REQUIRED!
SOLO SURVIVOR...THEY MEAN US!
SHH! THEY MEAN ME! GRAB MY HELMET AND JET PACK! I NEED TO GET OUT THERE AND TAKE THE FIGHT TO THOSE KILL BOTS.
BOOM
PARTY CRASHERS RECEIVE THE GIFT OF ANNIHILATION! WELCOME INVITED AND RARE GUESTS... I AM...

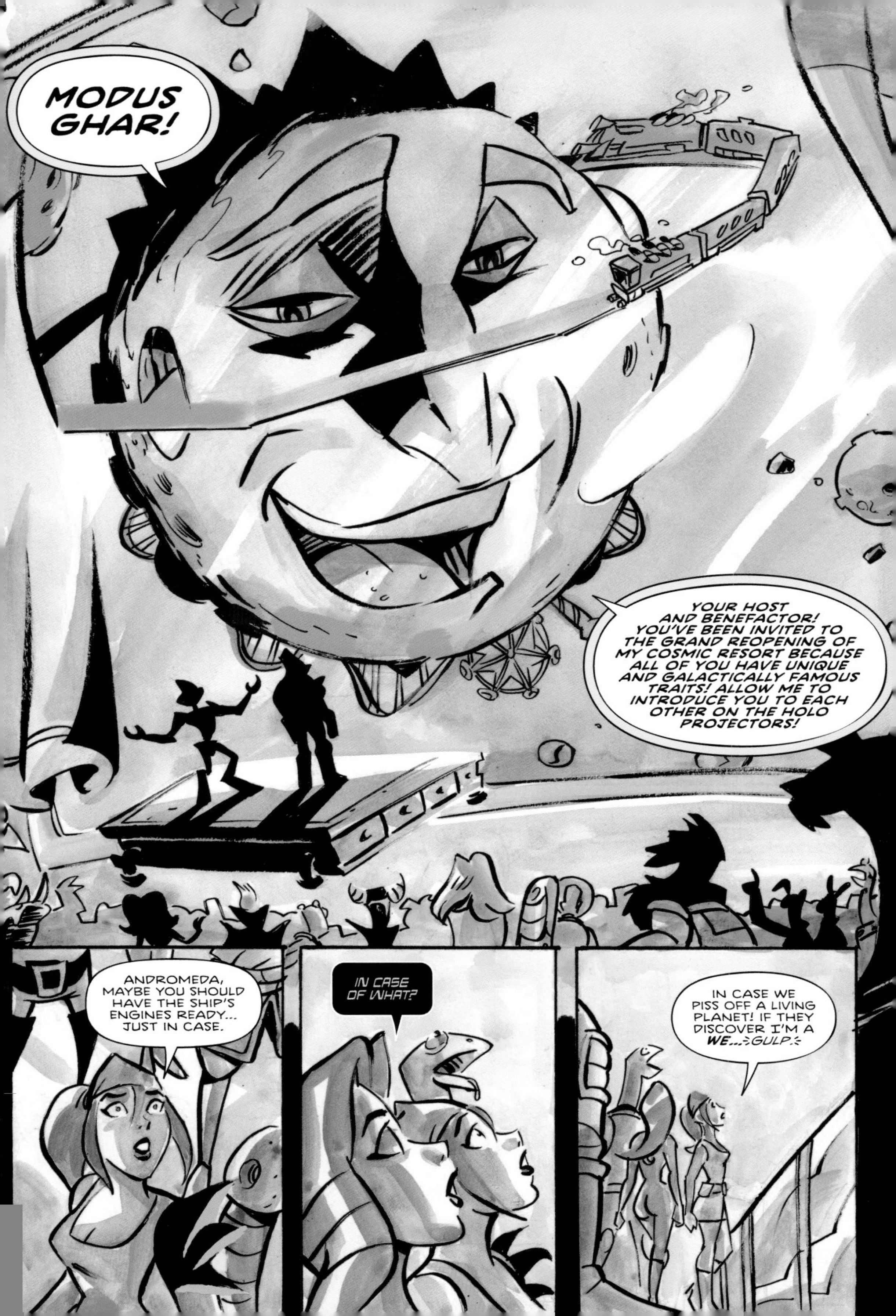
MODUS GHAR!
YOUR HOST AND BENEFACTOR! YOU'VE BEEN INVITED TO THE GRAND REOPENING OF MY COSMIC RESORT BECAUSE ALL OF YOU HAVE UNIQUE AND GALACTICALLY FAMOUS TRAITS! ALLOW ME TO INTRODUCE YOU TO EACH OTHER ON THE HOLO PROJECTORS!
ANDROMEDA, MAYBE YOU SHOULD HAVE THE SHIP'S ENGINES READY... JUST IN CASE.
IN CASE OF WHAT?
IN CASE WE PISS OFF A LIVING PLANET! IF THEY DISCOVER I'M A WE... GULP.

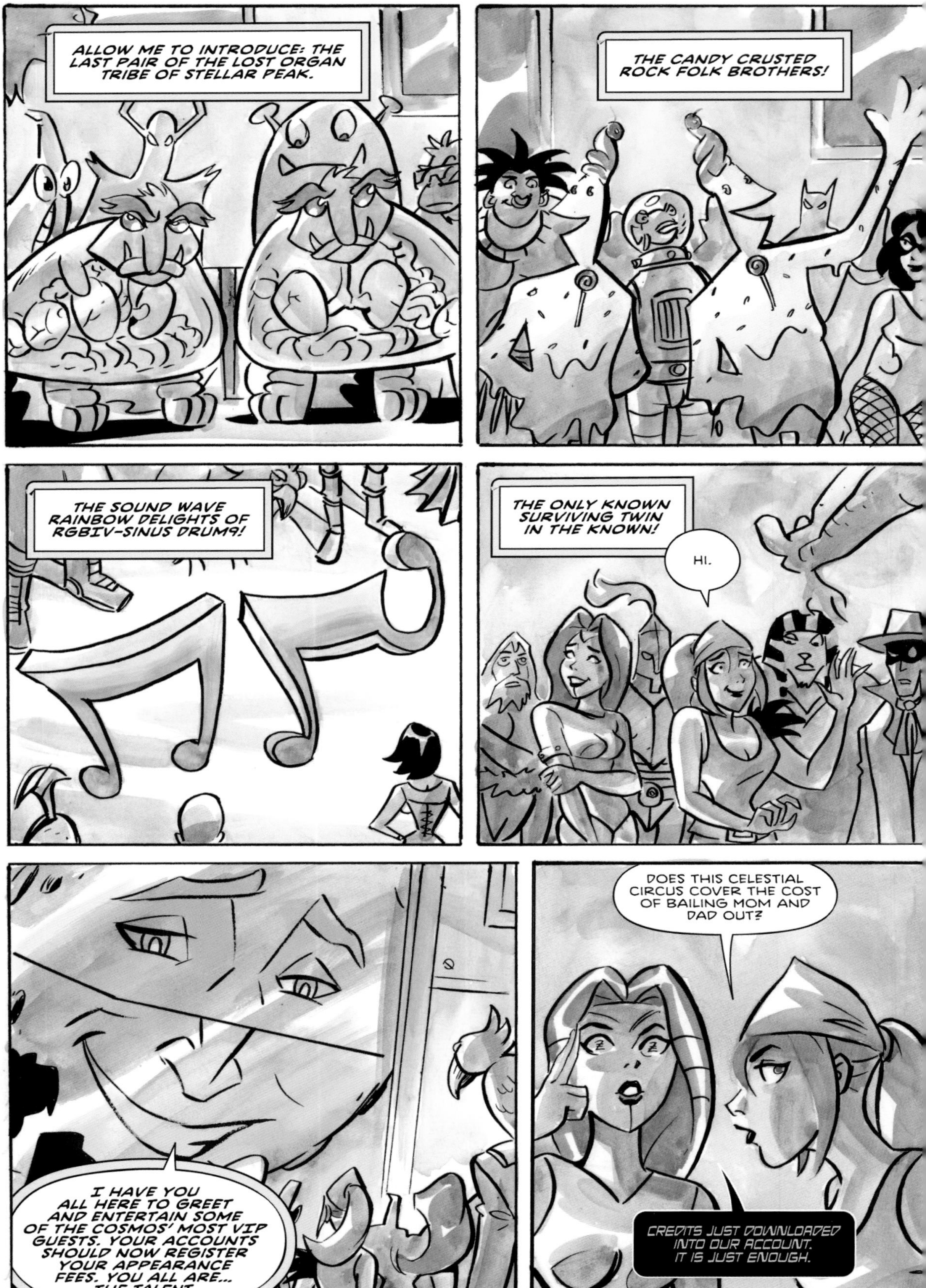
ALLOW ME TO INTRODUCE: THE LAST PAIR OF THE LOST ORGAN TRIBE OF STELLAR PEAK.
THE CANDY CRUSTED ROCK FOLK BROTHERS!
THE SOUND WAVE RAINBOW DELIGHTS OF RGBIV-SINUS DRUM9!
THE ONLY KNOWN SURVIVING TWIN IN THE KNOWN!
HI.
I HAVE YOU ALL HERE TO GREET AND ENTERTAIN SOME OF THE COSMOS' MOST VIP GUESTS. YOUR ACCOUNTS SHOULD NOW REGISTER YOUR APPEARANCE FEES. YOU ALL ARE... THE TALENT.
DOES THIS CELESTIAL CIRCUS COVER THE COST OF BAILING MOM AND DAD OUT?
CREDITS JUST DOWNLOADED INTO OUR ACCOUNT. IT IS JUST ENOUGH.

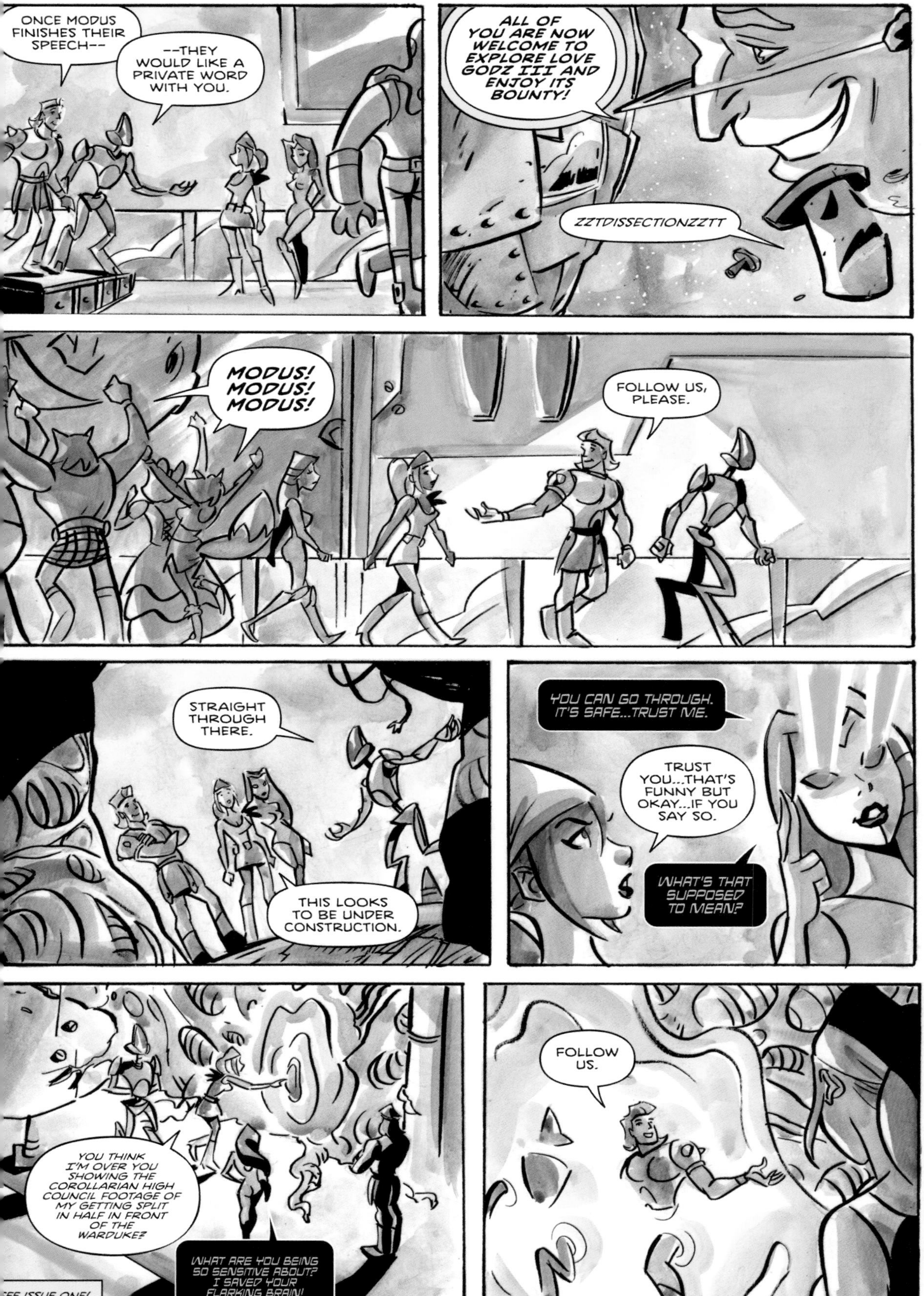

ONCE MODUS FINISHES THEIR SPEECH--
--THEY WOULD LIKE A PRIVATE WORD WITH YOU.
ALL OF YOU ARE NOW WELCOME TO EXPLORE LOVE GODZ III AND ENJOY ITS BOUNTY!
ZZTDISSECTIONZZTT
MODUS! MODUS! MODUS!
FOLLOW US, PLEASE.
STRAIGHT THROUGH THERE.
THIS LOOKS TO BE UNDER CONSTRUCTION.
YOU CAN GO THROUGH. IT'S SAFE...TRUST ME.
TRUST YOU...THAT'S FUNNY BUT OKAY...IF YOU SAY SO.
WHAT'S THAT SUPPOSED TO MEAN?
YOU THINK I'M OVER YOU SHOWING THE COROLLARIAN HIGH COUNCIL FOOTAGE OF MY GETTING SPLIT IN HALF IN FRONT OF THE WARDUKE?
WHAT ARE YOU BEING SO SENSITIVE ABOUT? I SAVED YOUR FLARKING BRAIN!
SEE ISSUE ONE!
FOLLOW US.

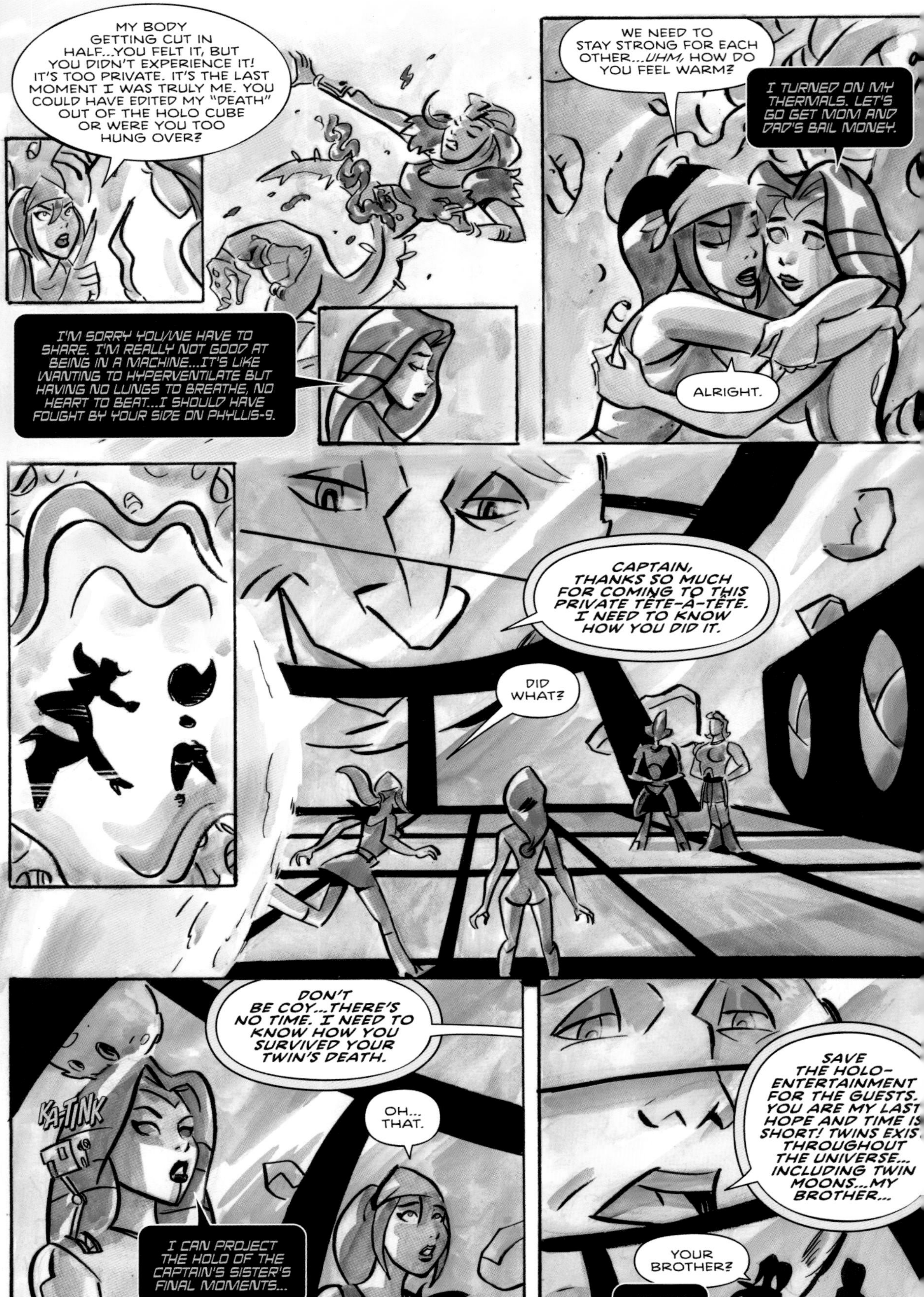
MY BODY GETTING CUT IN HALF...YOU FELT IT, BUT YOU DIDN'T EXPERIENCE IT! IT'S TOO PRIVATE. IT'S THE LAST MOMENT I WAS TRULY ME. YOU COULD HAVE EDITED MY "DEATH" OUT OF THE HOLO CUBE OR WERE YOU TOO HUNG OVER?
I'M SORRY YOU/WE HAVE TO SHARE. I'M REALLY NOT GOOD AT BEING IN A MACHINE...IT'S LIKE WANTING TO HYPERVENTILATE BUT HAVING NO LUNGS TO BREATHE, NO HEART TO BEAT...I SHOULD HAVE FOUGHT BY YOUR SIDE ON PHYLLIS-9.
WE NEED TO STAY STRONG FOR EACH OTHER...UHM, HOW DO YOU FEEL WARM?
I TURNED ON MY THERMALS. LET'S GO GET MOM AND DAD'S BAIL MONEY.
ALRIGHT.
CAPTAIN, THANKS SO MUCH FOR COMING TO THIS PRIVATE TÊTE-A-TÊTE. I NEED TO KNOW HOW YOU DID IT.
DID WHAT?
DON'T BE COY...THERE'S NO TIME. I NEED TO KNOW HOW YOU SURVIVED YOUR TWIN'S DEATH.
KA-TINK
OH... THAT.
I CAN PROJECT THE HOLO OF THE CAPTAIN'S SISTER'S FINAL MOMENTS...
SAVE THE HOLO-ENTERTAINMENT FOR THE GUESTS. YOU ARE MY LAST HOPE AND TIME IS SHORT! TWINS EXIST THROUGHOUT THE UNIVERSE... INCLUDING TWIN MOONS...MY BROTHER...
YOUR BROTHER?
HIS TWIN MOON!

"MY BROTHER, THE GREAT WARRIOR MOON-MODUS GHAZ, WAS STRUCK BY AN ENORMOUS ASTEROID."

Some time ago...

PZZZT PZZZT

"A NEARBY STAR WENT SUPER NOVA AND TEMPORARILY KNOCKED OUT OUR DEFENSE SATELLITES...WE NEVER SAW THE ASTEROID COMING."

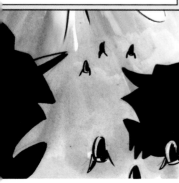

SMASH

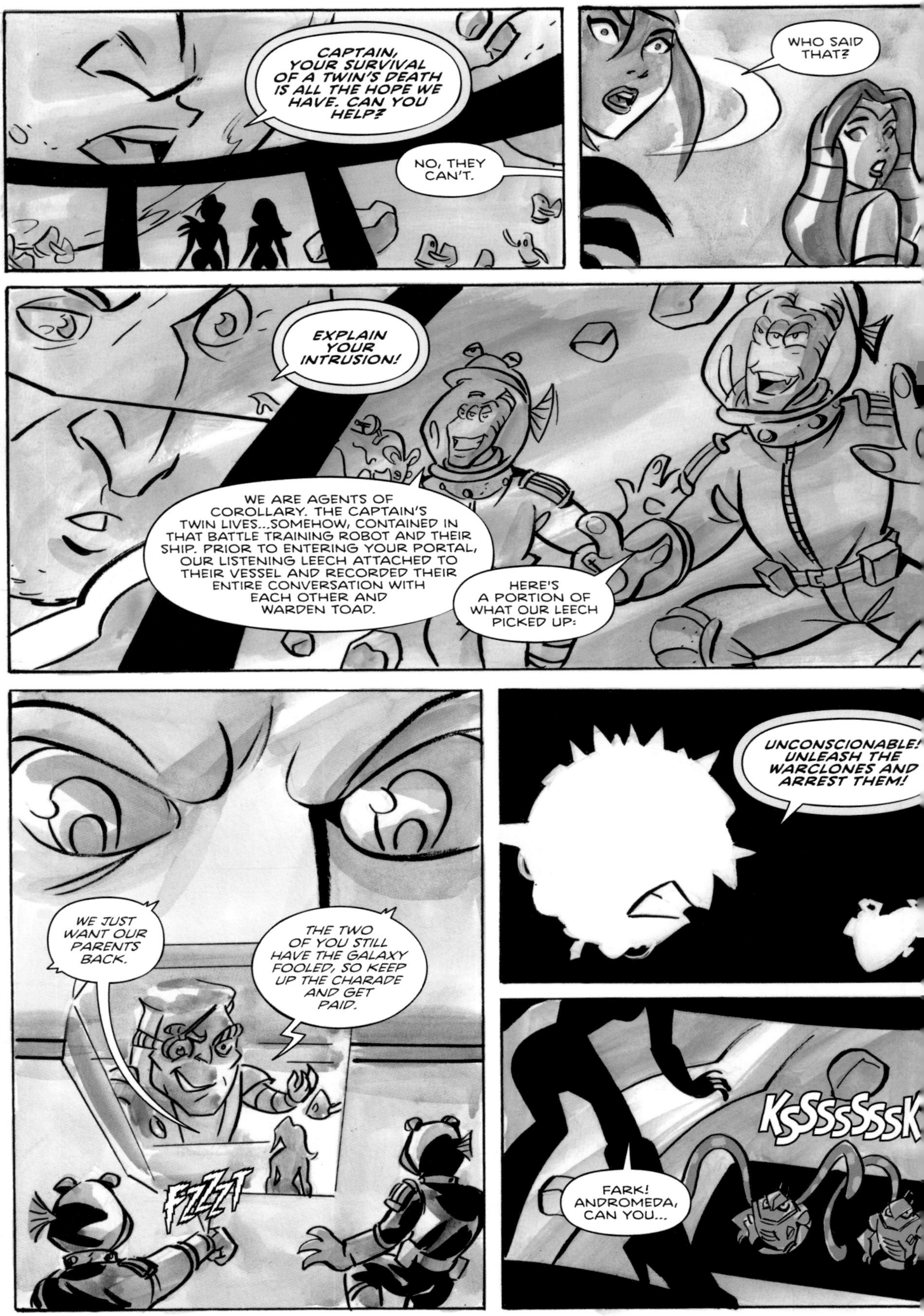
CAPTAIN, YOUR SURVIVAL OF A TWIN'S DEATH IS ALL THE HOPE WE HAVE. CAN YOU HELP?
NO, THEY CAN'T.
WHO SAID THAT?
EXPLAIN YOUR INTRUSION!
WE ARE AGENTS OF COROLLARY. THE CAPTAIN'S TWIN LIVES...SOMEHOW, CONTAINED IN THAT BATTLE TRAINING ROBOT AND THEIR SHIP. PRIOR TO ENTERING YOUR PORTAL, OUR LISTENING LEECH ATTACHED TO THEIR VESSEL AND RECORDED THEIR ENTIRE CONVERSATION WITH EACH OTHER AND WARDEN TOAD.
HERE'S A PORTION OF WHAT OUR LEECH PICKED UP:
WE JUST WANT OUR PARENTS BACK.
THE TWO OF YOU STILL HAVE THE GALAXY FOOLED, SO KEEP UP THE CHARADE AND GET PAID.
FZZZT
UNCONSCIONABLE! UNLEASH THE WARCLONES AND ARREST THEM!
KSSSSSSK
FARK! ANDROMEDA, CAN YOU...

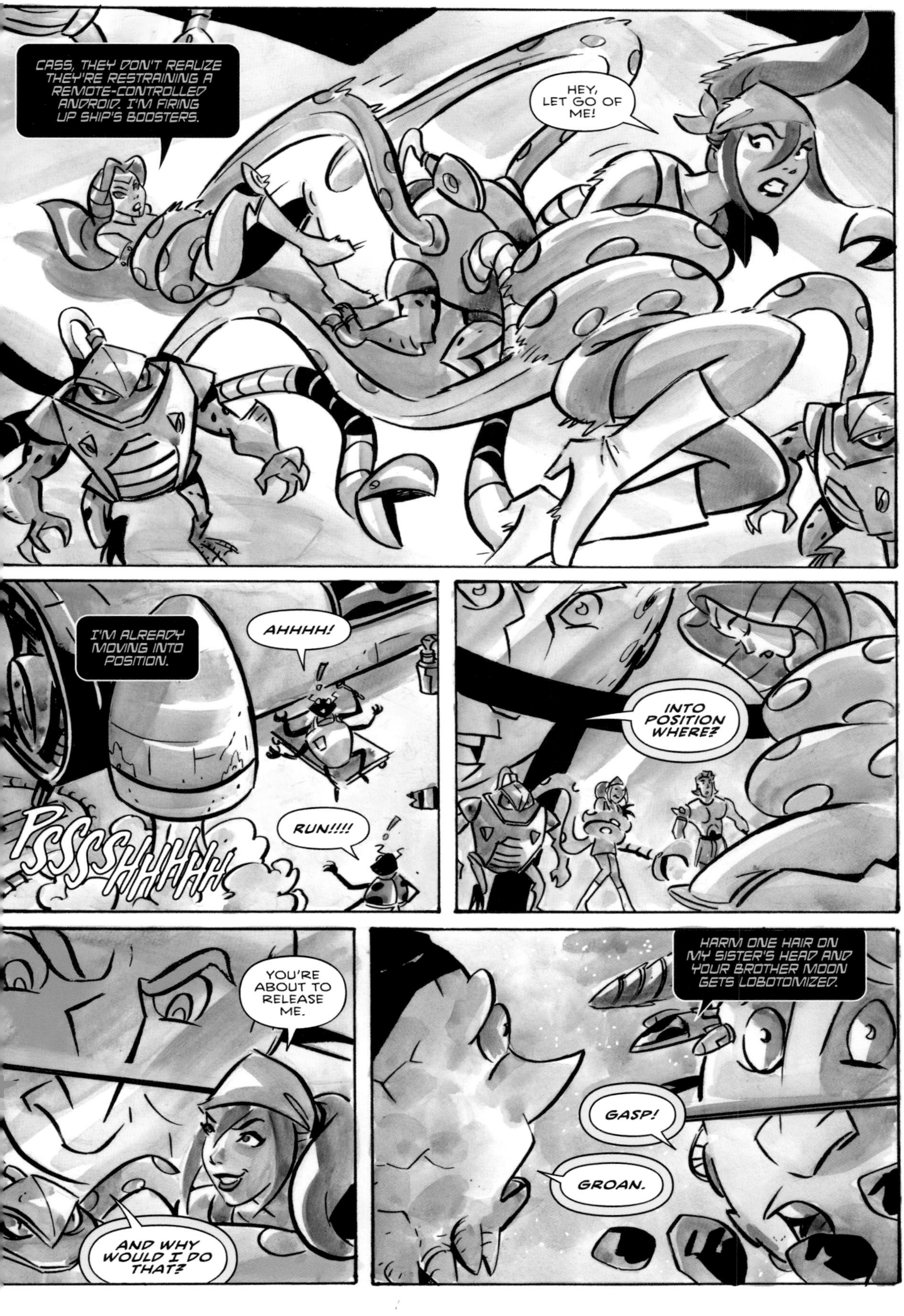
CASS, THEY DON'T REALIZE THEY'RE RESTRAINING A REMOTE-CONTROLLED ANDROID. I'M FIRING UP SHIP'S BOOSTERS.
HEY, LET GO OF ME!
I'M ALREADY MOVING INTO POSITION.
AHHHH!
RUN!!!!
PSSSSHHHHHH
INTO POSITION WHERE?
YOU'RE ABOUT TO RELEASE ME.
AND WHY WOULD I DO THAT?
HARM ONE HAIR ON MY SISTER'S HEAD AND YOUR BROTHER MOON GETS LOBOTOMIZED.
GASP!
GROAN.

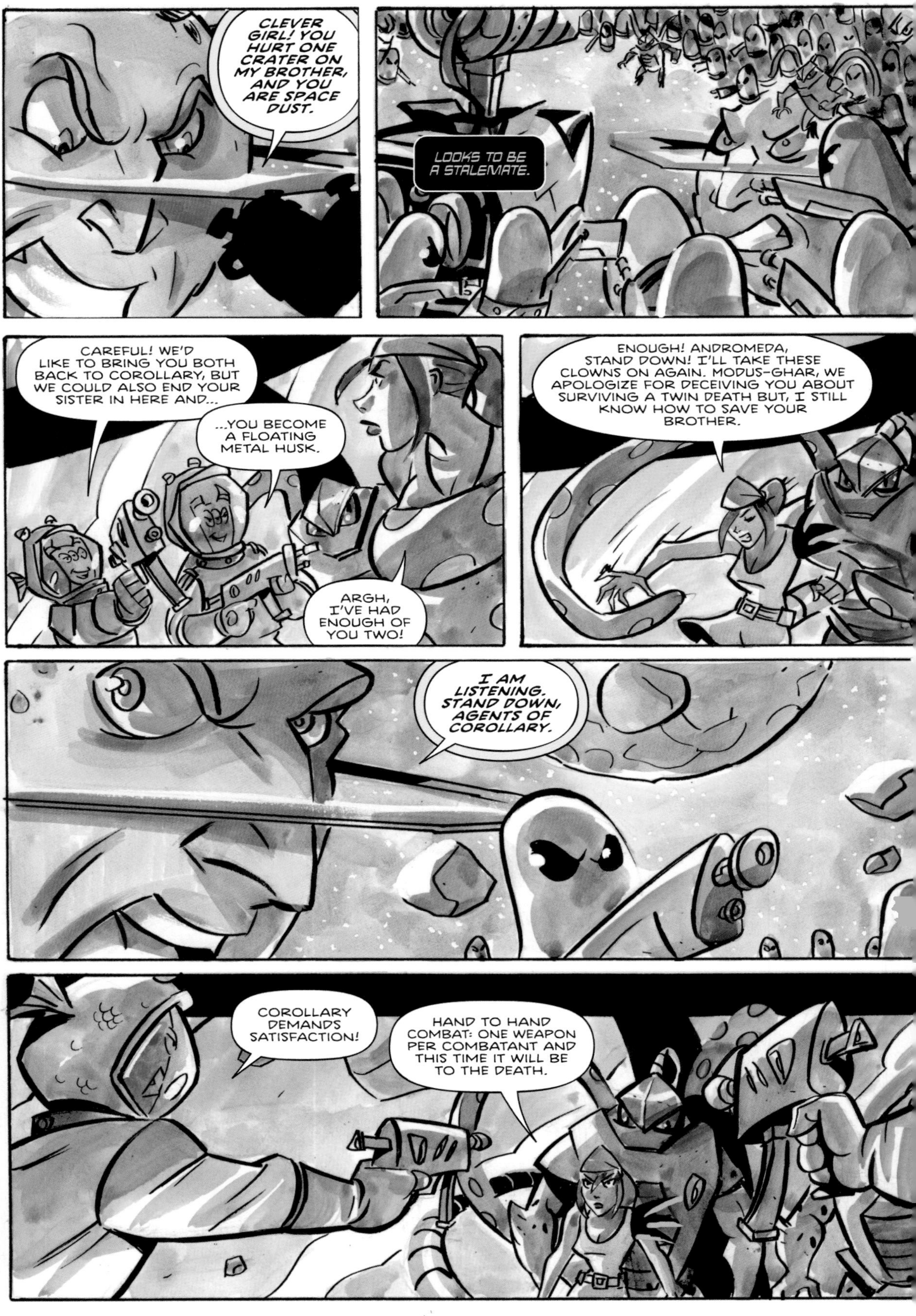
CLEVER GIRL! YOU HURT ONE CRATER ON MY BROTHER, AND YOU ARE SPACE DUST.
LOOKS TO BE A STALEMATE.
CAREFUL! WE'D LIKE TO BRING YOU BOTH BACK TO COROLLARY, BUT WE COULD ALSO END YOUR SISTER IN HERE AND...
...YOU BECOME A FLOATING METAL HUSK.
ARGH, I'VE HAD ENOUGH OF YOU TWO!
ENOUGH! ANDROMEDA, STAND DOWN! I'LL TAKE THESE CLOWNS ON AGAIN. MODUS-GHAR, WE APOLOGIZE FOR DECEIVING YOU ABOUT SURVIVING A TWIN DEATH BUT, I STILL KNOW HOW TO SAVE YOUR BROTHER.
I AM LISTENING. STAND DOWN, AGENTS OF COROLLARY.
COROLLARY DEMANDS SATISFACTION!
HAND TO HAND COMBAT: ONE WEAPON PER COMBATANT AND THIS TIME IT WILL BE TO THE DEATH.

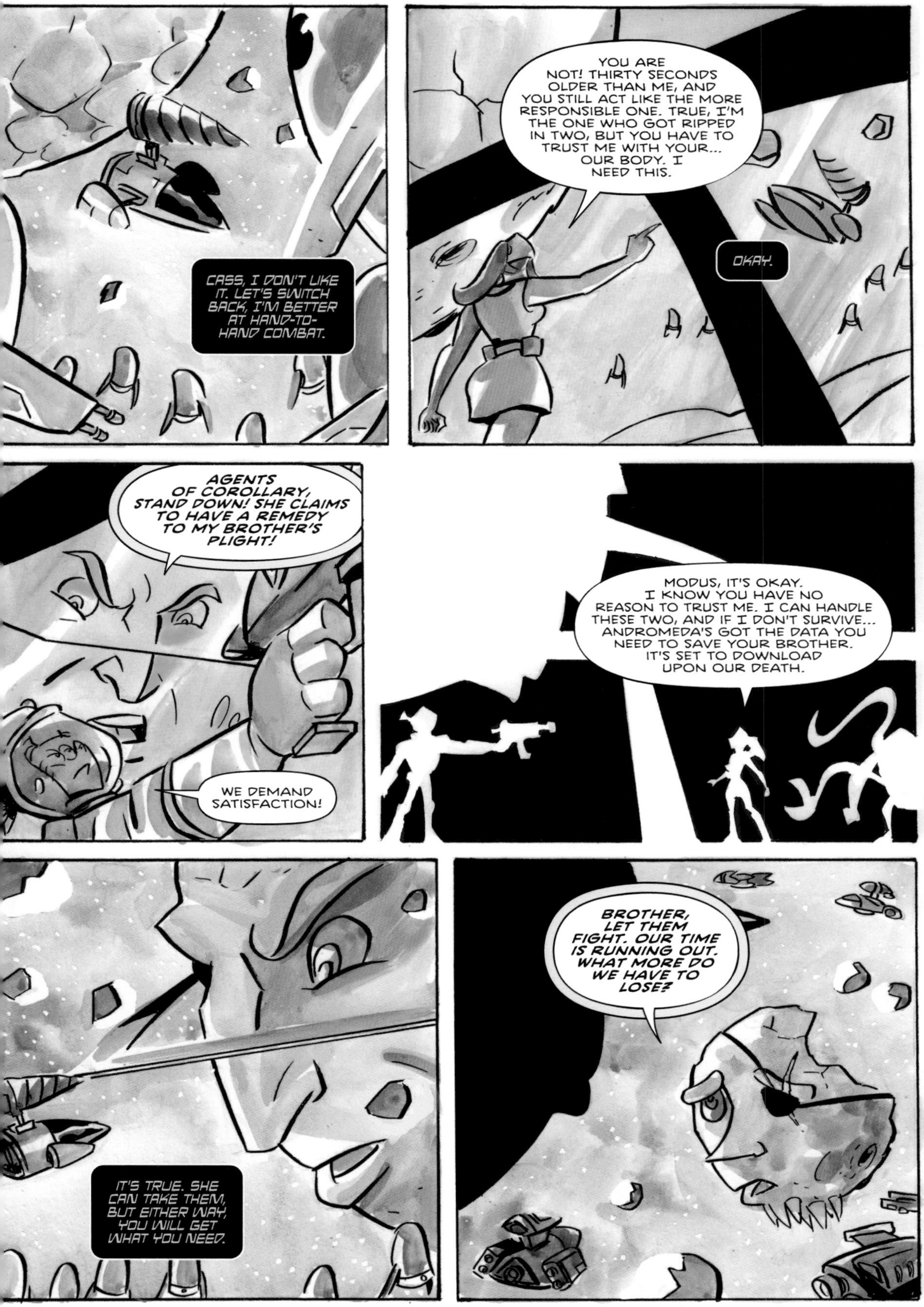
CASS, I DON'T LIKE IT. LET'S SWITCH BACK, I'M BETTER AT HAND-TO-HAND COMBAT.
YOU ARE NOT! THIRTY SECONDS OLDER THAN ME, AND YOU STILL ACT LIKE THE MORE RESPONSIBLE ONE. TRUE, I'M THE ONE WHO GOT RIPPED IN TWO, BUT YOU HAVE TO TRUST ME WITH YOUR... OUR BODY. I NEED THIS.
OKAY.
AGENTS OF COROLLARY, STAND DOWN! SHE CLAIMS TO HAVE A REMEDY TO MY BROTHER'S PLIGHT!
WE DEMAND SATISFACTION!
MODUS, IT'S OKAY. I KNOW YOU HAVE NO REASON TO TRUST ME. I CAN HANDLE THESE TWO, AND IF I DON'T SURVIVE... ANDROMEDA'S GOT THE DATA YOU NEED TO SAVE YOUR BROTHER. IT'S SET TO DOWNLOAD UPON OUR DEATH.
IT'S TRUE. SHE CAN TAKE THEM, BUT EITHER WAY, YOU WILL GET WHAT YOU NEED.
BROTHER, LET THEM FIGHT. OUR TIME IS RUNNING OUT. WHAT MORE DO WE HAVE TO LOSE?

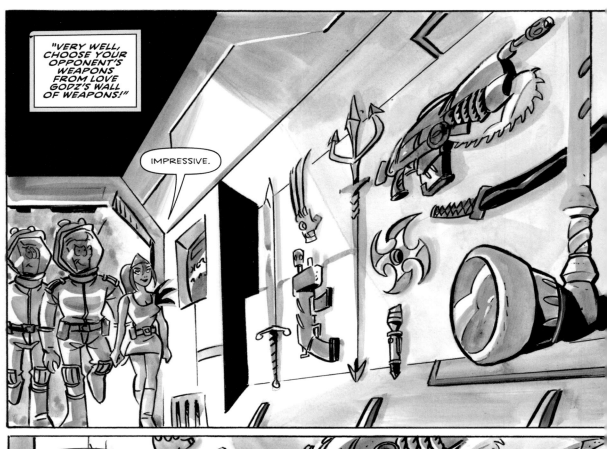

"VERY WELL, CHOOSE YOUR OPPONENT'S WEAPONS FROM LOVE GODZ'S WALL OF WEAPONS!"

IMPRESSIVE.

I'LL GO FIRST. THIS TRIDENT AND THAT SCARY LOOKING BROAD-SWORD.

LET'S HAVE YOU WIELD, GRUNT, THE METEOR HAMMER OF THWROCK.

∴GASP∴ THAT'S INCREDIBLY HEAVY.

DO ME A FAVOR?

YES?

DON'T UNDERESTIMATE ME.

WHOA.

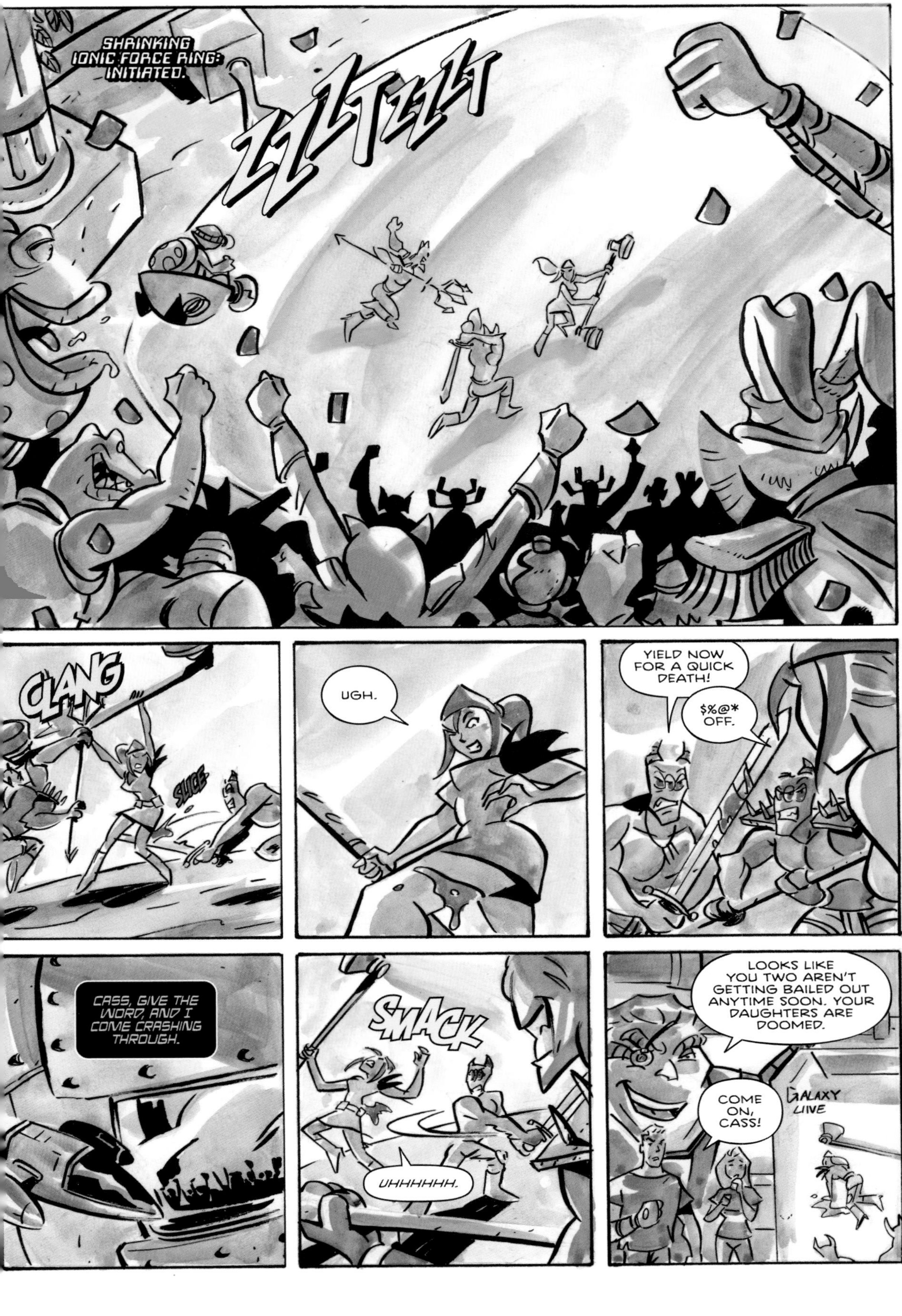
SHRINKING IONIC FORCE RING: INITIATED.
ZZZZTZZZZT
CLANG
SLICE
UGH.
YIELD NOW FOR A QUICK DEATH!
$%@* OFF.
CASS, GIVE THE WORD, AND I COME CRASHING THROUGH.
SMACK
UHHHHHH.
LOOKS LIKE YOU TWO AREN'T GETTING BAILED OUT ANYTIME SOON. YOUR DAUGHTERS ARE DOOMED.
COME ON, CASS!
GALAXY LIVE

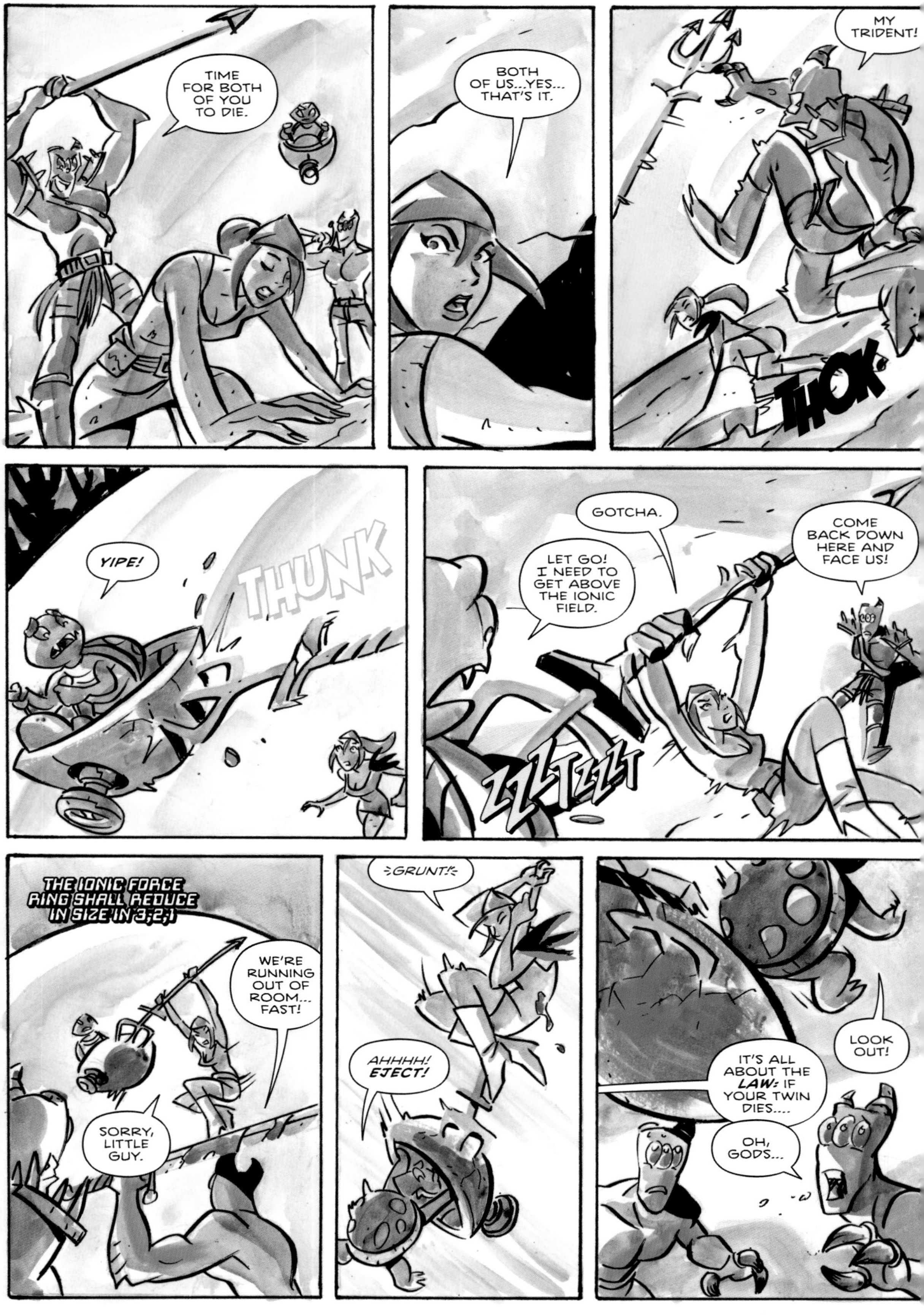
TIME FOR BOTH OF YOU TO DIE.
BOTH OF US... YES... THAT'S IT.
MY TRIDENT!
THOK
YIPE!
THUNK
GOTCHA.
LET GO! I NEED TO GET ABOVE THE IONIC FIELD.
COME BACK DOWN HERE AND FACE US!
ZZZTZZZT
THE IONIC FORCE RING SHALL REDUCE IN SIZE IN 3,2,1
WE'RE RUNNING OUT OF ROOM... FAST!
SORRY, LITTLE GUY.
GRUNT!
AHHHH! EJECT!
LOOK OUT!
IT'S ALL ABOUT THE LAW: IF YOUR TWIN DIES....
OH, GODS...

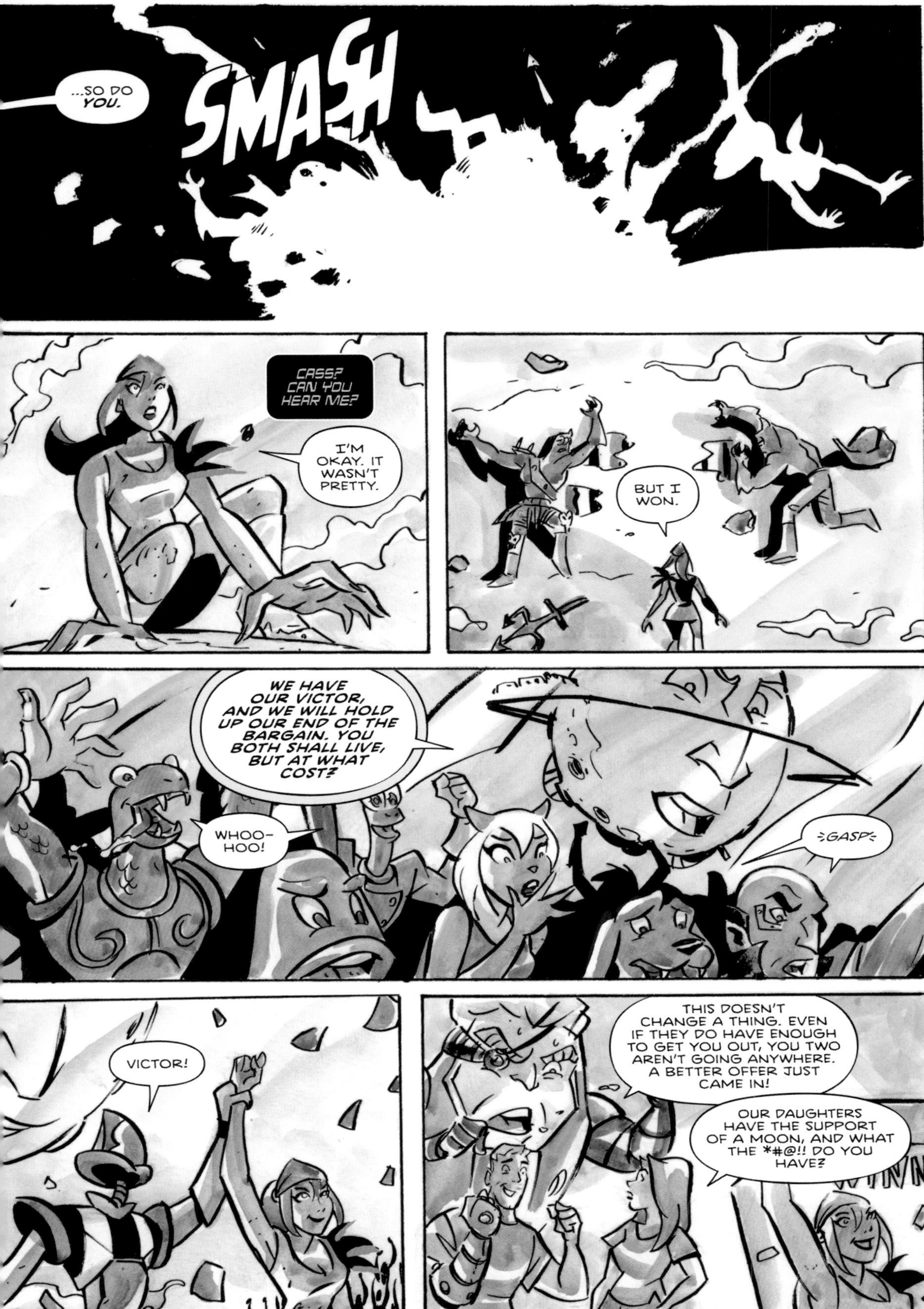
...SO DO YOU.
SMASH
CASS? CAN YOU HEAR ME?
I'M OKAY. IT WASN'T PRETTY.
BUT I WON.
WE HAVE OUR VICTOR, AND WE WILL HOLD UP OUR END OF THE BARGAIN. YOU BOTH SHALL LIVE, BUT AT WHAT COST?
WHOO-HOO!
GASP
VICTOR!
THIS DOESN'T CHANGE A THING. EVEN IF THEY DO HAVE ENOUGH TO GET YOU OUT, YOU TWO AREN'T GOING ANYWHERE. A BETTER OFFER JUST CAME IN!
OUR DAUGHTERS HAVE THE SUPPORT OF A MOON, AND WHAT THE *#@!! DO YOU HAVE?

PLEASE, LOWER YOUR WEAPON... OBVIOUSLY, YOU DON'T HAVE A WAY FOR US BOTH TO SURVIVE, BUT I STILL WANT WHATEVER TIME WE HAVE LEFT.

WHAT DO YOU THINK I'M TRYING TO DO HERE? THIS ISN'T A CANNON.

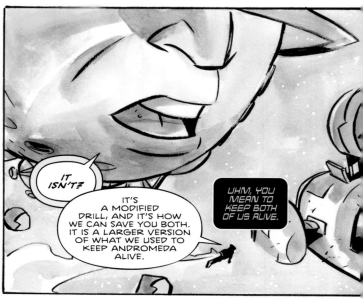

IT ISN'T?

IT'S A MODIFIED DRILL, AND IT'S HOW WE CAN SAVE YOU BOTH. IT IS A LARGER VERSION OF WHAT WE USED TO KEEP ANDROMEDA ALIVE.

UHM, YOU MEAN TO KEEP BOTH OF US ALIVE.

WELCOME BACK.

GOOD TO BE BACK.

CASS, I'M STARTING TO LOSE IT BEING STUCK AS SHIP. I NEED TO FEEL SOMETHING...ANYTHING. I AM BEGGING YOU TO LET US SWITCH.

≥GRUNT≤ ONE MORE SWITCH MIGHT BE ALL WE HAVE LEFT! ANDROMEDA, I GET THE CLAUSTROPHOBIA, BUT WE'RE VAPORIZED IF WE DON'T HELP THESE MOONS OUT FIRST.

THIS DRILL BORE THROUGH THE PETRIFIED ASTEROIDS OF GAMMA-63, SO MAKING IT TO YOUR BROTHER'S BRAIN-CORE SHOULDN'T BE A PROBLEM. AFTERWARDS, WE'LL NEED SOMETHING LARGE ENOUGH TO HOUSE HIS BRAIN-CORE.

OH MY! YOU WANT US TO TAKE TURNS IN MY PLANETARY SPHERE AND IN...

...LOVE GODZ ENGINE ROOM IS VAST ENOUGH TO HOST YOUR CORES, IT'S ALSO SHIELDED TO HANDLE THE KELVIN LEVEL TEMPS YOU TWO EMANATE.

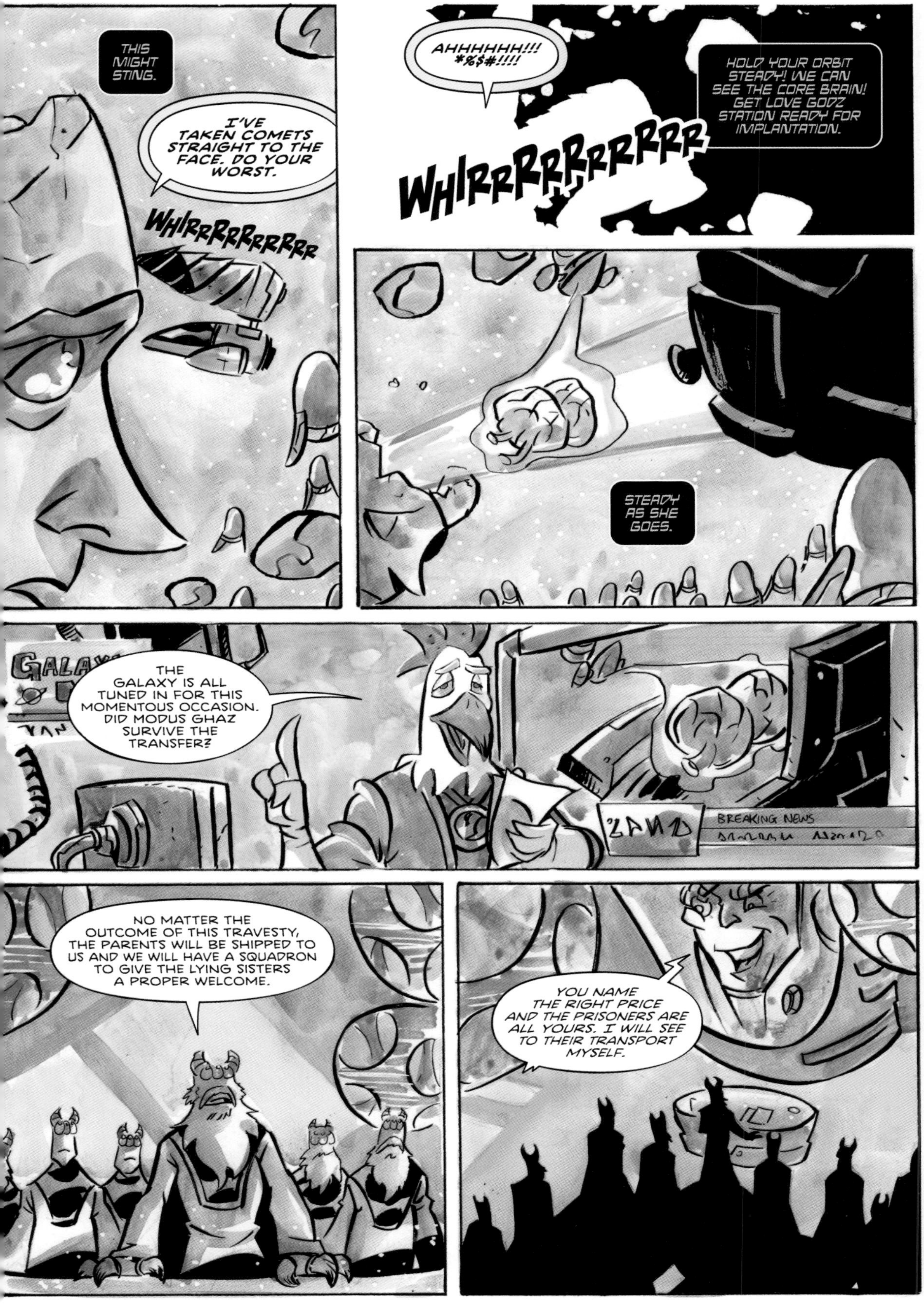
THIS MIGHT STING.
I'VE TAKEN COMETS STRAIGHT TO THE FACE. DO YOUR WORST.
WHIRRRRRRRRRRR
AHHHHHHH!!! *%$#!!!!
HOLD YOUR ORBIT STEADY! WE CAN SEE THE CORE BRAIN! GET LOVE GODZ STATION READY FOR IMPLANTATION.
WHIRRRRRRRRRR
STEADY AS SHE GOES.
THE GALAXY IS ALL TUNED IN FOR THIS MOMENTOUS OCCASION. DID MODUS GHAZ SURVIVE THE TRANSFER?
BREAKING NEWS
NO MATTER THE OUTCOME OF THIS TRAVESTY, THE PARENTS WILL BE SHIPPED TO US AND WE WILL HAVE A SQUADRON TO GIVE THE LYING SISTERS A PROPER WELCOME.
YOU NAME THE RIGHT PRICE AND THE PRISONERS ARE ALL YOURS. I WILL SEE TO THEIR TRANSPORT MYSELF.

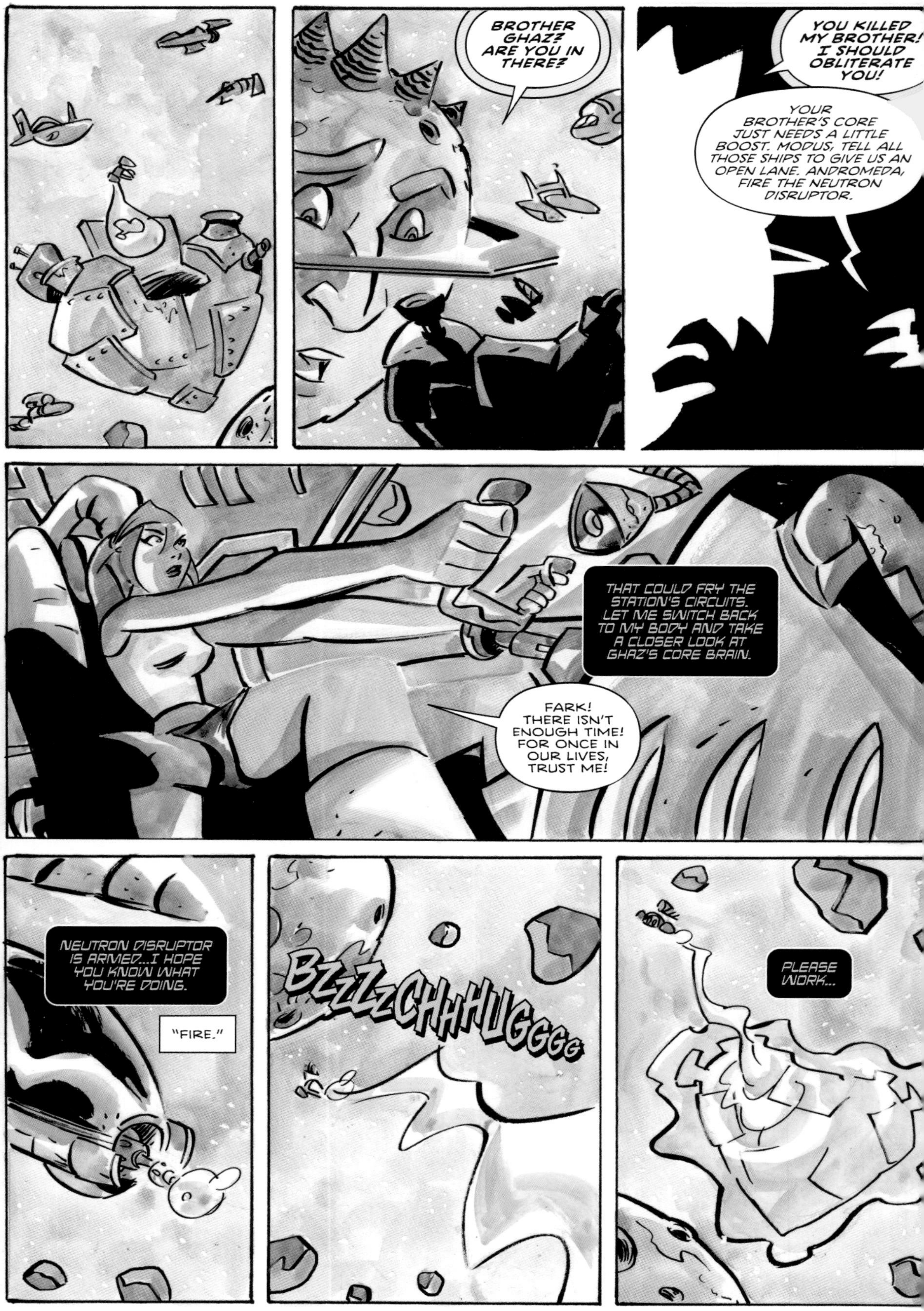
BROTHER GHAZ? ARE YOU IN THERE?
YOU KILLED MY BROTHER! I SHOULD OBLITERATE YOU!
YOUR BROTHER'S CORE JUST NEEDS A LITTLE BOOST. MODUS, TELL ALL THOSE SHIPS TO GIVE US AN OPEN LANE. ANDROMEDA, FIRE THE NEUTRON DISRUPTOR.
THAT COULD FRY THE STATION'S CIRCUITS. LET ME SWITCH BACK TO MY BODY AND TAKE A CLOSER LOOK AT GHAZ'S CORE BRAIN.
FARK! THERE ISN'T ENOUGH TIME! FOR ONCE IN OUR LIVES, TRUST ME!
NEUTRON DISRUPTOR IS ARMED...I HOPE YOU KNOW WHAT YOU'RE DOING.
"FIRE."
BZZZZCHHHUGGGGG
PLEASE WORK...

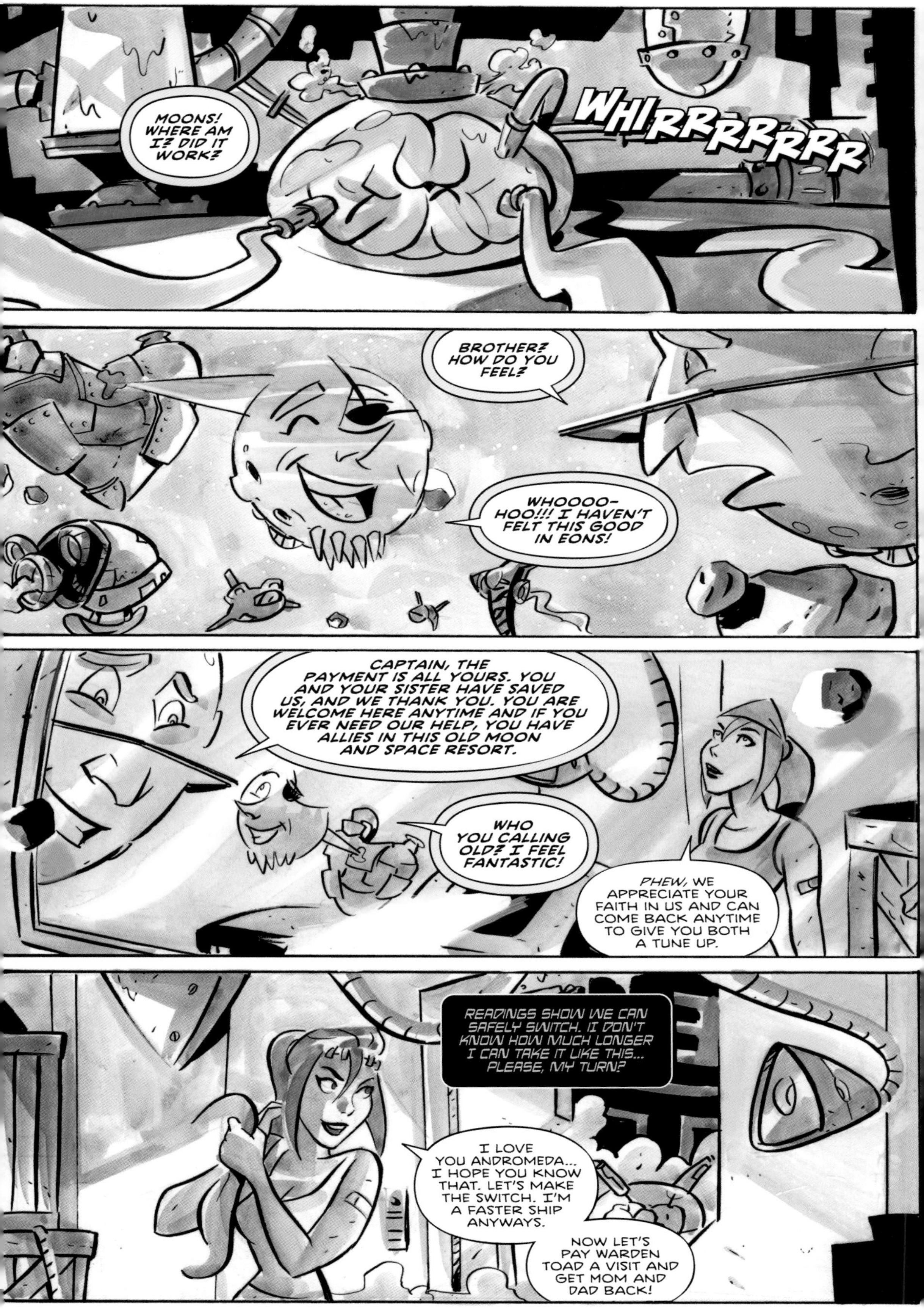
MOONS! WHERE AM I? DID IT WORK?
WHIRRRRRRRR
BROTHER? HOW DO YOU FEEL?
WHOOOO-HOO!!! I HAVEN'T FELT THIS GOOD IN EONS!
CAPTAIN, THE PAYMENT IS ALL YOURS. YOU AND YOUR SISTER HAVE SAVED US, AND WE THANK YOU. YOU ARE WELCOME HERE ANYTIME AND IF YOU EVER NEED OUR HELP, YOU HAVE ALLIES IN THIS OLD MOON AND SPACE RESORT.
WHO YOU CALLING OLD? I FEEL FANTASTIC!
PHEW, WE APPRECIATE YOUR FAITH IN US AND CAN COME BACK ANYTIME TO GIVE YOU BOTH A TUNE UP.
READINGS SHOW WE CAN SAFELY SWITCH. I DON'T KNOW HOW MUCH LONGER I CAN TAKE IT LIKE THIS... PLEASE, MY TURN?
I LOVE YOU ANDROMEDA... I HOPE YOU KNOW THAT. LET'S MAKE THE SWITCH. I'M A FASTER SHIP ANYWAYS.
NOW LET'S PAY WARDEN TOAD A VISIT AND GET MOM AND DAD BACK!

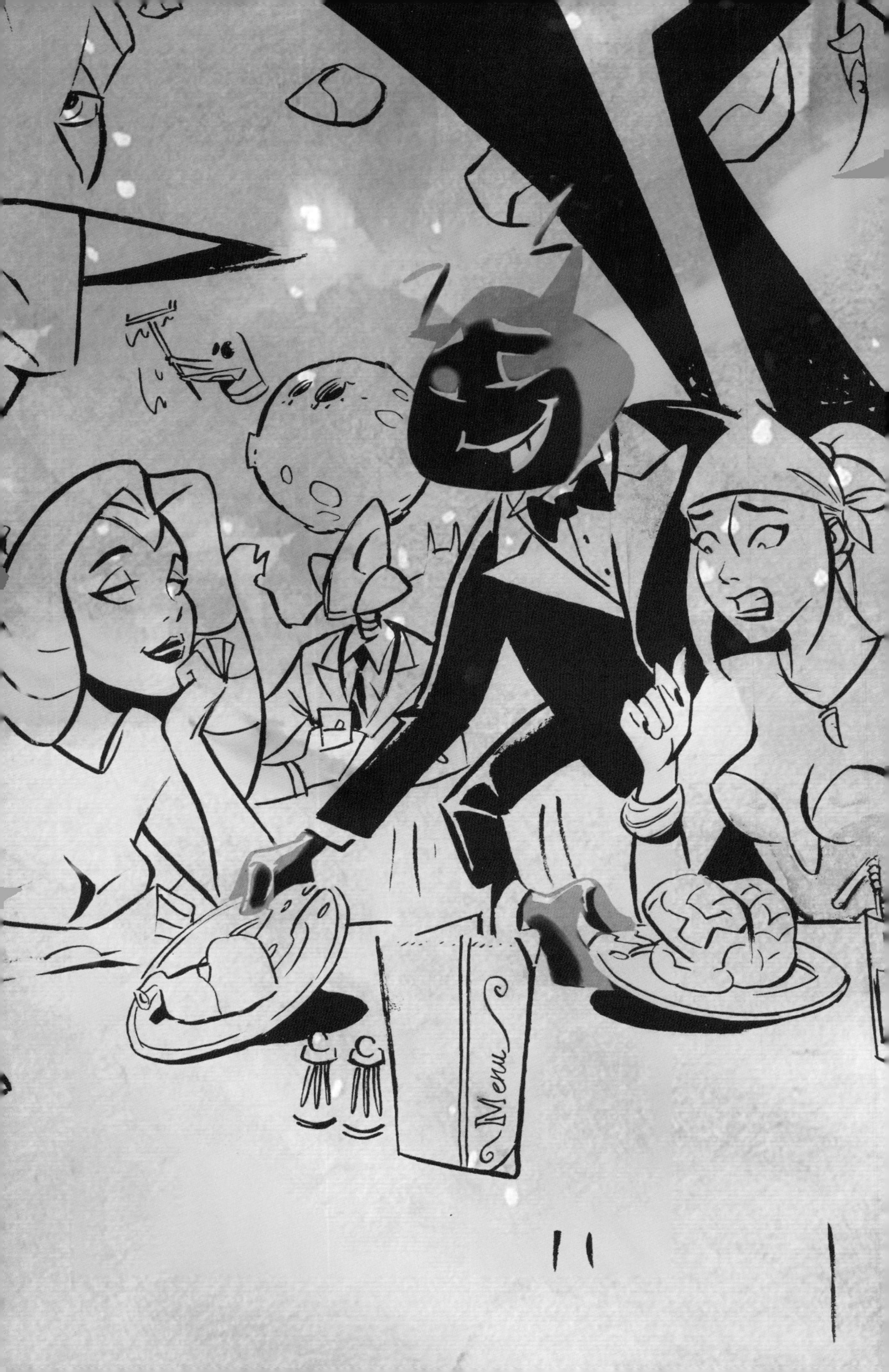
Menu

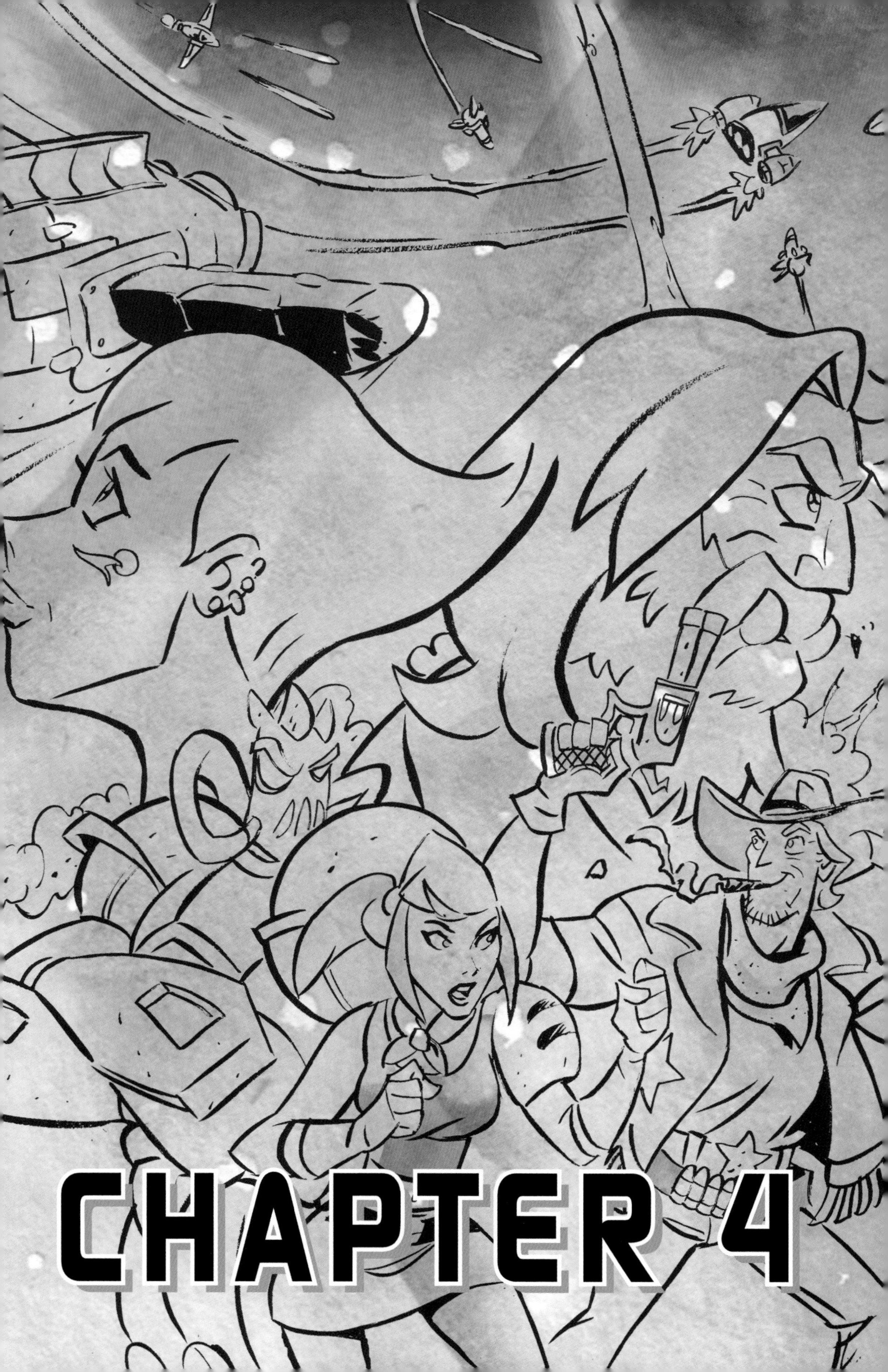
CHAPTER 4

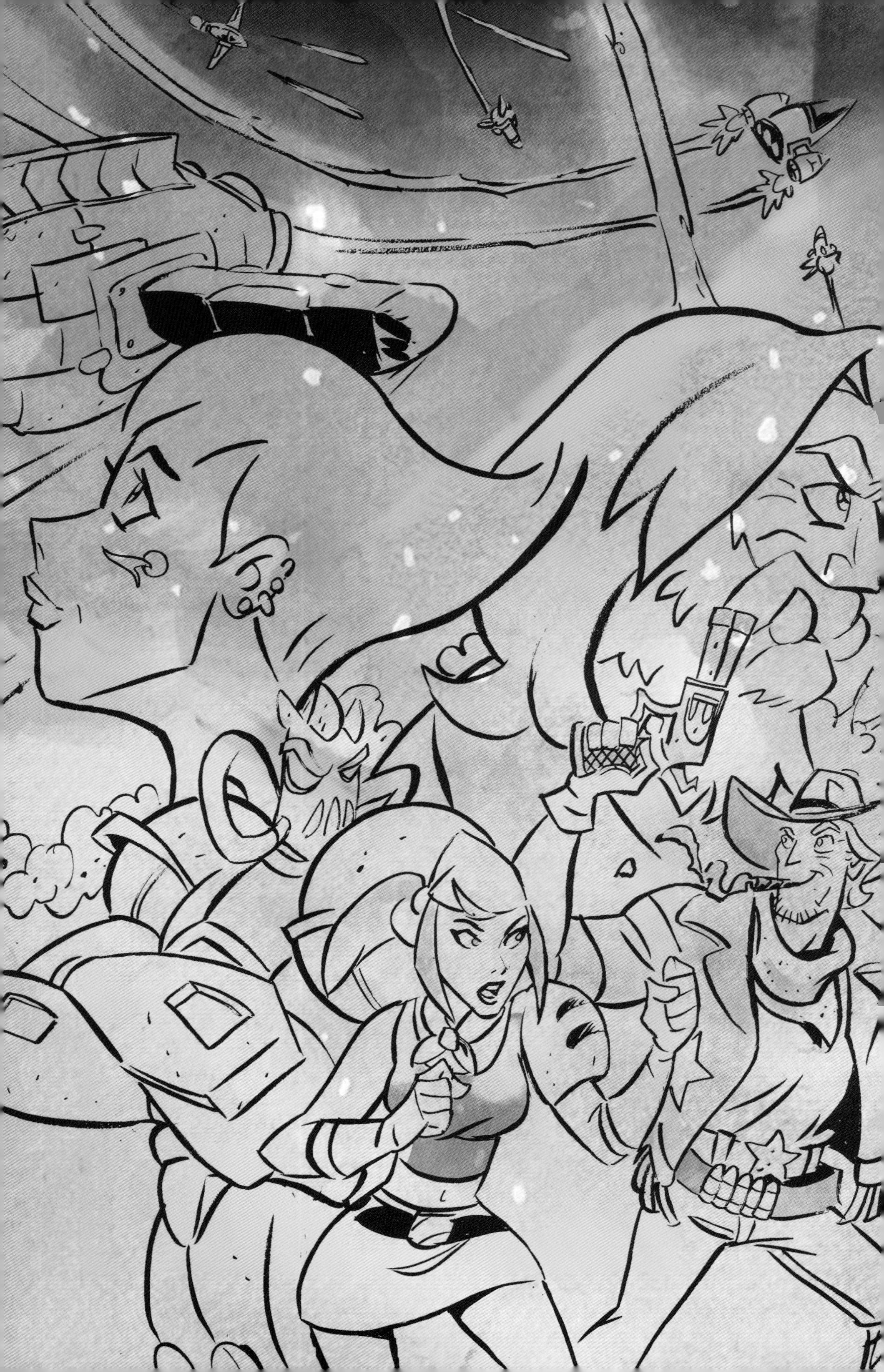

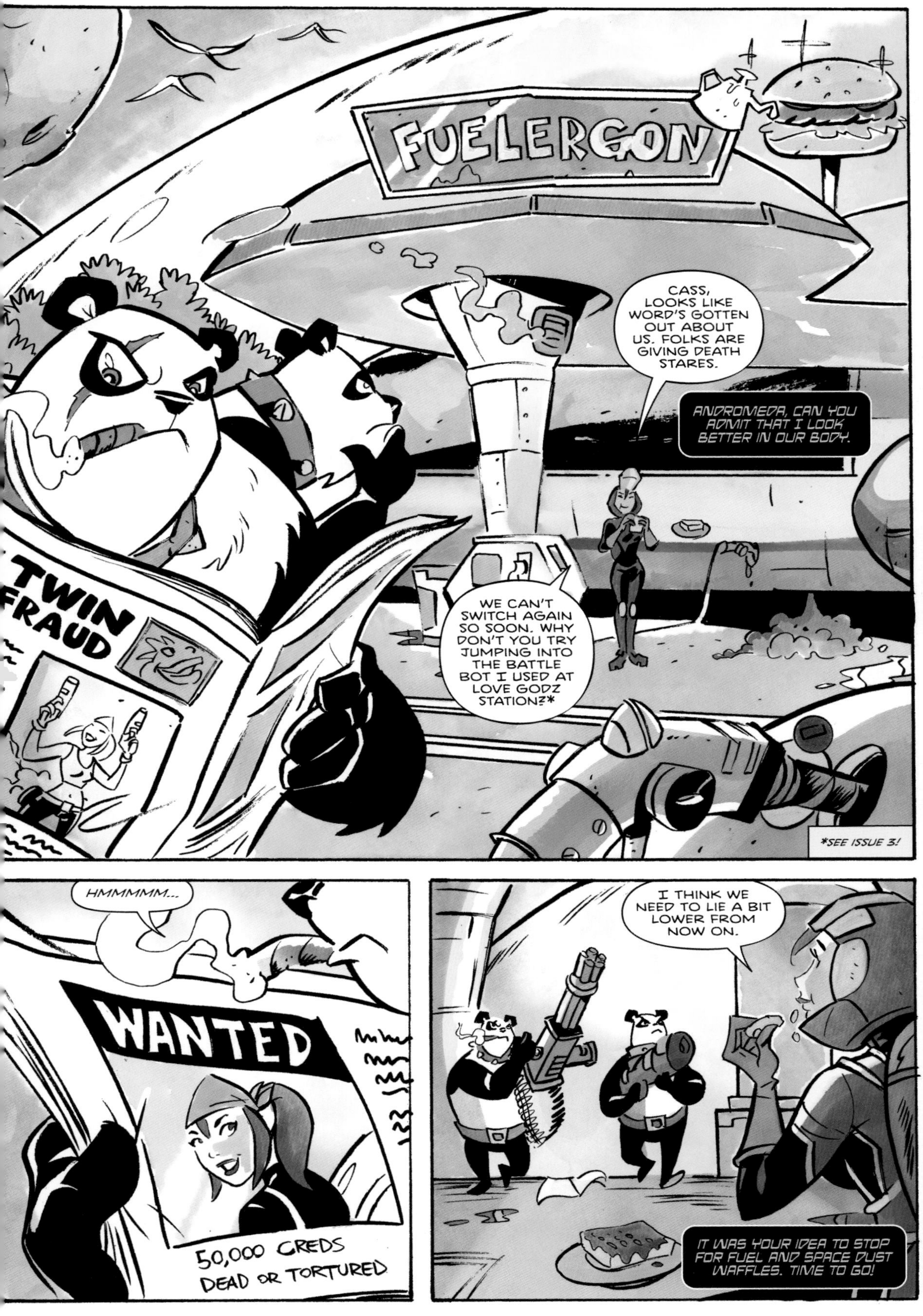
FUELERGON
CASS, LOOKS LIKE WORD'S GOTTEN OUT ABOUT US. FOLKS ARE GIVING DEATH STARES.
ANDROMEDA, CAN YOU ADMIT THAT I LOOK BETTER IN OUR BODY.
TWIN FRAUD
WE CAN'T SWITCH AGAIN SO SOON. WHY DON'T YOU TRY JUMPING INTO THE BATTLE BOT I USED AT LOVE GODZ STATION?*
*SEE ISSUE 3!
HMMMMM...
WANTED
50,000 CREDS DEAD OR TORTURED
I THINK WE NEED TO LIE A BIT LOWER FROM NOW ON.
IT WAS YOUR IDEA TO STOP FOR FUEL AND SPACE DUST WAFFLES. TIME TO GO!

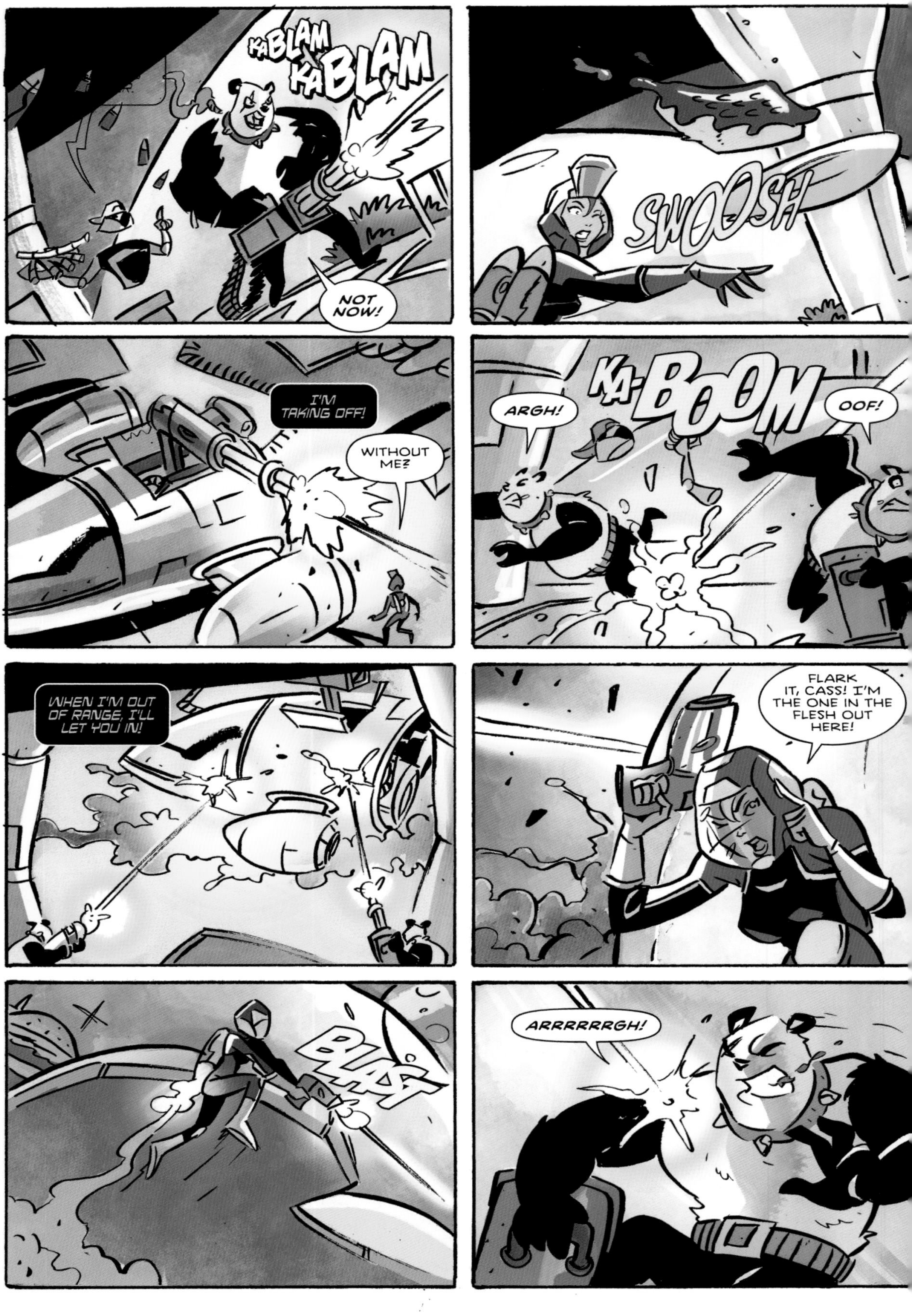
KABLAM KABLAM
NOT NOW!
SWOOSH
I'M TAKING OFF!
WITHOUT ME?
KA-BOOM
ARGH!
OOF!
WHEN I'M OUT OF RANGE, I'LL LET YOU IN!
FLARK IT, CASS! I'M THE ONE IN THE FLESH OUT HERE!
BLAST
ARRRRRRGH!

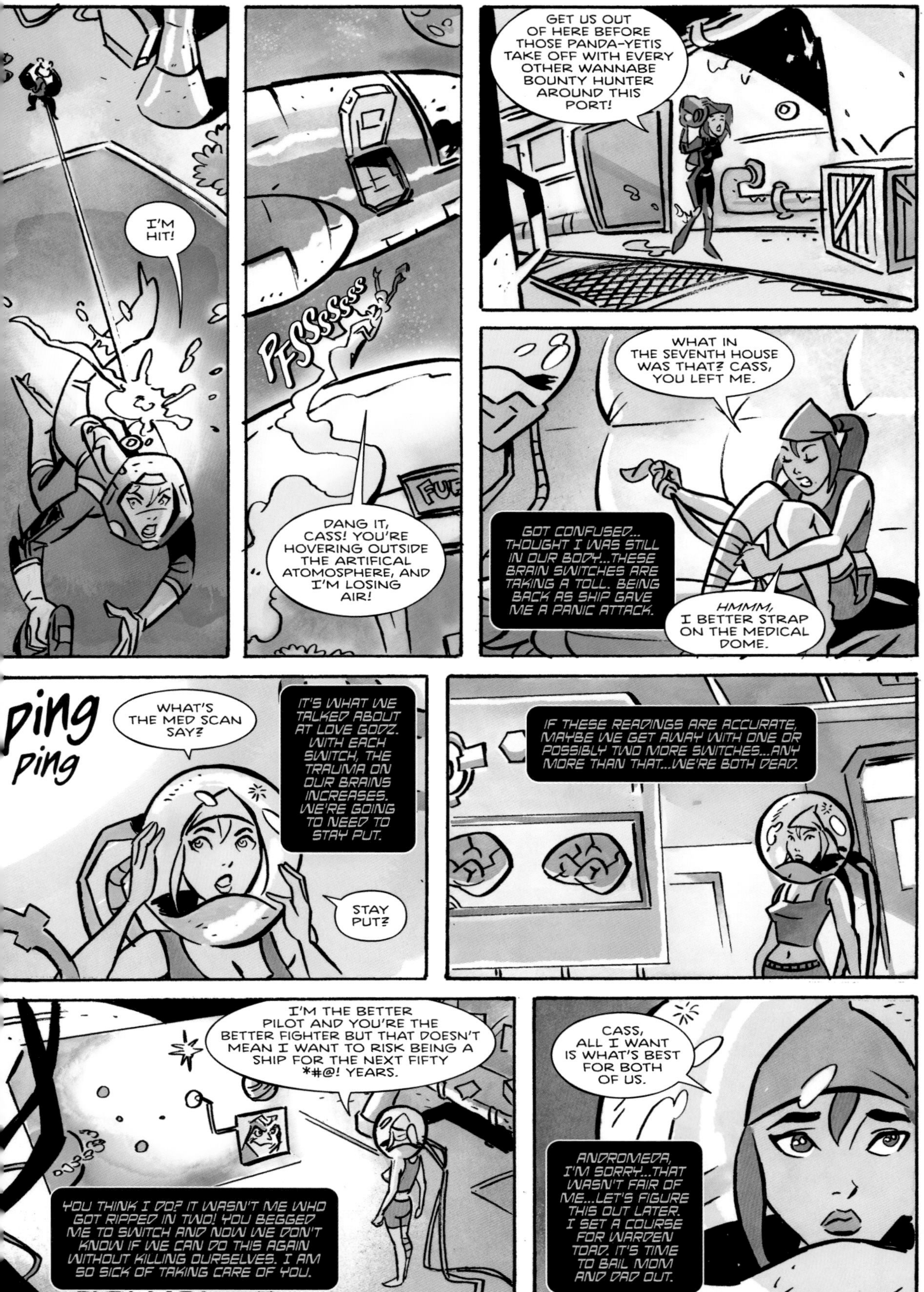
I'M HIT!
PFSSSSSSS
DANG IT, CASS! YOU'RE HOVERING OUTSIDE THE ARTIFICAL ATOMOSPHERE, AND I'M LOSING AIR!
GET US OUT OF HERE BEFORE THOSE PANDA-YETIS TAKE OFF WITH EVERY OTHER WANNABE BOUNTY HUNTER AROUND THIS PORT!
WHAT IN THE SEVENTH HOUSE WAS THAT? CASS, YOU LEFT ME.
GOT CONFUSED... THOUGHT I WAS STILL IN OUR BODY...THESE BRAIN SWITCHES ARE TAKING A TOLL. BEING BACK AS SHIP GAVE ME A PANIC ATTACK.
HMMM, I BETTER STRAP ON THE MEDICAL DOME.
ping ping
WHAT'S THE MED SCAN SAY?
IT'S WHAT WE TALKED ABOUT AT LOVE GODZ. WITH EACH SWITCH, THE TRAUMA ON OUR BRAINS INCREASES. WE'RE GOING TO NEED TO STAY PUT.
STAY PUT?
IF THESE READINGS ARE ACCURATE, MAYBE WE GET AWAY WITH ONE OR POSSIBLY TWO MORE SWITCHES...ANY MORE THAN THAT...WE'RE BOTH DEAD.
I'M THE BETTER PILOT AND YOU'RE THE BETTER FIGHTER BUT THAT DOESN'T MEAN I WANT TO RISK BEING A SHIP FOR THE NEXT FIFTY *#@! YEARS.
YOU THINK I DO? IT WASN'T ME WHO GOT RIPPED IN TWO! YOU BEGGED ME TO SWITCH AND NOW WE DON'T KNOW IF WE CAN DO THIS AGAIN WITHOUT KILLING OURSELVES. I AM SO SICK OF TAKING CARE OF YOU.
CASS, ALL I WANT IS WHAT'S BEST FOR BOTH OF US.
ANDROMEDA, I'M SORRY...THAT WASN'T FAIR OF ME...LET'S FIGURE THIS OUT LATER. I SET A COURSE FOR WARDEN TOAD. IT'S TIME TO BAIL MOM AND DAD OUT.

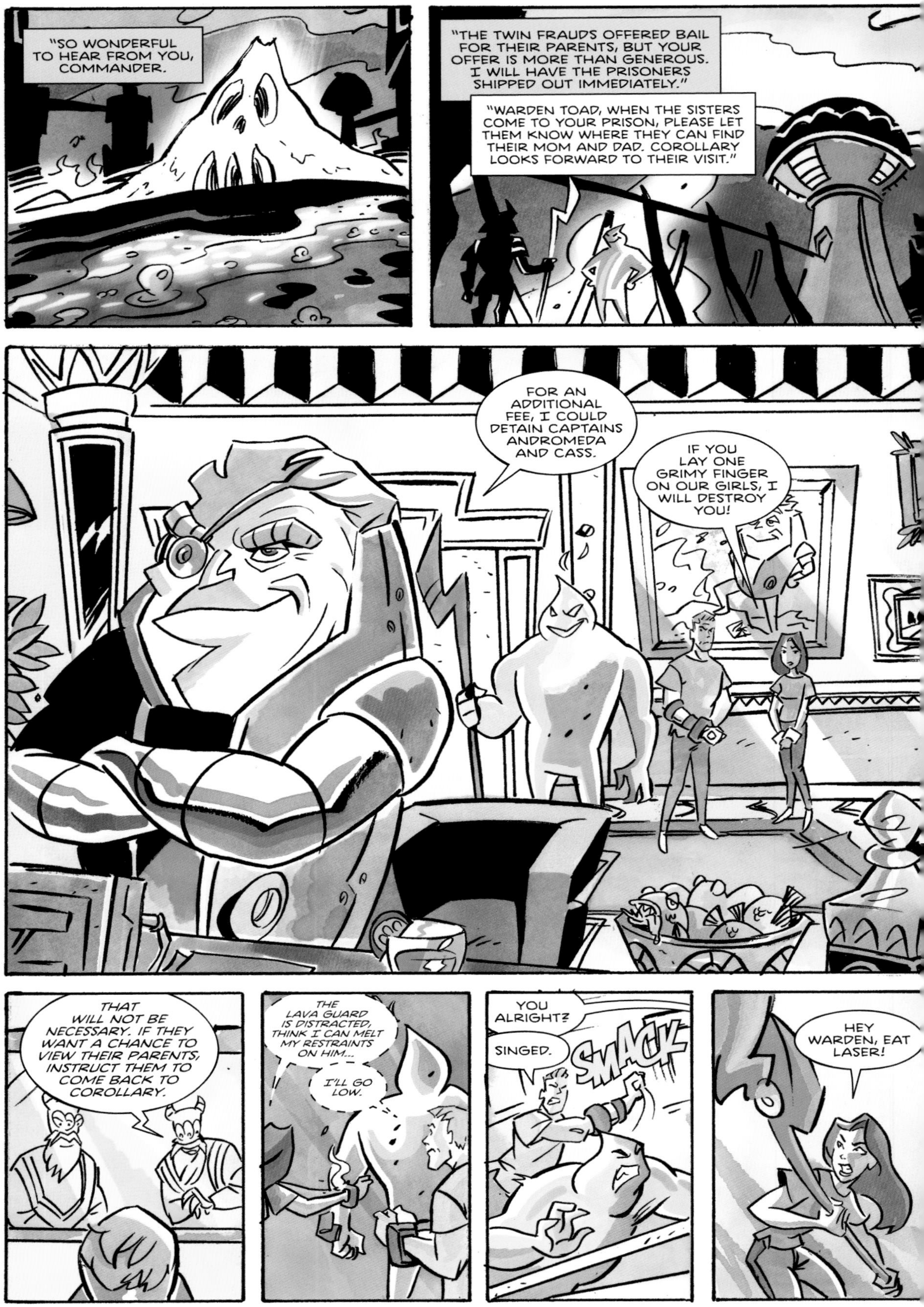
"SO WONDERFUL TO HEAR FROM YOU, COMMANDER.
"THE TWIN FRAUDS OFFERED BAIL FOR THEIR PARENTS, BUT YOUR OFFER IS MORE THAN GENEROUS. I WILL HAVE THE PRISONERS SHIPPED OUT IMMEDIATELY."
"WARDEN TOAD, WHEN THE SISTERS COME TO YOUR PRISON, PLEASE LET THEM KNOW WHERE THEY CAN FIND THEIR MOM AND DAD. COROLLARY LOOKS FORWARD TO THEIR VISIT."
FOR AN ADDITIONAL FEE, I COULD DETAIN CAPTAINS ANDROMEDA AND CASS.
IF YOU LAY ONE GRIMY FINGER ON OUR GIRLS, I WILL DESTROY YOU!
THAT WILL NOT BE NECESSARY. IF THEY WANT A CHANCE TO VIEW THEIR PARENTS, INSTRUCT THEM TO COME BACK TO COROLLARY.
THE LAVA GUARD IS DISTRACTED, THINK I CAN MELT MY RESTRAINTS ON HIM...
I'LL GO LOW.
YOU ALRIGHT?
SINGED.
SMACK
HEY WARDEN, EAT LASER!

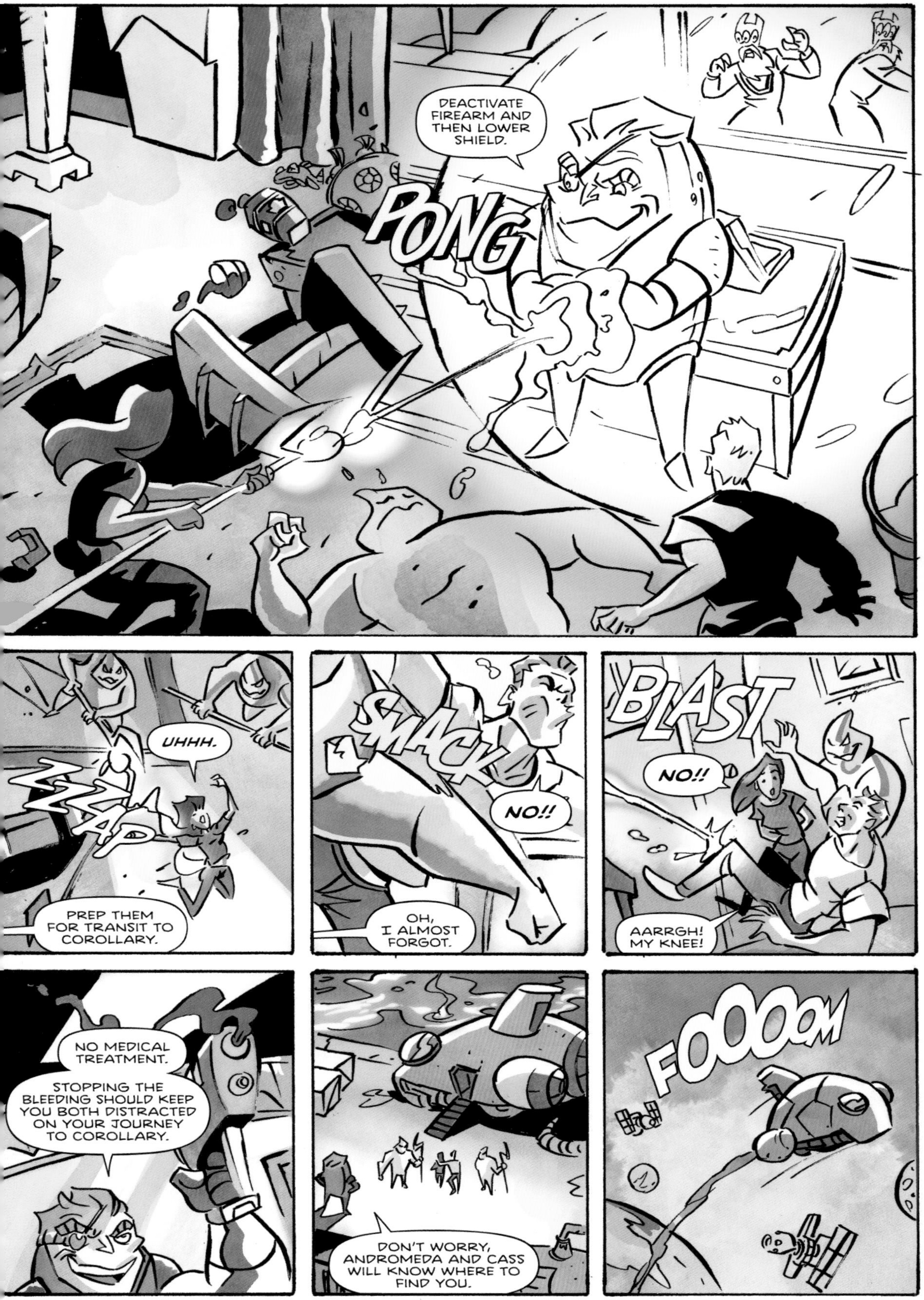
DEACTIVATE FIREARM AND THEN LOWER SHIELD.
PONG
UHHH.
ZZZAP
PREP THEM FOR TRANSIT TO COROLLARY.
SMACK
NO!!
OH, I ALMOST FORGOT.
BLAST
NO!!
AARRGH! MY KNEE!
NO MEDICAL TREATMENT.
STOPPING THE BLEEDING SHOULD KEEP YOU BOTH DISTRACTED ON YOUR JOURNEY TO COROLLARY.
DON'T WORRY, ANDROMEDA AND CASS WILL KNOW WHERE TO FIND YOU.
FOOOOOM

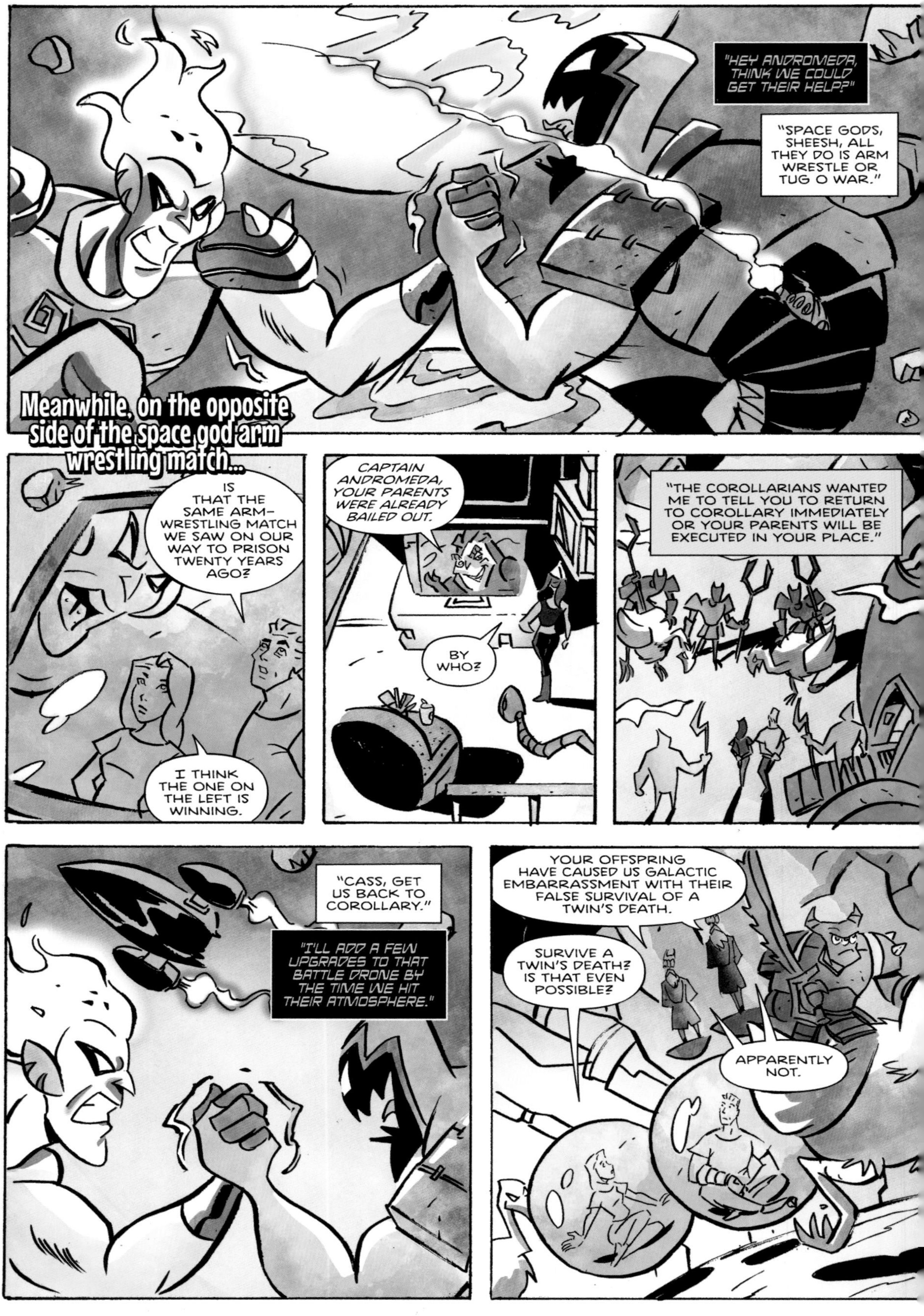

"HEY ANDROMEDA, THINK WE COULD GET THEIR HELP?"
"SPACE GODS, SHEESH, ALL THEY DO IS ARM WRESTLE OR TUG O WAR."
Meanwhile, on the opposite side of the space god arm wrestling match...
IS THAT THE SAME ARM-WRESTLING MATCH WE SAW ON OUR WAY TO PRISON TWENTY YEARS AGO?
I THINK THE ONE ON THE LEFT IS WINNING.
CAPTAIN ANDROMEDA, YOUR PARENTS WERE ALREADY BAILED OUT.
BY WHO?
"THE COROLLARIANS WANTED ME TO TELL YOU TO RETURN TO COROLLARY IMMEDIATELY OR YOUR PARENTS WILL BE EXECUTED IN YOUR PLACE."
"CASS, GET US BACK TO COROLLARY."
"I'LL ADD A FEW UPGRADES TO THAT BATTLE DRONE BY THE TIME WE HIT THEIR ATMOSPHERE."
YOUR OFFSPRING HAVE CAUSED US GALACTIC EMBARRASSMENT WITH THEIR FALSE SURVIVAL OF A TWIN'S DEATH.
SURVIVE A TWIN'S DEATH? IS THAT EVEN POSSIBLE?
APPARENTLY NOT.

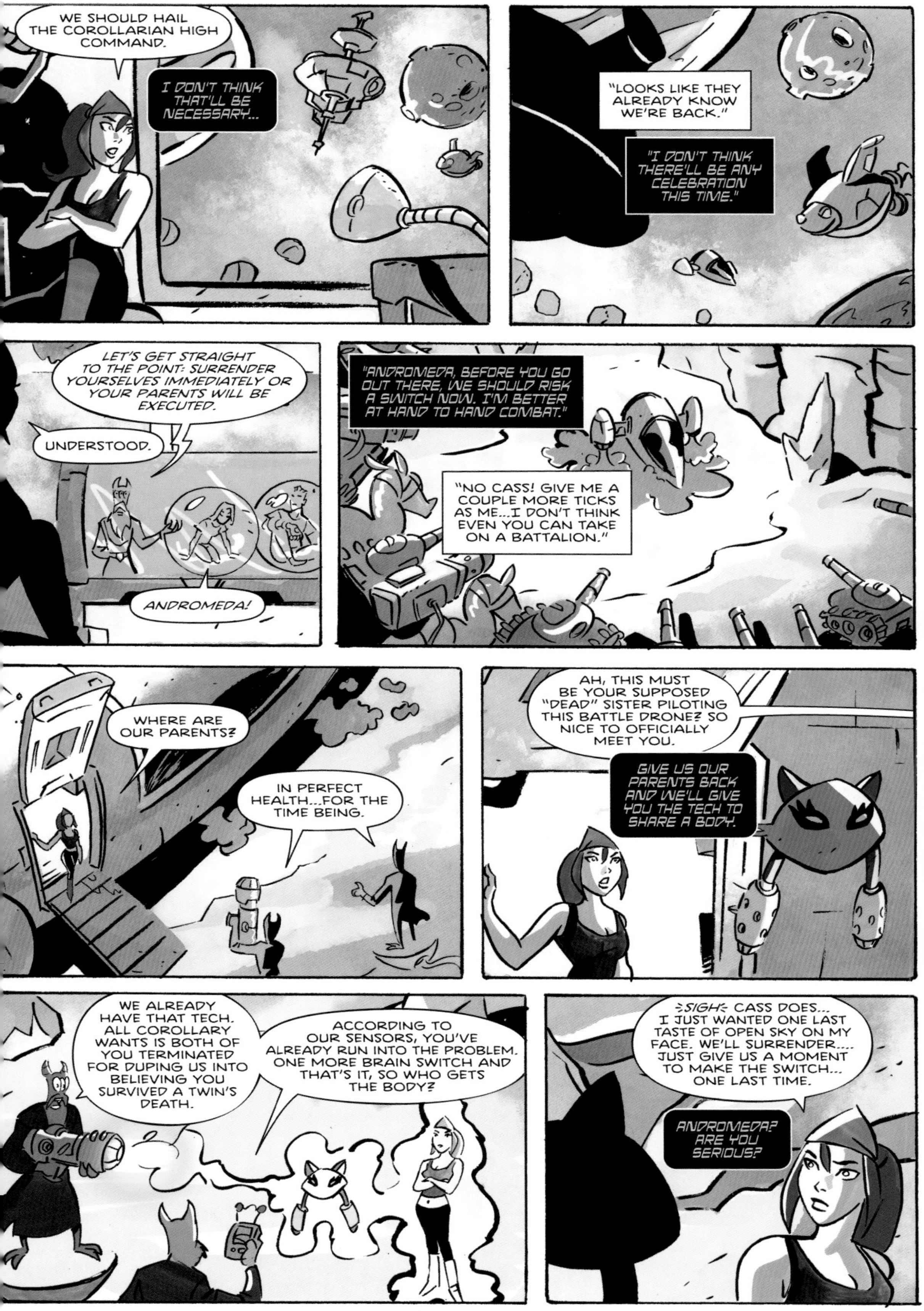
WE SHOULD HAIL THE COROLLARIAN HIGH COMMAND.
I DON'T THINK THAT'LL BE NECESSARY...
"LOOKS LIKE THEY ALREADY KNOW WE'RE BACK."
"I DON'T THINK THERE'LL BE ANY CELEBRATION THIS TIME."
LET'S GET STRAIGHT TO THE POINT: SURRENDER YOURSELVES IMMEDIATELY OR YOUR PARENTS WILL BE EXECUTED.
UNDERSTOOD.
ANDROMEDA!
"ANDROMEDA, BEFORE YOU GO OUT THERE, WE SHOULD RISK A SWITCH NOW. I'M BETTER AT HAND TO HAND COMBAT."
"NO CASS! GIVE ME A COUPLE MORE TICKS AS ME...I DON'T THINK EVEN YOU CAN TAKE ON A BATTALION."
WHERE ARE OUR PARENTS?
IN PERFECT HEALTH...FOR THE TIME BEING.
AH, THIS MUST BE YOUR SUPPOSED "DEAD" SISTER PILOTING THIS BATTLE DRONE? SO NICE TO OFFICIALLY MEET YOU.
GIVE US OUR PARENTS BACK AND WE'LL GIVE YOU THE TECH TO SHARE A BODY.
WE ALREADY HAVE THAT TECH. ALL COROLLARY WANTS IS BOTH OF YOU TERMINATED FOR DUPING US INTO BELIEVING YOU SURVIVED A TWIN'S DEATH.
ACCORDING TO OUR SENSORS, YOU'VE ALREADY RUN INTO THE PROBLEM. ONE MORE BRAIN SWITCH AND THAT'S IT, SO WHO GETS THE BODY?
=SIGH= CASS DOES... I JUST WANTED ONE LAST TASTE OF OPEN SKY ON MY FACE. WE'LL SURRENDER.... JUST GIVE US A MOMENT TO MAKE THE SWITCH... ONE LAST TIME.
ANDROMEDA? ARE YOU SERIOUS?

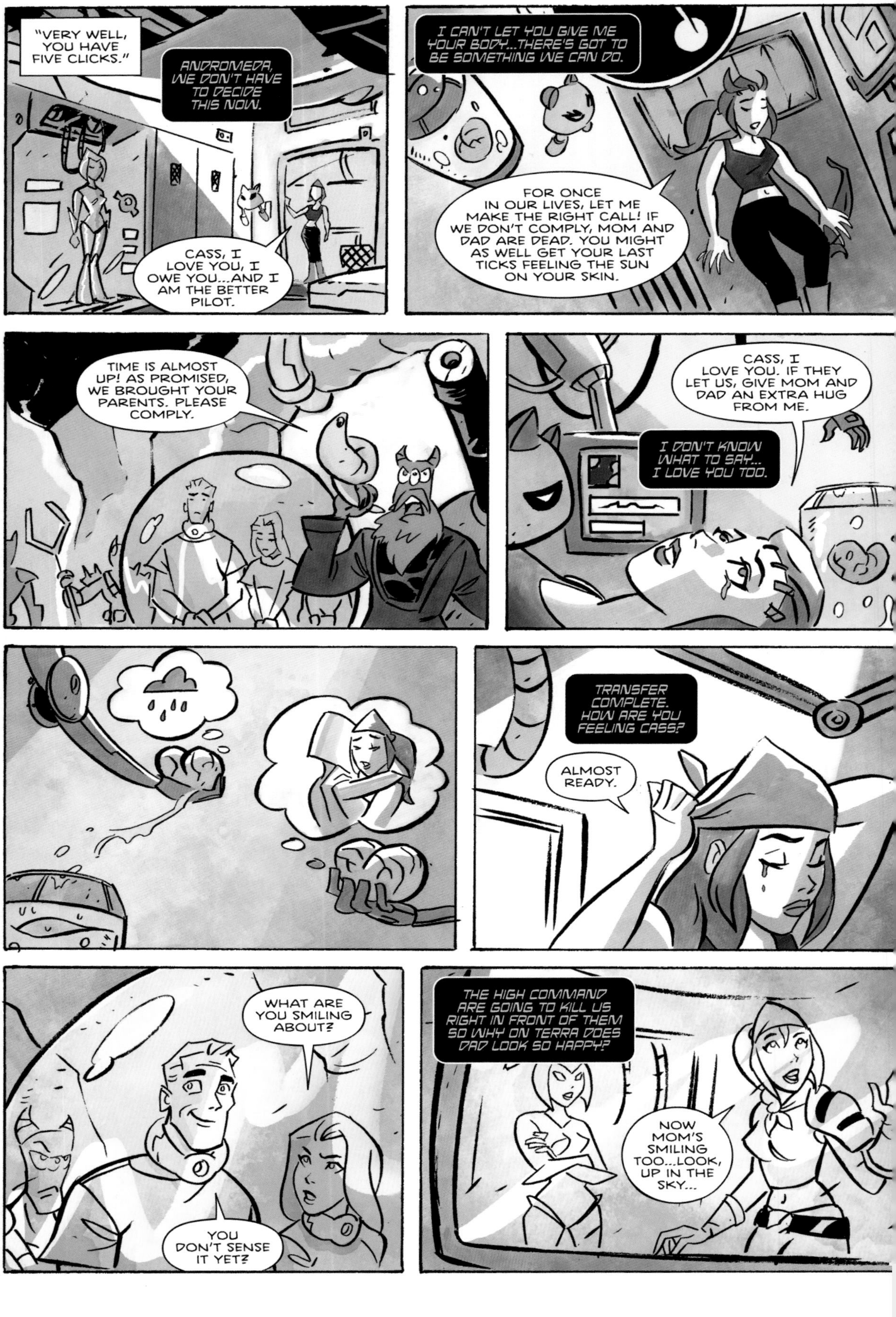

"VERY WELL, YOU HAVE FIVE CLICKS."
ANDROMEDA, WE DON'T HAVE TO DECIDE THIS NOW.
CASS, I LOVE YOU, I OWE YOU...AND I AM THE BETTER PILOT.
I CAN'T LET YOU GIVE ME YOUR BODY...THERE'S GOT TO BE SOMETHING WE CAN DO.
FOR ONCE IN OUR LIVES, LET ME MAKE THE RIGHT CALL! IF WE DON'T COMPLY, MOM AND DAD ARE DEAD. YOU MIGHT AS WELL GET YOUR LAST TICKS FEELING THE SUN ON YOUR SKIN.
TIME IS ALMOST UP! AS PROMISED, WE BROUGHT YOUR PARENTS. PLEASE COMPLY.
CASS, I LOVE YOU. IF THEY LET US, GIVE MOM AND DAD AN EXTRA HUG FROM ME.
I DON'T KNOW WHAT TO SAY... I LOVE YOU TOO.
TRANSFER COMPLETE. HOW ARE YOU FEELING CASS?
ALMOST READY.
WHAT ARE YOU SMILING ABOUT?
YOU DON'T SENSE IT YET?
THE HIGH COMMAND ARE GOING TO KILL US RIGHT IN FRONT OF THEM SO WHY ON TERRA DOES DAD LOOK SO HAPPY?
NOW MOM'S SMILING TOO...LOOK, UP IN THE SKY...

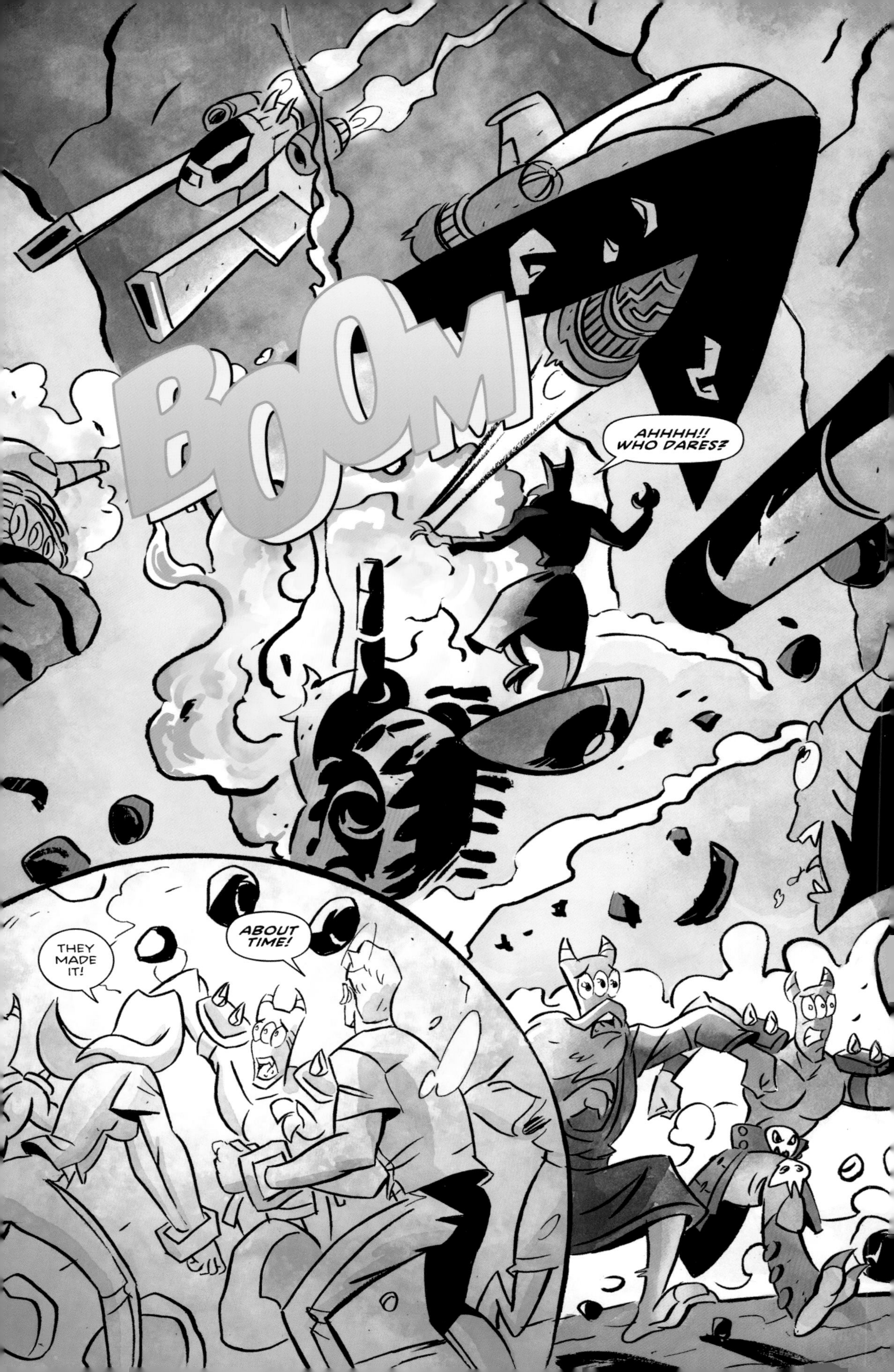
BOOM
AHHHH!! WHO DARES?
THEY MADE IT!
ABOUT TIME!

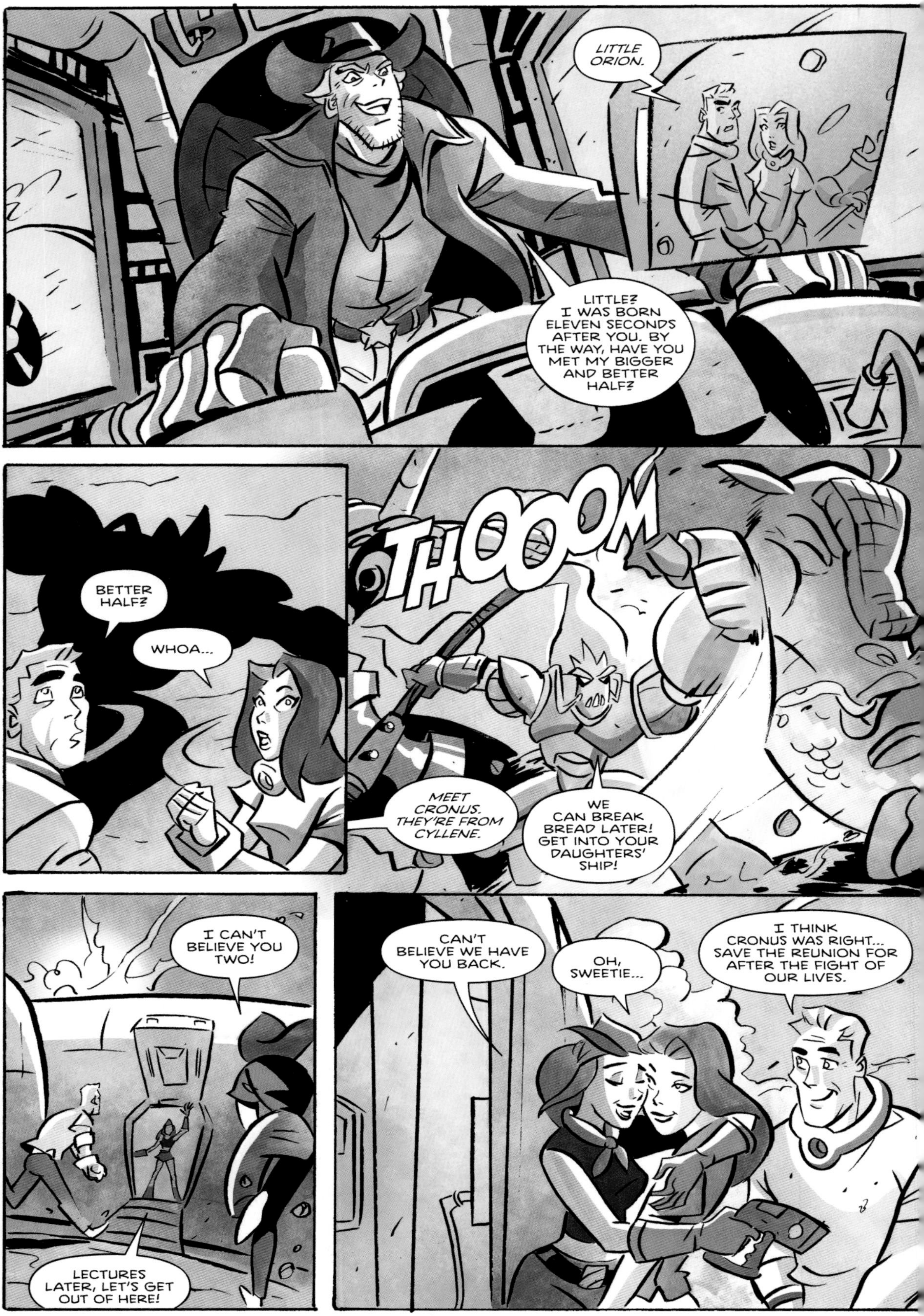
LITTLE ORION.
LITTLE? I WAS BORN ELEVEN SECONDS AFTER YOU. BY THE WAY, HAVE YOU MET MY BIGGER AND BETTER HALF?
BETTER HALF?
WHOA...
THOOOM
MEET CRONUS. THEY'RE FROM CYLLENE.
WE CAN BREAK BREAD LATER! GET INTO YOUR DAUGHTERS' SHIP!
I CAN'T BELIEVE YOU TWO!
LECTURES LATER, LET'S GET OUT OF HERE!
CAN'T BELIEVE WE HAVE YOU BACK.
OH, SWEETIE...
I THINK CRONUS WAS RIGHT... SAVE THE REUNION FOR AFTER THE FIGHT OF OUR LIVES.

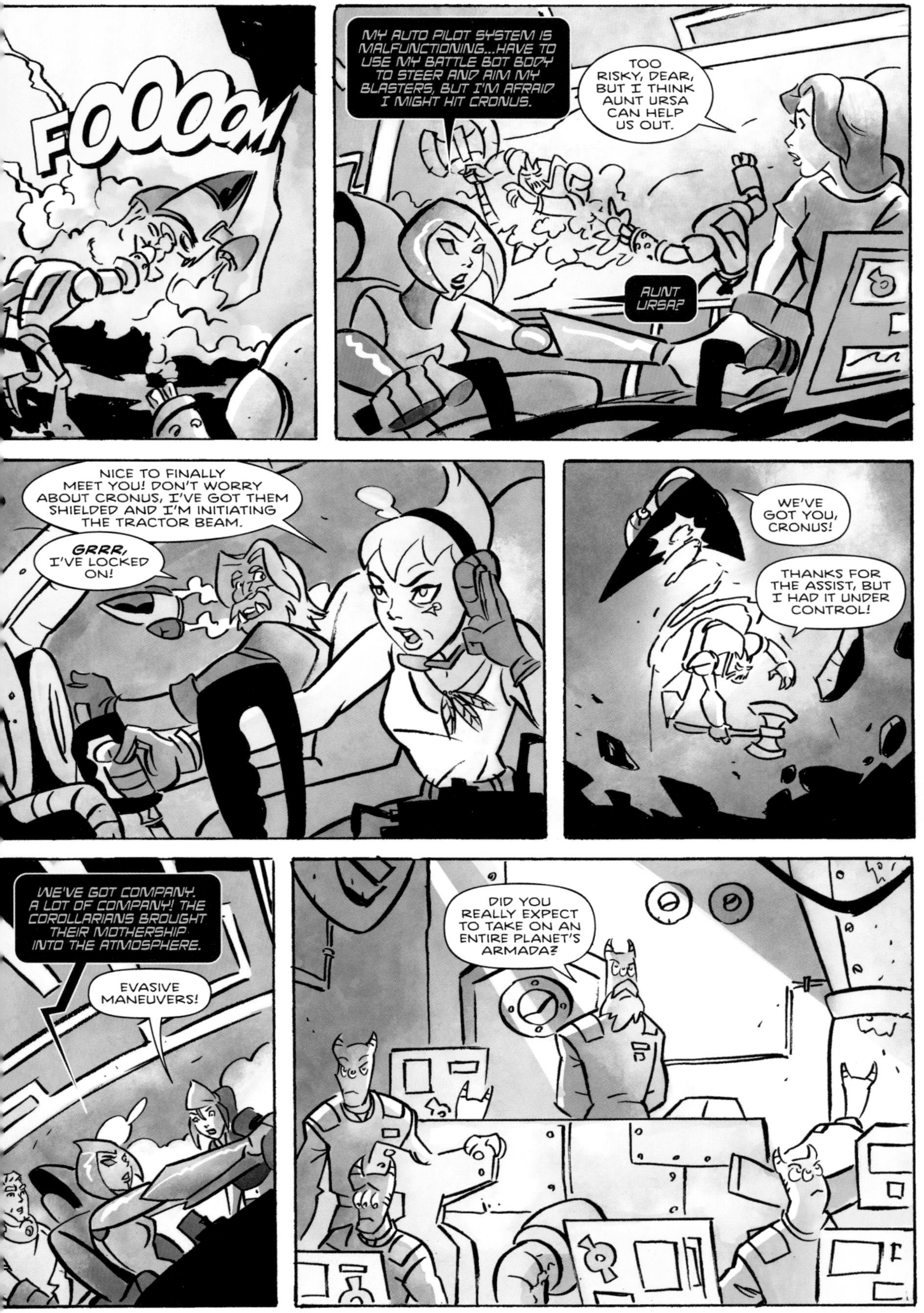
FOOOOM
MY AUTO PILOT SYSTEM IS MALFUNCTIONING...HAVE TO USE MY BATTLE BOT BODY TO STEER AND AIM MY BLASTERS, BUT I'M AFRAID I MIGHT HIT CRONUS.
TOO RISKY, DEAR, BUT I THINK AUNT URSA CAN HELP US OUT.
AUNT URSA?
NICE TO FINALLY MEET YOU! DON'T WORRY ABOUT CRONUS, I'VE GOT THEM SHIELDED AND I'M INITIATING THE TRACTOR BEAM.
GRRR, I'VE LOCKED ON!
WE'VE GOT YOU, CRONUS!
THANKS FOR THE ASSIST, BUT I HAD IT UNDER CONTROL!
WE'VE GOT COMPANY. A LOT OF COMPANY! THE COROLLARIANS BROUGHT THEIR MOTHERSHIP INTO THE ATMOSPHERE.
EVASIVE MANEUVERS!
DID YOU REALLY EXPECT TO TAKE ON AN ENTIRE PLANET'S ARMADA?

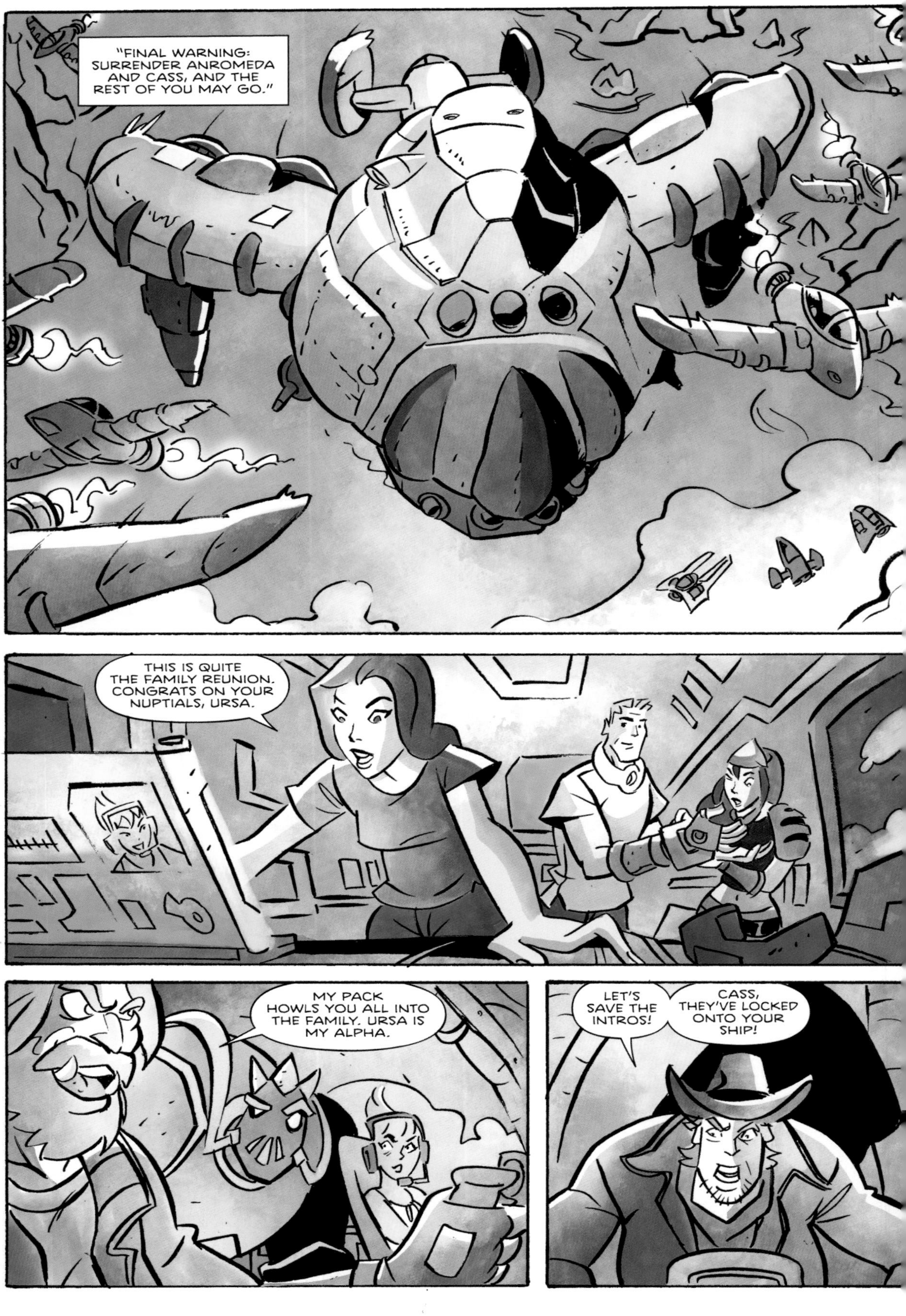
"FINAL WARNING: SURRENDER ANROMEDA AND CASS, AND THE REST OF YOU MAY GO."
THIS IS QUITE THE FAMILY REUNION. CONGRATS ON YOUR NUPTIALS, URSA.
MY PACK HOWLS YOU ALL INTO THE FAMILY. URSA IS MY ALPHA.
LET'S SAVE THE INTROS!
CASS, THEY'VE LOCKED ONTO YOUR SHIP!

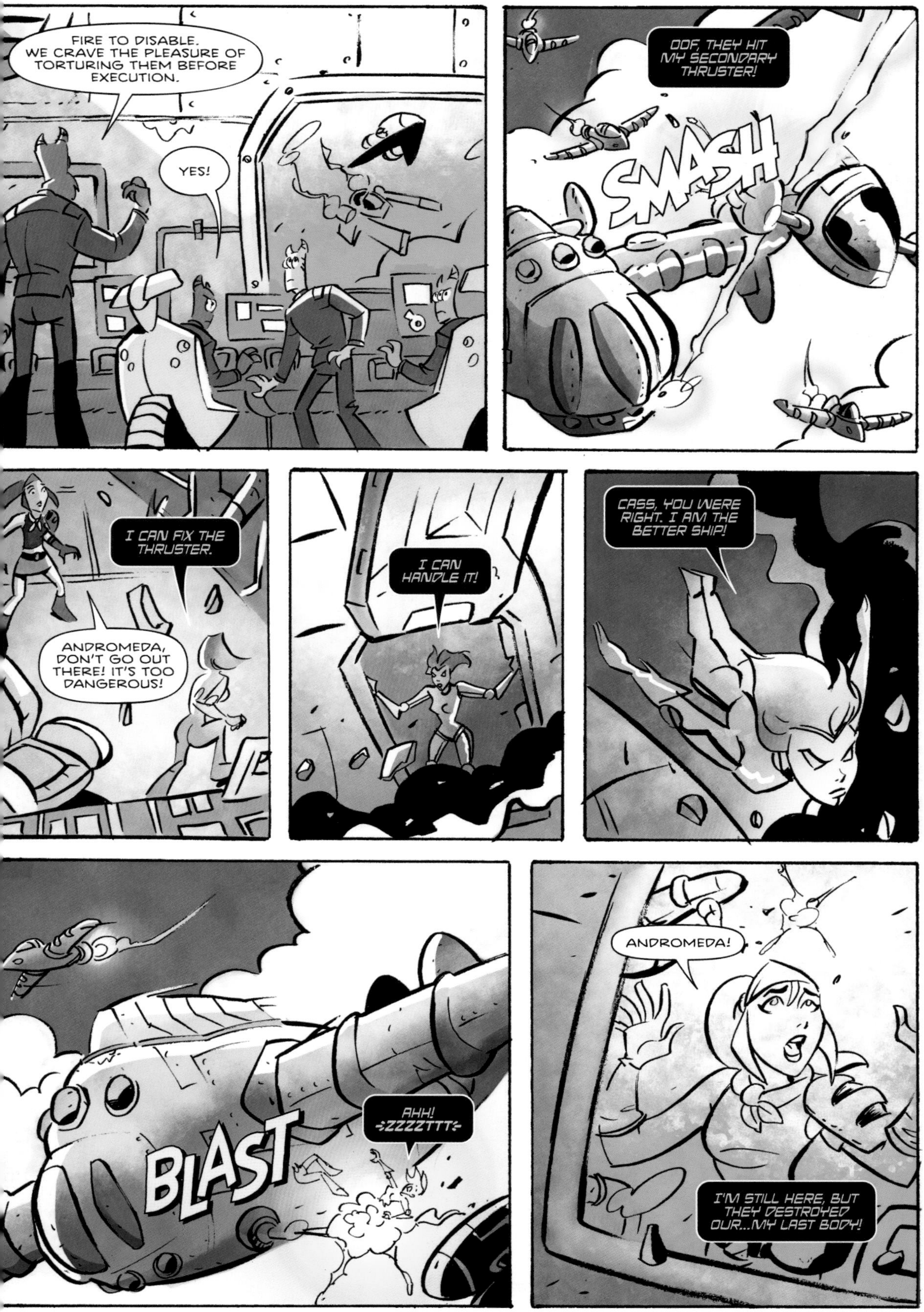

FIRE TO DISABLE. WE CRAVE THE PLEASURE OF TORTURING THEM BEFORE EXECUTION.
YES!
OOF, THEY HIT MY SECONDARY THRUSTER!
SMASH
I CAN FIX THE THRUSTER.
ANDROMEDA, DON'T GO OUT THERE! IT'S TOO DANGEROUS!
I CAN HANDLE IT!
CASS, YOU WERE RIGHT. I AM THE BETTER SHIP!
BLAST
AHH! ZZZZTTT
ANDROMEDA!
I'M STILL HERE, BUT THEY DESTROYED OUR...MY LAST BODY!

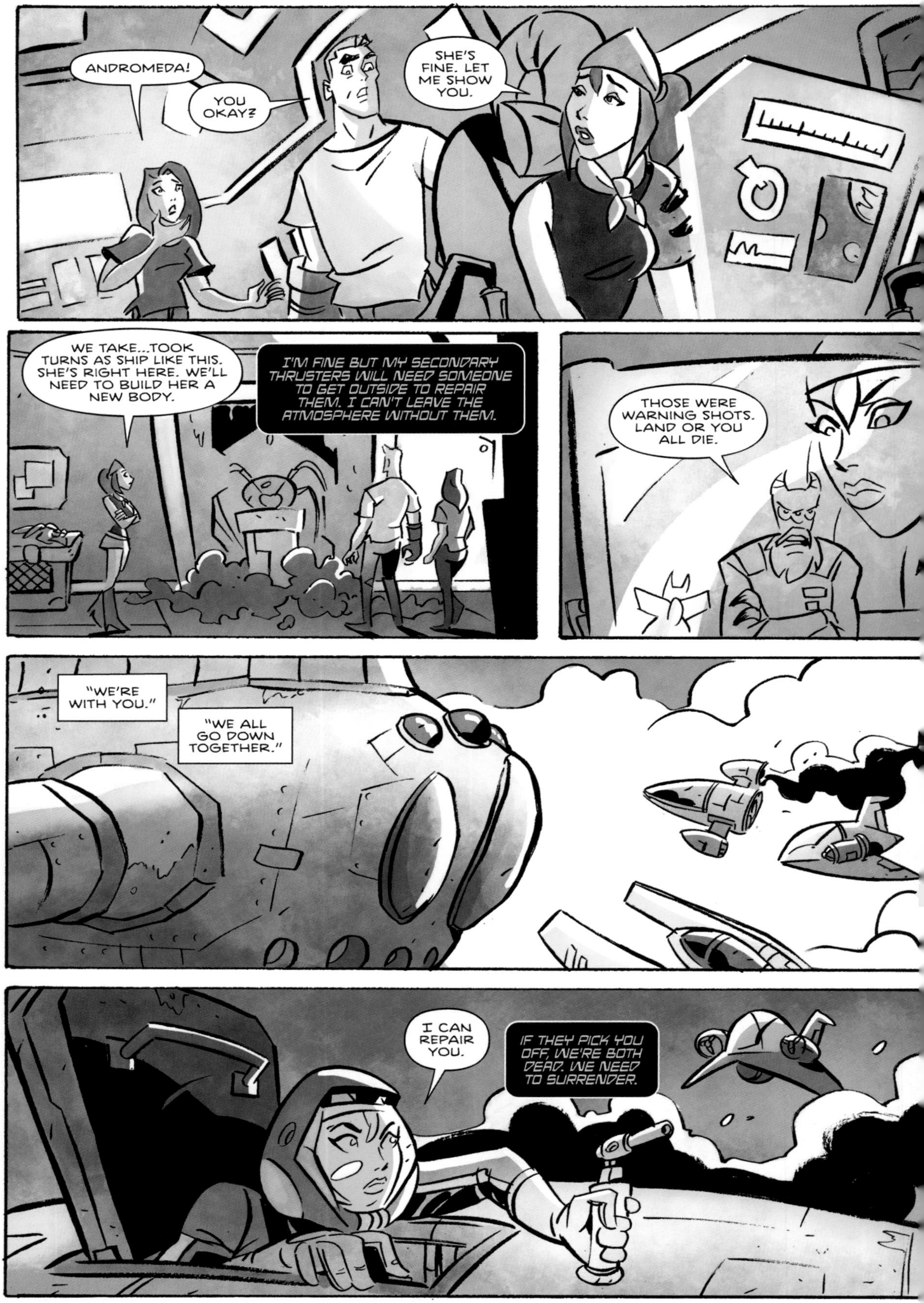
ANDROMEDA!
YOU OKAY?
SHE'S FINE. LET ME SHOW YOU.
WE TAKE...TOOK TURNS AS SHIP LIKE THIS. SHE'S RIGHT HERE. WE'LL NEED TO BUILD HER A NEW BODY.
I'M FINE BUT MY SECONDARY THRUSTERS WILL NEED SOMEONE TO GET OUTSIDE TO REPAIR THEM. I CAN'T LEAVE THE ATMOSPHERE WITHOUT THEM.
THOSE WERE WARNING SHOTS. LAND OR YOU ALL DIE.
"WE'RE WITH YOU."
"WE ALL GO DOWN TOGETHER."
I CAN REPAIR YOU.
IF THEY PICK YOU OFF, WE'RE BOTH DEAD. WE NEED TO SURRENDER.

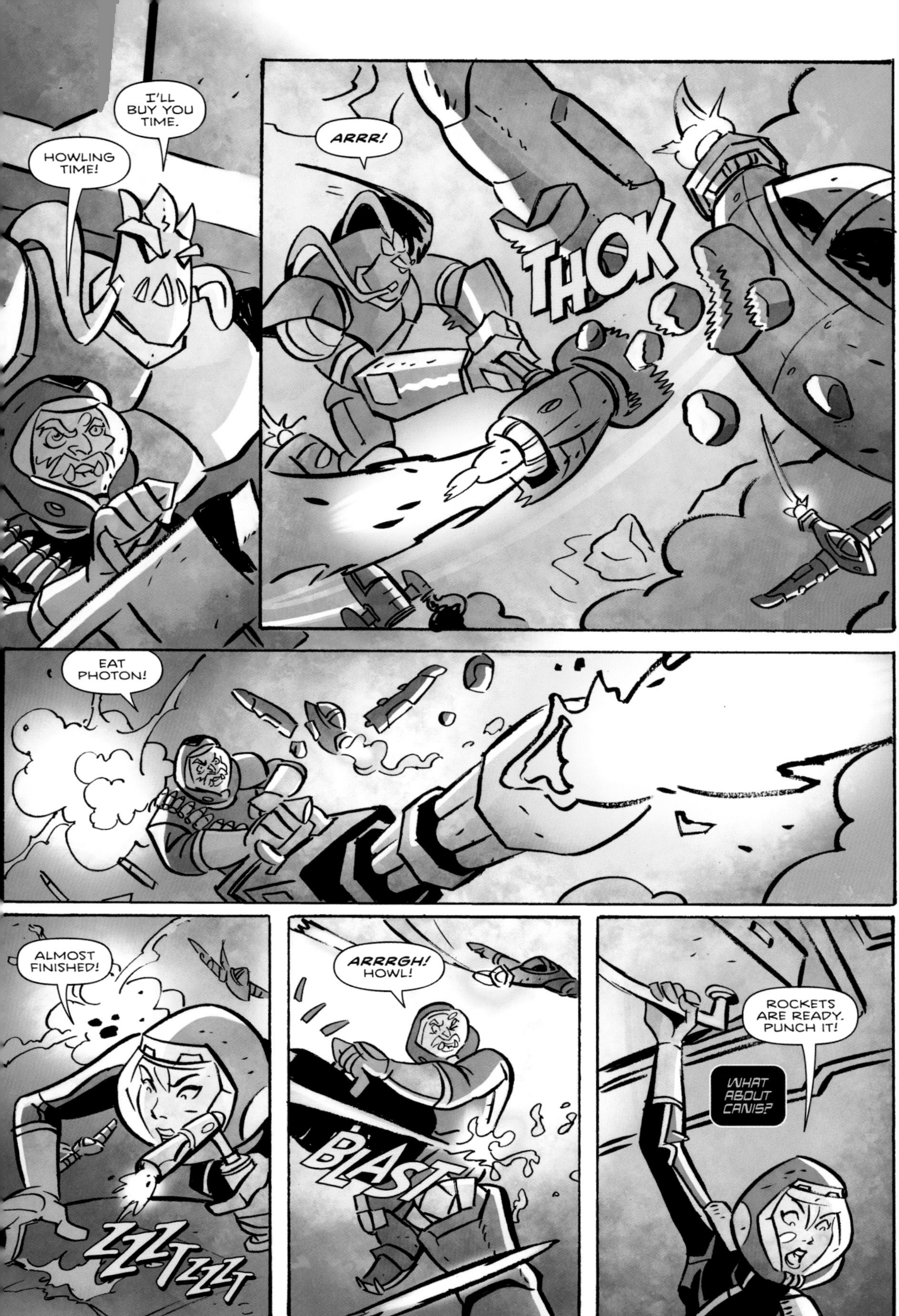

HOWLING TIME!
I'LL BUY YOU TIME.
ARRR!
THOK
EAT PHOTON!
ALMOST FINISHED!
ZZZTZZZT
ARRRGH! HOWL!
BLAST
ROCKETS ARE READY. PUNCH IT!
WHAT ABOUT CANIS?

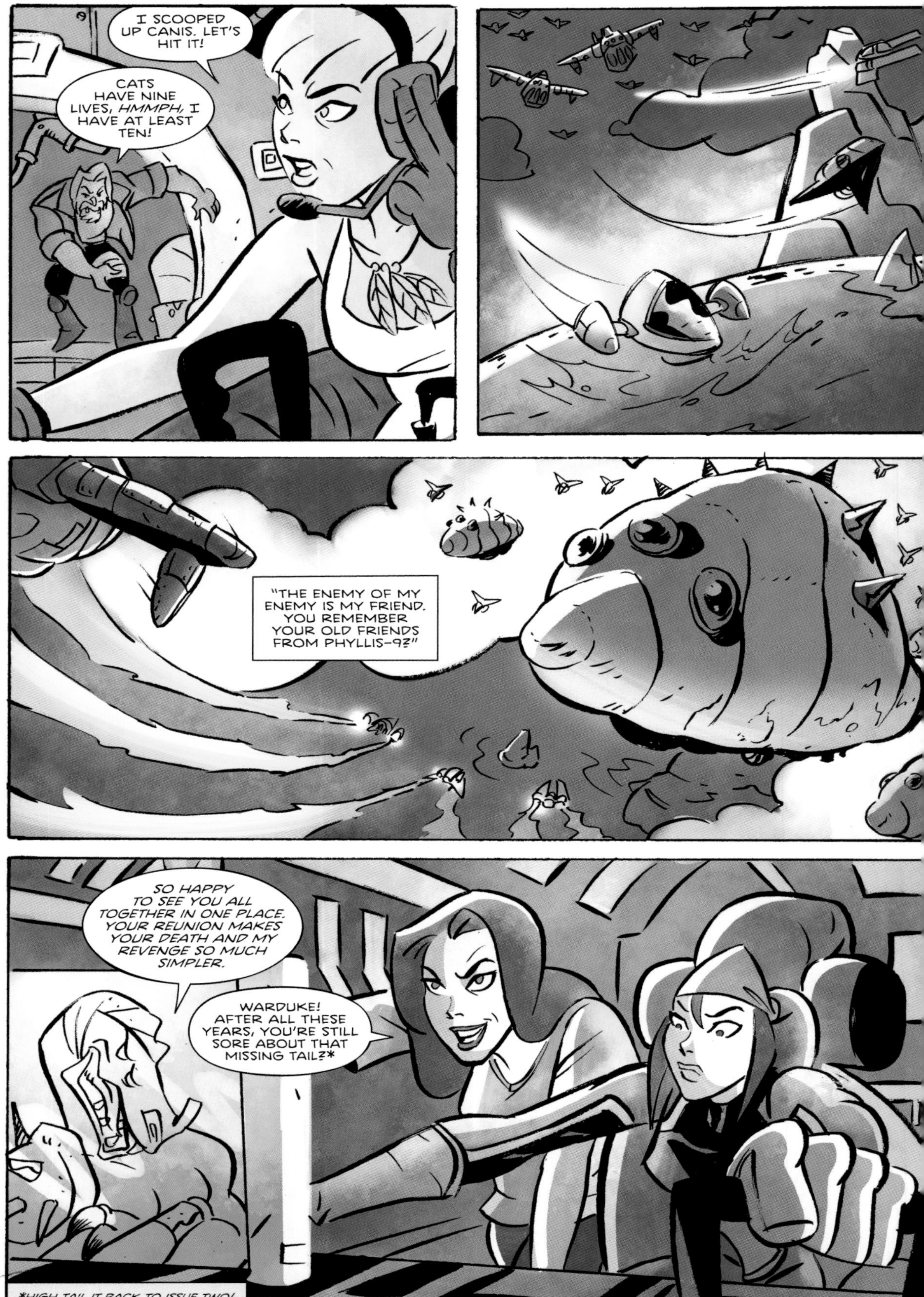
I SCOOPED UP CANIS. LET'S HIT IT!
CATS HAVE NINE LIVES, *HMMPH,* I HAVE AT LEAST TEN!
"THE ENEMY OF MY ENEMY IS MY FRIEND. YOU REMEMBER YOUR OLD FRIENDS FROM PHYLLIS-9?"
SO HAPPY TO SEE YOU ALL TOGETHER IN ONE PLACE. YOUR REUNION MAKES YOUR DEATH AND MY REVENGE SO MUCH SIMPLER.
WARDUKE! AFTER ALL THESE YEARS, YOU'RE STILL SORE ABOUT THAT MISSING TAIL?*
*HIGH TAIL IT BACK TO ISSUE TWO!

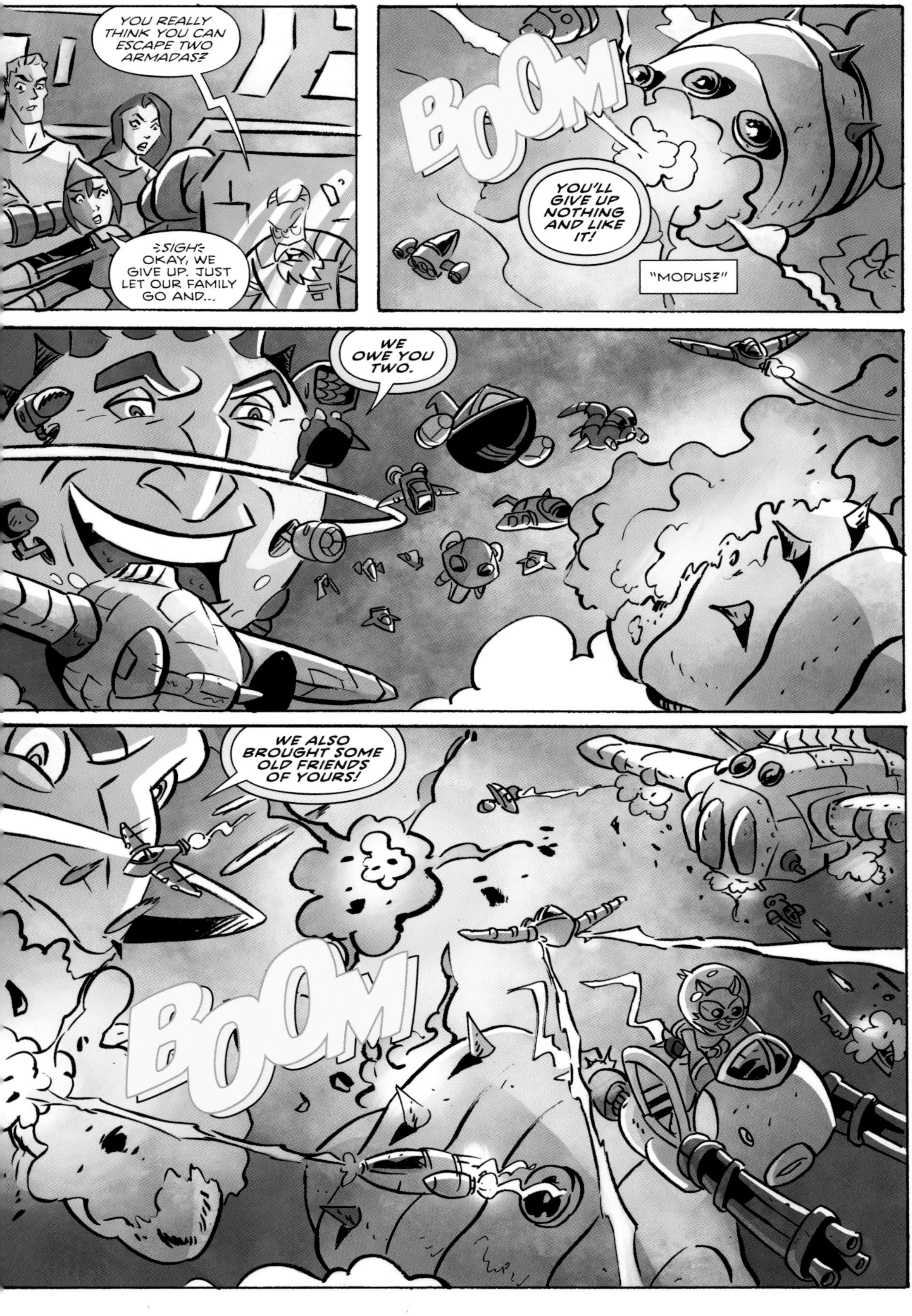

YOU REALLY THINK YOU CAN ESCAPE TWO ARMADAS?
SIGH OKAY, WE GIVE UP. JUST LET OUR FAMILY GO AND...
BOOM!
YOU'LL GIVE UP NOTHING AND LIKE IT!
"MODUS?"
WE OWE YOU TWO.
WE ALSO BROUGHT SOME OLD FRIENDS OF YOURS!
BOOM!

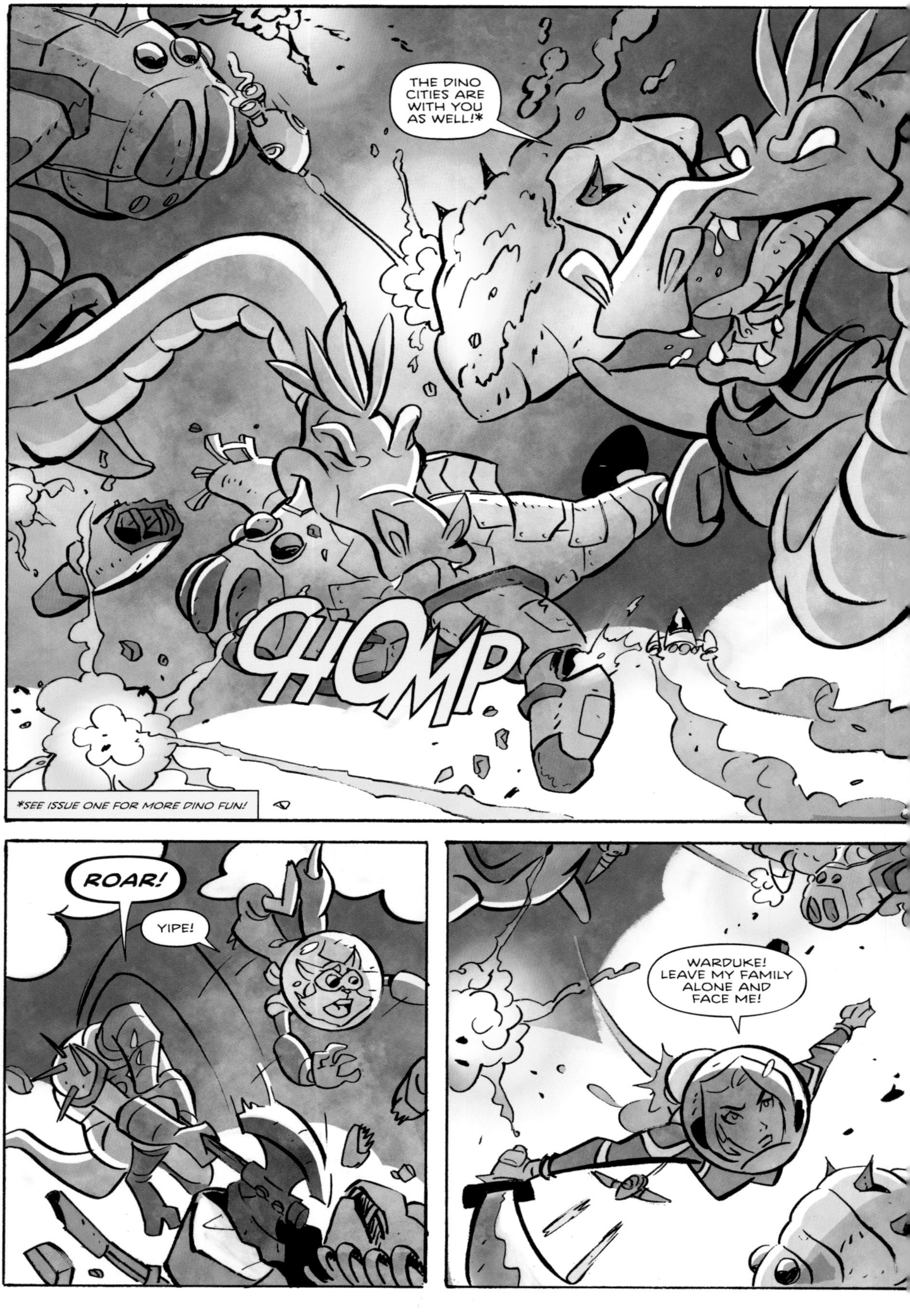
THE DINO CITIES ARE WITH YOU AS WELL!*
CHOMP
*SEE ISSUE ONE FOR MORE DINO FUN!
ROAR!
YIPE!
WARDUKE! LEAVE MY FAMILY ALONE AND FACE ME!

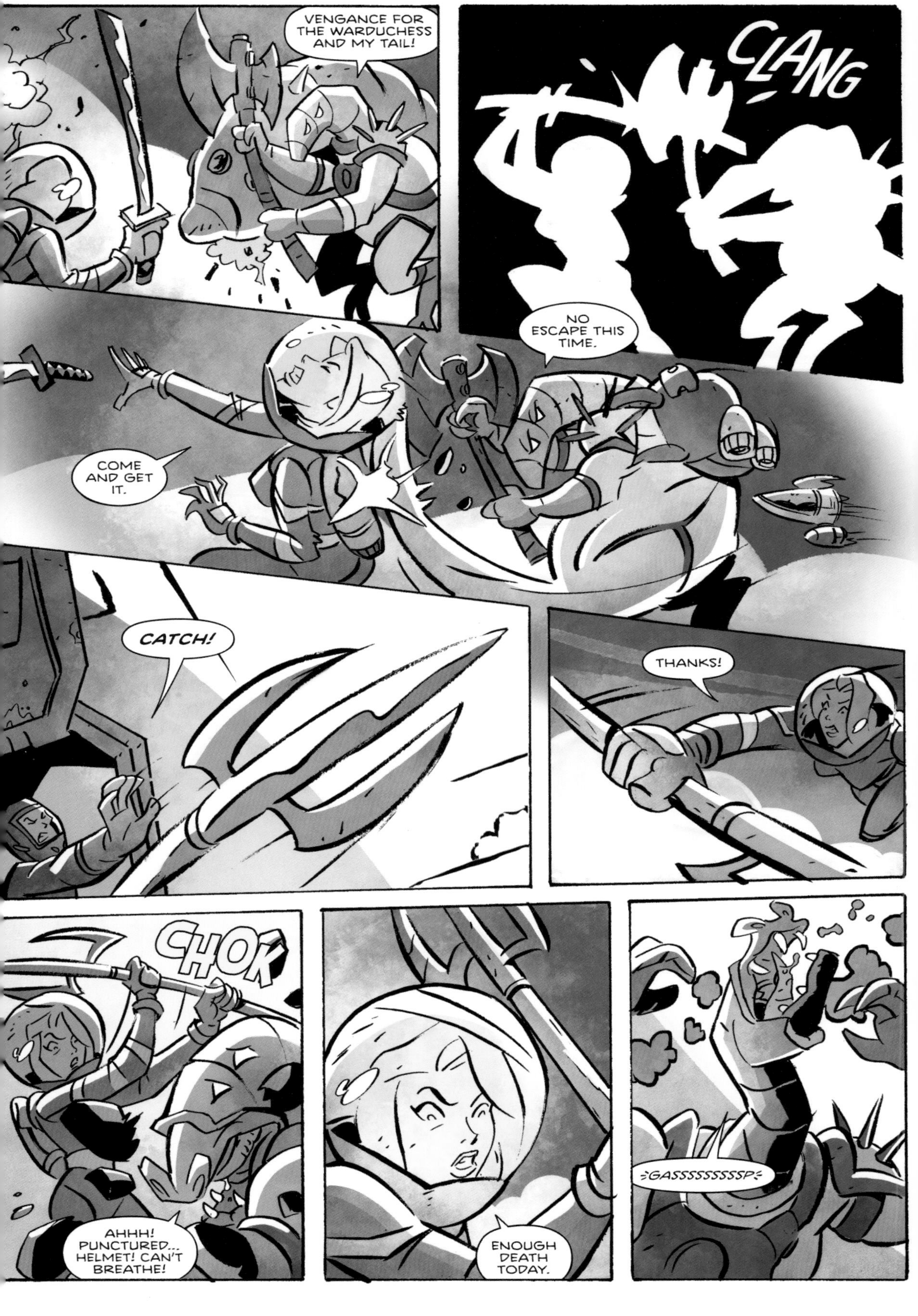
VENGANCE FOR THE WARDUCHESS AND MY TAIL!
CLANG
NO ESCAPE THIS TIME.
COME AND GET IT.
CATCH!
THANKS!
CHOK
AHHH! PUNCTURED... HELMET! CAN'T BREATHE!
ENOUGH DEATH TODAY.
GASSSSSSSSSP

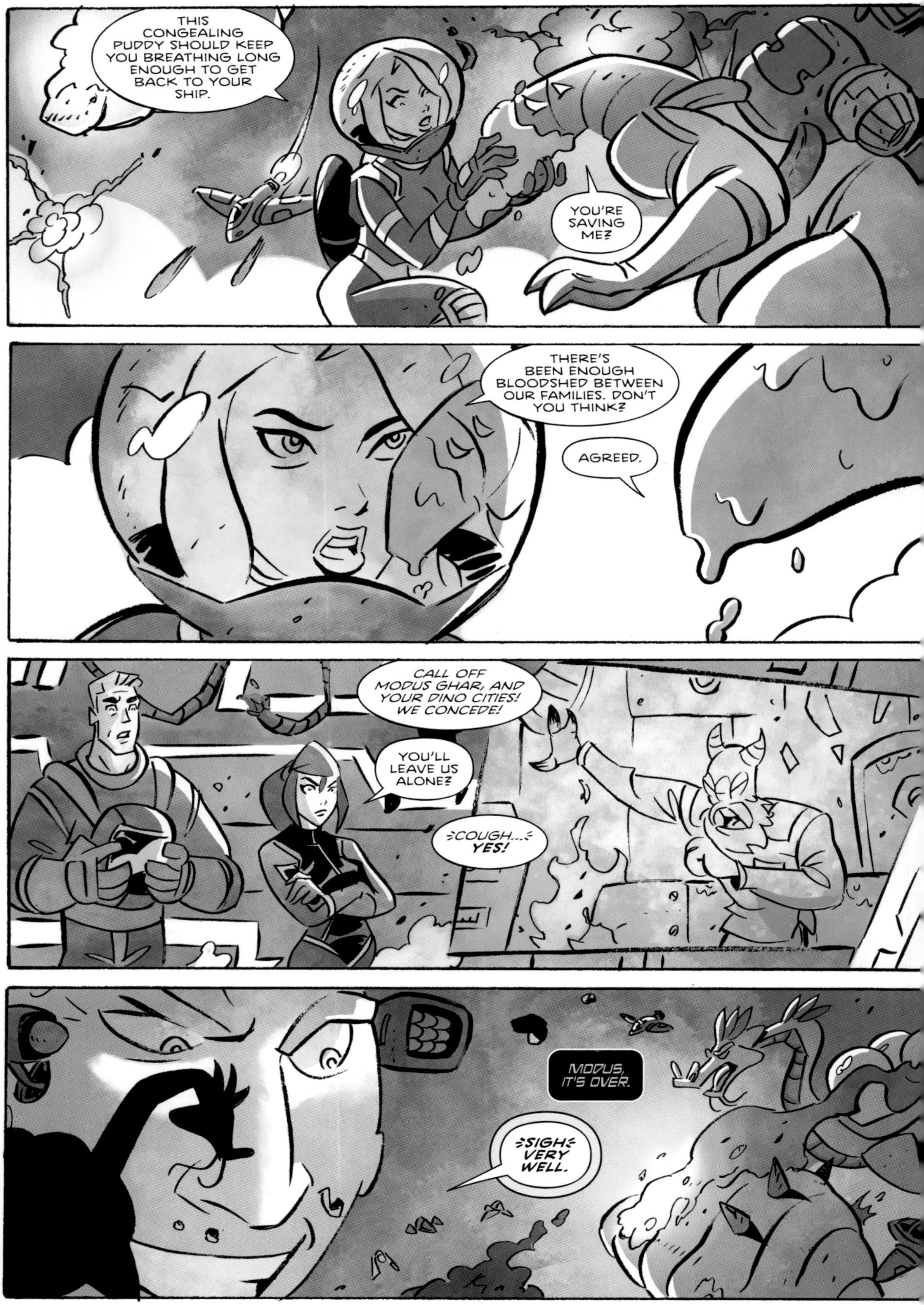

THIS CONGEALING PUDDY SHOULD KEEP YOU BREATHING LONG ENOUGH TO GET BACK TO YOUR SHIP.
YOU'RE SAVING ME?
THERE'S BEEN ENOUGH BLOODSHED BETWEEN OUR FAMILIES. DON'T YOU THINK?
AGREED.
CALL OFF MODUS GHAR, AND YOUR DINO CITIES! WE CONCEDE!
YOU'LL LEAVE US ALONE?
COUGH... YES!
MODUS, IT'S OVER.
SIGH VERY WELL.

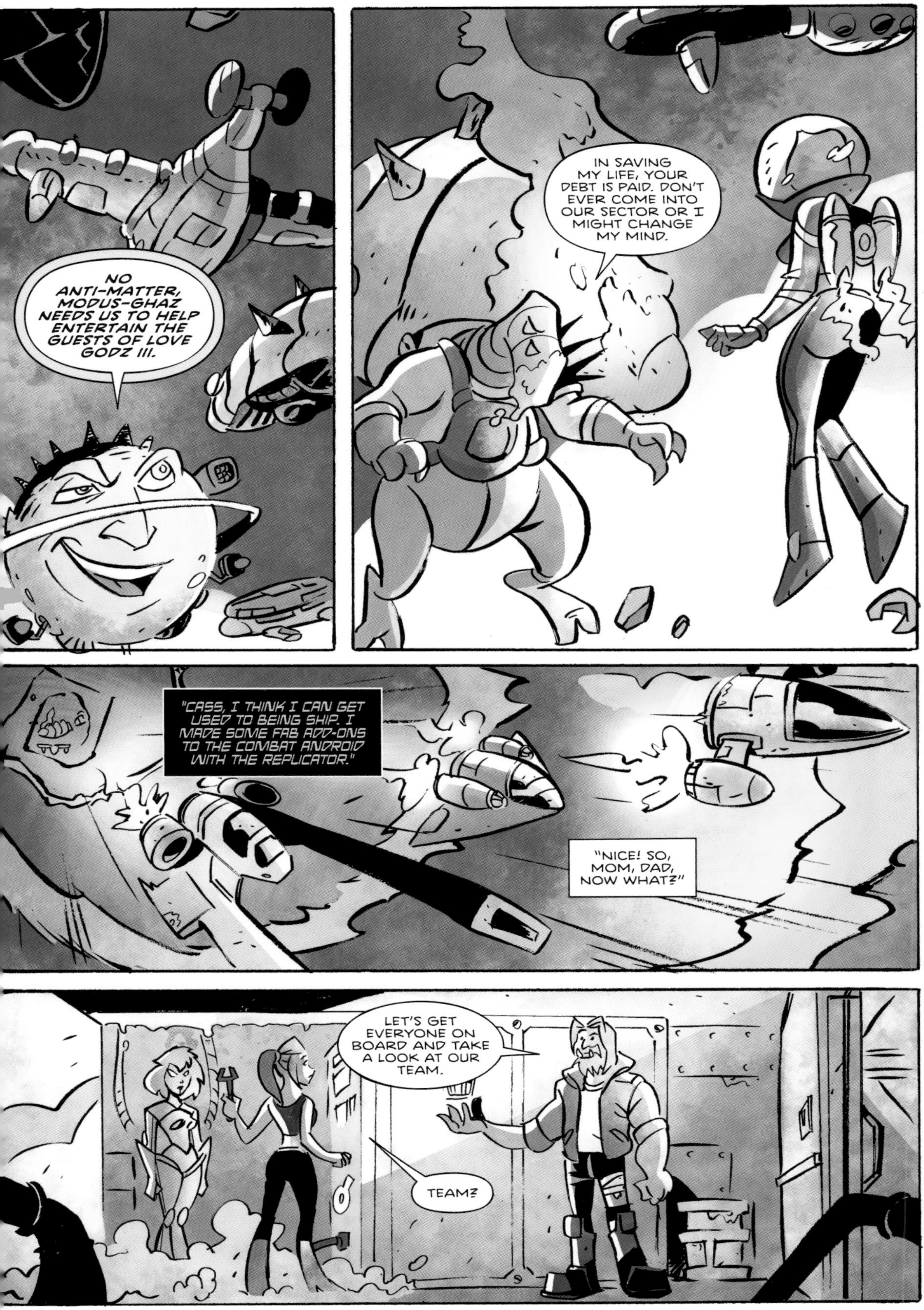
NO ANTI-MATTER, MODUS-GHAZ NEEDS US TO HELP ENTERTAIN THE GUESTS OF LOVE GODZ III.
IN SAVING MY LIFE, YOUR DEBT IS PAID. DON'T EVER COME INTO OUR SECTOR OR I MIGHT CHANGE MY MIND.
"CASS, I THINK I CAN GET USED TO BEING SHIP. I MADE SOME FAB ADD-ONS TO THE COMBAT ANDROID WITH THE REPLICATOR."
"NICE! SO, MOM, DAD, NOW WHAT?"
LET'S GET EVERYONE ON BOARD AND TAKE A LOOK AT OUR TEAM.
TEAM?

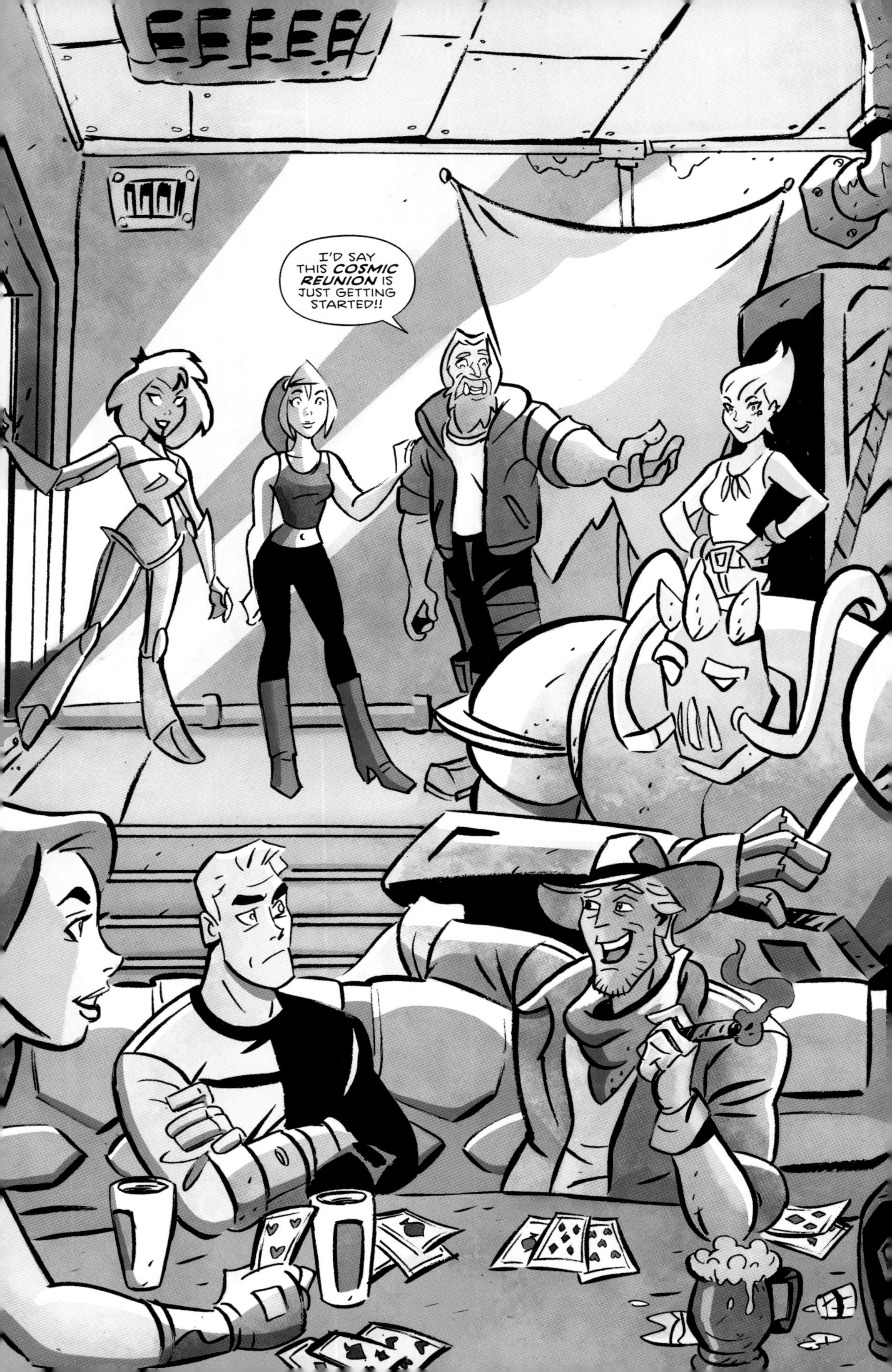
I'D SAY THIS COSMIC REUNION IS JUST GETTING STARTED!!

COVER GALLERY

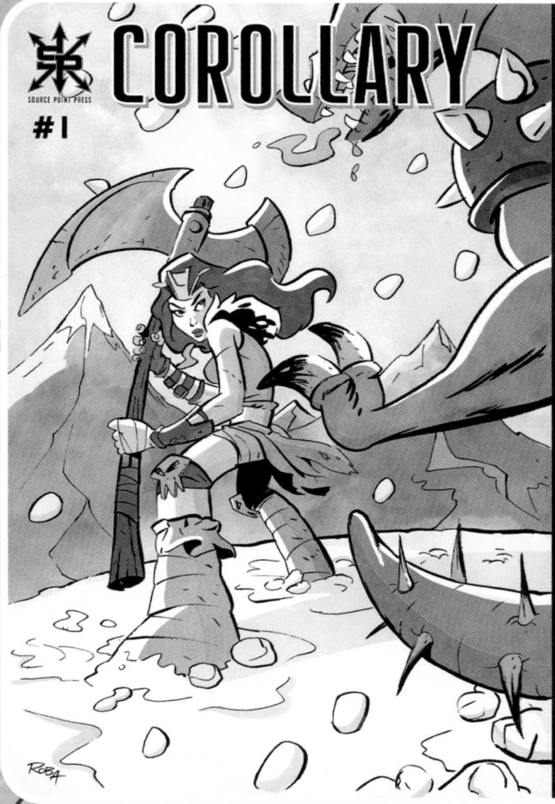

COROLLARY
SOURCE POINT PRESS
#1
ROBA

ISSUE 1
by Robert Ahmad

ISSUE 2
by Robert Ahmad

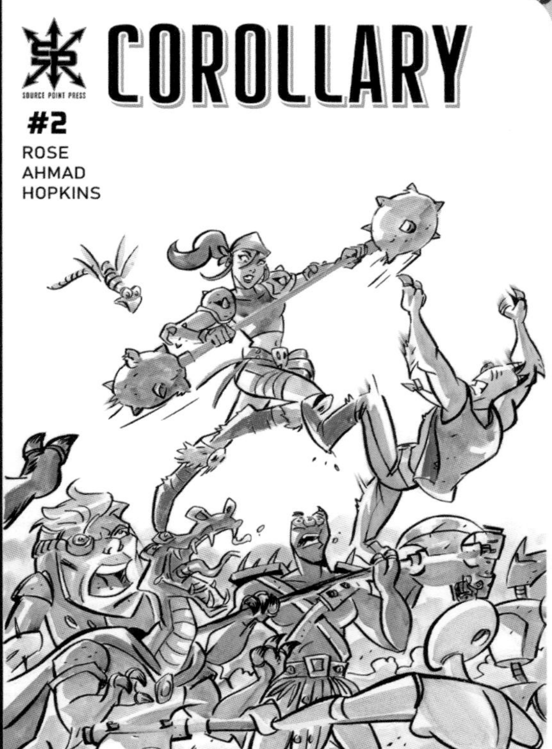

COROLLARY
SOURCE POINT PRESS
#2
ROSE
AHMAD
HOPKINS

COVER GALLERY

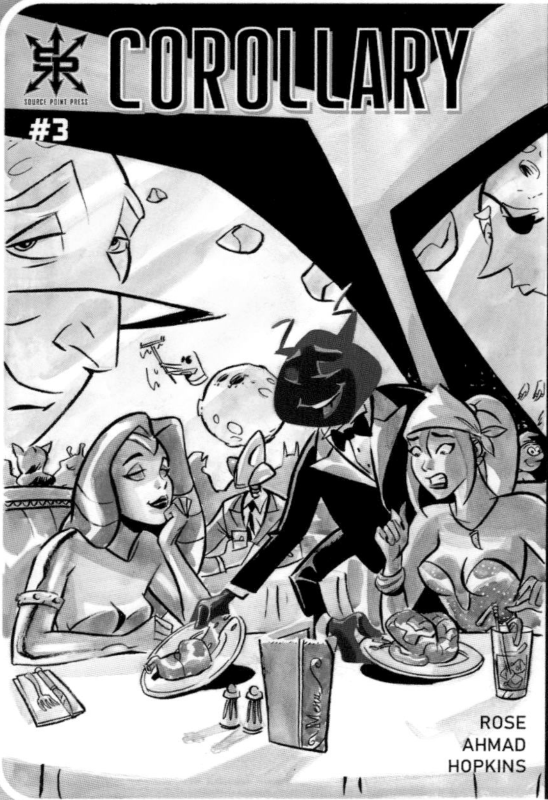
COROLLARY
SOURCE POINT PRESS
#3
ROSE
AHMAD
HOPKINS

ISSUE 3
by Robert Ahmad

ISSUE 4
by Robert Ahmad

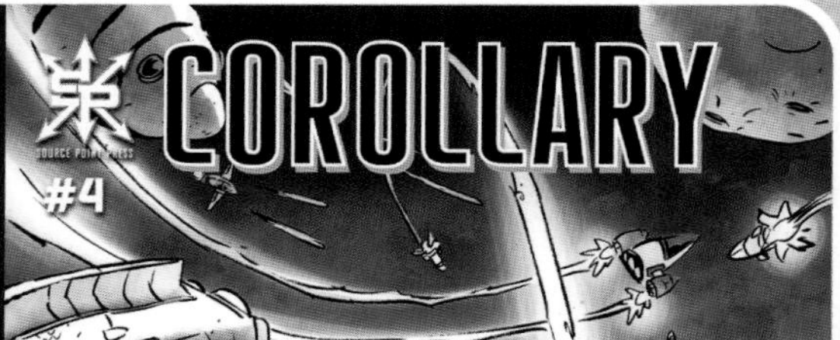
COROLLARY
SOURCE POINT PRESS
#4
ROSE
AHMAD
METZLER
HOPKINS

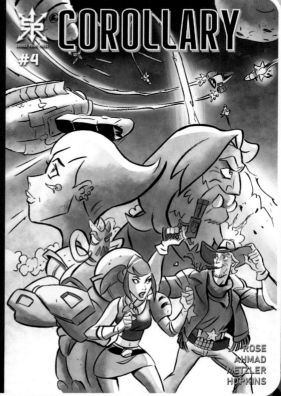

COVER GALLERY

SOURCE POINT PRESS
ASHCAN

COROLLARY
rose
ahmad
hopkins

ASHCAN
by Robert Ahmad

PINUP
by Dr. Shahin Chandrasoma

AFTERWORD AND SPECIAL THANKS

Since the first time my grandparents mailed me a care package of panel popping heroes and villains, comic books, graphic novels, and comic strips have been and continue to be an intrinsic part of my life. I envision my grandfather walking into a comic shop and asking what comics his nine-year-old grandson would enjoy. The answer: *all of them.*

I truly believe the medium of comics is magical. The magic lies in the gutters, the space between the panels where the reader fills in the cinematic story in their mind's eye. A comic manipulates time and space with those magical gutters. *Corollary* always had to exist as a comic and the spark of an idea came thanks to my daughter.

A few years back, after hearing the exciting news of some friends expecting twins, I tucked Karoline into bed, and as I turned off her galaxy light projector, she asked, "Dad, if a twin gets tickled, does the other one giggle?"

I said that was an excellent question, nestled her pink owl blankie in next to her, and allowed my mind to drift somewhere darker...*if your twin dies, so do you.* After leaving her room, I scrambled for a pen and notebook and got to writing. Karoline and her brother, Felix, might not be twins but they certainly have a love, push, pinch, hug kind of relationship. The main protagonists of *Corollary*: Andromeda and Cass, popped into existence as siblings with a lot to process about their definition of family; as well as, how to navigate their evolving relationship with one another and themselves.